DATE DUE

EVELYN WAUGH

BRIDESHEAD REVISITED

Evelyn Waugh restrained his magnificent satiric gift in writing his memory drama about the romantic entanglement of Charles Ryder with a great Anglo-Catholic family, and in the process he revealed himself as an elegiac, lyrical novelist of the utmost feeling and penetration. Conceived and created during the Second World War, BRIDESHEAD REVISITED is both a tribute to a dying aristocratic world, and a celebration of the civilization that gave that world form and meaning.

EVERYMAN,
I WILL GO WITH THEE,
AND BE THY GUIDE,
IN THY MOST NEED
TO GO BY THY SIDE

EVELYN WAUGH

Brideshead Revisited

with an Introduction by
Frank Kermode

EVERYMAN'S LIBRARY

Alfred A. Knopf New York Toronto

172

THIS IS A BORZOI BOOK

PUBLISHED BY ALFRED A. KNOPF, INC.

First included in Everyman's Library, 1993
Copyright © 1944, 1945 by Evelyn Waugh
Copyright renewed © 1972, 1973 by Mrs Laura Waugh
Published by arrangement with Little, Brown and Company, Inc.
Introduction, Bibliography, and Chronology Copyright © 1993 by
David Campbell Publishers Ltd.
Typography by Peter B. Willberg

ISBN 0-679-42300-1
LC 93-1854

Library of Congress Cataloging-in-Publication Data
Waugh, Evelyn, 1903–1966.
Brideshead revisited / Evelyn Waugh.
p.   cm.—(Everyman's library)
ISBN 0-679-42300-1 : $17.00
1. Upper classes—England—Fiction.
2. Catholics—England—Fiction. 3. Family—England—Fiction.
I. Title.
PR6045.A97B7   1993   93-1854
823'.912—dc20   CIP

Book Design by Barbara de Wilde and Carol Devine Carson

Typeset in the UK by MS Filmsetting Limited, Frome, Somerset

Printed and bound in Germany by
Mohndruck Graphische Betriebe GmbH, Gütersloh

BRIDESHEAD
REVISITED

———

INTRODUCTION

The pre-publication history of *Brideshead Revisited*, probably Evelyn Waugh's most successful novel, is complicated and unusual. Its last pages were written in London in June 1944, while the Allied forces were landing in Normandy. Waugh, by this time as disillusioned with the army as the army was with him, had served for years in various branches of the service – he had been a Marine and a Commando, seen action in Crete, and damaged himself in a parachute jump. Having sought and got leave to write a novel – in itself surely an unusual achievement for an officer in any service in 1944 – he must have supposed that as the end of the war approached he was, at forty-one, finished with active service. He was not; the proofs of *Brideshead* were revised in Yugoslavia, where he had been sent on a mission with Randolph Churchill. Much later that mission provided the basis for the last section of his last novel, *Unconditional Surrender*.

He had written nothing of much substance since *Put Out More Flags*, published in 1942; it celebrated the 'phoney war' and what he described as 'the Churchillian renaissance' at its end. The unfinished *Work Suspended* also belongs to that year. Meanwhile he had repeatedly demonstrated both his desire for military action, however desperate, and his constitutional reluctance to accept the role of a junior officer. Already in his late thirties, and unaccustomed to strenuous exercise, he struggled to comply with the requirement of physical fitness and the relatively hard life of wartime soldiering, but he was prone to insult senior officers in various ways, not least when drunk.

In these circumstances the 'marriage' between Waugh and the army headed for breakdown. He long retained an earnest if, as it sometimes appeared from the conduct of associates, idiosyncratic interest in the idea of combat, but other military qualities were lacking; one commanding officer rated him highest for 'Zeal' and lowest for 'Judgment'. Having taken part in a useless expedition against the Free French at Dakar (to be remembered in *Men at Arms*) and an abortive raid on Bardia in Libya, he arrived in Crete just in time to take part in the British evacuation, so bitterly recounted in *Officers and Gentlemen*, the second volume of the war trilogy that was to be his last work of fiction.

Waugh greatly resented what he took to be the shameful character of that retreat. He genuinely could not understand why people were not as brave as he was – or, if they were afraid, why they did not conceal their fear. He began to withdraw his interest from the war, saying he had come to think of it as a matter for others: there were really, he remarked, two wars in progress – Russia *v.* Germany, and USA *v.* Japan – and 'England', he now thought, 'had no part in either of them'. Disillusioned as to the value and purpose of the conflict, he decided he had no part to play in its continuance, and sought to resume his life as an artist, to labour in his true vocation. Feeling the onset of a very ambitious novel, he wrote to Brendan Bracken, an acquaintance who was then Minister of Information, and to the War Office, requesting leave for three months. He explained that he was over forty, that he lacked physical agility and also such qualities as might make up for that lack – a knowledge of useful foreign languages, and so on. However, he remained able to write novels, and he asked for time to write one now, promising that three months would suffice for the purpose.

He eventually got his leave (though it was to be interrupted somewhat by the interference of military bureaucrats). Bracken earned little gratitude for his part in making this possible, for he was made to contribute to the character of Rex Mottram in the book that resulted. Waugh was contemplating, he said, a *magnum opus*, and for such a purpose the period of leave he requested might, though lengthy in view of the military situation, have looked barely adequate; but he was confident that he could bring it off, and indeed the book got written in a little over four months.

The story of its writing is as follows. From his diary we know he began it on 1 February 1944 in a hotel in Chagford, Devon: 'Up at 8.30, two and a half hours earlier than in London, and at work before 10. I found my mind stiff and my diction stilted but by dinner-time I had finished 1,300 words all of which were written twice and many three times before I got the time sequence and the transitions satisfactorily, but I think it is now all right.' On the following day we have 'Score at close of play 3,000 words odd.' Constantly rewriting, and under repeated threats of military recall, he was within a week managing 1,500–2,000 words a day, and on 14 February he wrote 3,000 words in three hours. By the 26th he had done 33,000 words, but was then forced back to 'military frivolities'. However, he managed to get another six weeks' leave and resumed work on 16 March (2,700 words). He then proceeded with extraordinary despatch, and by the end of March had half finished. On 4 May he complained about the difficulty of writing about 'love-making on a liner'. On 21 May he records that he has 'written about 15,000 words in the last week and am in alternate despondency and exultation about the book'. Lord Marchmain died on D-Day, 6 June: 'There only remains now the epilogue which is easy meat.' 'On Corpus Christi Day 1944 [10 June] ... I finished the last version of *Brideshead Revisited* and sent it to be typed.' It was, he wrote in a letter to his wife, the dedicatee, his first important book, and he was somewhat impatient for it to be recognized as such.

Waugh usually wrote fast when sure what he wanted to do, and if there is an unexpected touch of Trollope in this proud word-counting (and in the appended '*Chagford, February–June, 1944*') it is not to be thought that the work was as easily achieved as its completion in so short a time might suggest. The researches of Robert Murray Davis in the archives at Austin, Texas, and elsewhere have demonstrated the intensity of the labour devoted to the manuscript while the writing was in progress.

Waugh long wished to revise the book as it stood in 1944, and minor corrections were made in subsequent editions. In 1959 the publisher invited him to make any changes he wanted for a new edition, to be wholly reset, and the result was the version here reprinted. It differs in various respects from the first edition, even in physical characteristics – the trade edition of 1944 is printed on wartime 'economy' paper, the pages grey and fragile. More important were the alterations made, after mature consideration, to the structure and style of the work. These are referred to in the author's Preface. Observing that this book had won him celebrity but lost him esteem, he goes on to endorse its theme but criticizes its form and some aspects of its style. He deplores but excuses its celebration of gluttony; this, he says, he has now qualified, though not everything proper to the mood of 1944 could be removed simply because it seemed excessive in 1959. 'It would be impossible to bring it up to date without totally destroying it.'

The changes can be summarized thus. Waugh reverted to the three-book structure he had planned in the manuscript but reduced to two books in the 1944 version. He cut out or altered some of what he calls 'the grosser passages', trimming nostalgic accounts of luxurious eating and drinking (forgive-able as the self-indulgent reveries of the age of austerity in which the novel was written) and also instances of what Conor Cruise O'Brien, in an essay that mildly upset Waugh, referred to as 'elegiac afflatus'. But even after these changes the prose of *Brideshead* remains heavier, more elaborate, than that of any novel he had written before, and this is understandable considering that the subject is one of the gravest importance to the author – no less than 'the operation of divine grace on a group of diverse but closely connected characters'. Since the house itself has stood for the survival in apostate England of a remnant of Catholic aristocracy, though on the point of succumbing to atheistic modernity and the reign of the Hoopers, it seemed right to 'pile it on rather', and the same might be said for the reminiscences of the Oxford of Waugh's youth, which, as he says in his autobiography, was to him 'a Kingdom of Cockayne'.

To give a few instances of the reduction of the pile: Oxford, which in 1944 'exhaled the soft vapours of a thousand years of learning', in 1960 'exhaled the soft airs of centuries of youth' – a less extravagant and perhaps more accurate claim. In the account of the dinner at which Charles Ryder sees through the pretensions of Rex Mottram there was a long elegiac speech about Burgundy, now curtailed though not eliminated. Similarly there are beneficial cuts in the account of Sebastian

Flyte's Oxford luncheon party, which began 'a new epoch' in Charles Ryder's life. The beginning of Book Three is quite heavily cut. Anthony Blanche is introduced far less extravagantly in the final than in the original version, no longer quite as 'foreign as a Martian'.

On the other hand the blue pencil spared some rather weighty editorializing, as at the opening of Book One, Chapter 4: 'The languor of Youth – how unique and quintessential it is!', and so on to a comparison between that languor and the experience of the Beatific Vision. In Book One, Chapter 5, there is a passage, beginning 'The Charity matinée was over', which explains how grievously Anthony Blanche was missed when he failed to return to Oxford. It develops an extremely elaborate theatrical figure and its success depends on the ingenuity of that figure, and on the gravity of tone that conveys it. It now seems strained or overdone, and as it was surely dispensable one is surprised that it was spared.

There are more such passages: one in particular at the outset of Book Three describes the behaviour of the pigeons in the piazza of San Marco, and indicates their fugitive resemblance to human memories. The comparison near the beginning, between Ryder's disillusion with the army and the decay of a marriage, extends over some three hundred words and feels laboured. There is the very elaborate figure that occurs after Charles' conversation with his boring and proper cousin, to suggest that the wickedness of Oxford undergraduates can be compared with the slow fermentation of port. (Waugh liked this simile well enough to quote it in his autobiography.)

Such elaborately extended metaphors add a new gravity to the tone of the novel. Waugh's prose, like his handling of displaced autobiography, has induced some critics to compare *Brideshead* with Proust's *A la Recherche du temps perdu*, but its scale, though quite grand, is modest compared with that of Proust, and the author's avowed purpose, to demonstrate the workings of divine grace, wholly different.

One change in the final version has probably given rise to more comment than any of the others. As I have already noted, Waugh was not happy about the scene of love-making on the liner, complaining that it was difficult to render sex without being able to describe the sexual act in detail.

'I feel very much the futility of describing sexual emotions without describing the sexual act; I should like to give as much detail as I have of the meals, to the two coitions – with his wife and Julia. It would be no more or less obscene than to leave them to the reader's imagination, which in this case cannot be as acute as mine. There is a gap in which the reader will insert his own sexual habits instead of those of my characters.'

(*Diaries*, 9 May 1944)

In 1944 the love-making with Julia on the liner avoids any imputation of sexual excitement but goes in for rhetorical excess instead: 'I took formal possession of her as a lover ... Now on the rough water I was made free of her narrow loins and, it seemed now, assuaging that fierce appetite, cast a burden which I had borne all my life, toiled under, not knowing its nature – now, while the waves still broke and thundered on the prow, the act of possession was a symbol, a rite of ancient origin and solemn meaning.' Understandably discontented with this uneasily inflated prose, Waugh shortened the passage in 1960: 'Now on the rough water there was a formality to be observed, no more. It was as though a deed of conveyance of her narrow loins had been drawn and sealed. I was making my first entry as the freeholder of a property I would enjoy and develop at leisure.'

Not everybody will think this much of an improvement. From a rite observed in bad weather – accompanied by what Martin Stannard calls 'the lamentable phallic imagery of the ship' (Stannard, p. 106) – the lovemaking becomes an act of formal possession, as of a house. The figure of 'possession' and being made free of something has swollen into an elaborate trope about property, complete with a deed of conveyance; no fierce appetite is assuaged. Not surprisingly, some have complained that Ryder might almost be thinking about the inheritance of Brideshead made possible by this union, treating the coition as merely part of the negotiations for that supremely desirable residence.

Since these remarks about elaborate tropes and mannered gravity may have sounded a little disparaging, it should here be said that Waugh's dialogue is as edged and witty as ever; that he is extraordinarily skilful in making each of his characters speak in his or her own way, from Ryder's very original father to the bright child Cordelia. Waugh once argued for the value to writers of aristocratic English: 'only a continuous tradition of gentle speech, with all its implications – the avoidance of boredom and vulgarity, the exchange of complicated ideas, the observance of subtle nuances of word and phrase – can preserve the written tongue from death, and lifelong habitude to such speech alone schools a man to write his own tongue'. This rule may be of less general application than is here suggested, but it was one that the author himself obeyed, and with notable results. Nor is it merely a matter of upper-class dialect; one feels he heard his characters, distinguished their usages, reported idiolects.

On the whole most readers, I think, would agree that the purgation of the first version – not over-rigorous, for reasons Waugh suggests in his Preface – makes for improvement: the final version of the novel is preferable. Enough of the grand grave elaboration persists to convey the impression that this is the manner best suited to the mood in which the author attempted the work, the manner that best conveys the sense in which the novel is a personal record. To call the book displaced autobiography is of course not to suggest that Ryder is a self-portrait, but Waugh would certainly have seen conversion to Catholicism, with the attendant benefits and sacrifices, as evidence of the operation of grace in both his own life and his character's.

There are certainly reminiscences, however fictionalized, of episodes in the author's life. Important elements of the plot concern the Catholic prohibition of remarriage while a spouse remains alive, a difficulty Waugh had himself experienced, and one not to be dismissed as easily as Rex Mottram believed. Even more instrumental in the conception of the book was Waugh's anxiety about friends who remained, as he saw the matter, in schism (Anglicans, for instance, like John Betjeman) or others who had apostasized. He worried about the faith of Graham Greene, and at one remarkable moment succeeded in inducing a dying friend, Hubert Duggan, to see a priest. Duggan had lived out of wedlock with a woman now dead, and apparently felt it would be an insult to her memory if he were now to declare himself repentant on account of that relationship. A priest was brought in all the same, and succeeded in giving the dying man absolution; he was held to have assented and crossed himself (*Diaries*, 13 October 1943). This moment, a palpable intervention, as it was taken to be, of divine grace in a human life, was Waugh's inspiration for the account of the death of Lord Marchmain, who had also lived in sin.

*

The novel begins in a tedious and sleazy wartime present, in a military setting of that lowering variety, well known to survivors of Word War II, in which the absence or remoteness of action makes routine duties, moves, drills, orders and reprimands seem banal or irrelevant, causing all manner of petty irritation and bringing out the worst in everybody. This helps to account for Ryder's discontent, and has the additional thematic value of introducing the contemptibly irritating Hooper, the lowborn lowminded subaltern regarded by Ryder as representative of a new generation – a fellow innately incapable of understanding fine points of honour or discipline or indeed language, an enemy of the faith, and a threat, however negligible in himself, to the best people. Aimless troop movements undertaken in this company and this mood bring Ryder unexpectedly to Brideshead; whereupon the narrative retreats to the early twenties, when Ryder as an undergraduate fell under the spell of Sebastian Flyte, inhabitant of the paradisial Brideshead, Brideshead before the fall.

The Oxford memories in *Brideshead* may be thought of less as displaced than as transfigured autobiography. Waugh later wrote lovingly of his undergraduate life in *A Little Learning*, and others have contributed, in memoirs and admiring historical studies, to our idea of the place as Waugh experienced it in the early twenties. The beauty of the city itself, in the days before it was quite ruined by the motor car, was enhanced, at any rate for its transient occupants, by its being an almost exclusively male community. Waugh remarks that few of his contemporaries had 'any serious interest in women' though 'very few have developed into homosexuals'. They were in some respects, he says, sophisticated, in others barely adolescent. It was a time for warm male friendships, and that suited Waugh very well. At Oxford he was 'reborn'. He drank a lot, formed one homosexual relationship, and made friends with grander people from grander colleges than Hertford, where he was a scholar. He read too little and did not get on very well with dons, against one of whom he later conducted one of his relentless campaigns of teasing. He was fortunate in having as his Oxford contemporaries men of the calibre of Graham Greene, Henry Green, Anthony Powell, John Betjeman and Cyril Connolly, and he made several close friendships, but seems to have reserved his highest admiration for the affluent Alastair Graham and for Harold Acton and Brian Howard – 'a rich source of anecdote' who contributed much to the character of Anthony Blanche in *Brideshead*.

Oxford had also provided the opening scene of Waugh's first novel, *Decline and Fall*, which describes, with a degree of *schadenfreude* and teasing, the discomfiture of Paul Pennyfeather at the hands of drunken aristocratic rowdies of the 'Bollinger' Club, really the Bullingdon at Christ Church. (Tom Driberg remarked that the opening chapter of *Decline and Fall* gave 'a mild account of the night of any Bullingdon Club dinner'.) In *Brideshead* such people are not absent, nor is the slightly cruel fun – Blanche is an obvious quarry – but all is bathed in an elegiac glow, partly attributable to the 'mood of sentimental delusion' in which the novel was written.

Book One of the novel has an epigraph, 'Et in Arcadia Ego', a tag often used to suggest memories of a past idyllic time, though in fact the words, as Waugh understood very well, are supposed to be spoken by Death ('All fates,' said Waugh much later, 'are "worse than death"' (*Diaries*, p. 787). That time, like any time, could hold in perfection but a little moment, and the shadow of decay or death must be on Ryder's first outing with Sebastian, his first visit to Brideshead. Sebastian the beautiful, in any secular sense the doomed, the winsome lover of a teddy-bear, had vomited through the window into Ryder's room, so binding together two lives which, each in its way but also in concert, will illustrate the operation of grace in human existence, so that the mess left for the scout to clean up is, in a way, evidence of that operation.

After their meeting we are at once introduced to Ryder's father, eccentric, drily teasing, mildly malevolent, and his pompous cousin Jasper; they are from a world elsewhere, not the Flyte world, so 'madly charming'. What Ryder had already learnt, and what neither pompous cousin nor self-absorbed, ironic father ever would, was 'that to know and love one other human being is the root of all wisdom'. Like Blanche in his way, he had, in loving Sebastian, discovered a kind of holiness. He had also discovered, from Blanche, the delights of ostentatious and luxurious self-indulgence as well as a malevolence altogether preferable to his father's, as when Blanche at the George, having ordered 'four Alexandra cocktails' at once, gossips wickedly about Sebastian's family. (In fact the cocktail was called an Alexander, not an Alexandra; but we cannot suppose the mistake to have been Blanche's.)

Eventually Sebastian allows Ryder to meet them, first Julia, who at once faintly arouses him; sex is also an agent, though a devious one, of grace. To be at Brideshead was for various reasons, and not only for its luxuries, to be 'very near heaven'. The spirit of that first stay is not particularly numinous or even very religious; Brideshead is 'not an old-established centre of Catholicism', and Ryder is aware of no supernatural solicitations. Yet the family is, as it were, vexed by its difference, its openness to calls unheard by those from whom they are different, including the young Ryder – its awareness of the enormous gulf existing between Catholics and others. Lord Marchmain, on his marriage, had entered into that difference; he tried to go back, but the end of the story is that when death approached he found himself, for all his worldliness and all his rage against the wife who had made him Catholic, compelled by the 'twitch upon the thread' to return to the condition of difference from which he had defected.

The twitch upon the thread is a central theme. The history of Lady Marchmain's relations with her husband and with Sebastian causes the latter to call her 'a femme fatale ... She killed at a touch.' Halfway through the book she announces that 'we must make a Catholic of Charles'. He will succumb to grace as it operates through the Flytes, and, eventually, concur even in her arguments in favour of wealth: '... it is possible for the rich to sin by coveting the privileges of the poor. The poor have always been the favourites of God.' Ryder is not at that point persuaded; he is preoccupied by Sebastian's apparent plight, described in another over-wrought figure as that of a Polynesian threatened by a colonist. But he is affected, and we are already wondering how the 'twitch on the thread' will be applied. That phrase, used as the title of Book Three, derives from one of Chesterton's Father Brown stories, earlier read as one of Lady Marchmain's after-dinner performances; in the words of Mark Amory, it is 'a fishing metaphor ... meaning that once someone has seen the Grace of God, however much time and space remove him, he can be retrieved' (*Letters*, p. 207).

There are different manifestations, many of which may seem improbable to sceptics, of the angling operations of grace. Sebastian's drunken decline, the interventions of Mr Samgrass, even Sebastian's running away like his father before him; or Lady Marchmain's introducing Ryder into her 'femi-nine' world, and telling him she had prayed for him: all these are part of the divine sport. All manner of apparently random events can constitute a divine plot.

Ryder cannot escape: professing to be with Sebastian *contra mundum*, seeing through what he takes to be the tricks of Lady Marchmain, he is nevertheless confounded in a conversation with Lord Brideshead, the pious, dull elder brother, regarded by Rex Mottram as just a 'half-baked monk'. Ryder cannot understand why Brideshead brings 'God into everything' and says, 'It seems to me that without your religion Sebastian would have a chance to be a happy and healthy man.' 'It's arguable,' replies Brideshead. Here the 'difference' is clearly expressed; Ryder cannot yet see either why God has to be in everything, nor why that chance of health and happiness is relatively unimportant; it will take time and much plotting to bring him to such an understanding.

Brideshead is fortunate in his unquestioned acceptance; he may be absurd in some ways (as he is, on the face of it, in his

choice of wife) but in the one thing truly necessary he is both
wise and lucky. His sister Julia, on the other hand, resents
what seems to her the misfortune of being Catholic, but cannot
break away: 'if she apostasized now, having been brought up
in the Church, she would go to hell, while the Protestant girls
of her acquaintance, schooled in happy ignorance, could
marry eldest sons, live at peace with their world, and get to
heaven before her'. The suggestion seems to be that to have
the certain knowledge that comes with Catholicism can, for
some, amount to a sort of curse; ignorant Protestants can
avoid the troubles of conscience and deprivation entailed by
adherence to the true religion and at the same time avoid the
risk of hell. But out of love for Mottram, who has no
understanding at all of the 'difference' – as the Jesuit who
instructs him puts it, he has 'no sense of reality', is almost a
'semi-imbecile' – she does apostasize, or try to: 'I can't get all
that sort of thing out of my mind, quite – Death, Judgment,
Heaven, Hell, Nanny Hawkins and the catechism.' Mottram
indeed turns out not to be 'a complete human being', but
'something absolutely modern that only this ghastly age could
produce. A tiny bit of a man', rather like a Hooper become
rich and powerful.

Wholeness in humanity is normally to be sought in the
Catholic and well born; but the cost of being whole can be
great. It is great for Sebastian, if only on a secular view; he
comes to no earthly good. It is great for the family, who lose
the chapel and Marchmain House. As Cordelia understands,
it is a question of doing what the great plot irresistibly requires
of you. 'If you haven't a vocation it's no good ... and if you
have a vocation you can't get away from it, however much
you hate it.'

Ryder's understanding of these matters is deferred. When
the third and final book begins, after a lapse of ten years, he
has become quite famous as an artist; he has travelled much
and married badly; but, he says, 'I remained unchanged, still
a small part of myself pretending to be a whole', and in that
resembling Mottram more than a Catholic.

The understanding that there is a genuine impediment to
his marriage with Julia, and that there is such a condition as

'living in sin', is the beginning of the twitch on Ryder's thread. Julia, it appears, is, like Sebastian, not an end but a 'forerunner'. That understanding is also occasion for Julia's extraordinary outburst, partly excused, along with the moribund monologue of Lord Marchmain, by Waugh in his Preface. She thinks there is no turning back; wrongly, of course. The important thing is to be turned back before dying.

The death foreseen by Cordelia for Sebastian is that he will be picked up dying after a drinking bout and 'show by a mere flicker of the eyelid that he is conscious when they give him the last sacraments'. Ryder is by such speculations brought up close to the fence he had not known he must take before his own death. Dying is the most important moment in a life. It is fitting that the book should end with the peaceful death of Lord Marchmain ('They mean something so different by "peace"'). Julia, naturally understanding the importance of the moment, goes for a priest; Ryder deplores this act, but kneels in prayer as the absolution is given, and his prayer is answered. His reward is to be parted from Julia. By the time he returns in uniform to Brideshead it has been defiled by billeted troops, by the incursion of the age of Hooper; but the lamp burns again in the sanctuary of the chapel.

The reasons why, in the 1960 Preface, Waugh can say that this novel 'lost me such esteem as I once enjoyed among my contemporaries' are probably two. First, some readers, accustomed to the stringency and economy of his earlier prose, found his manner self-indulgent. Secondly, he was now angrily accused of snobbery, a snobbery that seemed to be closely associated with his championship of the religion to which he had been converted. Henry Reed's review in the *New Statesman* (23 June 1945), on the whole admiring, began with a condemnation of this snobbery: 'A burden of respect for the peerage and for Eton, which those who belong to the former, or have been to the latter, seem able lightly to discard, weighs heavily upon him.' Reed singles out the scene with Mottram in the Paris restaurant as an instance of the narrator scoring off the lower-caste characters; in Waugh's 'testiness at other people's bad taste' he detects 'a special vulgarity'.

Waugh claimed not to be worried by such charges. 'Class

consciousness, particularly in England, has been so much inflamed these days that to mention a nobleman is like mentioning a prostitute sixty years ago. The new prudes say, "No doubt such people do exist but we would sooner not hear about them". I reserve the right to deal with the kind of people I know best.' He would not have wished to apologize for the famous passage in which Ryder reflects that Lady March-main's brothers, representative sons of 'the Catholic squires of England', were sacrificed in World War I 'to make a world for Hooper; they were the aborigines, vermin by right of law, to be shot off at leisure so that things might be safe for the travelling salesman, with his polygonal pince-nez, his fat wet hand-shake, his grinning dentures'.

What did upset him was any imputation that he believed the Catholic aristocracy to warrant special attentions from grace, attentions withheld from Mottrams and Hoopers and *hoi polloi*. Lady Marchmain's remarks about the spiritual privileges of the poor were perhaps inserted to forestall such interpretations; but they were forthcoming nevertheless. Conor Cruise O'Brien, an authority on the Catholic novel, pointed out, in the largely polite and admiring essay to which I referred earlier, that in Catholic countries (Ireland was perhaps in his mind) 'Catholicism is not romantic, not invaria-bly associated with big houses, or the fate of an aristocracy', adding that Waugh's Catholicism is 'dark and defeatist'. In a response to this article Waugh again admitted snobbery, but pointed out that at least two aristocrats in *Brideshead Revisited* – Mottram and Celia – are represented as 'worldly', and not 'sanctified' by his 'reverence for money and rank'. Given that Mottram is, in matters of religion, an ignoramus like Box-Bender in the later war trilogy, and Celia one of Waugh's pagan, rather dissolute upper-class women, like Guy Crouch-back's wife in the later work, this may seem a less than wholly satisfactory defence. But his main purpose in replying to O'Brien was 'the fear that a hasty reader [of O'Brien's notice] might conceive the doubt, which your reviewer scrupulously refrains from expressing, of the good faith of my conversion to Catholicism'.

Waugh expressed his shocked repudiation of such interpretations in a reply to an article by the present writer on the occasion of the publication of the 1960 edition of *Brideshead Revisited*. 'He imputes to me the absurd and blasphemous opinion that divine grace is "confined" to the highest and lowest class,' he wrote, citing a passage from *Helena* as proof that he did not hold that opinion.

My article had in fact emphasized, with evidence from *Helena*, Waugh's passionate concern for the *facts* of Catholic Christianity, and his confidence that 'the Faith is absolutely satisfactory to the mind ... that it is completely compelling to any who give it "indifferent and quiet audience"' – a quotation from Waugh's book about the martyr Campion. I did not, when I wrote the piece, know Mr O'Brien's essay, and said at more length many of the same things, with a similar degree of admiration and respect, and with some quite modestly expressed reservations. The offensive words were these: 'But the operation of divine grace seems to be confined to those who say "chimney-piece" and the enviable poor. Hooper and his brothers may be hard to bear, but it seems outrageous to damn them for their manners.' This is too strongly expressed, though to take it in isolation from the lengthy (and, I find on re-reading it, accurate) characterization of the faith expressed in this and other novels was unfair. Unfairness of course is essential to Waugh's controversial manner, as it is to the fun and to the power of these works.

Returning to *Brideshead Revisited* after so many years, one is again impressed less by its preoccupation with luxury than by its preoccupation with death. Ryder speaks of the 'tragedy' in which he had participated, a tragedy which resulted from the acceptance of the truth, a truth of separation and death. There is, to use the word in a sense only indirectly related to the quality of aristocracy, a certain nobility in this attitude. Ryder, in the final pages, can, rather surprisingly, allow himself to tell Hooper that he is 'homeless, childless, middle-aged, loveless'. Waugh never pretended that religious belief should make one happy. In his ruined world, symbolized at the end by the great house now defaced, there is no abiding city, but there is the hope of heaven signified by the lamp 'of deplorable design'. All fates are worse than death, though many of them are amusing or even beautiful. Waugh, tired of the army, chose to be an artist in this book, and he never dissociated art from skill. This skill, devoted as it is to the narrative expression of a clear and unwavering faith, makes *Brideshead Revisited*, after all the necessary reservations are stated, a memorable work of art.

Frank Kermode

SELECT BIBLIOGRAPHY

———

THE NOVELS OF EVELYN WAUGH
(all published by Chapman & Hall)

Decline and Fall, 1928.
Vile Bodies, 1930.
Black Mischief, 1932.
A Handful of Dust, 1934.
Scoop, 1938.
Put Out More Flags, 1942.
Brideshead Revisited, 1945.
The Loved One, 1948.
Helena, 1950.
Men at Arms, 1952.
Officers and Gentlemen, 1955.
The Ordeal of Gilbert Pinfold, 1957.
Unconditional Surrender, 1961.
(*Men at Arms, Officers and Gentlemen,* and *Unconditional Surrender* form a trilogy later published in a revised version as *Sword of Honour,* 1965.)

BIOGRAPHY
The best biography of Evelyn Waugh is by Martin Stannard: vol. 1, *Evelyn Waugh: The Early Years,* Dent, 1986; vol. 2, *Evelyn Waugh: No Abiding City,* Dent, 1992. There is an earlier biography by the author's friend Christopher Sykes (*Evelyn Waugh: A Biography,* Collins, 1975). There are details in many memoirs and in the biographies of Waugh's contemporaries, e.g., the autobiographies of his brother Alec (*My Brother Evelyn and Other Profiles,* Cassell, 1967), of Anthony Powell, *To Keep the Ball Rolling,* vol. 2, Heinemann, 1978), and in Bevis Hillier's *Young Betjeman* (Murray, 1988). Waugh's *Letters* were edited by Mark Amory (Weidenfeld & Nicolson, 1980) and there are more letters in Artemis Cooper, ed., *Mr Wu and Mrs Stitch: The Letters of Evelyn Waugh and Diana Cooper* (Hodder & Stoughton, 1991). Michael Davie edited *The Diaries of Evelyn Waugh* (Methuen, 1983). Humphrey Carpenter's *The Brideshead Generation* (Weidenfeld & Nicolson, 1989) is a biography, written with special attention to the lives of Waugh's Oxford contemporaries.

CRITICISM
Criticism of Waugh's novels is well selected in Martin Stannard's

Evelyn Waugh: The Critical Heritage (Routledge & Kegan Paul, 1984). Waugh himself approved of Frederick J. Stopp's *Evelyn Waugh: The Portrait of an Artist* (Chapman & Hall, 1958). Other valuable works are 'Donat O'Donnel' [Conor Cruise O'Brien], *Maria Cross: Imaginative Patterns in a Group of Modern Catholic Writers* (Oxford, 1952) and Robert Murray Davis, *Evelyn Waugh, Writer* (Oklahoma, Pilgrim Books, 1981).

CHRONOLOGY

DATE	AUTHOR'S LIFE	LITERARY CONTEXT
1897	Birth of Alec Waugh, Evelyn's brother.	
1903	Birth of Evelyn Waugh to Arthur and Catherine Waugh in Hampstead.	James: *The Ambassadors.* Shaw: *Man and Superman.*
1904		James: *The Golden Bowl.* Conrad: *Nostromo.*
1907		Conrad: *The Secret Agent.*
1908		Forster: *A Room with a View.* Bennett: *The Old Wives' Tale.*
1910	Attends Heath Mount preparatory school. *The Curse of the Horse Race* (unpublished).	Forster: *Howards End.*
1911		Lawrence: *The White Peacock.*
1913		Lawrence: *Sons and Lovers.* Proust: *A la Recherche du temps perdu.*
1914		Conrad: *Chance.* Joyce: *Dubliners.*
1915		Madox Ford: *The Good Soldier.* Conrad: *Victory.* Buchan: *The Thirty-Nine Steps.* Woolf: *The Voyage Out.*
1916	Attends Lancing College. Starts to write diaries which continue throughout his life.	Joyce: *A Portrait of the Artist as a Young Man.* Shaw: *Pygmalion.*
1917		Yeats: *The Wild Swans at Coole.* Eliot: *Prufrock and Other Observations.*
1918		Brooke: *Collected Poems.* Pirandello: *Six Characters in Search of an Author.*
1919		Shaw: *Heartbreak House.*
1920		Pound: *Hugh Selwyn Mauberley.*
1921	Attends Hertford College, Oxford; also studies at the Ruskin School of Art.	Huxley: *Crome Yellow.*

Emmeline Pankhurst founds the Women's Social and Political Union.

Russo-Japanese War.

Asquith becomes Prime Minister.
Death of Edward VII. Liberals back in power.

Coronation of George V. Agadir crisis. Suffragette riots.

Outbreak of World War I.
Asquith forms coalition government with Balfour.

First battle of the Somme. Lloyd George becomes Prime Minister.

Russian revolution. US joins war. Third Battle of Ypres.

Armistice. Women over thirty gain vote.

Versailles peace conference.
League of Nations formed. Prohibition in the US.

DATE	AUTHOR'S LIFE	LITERARY CONTEXT
1922		Joyce: *Ulysses*. Eliot: *The Waste Land*. Housman: *Last Poems*. Fitzgerald: *The Beautiful and the Damned*.
1923	*Anthony, Who Sought Things That Were Lost*.	e e cummings: *The Enormous Room*. Huxley: *Antic Hay*.
1924	Leaves Oxford with a third class honours degree. Waugh then becomes a master at a preparatory school. *The Temple at Thatch* (unpublished).	Forster: *A Passage to India*. Shaw: *Saint Joan*.
1925		Fitzgerald: *The Great Gatsby*. Kafka: *The Trial*.
1926	Trains as a carpenter. *P.R.B. An Essay on the Pre-Raphaelite Brotherhood* (printed privately). *The Balance* (Georgian Papers).	Faulkner: *Soldiers' Pay*. Nabokov: *Mary*. Henry Green: *Blindness*.
1927	Meets and marries Evelyn Gardner. Publishes his first book, a biography of Dante Gabriel Rossetti.	Woolf: *To the Lighthouse*. Hemingway: *Men Without Women*. Dunne: *An Experiment with Time*.
1928	*Decline and Fall*.	Lawrence: *Lady Chatterley's Lover*. Woolf: *Orlando*. Yeats: *The Tower*. Lewis: *The Childermass*. Nabokov: *King, Queen, Knave*.
1929	Divorces his wife Evelyn.	Faulkner: *The Sound and the Fury*. Cocteau: *Les Enfants terribles*. Hemingway: *A Farewell to Arms*. Priestley: *The Good Companions*. Remarque: *All Quiet on the Western Front*.
1930	Converts to Roman Catholicism. *Vile Bodies*, *Labels*.	Eliot: *Ash Wednesday*. Faulkner: *As I Lay Dying*. Nabokov: *The Defence*.
1931	Travels around Africa and South America. *Remote People*.	Faulkner: *Sanctuary*.

HISTORICAL EVENTS

Stalin becomes General Secretary of the Communist party Central Committee. Mussolini marches on Rome. Coalition falls and Bonar Law forms Conservative ministry.

Baldwin becomes Prime Minister. Hitler's coup in Munich fails. Women gain legal equality in divorce suits.

First Labour government formed by Ramsay MacDonald. Hitler in prison. Death of Lenin. Baldwin becomes Prime Minister again after a Conservative election victory.

Locarno conference.

British general strike. First television demonstrated. Stalin begins to oust Trotsky. French financial crisis.

German economy collapses.

Hoover becomes US president.

Wall Street crash.

Gandhi begins civil disobedience campaign in India. Nazis win seats from the moderates in German election.

DATE	AUTHOR'S LIFE	LITERARY CONTEXT
1932	*Black Mischief, Cruise, Bella Fleace Gave a Party, Incident in Anzania.*	Huxley: *Brave New World.* Faulkner: *Light in August.* Nabokov: *Glory.*
1933	*Out of Depth.*	Malraux: *La Condition humaine.* Stein: *The Autobiography of Alice B. Toklas.*
1934	*A Handful of Dust, Mr. Loveday's Little Outing, On Guard, Ninety-Two Days.*	
1935	*Winner Takes All*, also a biography of Edmund Campion.	Isherwood: *Mr. Norris Changes Trains.* Eliot: *Murder in the Cathedral.* Odets: *Waiting for Lefty.* Graham Greene: *England Made Me.*
1936	*Period Piece, Excursion in Reality, Waugh in Abyssinia, Love in the Slumps.*	Faulkner: *Absalom, Absalom!* Nabokov: *Despair.*
1937	Marries Laura Herbert.	Hemingway: *To Have and Have Not.* Orwell: *The Road to Wigan Pier.* Sartre: *La Nausée.* Steinbeck: *Of Mice and Men.*
1938	Birth of his daughter Teresa. *Scoop.*	Graham Greene: *Brighton Rock.* Beckett: *Murphy.* Orwell: *Homage to Catalonia.*
1939	Birth of his son Auberon. Joins the Royal Marines and then the Commandos, serving throughout the war. *An Englishman's Home, Robbery Under Law.*	Joyce: *Finnegans Wake.* Eliot: *The Family Reunion.* Steinbeck: *The Grapes of Wrath.* Henry Green: *Party Going.* Auden: *Journey to a War.* Isherwood: *Goodbye to Berlin.*
1940		Hemingway: *For Whom the Bell Tolls.* Graham Greene: *The Power and the Glory.* Dylan Thomas: *Portrait of the Artist as a Young Dog.* Faulkner: *The Hamlet.* Henry Green: *Pack my Bag: A Self-Portrait.*
1941		Acton: *Peonies and Ponies.* Fitzgerald: *The Last Tycoon.*

CHRONOLOGY

Hunger marches in Britain. F. D. Roosevelt's landslide victory.

Hitler becomes Chancellor of Germany. Nazi persecution of Jews begins.

Riots in Paris.

Italy invades Abyssinia.

Spanish civil war begins. Abdication crisis in Britain.

Japanese invade China. Attempts are made to appease Hitler. Discovery of Fascist plot in Paris. Baldwin retires and Neville Chamberlain becomes Prime Minister.

Germany annexes Austria. Munich crisis.

Germany invades Czechoslovakia and Poland; Britain and France declare war (September 3).

Churchill becomes Prime Minister. France falls and Italy joins the war in alliance with Germany.

USSR is invaded. Japanese attack Pearl Harbor. US joins war.

DATE	AUTHOR'S LIFE	LITERARY CONTEXT
1942	Birth of his daughter Margaret (died 1986). *Put Out More Flags* (a sequel to *Black Mischief*), *Work Suspended*.	Anouilh: *Eurydice*. Sartre: *Les Mouches*. Camus: *L'Etranger*. Camus: *Le Mythe de Sisyphe*.
1943		Davies: *Collected Poems*. Henry Green: *Caught*.
1944	Birth of his daughter Harriet.	Eliot: *Four Quartets*. Anouilh: *Antigone*. Camus: *Caligula*. Sartre: *Huis Clos*.
1945	*Brideshead Revisited, Charles Ryder's School Days*.	Broch: *The Death of Virgil*. Betjeman: *New Bats in Old Belfries*. Orwell: *Animal Farm*. Henry Green: *Loving*.
1946	Birth of his son James. *Scott-King's Modern Europe, When the Going Was Good*.	Rattigan: *The Winslow Boy*. Cocteau: *L'Aigle à deux têtes*. Henry Green: *Back*. Dylan Thomas: *Deaths and Entrances*.
1947	*Wine in Peace and War*.	Mann: *Doctor Faustus*. Camus: *La Peste*. Diary of Anne Frank is published. Henry Green: *Concluding*.
1948	*The Loved One*.	Eliot: *Notes Towards the Definition of Culture*. Graham Greene: *The Heart of the Matter*. Faulkner: *Intruder in the Dust*. Henry Green: *Nothing*. Acton: *Memoirs of an Aesthete*.
1949		Orwell: *Nineteen Eighty-Four*. De Beauvoir: *The Second Sex*. Graham Greene: *The Third Man*. Miller: *Death of a Salesman*.
1950	Birth of his son Septimus. *Helena*.	Lawrence Durrell: *Sappho*. Hemingway: *Across the River and into the Trees*. Eliot: *The Cocktail Party*. Henry Green: *Doting*.
1951		Salinger: *The Catcher in the Rye*. Powell: *A Question of Upbringing* (the first of the 12 novels comprising *A Dance to the Music of Time*: 1952–75).

Germans retreat in Russia, Africa and Italy.

Germany is besieged.

Hitler commits suicide. World War II ends after atom bombs are dropped on Hiroshima and Nagasaki.

Iron curtain speech by Churchill.

Gruppe 47 founded by Young German Writers. Dead Sea scrolls are discovered.

Erhard launches the Deutschemark.

Germany is divided: Adenauer is Chancellor of West Germany, Ulbricht rules East.

Korea declares itself an independent state. Macarthy witch hunts – persecution of Communists throughout US.

DATE	AUTHOR'S LIFE	LITERARY CONTEXT
1952	*Men at Arms*, the first part of the *Sword of Honour* trilogy. *The Holy Places*.	Beckett: *Waiting for Godot*. Miller: *The Crucible*.
1953	*Love Among the Ruins*.	Hartley: *The Go-Between*.
1955	Moves to a large country house in Somerset with his family. *Officers and Gentlemen*, the second part of the *Sword of Honour* trilogy.	Nabokov: *Lolita*. Miller: *A View from the Bridge*. Graham Greene: *Loser Takes All*; *The Quiet American*. Murdoch: *Under The Net*.
1956		Beckett: *Molloy*. Camus: *The Fall*. Faulkner: *Requiem for a Nun*.
1957	*The Ordeal of Gilbert Pinfold*.	Camus: *L'Exil et le Royaume*. Pasternak: *Doctor Zhivago*. Pinter: *The Birthday Party*. Nabokov: *Pnin*. Spark: *The Comforters*.
1959	Publishes a biography of Ronald Knox.	Spark: *Memento Mori*. Eliot: *The Elder Statesman*. Graham Greene: *The Complaisant Lover*. Beckett: *Endgame*.
1960	*A Tourist in Africa*.	Spark: *The Ballad of Peckham Rye*. Updike: *Rabbit, Run*. Pinter: *The Caretaker*. Betjeman: *Summoned by Bells*.
1961	*Unconditional Surrender*, the final part of the *Sword of Honour* trilogy.	Graham Greene: *A Burnt-Out Case*. Albee: *The American Dream*. Huxley: *Religion without Revelation*. Spark: *The Prime of Miss Jean Brodie*.
1962	*Tactical Exercise*.	Albee: *Who's Afraid of Virginia Woolf?* Isherwood: *Down There on a Visit*.
1963	*Basil Seal Rides Again*.	Stoppard: *A Walk on Water*. Pinter: *The Lover*. Spark: *The Girls of Slender Means*.
1964	*A Little Learning*, an autobiography.	Sartre: *Les Mots*. Ayme: *The Minotaur*. Isherwood: *A Single Man*.
1965		Pinter: *The Homecoming*. Albee: *Tiny Alice*.
1966	Waugh dies at his home after Mass on Easter Sunday.	Albee: *A Delicate Balance*.

CHRONOLOGY

BRIDESHEAD REVISITED

The sacred and profane Memories
of Captain Charles Ryder

AUTHOR'S NOTE

I am not I: thou art not he or she:
they are not they
E.W.

CONTENTS

To
LAURA

PREFACE

THIS novel, which is here re-issued with many small additions and some substantial cuts, lost me such esteem as I once enjoyed among my contemporaries and led me into an unfamiliar world of fan-mail and press photographers. Its theme – the operation of divine grace on a group of diverse but closely connected characters – was perhaps presumptuously large, but I make no apology for it. I am less happy about its form, whose more glaring defects may be blamed on the circumstances in which it was written.

In December 1943 I had the good fortune when parachuting to incur a minor injury which afforded me a rest from military service. This was extended by a sympathetic commanding officer, who let me remain unemployed until June 1944 when the book was finished. I wrote with a zest that was quite strange to me and also with impatience to get back to the war. It was a bleak period of present privation and threatening disaster – the period of soya beans and Basic English – and in consequence the book is infused with a kind of gluttony, for food and wine, for the splendours of the recent past, and for rhetorical and ornamental language, which now with a full stomach I find distasteful. I have modified the grosser passages but have not obliterated them because they are an essential part of the book.

I have been in two minds as to the treatment of Julia's outburst about mortal sin and Lord Marchmain's dying soliloquy. These passages were never, of course, intended to report words actually spoken. They belong to a different way of writing from, say, the early scenes between Charles and his father. I would not now introduce them into a novel which elsewhere aims at verisimilitude. But I have retained them here in something near their original form because, like the

Burgundy (misprinted in many editions) and the moonlight they were essentially of the mood of writing; also because many readers liked them, though that is not a consideration of first importance.

It was impossible to foresee, in the spring of 1944, the present cult of the English country house. It seemed then that the ancestral seats which were our chief national artistic achievement were doomed to decay and spoliation like the monasteries in the sixteenth century. So I piled it on rather, with passionate sincerity. Brideshead today would be open to trippers, its treasures rearranged by expert hands and the fabric better maintained than it was by Lord Marchmain. And the English aristocracy has maintained its identity to a degree that then seemed impossible. The advance of Hooper has been held up at several points. Much of this book therefore is a panegyric preached over an empty coffin. But it would be impossible to bring it up to date without totally destroying it. It is offered to a younger generation of readers as a souvenir of the Second War rather than of the twenties or of the thirties, with which it ostensibly deals.

E. W.

Combe Florey 1959

PROLOGUE
Brideshead Revisited

WHEN I reached 'C' Company lines, which were at the top of the hill, I paused and looked back at the camp, just coming into full view below me through the grey mist of early morning. We were leaving that day. When we marched in, three months before, the place was under snow; now the first leaves of spring were unfolding. I had reflected then that, whatever scenes of desolation lay ahead of us, I never feared one more brutal than this, and I reflected now that it had no single happy memory for me.

Here love had died between me and the army.

Here the tram-lines ended, so that men returning fuddled from Glasgow could doze in their seats until roused by their journey's end. There was some way to go from the tram-stop to the camp gates; quarter of a mile in which they could button their blouses and straighten their caps before passing the guard-room, quarter of a mile in which concrete gave place to grass at the road's edge. This was the extreme limit of the city. Here the close, homogeneous territory of housing estates and cinemas ended and the hinterland began.

The camp stood where, until quite lately, had been pasture and ploughland; the farmhouse still stood in a fold of the hill and had served us for battalion offices; ivy still supported part of what had once been the walls of a fruit garden; half an acre of mutilated old trees behind the wash-houses survived of an orchard. The place had been marked for destruction before the army came to it. Had there been another year of peace, there would have been no farmhouse, no wall, no apple trees. Already half a mile of concrete road lay between bare clay banks, and on either side a chequer of open ditches showed where the municipal contractors had designed a system of drainage. Another

year of peace would have made the place part of the neighbouring suburb. Now the huts where we had wintered waited their
turn for destruction.

Over the way, the subject of much ironical comment, half
hidden even in winter by its embosoming trees, lay the municipal lunatic asylum, whose cast-iron railings and noble gates put
our rough wire to shame. We could watch the madmen, on
clement days, sauntering and skipping among the trim gravel
walks and pleasantly planted lawns; happy collaborationists
who had given up the unequal struggle, all doubts resolved, all
duty done, the undisputed heirs-at-law of a century of progress,
enjoying the heritage at their ease. As we marched past, the
men used to shout greetings to them through the railings –
'Keep a bed warm for me, chum. I shan't be long' – but
Hooper, my newest-joined platoon-commander, grudged them
their life of privilege; 'Hitler would put them in a gas chamber,'
he said; 'I reckon we can learn a thing or two from him.'

Here, when we marched in at mid-winter, I brought a
company of strong and hopeful men; word had gone round
among them, as we moved from the moors to this dockland
area, that we were at last in transit for the Middle East. As the
days passed and we began clearing the snow and levelling a
parade ground, I saw their disappointment change to resignation. They snuffed the smell of the fried-fish shops and cocked
their ears to familiar, peace-time sounds of the works' siren and
the dance-hall band. On off-days they slouched now at street
corners and sidled away at the approach of an officer for fear
that, by saluting, they would lose face with their new mistresses.
In the company office there was a crop of minor charges and
requests for compassionate leave; while it was still half-light,
day began with the whine of the malingerer and the glum face
and fixed eye of the man with a grievance.

And I, who by every precept should have put heart into
them – how could I help them, who could so little help myself?
Here the colonel under whom we had formed, was promoted
out of our sight and succeeded by a younger and less lovable
man, cross-posted from another regiment. There were few left in

the mess now of the batch of volunteers who trained together at the outbreak of war; one way and another they were nearly all gone – some had been invalided out, some promoted to other battalions, some posted to staff jobs, some had volunteered for special service, one had got himself killed on the field firing range, one had been court-martialled – and their places were taken by conscripts; the wireless played incessantly in the ante-room nowadays, and much beer was drunk before dinner; it was not as it had been.

Here at the age of thirty-nine I began to be old. I felt stiff and weary in the evenings and reluctant to go out of camp; I developed proprietary claims to certain chairs and newspapers; I regularly drank three glasses of gin before dinner, never more or less, and went to bed immediately after the nine o'clock news. I was always awake and fretful an hour before reveille.

Here my last love died. There was nothing remarkable in the manner of its death. One day, not long before this last day in camp, as I lay awake before reveille, in the Nissen hut, gazing into the complete blackness, amid the deep breathing and muttering of the four other occupants, turning over in my mind what I had to do that day – had I put in the names of two corporals for the weapon-training course? Should I again have the largest number of men overstaying their leave in the batch due back that day? Could I trust Hooper to take the candidates class out map-reading? – as I lay in that dark hour, I was aghast to realize that something within me, long sickening, had quietly died, and felt as a husband might feel, who, in the fourth year of his marriage, suddenly knew that he had no longer any desire, or tenderness, or esteem, for a once-beloved wife; no pleasure in her company, no wish to please, no curiosity about anything she might ever do or say or think; no hope of setting things right, no self-reproach for the disaster. I knew it all, the whole drab compass of marital disillusion; we had been through it together, the Army and I, from the first importunate courtship until now, when nothing remained to us except the chill bonds of law and duty and custom. I had played every scene in the domestic tragedy, had found the early tiffs become more frequent, the tears less affecting, the reconciliations less sweet, till they engendered a mood of aloofness and cool criticism, and the growing conviction that it was not myself but the loved one who was at fault. I caught the false notes in her voice and learned to listen for them apprehensively; I recognized the blank, resentful stare of incomprehension in her eyes, and the selfish, hard set of the corners of her mouth. I learned her, as one must learn a woman one has kept house with, day in, day out, for three and a half years; I learned her slatternly ways, the routine and mechanism of her charm, her jealousy and self-seeking, and her nervous trick with the fingers when she was lying. She was stripped of all enchantment now and I knew her for an uncongenial stranger to whom I had bound myself indissolubly in a moment of folly.

So, on this morning of our move, I was entirely indifferent as to our destination. I would go on with my job, but I could bring to it nothing more than acquiescence. Our orders were to entrain at 0915 hours at a nearby siding, taking in the haver-sack the unexpired portion of the day's ration; that was all I needed to know. The company second-in-command had gone on with a small advance party. Company stores had been packed the day before. Hooper had been detailed to inspect the lines. The company was parading at 0730 hours with their kit-bags piled before the huts. There had been many such moves since the wildly exhilarating morning in 1940 when we had erroneously believed ourselves destined for the defence of Calais. Three or four times a year since then we had changed our location; this time our new commanding officer was making an unusual display of 'security' and had even put us to the trouble of removing all distinguishing badges from our uniforms and transport. It was 'valuable training in active service conditions', he said. 'If I find any of these female camp followers waiting for us the other end, I'll know there's been a leakage.'

The smoke from the cook-houses drifted away in the mist and the camp lay revealed as a planless maze of short-cuts, superimposed on the unfinished housing-scheme, as though disinterred at a much later date by a party of archaeologists.

'*The Pollock diggings provide a valuable link between the citizen-slave communities of the twentieth century and the tribal anarchy which succeeded them. Here you see a people of advanced culture, capable of an elaborate draining system and the construction of permanent highways, over-run by a race of the lowest type.*'

Thus, I thought, the pundits of the future might write; and, turning away, I greeted the company sergeant-major: 'Has Mr Hooper been round?'

'Haven't seen him at all this morning, sir.'

We went to the dismantled company office, where I found a window newly broken since the barrack-damages book was completed. 'Wind-in-the-night, sir,' said the sergeant-major.

(All breakages were thus attributable or to 'Sappers'-demonstration, sir.')

Hooper appeared; he was a sallow youth with hair combed back, without parting, from his forehead, and a flat, Midland accent; he had been in the company two months.

The troops did not like Hooper because he knew too little about his work and would sometimes address them individually as 'George' at stand-easies, but I had a feeling which almost amounted to affection for him, largely by reason of an incident on his first evening in mess.

The new colonel had been with us less than a week at the time and we had not yet taken his measure. He had been standing rounds of gin in the ante-room and was slightly boisterous when he first took notice of Hooper.

'That young officer is one of yours, isn't he, Ryder?' he said to me. 'His hair wants cutting.'

'It does, sir,' I said. It did. 'I'll see that it's done.'

The colonel drank more gin and began to stare at Hooper, saying audibly, 'My God, the officers they send us now!'

Hooper seemed to obsess the colonel that evening. After dinner he suddenly said very loudly: 'In my late regiment if a young officer turned up like that, the other subalterns would bloody well have cut his hair for him.'

No one showed any enthusiasm for this sport, and our lack of response seemed to inflame the colonel. 'You,' he said, turning to a decent boy in 'A' Company, 'go and get a pair of scissors and cut that young officer's hair for him.'

'Is that an order, sir?'

'It's your commanding officer's wish and that's the best kind of order I know.'

'Very good, sir.'

And so, in an atmosphere of chilly embarrassment, Hooper sat in a chair while a few snips were made at the back of his head. At the beginning of the operation I left the ante-room, and later apologized to Hooper for his reception. 'It's not the sort of thing that usually happens in this regiment,' I said.

'Oh, no hard feelings,' said Hooper. 'I can take a bit of sport.'

Hooper had no illusions about the Army – or rather no special illusions distinguishable from the general, enveloping fog from which he observed the universe. He had come to it reluctantly, under compulsion, after he had made every feeble effort in his power to obtain deferment. He accepted it, he said, 'like the measles'. Hooper was no romantic. He had not as a child ridden with Rupert's horse or sat among the camp fires at Xanthus-side; at the age when my eyes were dry to all save poetry – that stoic, redskin interlude which our schools introduce between the fast-flowing tears of the child and the man – Hooper had wept often, but never for Henry's speech on St Crispin's day, nor for the epitaph at Thermopylae. The history they taught him had had few battles in it but, instead, a profusion of detail about humane legislation and recent industrial change. Gallipoli, Balaclava, Quebec, Lepanto, Bannockburn, Roncevales, and Marathon – these, and the Battle in the West where Arthur fell, and a hundred such names whose trumpet-notes, even now in my sere and lawless state, called to me irresistibly across the intervening years with all the clarity and strength of boyhood, sounded in vain to Hooper.

He seldom complained. Though himself a man to whom one could not confidently entrust the simplest duty, he had an over-mastering regard for efficiency and, drawing on his modest commercial experience, he would sometimes say of the ways of the Army in pay and supply and the use of 'man-hours': 'They couldn't get away with that in business.'

He slept sound while I lay awake fretting.

In the weeks that we were together Hooper became a symbol to me of Young England, so that whenever I read some public utterance proclaiming what Youth demanded in the Future and what the world owed to Youth, I would test these general statements by substituting 'Hooper' and seeing if they still seemed as plausible. Thus in the dark hour before reveille I sometimes pondered: 'Hooper Rallies', 'Hooper Hostels', 'International Hooper Cooperation', and 'the Religion of Hooper'. He was the acid test of all these alloys.

So far as he had changed at all, he was less soldierly now than when he arrived from his OCTU. This morning, laden with full equipment, he looked scarcely human. He came to attention with a kind of shuffling dance-step and spread a wool-gloved palm across his forehead.

'I want to speak to Mr Hooper, sergeant-major ... well, where the devil have you been? I told you to inspect the lines.'

''M I late? Sorry. Had a rush getting my gear together.'

'That's what you have a servant for.'

'Well, I suppose it is, strictly speaking. But you know how it is. He had his own stuff to do. If you get on the wrong side of these fellows they take it out of you other ways.'

'Well, go and inspect the lines now.'

'Rightyoh.'

'And for Christ's sake don't say "rightyoh".'

'Sorry. I do try to remember. It just slips out.'

When Hooper left the sergeant-major returned.

'C.O. just coming up the path, sir,' he said.

I went out to meet him.

There were beads of moisture on the hog-bristles of his little red moustache.

'Well, everything squared up here?'

'Yes, I think so, sir.'

'*Think so?* You ought to know.'

His eyes fell on the broken window. 'Has that been entered in the barrack damages?'

'Not yet, sir.'

'*Not yet?* I wonder when it would have been, if I hadn't seen it.'

He was not at ease with me, and much of his bluster rose from timidity, but I thought none the better of it for that.

He led me behind the huts to a wire fence which divided my area from the carrier-platoon's, skipped briskly over, and made for an overgrown ditch and bank which had once been a field boundary on the farm. Here he began grubbing with his walking-stick like a truffling pig and presently gave a cry of triumph. He had disclosed one of those deposits of rubbish, which are dear to the private soldier's sense of order: the head of a broom, the lid of a stove, a bucket rusted through, a sock, a loaf of bread, lay under the dock and nettle among cigarette packets and empty tins.

'Look at that,' said the commanding officer. 'Fine impression that gives to the regiment taking over from us.'

'That's bad,' I said.

'It's a disgrace. See everything there is burned before you leave camp.'

'Very good, sir. Sergeant-major, send over to the carrier-platoon and tell Captain Brown that the C.O. wants this ditch cleared up.'

I wondered whether the colonel would take this rebuff; so did he. He stood a moment irresolutely prodding the muck in the ditch, then he turned on his heel and strode away.

'You shouldn't do it, sir,' said the sergeant-major, who had been my guide and prop since I joined the company. 'You shouldn't really.'

'That wasn't our rubbish.'

'Maybe not, sir, but you know how it is. If you get on the wrong side of senior officers they take it out of you other ways.'

As we marched past the madhouse, two or three elderly inmates gibbered and mouthed politely behind the railings.

'Cheeroh, chum, we'll be seeing you'; 'We shan't be long now'; 'Keep smiling till we meet again', the men called to them.

I was marching with Hooper at the head of the leading platoon.

'I say, any idea where we're off to?'

'None.'

'D'you think it's the real thing?'

'No.'

'Just a flap?'

'Yes.'

'Everyone's been saying we're for it. I don't know what to think really. Seems so silly somehow, all this drill and training if we never go into action.'

'I shouldn't worry. There'll be plenty for everyone in time.'

'Oh, I don't want *much* you know. Just enough to say I've been in it.'

A train of antiquated coaches was waiting for us at the siding; an R.T.O. was in charge; a fatigue party was loading the last of the kit-bags from the trucks to the luggage vans. In half an hour we were ready to start and in an hour we started.

My three platoon commanders and myself had a carriage to ourselves. They ate sandwiches and chocolate, smoked and slept. None of them had a book. For the first three or four hours they noted the names of the towns and leaned out of the windows when, as often happened, we stopped between stations. Later they lost interest. At midday and again at dark some tepid cocoa was ladled from a container into our mugs. The train moved slowly south through flat, drab main-line scenery.

The chief incident in the day was the C.O.'s 'order group'. We assembled in his carriage, at the summons of an orderly, and found him and the adjutant wearing their steel helmets and equipment. The first thing he said was: 'This is an Order Group. I expect you to attend properly dressed. The fact that we happen to be in a train is immaterial.' I thought he was going to send us back but, after glaring at us, he said, 'Sit down.'

'The camp was left in a disgraceful condition. Wherever I went I found evidence that officers are not doing their duty. The state in which a camp is left is the best possible test of the efficiency of regimental officers. It is on such matters that the reputation of a battalion and its commander rests. And' – did he in fact say this or am I finding words for the resentment in his voice and eye? I think he left it unsaid – 'I do not intend to have my professional reputation compromised by the slackness of a few temporary officers.'

We sat with our note-books and pencils waiting to take down the details of our next jobs. A more sensitive man would have seen that he had failed to be impressive; perhaps he saw, for he added in a petulant schoolmasterish way: 'All I ask is loyal cooperation.'

Then he referred to his notes and read:

'Orders.

'Information. The battalion is now in transit between location A and location B. This is a major L of C and is liable to bombing and gas attack from the enemy.

'Intention. I intend to arrive at location B.

'Method. Train will arrive at destination at approximately 2315 hours ...' and so on.

The sting came at the end under the heading, 'Administration'. 'C' Company, less one platoon, was to unload the train on arrival at the siding where three three-tonners would be available for moving all stores to a battalion dump in the new camp; work to continue until completed; the remaining platoon was to find a guard on the dump and perimeter sentries for the camp area.

'Any questions?'

'Can we have an issue of cocoa for the working party?'

'No. Any more questions?'

When I told the sergeant-major of these orders he said: 'Poor old "C" Company struck unlucky again'; and I knew this to be a reproach for my having antagonized the commanding officer.

I told the platoon commanders.

'I say,' said Hooper, 'it makes it awfully awkward with the

chaps. They'll be fairly browned off. He always seems to pick on us for the dirty work.'

'You'll do guard.'

'Okeydoke. But I say, how am I to find the perimeter in the dark?'

Shortly after blackout we were disturbed by an orderly making his way lugubriously down the length of the train with a rattle. One of the more sophisticated sergeants called out '*Deuxième service.*'

'We are being sprayed with liquid mustard-gas,' I said. 'See that the windows are shut.' I then wrote a neat little situation-report to say that there were no casualties and nothing had been contaminated; that men had been detailed to decontaminate the outside of the coach before detraining. This seemed to satisfy the commanding officer, for we heard no more from him. After dark we all slept.

At last, very late, we came to our siding. It was part of our training in security and active service conditions that we should eschew stations and platforms. The drop from the running board to the cinder track made for disorder and breakages in the darkness.

'Fall in on the road below the embankment. "C" Company seem to be taking their time as usual, Captain Ryder.'

'Yes, sir. We're having a little difficulty with the bleach.'

'Bleach?'

'For decontaminating the outside of the coaches, sir.'

'Oh, very conscientious, I'm sure. Skip it and get a move on.'

By now my half-awake and sulky men were clattering into shape on the road. Soon Hooper's platoon had marched off into the darkness; I found the lorries, organized lines of men to pass the stores from hand to hand down the steep bank, and, presently, as they found themselves doing something with an apparent purpose in it, they got more cheerful. I handled stores with them for the first half hour; then broke off to meet the company second-in-command who came down with the first returning truck.

'It's not a bad camp,' he reported; 'big private house with

two or three lakes. Looks as if we might get some duck if we're lucky. Village with one pub and a post office. No town within miles. I've managed to get a hut between the two of us.'

By four in the morning the work was done. I drove in the last lorry, through tortuous lanes where the overhanging boughs whipped the windscreen; somewhere we left the lane and turned into a drive; somewhere we reached an open space where two drives converged and a ring of storm lanterns marked the heap of stores. Here we unloaded the truck and, at long last, followed the guides to our quarters, under a starless sky, with a fine drizzle of rain beginning now to fall.

I slept until my servant called me, rose wearily, dressed and shaved in silence. It was not till I reached the door that I asked the second-in-command, 'What's this place called?'

He told me and, on the instant, it was as though someone had switched off the wireless, and a voice that had been bawling in my ears, incessantly, fatuously, for days beyond number, had been suddenly cut short; an immense silence followed, empty at first, but gradually, as my outraged sense regained authority, full of a multitude of sweet and natural and long forgotten sounds: for he had spoken a name that was so familiar to me, a conjuror's name of such ancient power, that, at its mere sound, the phantoms of those haunted late years began to take flight.

Outside the hut I stood bemused. The rain had ceased but the clouds hung low and heavy overhead. It was a still morning and the smoke from the cook-house rose straight to the leaden sky. A cart-track, once metalled, then overgrown, now rutted and churned to mud, followed the contour of the hillside and dipped out of sight below a knoll, and on either side of it lay the haphazard litter of corrugated iron, from which rose the rattle and chatter and whistling and catcalls, all the zoo-noises of the battalion beginning a new day. Beyond and about us, more familiar still, lay an exquisite man-made landscape. It was a sequestered place, enclosed and embraced in a single, winding valley. Our camp lay along one gentle slope; opposite us the ground led, still unravished, to the neighbourly horizon, and between us flowed a stream – it was named the Bride and rose not two miles away at a farm called Bridesprings, where we used sometimes to walk to tea; it became a considerable river lower down before it joined the Avon – which had been dammed here to form three lakes, one no more than a wet slate among the reeds, but the others more spacious, reflecting the clouds and the mighty beeches at their margin. The woods were all of oak and beech, the oak grey and bare, the beech faintly dusted with green by the breaking buds; they made a simple, carefully designed pattern with the green glades and the wide green spaces – Did the fallow deer graze here still? – and, lest the eye wander aimlessly, a Doric temple stood by the water's edge, and an ivy-grown arch spanned the lowest of the connecting weirs. All this had been planned and planted a century and a half ago so that, at about this date, it might be seen in its maturity. From where I stood the house was hidden by a green spur, but I knew well how and where it lay, couched among the lime trees like a hind in the bracken.

Hooper came sidling up and greeted me with his much imitated but inimitable salute. His face was grey from his night's vigil and he had not yet shaved.

'"B" Company relieved us. I've sent the chaps off to get cleaned up.'

'Good.'

'The house is up there, round the corner.'

'Yes,' I said.

'Brigade Headquarters are coming there next week. Great barrack of a place. I've just had a snoop round. Very ornate, I'd call it. And a queer thing, there's a sort of R.C. Church attached. I looked in and there was a kind of service going on – just a padre and one old man. I felt very awkward. More in your line than mine.' Perhaps I seemed not to hear; in a final effort to excite my interest he said: 'There's a frightful great fountain, too, in front of the steps, all rocks and sort of carved animals. You never saw such a thing.'

'Yes, Hooper, I did. I've been here before.'

The words seemed to ring back to me enriched from the vaults of my dungeon.

'Oh well, you know all about it. I'll go and get cleaned up.'

I had been there before; I knew all about it.

BOOK ONE

ET IN ARCADIA EGO

CHAPTER I

'I HAVE been here before,' I said; I had been there before; first with Sebastian more than twenty years ago on a cloudless day in June, when the ditches were creamy with meadowsweet and the air heavy with all the scents of summer; it was a day of peculiar splendour, and though I had been there so often, in so many moods, it was to that first visit that my heart returned on this, my latest.

That day, too, I had come not knowing my destination. It was Eights Week. Oxford – submerged now and obliterated, irrecoverable as Lyonnesse, so quickly have the waters come flooding in – Oxford, in those days, was still a city of aquatint. In her spacious and quiet streets men walked and spoke as they had done in Newman's day; her autumnal mists, her grey springtime, and the rare glory of her summer days – such as that day – when the chestnut was in flower and the bells rang out high and clear over her gables and cupolas, exhaled the soft airs of centuries of youth. It was this cloistral hush which gave our laughter its resonance, and carried it still, joyously, over the intervening clamour. Here, discordantly, in Eights Week, came a rabble of womankind, some hundreds strong, twittering and fluttering over the cobbles and up the steps, sight-seeing and pleasure-seeking, drinking claret cup, eating cucumber sandwiches; pushed in punts about the river, herded in droves to the college barges; greeted in the *Isis* and in the Union by a sudden display of peculiar, facetious, wholly distressing Gilbert-and-Sullivan badinage, and by peculiar choral effects in the College chapels. Echoes of the intruders penetrated every corner, and in my own College was no echo, but an original fount of the grossest disturbance. We were giving a ball. The front quad, where I lived, was floored and tented; palms and azaleas were banked round the porter's lodge; worst of all, the don who lived above me, a mouse of a man connected with the Natural Sciences, had lent his rooms for a Ladies' Cloakroom, and a printed notice proclaiming this outrage hung not six inches from my oak.

No one felt more strongly about it than my scout.

'Gentlemen who haven't got ladies are asked as far as possible to take their meals out in the next few days,' he announced despondently. 'Will you be lunching in?'

'No, Lunt.'

'So as to give the servants a chance, they say. What a chance! I've got to buy a *pin-cushion* for the Ladies' Cloakroom. What do they want with dancing? I don't see the reason in it. There never was dancing before in Eights Week. Commem. now is another matter being in the vacation, but not in Eights Week, as if teas and the river wasn't enough. If you ask me, sir, it's all on account of the war. It couldn't have happened but for that.' For this was 1923 and for Lunt, as for thousands of others, things could never be the same as they had been in 1914. 'Now wine in the evening,' he continued, as was his habit half in and half out of the door, 'or one or two gentlemen to luncheon, there's reason in. But not dancing. It all came in with the men back from the war. They were too old and they didn't know and they wouldn't learn. That's the truth. And there's some even goes dancing with the town at the Masonic – but the proctors will get *them*, you see ... Well, here's Lord Sebastian. I mustn't stand here talking when there's pin-cushions to get.'

Sebastian entered – dove-grey flannel, white *crêpe de Chine*, a Charvet tie, my tie as it happened, a pattern of postage stamps – 'Charles – what in the world's happening at your college? Is there a circus? I've seen everything except elephants. I must say the whole of Oxford has become *most* peculiar suddenly. Last night it was pullulating with women. You're to come away at once, out of danger. I've got a motor-car and a basket of strawberries and a bottle of Château Peyraguey – which isn't a wine you've ever tasted, so don't pretend. It's heaven with strawberries.'

'Where are we going?'

'To see a friend.'

'Who?'

'Name of Hawkins. Bring some money in case we see anything we want to buy. The motor-car is the property of a man called Hardcastle. Return the bits to him if I kill myself; I'm not very good at driving.'

Beyond the gate, beyond the winter garden that was once the lodge, stood an open, two-seater Morris-Cowley. Sebastian's teddy-bear sat at the wheel. We put him between us – 'Take care he's not sick' – and drove off. The bells of St Mary's were chiming nine; we escaped collision with a clergyman, black-straw-hatted, white-bearded, pedalling quietly down the wrong side of the High Street, crossed Carfax, passed the station, and were soon in open country on the Botley Road; open country was easily reached in those days.

'Isn't it early?' said Sebastian. 'The women are still doing whatever women do to themselves before they come downstairs. Sloth has undone them. We're away. God bless Hardcastle.'

'Whoever he may be.'

'He thought he was coming with us. Sloth undid him too. Well, I did tell him *ten*. He's a very gloomy man in my college. He leads a double life. At least I assume he does. He couldn't go on being Hardcastle, day and night, always, could he? – or he'd die of it. He says he knows my father, which is impossible.'

'Why?'

'No one knows papa. He's a social leper. Hadn't you heard?'

'It's a pity neither of us can sing,' I said.

At Swindon we turned off the main road and, as the sun mounted high, we were among dry-stone walls and ashlar houses. It was about eleven when Sebastian, without warning, turned the car into a cart-track and stopped. It was hot enough now to make us seek the shade. On a sheep-cropped knoll under a clump of elms we ate the strawberries and drank the wine – as Sebastian promised, they were delicious together – and we lit fat, Turkish cigarettes and lay on our backs, Sebastian's eyes on the leaves above him, mine on his profile, while the blue-grey smoke rose, untroubled by any wind, to the blue-green shadows of foliage, and the sweet scent of the tobacco merged with the sweet summer scents around us and the fumes of the sweet, golden wine seemed to lift us a finger's breadth above the turf and hold us suspended.

'Just the place to bury a crock of gold,' said Sebastian. 'I should like to bury something precious in every place where I've been happy and then, when I was old and ugly and miserable, I could come back and dig it up and remember.'

This was my third term since matriculation, but I date my Oxford life from my first meeting with Sebastian, which had happened, by chance, in the middle of the term before. We were in different colleges and came from different schools; I might well have spent my three or four years in the University and never have met him, but for the chance of his getting drunk one evening in my college and of my having ground-floor rooms in the front quadrangle.

I had been warned against the dangers of these rooms by my cousin Jasper, who alone, when I first came up, thought me a suitable subject for detailed guidance. My father offered me none. Then, as always, he eschewed serious conversation with me. It was not until I was within a fortnight of going up that he mentioned the subject at all; then he said, shyly and rather slyly: 'I've been talking about you. I met your future Warden at the Athenaeum. I wanted to talk about Etruscan notions of immortality; he wanted to talk about extension lectures for the working class; so we compromised and talked about you. I asked him what your allowance should be. He said, 'Three hundred a year; on no account give him more; that's all most men have.' I thought that a deplorable answer. *I* had more than most men when *I* was up, and my recollection is that nowhere else in the world and at no other time, do a few hundred pounds, one way or the other, make so much difference to one's importance and popularity. I toyed with the idea of giving you six hundred,' said my father, snuffling a little, as he did when he was amused, 'but I reflected that, should the Warden come to hear of it, it might sound deliberately impolite. So I shall give you five hundred and fifty.'

I thanked him.

'Yes, it's indulgent of me, but it all comes out of capital, you know. . . . I suppose this is the time I should give you advice. I never had any myself except once from your cousin Alfred. Do you know, in the summer before I was going up, your cousin Alfred rode over to Boughton especially to give me a piece of advice? And do you know what that advice was? 'Ned,' he said, 'there's one thing I must beg of you. *Always* wear a tall hat on Sundays during term. It is by that, more than anything, that a man is judged.' And do you know,' continued my father, snuffling deeply, 'I *always did*? Some men did, some didn't. I never saw any difference between them or heard it commented on, but I *always wore mine*. It only shows what effect judicious advice can have, properly delivered at the right moment. I wish I had some for you, but I haven't.'

My cousin Jasper made good the loss; he was the son of my father's elder brother, to whom he referred more than once, only half facetiously, as 'the Head of the Family'; he was in his fourth year and, the term before, had come within appreciable distance of getting his rowing blue; he was secretary of the Canning and president of the J.C.R.; a considerable person in college. He called on me formally during my first week and stayed to tea; he ate a very heavy meal of honey-buns, anchovy toast, and Fuller's walnut cake, then he lit his pipe and, lying back in the basket-chair, laid down the rules of conduct which I should follow; he covered most subjects; even today I could repeat much of what he said, word for word. '. . . You're reading History? A perfectly respectable school. The very worst is English literature and the next worst is Modern Greats. You want either a first or a fourth. There is no value in anything between. Time spent on a good second is time thrown away. You should go to the best lectures – Arkwright on Demosthenes for instance – irrespective of whether they are in your school or not. . . . Clothes. Dress as you do in a country house. Never wear a tweed coat and flannel trousers – always a suit. And go to a

London tailor; you get better cut and longer credit. ... Clubs. Join the Carlton now and the Grid at the beginning of your second year. If you want to run for the Union – and it's not a bad thing to do – make your reputation *outside* first, at the Canning or the Chatham, and begin by speaking on the paper. ... Keep clear of Boar's Hill. ...' The sky over the opposing gables glowed and then darkened; I put more coal on the fire and turned on the light, revealing in their respectability his London-made plus-fours and his Leander tie. ... 'Don't treat dons like schoolmasters; treat them as you would the vicar at home. ... You'll find you spend half your second year shaking off the undesirable friends you made in your first. ... Beware of the Anglo-Catholics – they're all sodomites with unpleasant accents. In fact, steer clear of all the religious groups; they do nothing but harm. ...'

Finally, just as he was going, he said, 'One last point. Change your rooms.' – They were large, with deeply recessed windows and painted, eighteenth-century panelling; I was lucky as a freshman to get them. 'I've seen many a man ruined through having ground-floor rooms in the front quad,' said my cousin with deep gravity. 'People start dropping in. They leave their gowns here and come and collect them before hall; you start giving them sherry. Before you know where you are, you've opened a free bar for all the undesirables of the college.'

I do not know that I ever, consciously, followed any of this advice. I certainly never changed my rooms; there were gilly-flowers growing below the windows which on summer evenings filled them with fragrance.

It is easy, retrospectively, to endow one's youth with a false precocity or a false innocence; to tamper with the dates marking one's stature on the edge of the door. I should like to think – indeed I sometimes do think – that I decorated those rooms with Morris stuffs and Arundel prints and that my shelves were filled with seventeenth-century folios and French novels of the second empire in Russia-leather and watered silk. But this was not the truth. On my first afternoon I proudly hung a reproduction of Van Gogh's *Sunflowers* over the fire and set up a screen,

painted by Roger Fry with a Provençal landscape, which I had
bought inexpensively when the Omega workshops were sold up.
I displayed also a poster by McKnight Kauffer and Rhyme
Sheets from the Poetry Bookshop, and, most painful to recall, a
porcelain figure of Polly Peachum which stood between black
tapers on the chimney-piece. My books were meagre and
commonplace – Roger Fry's *Vision and Design*, the Medici Press
edition of *A Shropshire Lad*, *Eminent Victorians*, some volumes of
Georgian Poetry, *Sinister Street* and *South Wind* – and my earliest
friends fitted well into this background; they were Collins, a
Wykehamist, an embryo don, a man of solid reading and
childlike humour, and a small circle of college intellectuals, who
maintained a middle course of culture between the flamboyant
'aesthetes' and the proletarian scholars who scrambled fiercely
for facts in the lodging-houses of the Iffley Road and Wellington
Square. It was by this circle that I found myself adopted during
my first term; they provided the kind of company I had enjoyed
in the sixth form at school, for which the sixth form had
prepared me; but even in the earliest days, when the whole
business of living at Oxford, with rooms of my own and my own
cheque book, was a source of excitement, I felt at heart that this
was not all which Oxford had to offer.

At Sebastian's approach these grey figures seemed quietly to
fade into the landscape and vanish, like highland sheep in the
misty heather. Collins had exposed the fallacy of modern
aesthetics to me: '. . . the whole argument from Significant Form
stands or falls by *volume*. If you allow Cézanne to represent a
third dimension on his two-dimensional canvas, then you must
allow Landseer his gleam of loyalty in the spaniel's eye' . . . but
it was not until Sebastian, idly turning the page of Clive Bell's
Art, read: "Does anyone feel the same kind of emotion for a
butterfly or a flower that he feels for a cathedral or a picture?"
Yes. *I* do,' that my eyes were opened.

I knew Sebastian by sight long before I met him. That was
unavoidable for, from his first week, he was the most conspicuous man of his year by reason of his beauty, which was
arresting, and his eccentricities of behaviour, which seemed to

know no bounds. My first sight of him was in the door of Germer's, and, on that occasion, I was struck less by his looks than by the fact that he was carrying a large teddy-bear.

'That,' said the barber, as I took his chair, 'was Lord Sebastian Flyte. A *most* amusing young gentleman.'

'Apparently,' I said coldly.

'The Marquis of Marchmain's second boy. His brother, the Earl of Brideshead, went down last term. Now he was *very* different, a very quiet gentleman, quite like an old man. What do you suppose Lord Sebastian wanted? A hair brush for his teddy-bear; it had to have very stiff bristles, *not*, Lord Sebastian said, to brush him with, but to threaten him with a spanking when he was sulky. He bought a very nice one with an ivory back and he's having "Aloysius" engraved on it – that's the bear's name.' The man, who, in his time, had had ample chance to tire of undergraduate fantasy, was plainly captivated. I, however, remained censorious, and subsequent glimpses of him, driving in a hansom cab and dining at the George in false whiskers, did not soften me, although Collins, who was reading Freud, had a number of technical terms to cover everything.

Nor, when at last we met, were the circumstances propitious. It was shortly before midnight in early March; I had been entertaining the college intellectuals to mulled claret; the fire was roaring, the air of my room heavy with smoke and spice, and my mind weary with metaphysics. I threw open my windows and from the quad outside came the not uncommon sounds of bibulous laughter and unsteady steps. A voice said: 'Hold up'; another, 'Come on'; another, 'Plenty of time ... House ... till Tom stops ringing'; and another, clearer than the rest, 'D'you know I feel most unaccountably unwell. I must leave you a minute,' and there appeared at my window the face I knew to be Sebastian's, but not, as I had formerly seen it, alive and alight with gaiety; he looked at me for a moment with unfocused eyes and then, leaning forward well into the room, he was sick.

It was not unusual for dinner parties to end in that way; there was in fact a recognized tariff for the scout on such occasions; we were all learning, by trial and error, to carry our wine. There was also a kind of insane and endearing orderliness about Sebastian's choice, in his extremity, of an open window. But, when all is said, it remained an unpropitious meeting.

His friends bore him to the gate and, in a few minutes, his host, an amiable Etonian of my year, returned to apologize. He, too, was tipsy and his explanations were repetitive and, towards the end, tearful. 'The wines were too various,' he said: 'it was neither the quality nor the quantity that was at fault. It was the mixture. Grasp that and you have the root of the matter. To understand all is to forgive all.'

'Yes,' I said, but it was with a sense of grievance that I faced Lunt's reproaches next morning.

'A couple of jugs of mulled claret between the five of you,' Lunt said, 'and *this* had to happen. Couldn't even get to the window. Those that can't keep it down are better without it.'

'It wasn't one of my party. It was someone from out of college.'

'Well, it's just as nasty clearing it up, whoever it was.'

'There's five shillings on the sideboard.'

'So I saw and thank you, but I'd rather not have the money and not have the mess, *any* morning.'

I took my gown and left him to his task. I still frequented the lecture-room in those days, and it was after eleven when I returned to college. I found my room full of flowers; what looked like, and, in fact, was, the entire day's stock of a market-stall stood in every conceivable vessel in every part of the room. Lunt was secreting the last of them in brown paper preparatory to taking them home.

'Lunt, *what* is all this?'

'The gentleman from last night, sir, he left a note for you.'

The note was written in *conté* crayon on a whole sheet of my choice Whatman H.P. drawing paper: *I am very contrite. Aloysius won't speak to me until he sees I am forgiven, so please come to luncheon today. Sebastian Flyte.* It was typical of him, I reflected, to assume I knew where he lived; but, then, I *did* know.

'A most amusing gentleman, I'm sure it's quite a pleasure to clean up after him. I take it you're lunching out, sir. I told Mr Collins and Mr Partridge so – they wanted to have their commons in here with you.'

'Yes, Lunt, lunching out.'

That luncheon party – for party it proved to be – was the beginning of a new epoch in my life.

I went there uncertainly, for it was foreign ground and there was a tiny, priggish, warning voice in my ear which in the tones of Collins told me it was seemly to hold back. But I was in search of love in those days, and I went full of curiosity and the faint, unrecognized apprehension that here, at last, I should find that low door in the wall, which others, I knew, had found before me, which opened on an enclosed and enchanted garden, which was somewhere, not overlooked by any window, in the heart of that grey city.

Sebastian lived at Christ Church, high in Meadow Buildings. He was alone when I came, peeling a plover's egg taken from the large nest of moss in the centre of his table.

'I've just counted them,' he said. 'There were five each and two over, so I'm having the two. I'm unaccountably hungry today. I put myself unreservedly in the hands of Dolbear and Goodall, and feel so drugged that I've begun to believe that the whole of yesterday evening was a dream. Please don't wake me up.'

He was entrancing, with that epicene beauty which in extreme youth sings aloud for love and withers at the first cold wind.

His room was filled with a strange jumble of objects – a harmonium in a gothic case, an elephant's-foot waste-paper basket, a dome of wax fruit, two disproportionately large Sèvres vases, framed drawings by Daumier – made all the more incongruous by the austere college furniture and the large luncheon table. His chimney-piece was covered in cards of invitation from London hostesses.

'That beast Hobson has put Aloysius next door,' he said. 'Perhaps it's as well, as there wouldn't have been any plovers' eggs for him. D'you know, Hobson hates Aloysius. I wish I had a scout like yours. He was sweet to me this morning where some people might have been quite strict.'

The party assembled. There were three Etonian freshmen, mild, elegant, detached young men who had all been to a dance in London the night before, and spoke of it as though it had been the funeral of a near but unloved kinsman. Each as he came into the room made first for the plovers' eggs, then noticed Sebastian and then myself with a polite lack of curiosity which seemed to say: 'We should not dream of being so offensive as to suggest that you never met us before.'

'The first this year,' they said. 'Where do you get them?'

'Mummy sends them from Brideshead. They always lay early for her.'

When the eggs were gone and we were eating the lobster Newburg, the last guest arrived.

'My dear,' he said, 'I couldn't get away before. I was lunching with my p-p-preposterous tutor. He thought it very odd my leaving when I did. I told him I had to change for *F-f-footer*.'

He was tall, slim, rather swarthy, with large saucy eyes. The rest of us wore rough tweeds and brogues. He had on a smooth chocolate-brown suit with loud white stripes, suède shoes, a large bow-tie and he drew off yellow, wash-leather gloves as he came into the room; part Gallic, part Yankee, part, perhaps, Jew; wholly exotic.

This, I did not need telling, was Anthony Blanche, the 'aesthete' *par excellence*, a byword of iniquity from Cherwell Edge to Somerville. He had been pointed out to me often in the streets, as he pranced along with his high peacock tread; I had heard his voice in the George challenging the conventions; and now meeting him, under the spell of Sebastian, I found myself enjoying him voraciously.

After luncheon he stood on the balcony with a megaphone which had appeared surprisingly among the bric-à-brac of Sebastian's room, and in languishing tones recited passages from *The Waste Land* to the sweatered and muffled throng that was on its way to the river.

'*I, Tiresias, have foresuffered all*,' he sobbed to them from the Venetian arches;

> '*Enacted on this same d-divan or b-bed,*
> *I who have sat by Thebes below the wall*
> *And walked among the l-l-lowest of the dead ...*'

And then, stepping lightly into the room, 'How I have surprised them! All b-boatmen are Grace Darlings to me.'

We sat on sipping Cointreau while the mildest and most detached of the Etonians sang: 'Home they brought her warrior dead' to his own accompaniment on the harmonium.

It was four o'clock before we broke up.

Anthony Blanche was the first to go. He took formal and complimentary leave of each of us in turn. To Sebastian he said: 'My dear, I should like to stick you full of barbed arrows like a p-p-pin-cushion,' and to me: 'I think it's perfectly brilliant of Sebastian to have discovered you. Where do you lurk? I shall come down your burrow and ch-chivvy you out like an old st-t-toat.'

The others left soon after him. I rose to go with them, but Sebastian said: 'Have some more Cointreau,' so I stayed and later he said, 'I must go to the Botanical Gardens.'

'Why?'

'To see the ivy.'

It seemed a good enough reason and I went with him. He took my arm as we walked under the walls of Merton.

'I've never been to the Botanical Gardens,' I said.

'Oh, Charles, what a lot you have to learn! There's a beautiful arch there and more different kinds of ivy than I knew existed. I don't know where I should be without the Botanical Gardens.'

When at length I returned to my rooms and found them exactly as I had left them that morning, I detected a jejune air that had not irked me before. What was wrong? Nothing except the golden daffodils seemed to be real. Was it the screen? I turned it face to the wall. That was better.

It was the end of the screen. Lunt never liked it, and after a few days he took it away, to an obscure refuge he had under the stairs, full of mops and buckets.

That day was the beginning of my friendship with Sebastian, and thus it came about, that morning in June, that I was lying beside him in the shade of the high elms watching the smoke from his lips drift up into the branches.

Presently we drove on and in another hour were hungry. We stopped at an inn, which was half farm also, and ate eggs and bacon, pickled walnuts and cheese, and drank our beer in a sunless parlour where an old clock ticked in the shadows and a cat slept by the empty grate.

We drove on and in the early afternoon came to our destination: wrought-iron gates and twin, classical lodges on a village green, an avenue, more gates, open parkland, a turn in the drive; and suddenly a new and secret landscape opened before us. We were at the head of a valley and below us, half a mile distant, grey and gold amid a screen of boskage, shone the dome and columns of an old house.

'Well?' said Sebastian, stopping the car. Beyond the dome lay receding steps of water and round it, guarding and hiding it, stood the soft hills.

'Well?'

'What a place to live in!' I said.

'You must see the garden front and the fountain.' He leaned forward and put the car into gear. 'It's where my family live'; and even then, rapt in the vision, I felt, momentarily, an ominous chill at the words he used – not, 'that is my house', but 'it's where my family live'.

'Don't worry,' he continued, 'they're all away. You won't have to meet them.'

'But I should like to.'

'Well, you can't. They're in London.'

We drove round the front into a side court – 'Everything's shut up. We'd better go in this way' – and entered through the fortress-like, stone-flagged, stone-vaulted passages of the servants' quarters – 'I want you to meet Nanny Hawkins. That's what we've come for' – and climbed uncarpeted, scrubbed elm stairs, followed more passages of wide boards covered in the centre by a thin strip of drugget, through passages covered by linoleum, passing the wells of many minor staircases and many rows of crimson and gold fire buckets, up a final staircase, gated at the head. The dome was false, designed to be seen from below like the cupolas of Chambord. Its drum was merely an additional storey full of segmental rooms. Here were the nurseries.

Sebastian's nanny was seated at the open window; the fountain lay before her, the lakes, the temple, and, far away on the last spur, a glittering obelisk; her hands lay open in her lap and, loosely between them, a rosary; she was fast asleep. Long hours of work in her youth, authority in middle life, repose and security in her age, had set their stamp on her lined and serene face.

'Well,' she said, waking; 'this *is* a surprise.'

Sebastian kissed her.

'Who's this?' she said, looking at me. 'I don't think I know him.'

Sebastian introduced us.

'You've come just the right time. Julia's here for the day. Such a time they're all having. It's dull without them. Just Mrs Chandler and two of the girls and old Bert. And then they're all going on holidays and the boiler's being done out in August and you going to see his Lordship in Italy, and the rest on visits, it'll be October before we're settled down again. Still, I suppose Julia must have her enjoyment the same as other young ladies, though what they always want to go to London for in the best of the summer and the gardens all out, I never have understood. Father Phipps was here on Thursday and I said exactly the same to him,' she added as though she had thus acquired sacerdotal authority for her opinion.

'D'you say Julia's here?'

'Yes, dear, you must have just missed her. It's the Conservative Women. Her Ladyship was to have done them, but she's poorly. Julia won't be long; she's leaving immediately after her speech, before the tea.'

'I'm afraid we may miss her again.'

'Don't do that, dear, it'll be such a surprise to her seeing you, though she ought to wait for the tea, I told her, it's what the Conservative Women come for. Now what's the news? Are you studying hard at your books?'

'Not very, I'm afraid, nanny.'

'Ah, cricketing all day long I expect, like your brother. He found time to study, too, though. He's not been here since Christmas, but he'll be here for the Agricultural, I expect. Did you see this piece about Julia in the paper? She brought it down for me. Not that it's nearly good enough of her, but what it says is *very* nice. "The lovely daughter whom Lady Marchmain is bringing out this season ... witty as well as ornamental ... the most popular débutante", well that's no more than the truth, though it was a shame to cut her hair; such a lovely head of hair she had, just like her Ladyship's. I said to Father Phipps it's not natural. He said: "Nuns do it," and I said, "Well, surely, father, you aren't going to make a nun out of Lady Julia? The very idea!"'

Sebastian and the old woman talked on. It was a charming room, oddly shaped to conform with the curve of the dome. The walls were papered in a pattern of ribbon and roses. There was a rocking-horse in the corner and an oleograph of the Sacred Heart over the mantelpiece; the empty grate was hidden by a bunch of pampas grass and bulrushes; laid out on the top of the chest of drawers and carefully dusted, were the collection of small presents which had been brought home to her at various times by her children, carved shell and lava, stamped leather, painted wood, china, bog-oak, damascened silver, blue-john, alabaster, coral, the souvenirs of many holidays.

Presently nanny said: 'Ring the bell, dear, and we'll have some tea. I usually go down to Mrs Chandler, but we'll have it up here today. My usual girl has gone to London with the others. The new one is just up from the village. She didn't know anything at first, but she's coming along nicely. Ring the bell.'

But Sebastian said we had to go.

'And miss Julia? She *will* be upset when she hears. It would have been *such* a surprise for her.'

'Poor nanny,' said Sebastian when we left the nursery. 'She does have such a dull life. I've a good mind to bring her to Oxford to live with me, only she'd always be trying to send me to church. We must go quickly before my sister gets back.'

'Which are you ashamed of, her or me?'

'I'm ashamed of myself,' said Sebastian gravely. 'I'm not going to have you get mixed up with my family. They're so madly charming. All my life they've been taking things away from me. If they once got hold of you with their charm, they'd make you *their* friend not mine, and I won't let them.'

'All right,' I said. 'I'm perfectly content. But am I not going to be allowed to see any more of the house?'

'It's all shut up. We came to see nanny. On Queen Alexandra's day it's all open for a shilling. Well, come and look if you want to. ...'

He led me through a baize door into a dark corridor; I could dimly see a gilt cornice and vaulted plaster above; then, opening a heavy, smooth-swinging, mahogany door, he led me into a darkened hall. Light streamed through the cracks in the shutters. Sebastian unbarred one, and folded it back; the mellow afternoon sun flooded in, over the bare floor, the vast, twin fireplaces of sculptured marble, the coved ceiling frescoed with classic deities and heroes, the gilt mirrors and *scagliola* pilasters, the islands of sheeted furniture. It was a glimpse only, such as might be had from the top of an omnibus into a lighted ballroom; then Sebastian quickly shut out the sun. 'You see,' he said, 'it's like this.'

His mood had changed since we had drunk our wine under the elm trees, since we had turned the corner of the drive and he had said: 'Well?'

'You see, there's nothing to see. A few pretty things I'd like to show you one day – not now. But there's the chapel. You must see that. It's a monument of *art nouveau*.'

The last architect to work at Brideshead had added a colonnade and flanking pavilions. One of these was the chapel. We entered it by the public porch (another door led direct to the house); Sebastian dipped his fingers in the water stoup, crossed himself, and genuflected; I copied him. 'Why do you do that?' he asked crossly.

'Just good manners.'

'Well, you needn't on my account. You wanted to do sight-seeing; how about this?'

The whole interior had been gutted, elaborately refurnished and redecorated in the arts-and-crafts style of the last decade of the nineteenth century. Angels in printed cotton smocks, rambler-roses, flower-spangled meadows, frisking lambs, texts in Celtic script, saints in armour, covered the walls in an intricate pattern of clear, bright colours. There was a triptych of pale oak, carved so as to give it the peculiar property of seeming to have been moulded in Plasticine. The sanctuary lamp and all the metal furniture were of bronze, hand-beaten to the patina of a pock-marked skin; the altar steps had a carpet of grass-green, strewn with white and gold daisies.

'Golly,' I said.

'It was papa's wedding present to mama. Now, if you've seen enough, we'll go.'

On the drive we passed a closed Rolls-Royce driven by a chauffeur; in the back was a vague, girlish figure who looked round at us through the window.

'Julia,' said Sebastian. 'We only just got away in time.'

We stopped to speak to a man with a bicycle – 'That was old Bat,' said Sebastian – and then were away, past the wrought-iron gates, past the lodges, and out on the road heading back to Oxford.

'I'm sorry,' said Sebastian after a time. 'I'm afraid I wasn't very nice this afternoon. Brideshead often has that effect on me. But I had to take you to see nanny.'

Why? I wondered; but said nothing – Sebastian's life was governed by a code of such imperatives. 'I *must* have pillar-box red pyjamas,' 'I *have* to stay in bed until the sun works round to the windows,' 'I've absolutely *got* to drink champagne tonight!' – except, 'It had quite the reverse effect on me.'

After a long pause he said petulantly, 'I don't keep asking you questions about *your* family.'

'Neither do I about yours.'

'But you look inquisitive.'

'Well, you're so mysterious about them.'

'I hoped I was mysterious about everything.'

'Perhaps I am rather curious about people's families – you see, it's not a thing I know about. There is only my father and myself. An aunt kept an eye on me for a time but my father drove her abroad. My mother was killed in the war.'

'Oh ... how very unusual.'

'She went to Serbia with the Red Cross. My father has been rather odd in the head ever since. He just lives alone in London with no friends and footles about collecting things.'

Sebastian said, 'You don't know what you've been saved. There are lots of us. Look them up in Debrett.'

His mood was lightening now. The further we drove from Brideshead, the more he seemed to cast off his uneasiness – the almost furtive restlessness and irritability that had possessed him. The sun was behind us as we drove, so that we seemed to be in pursuit of our own shadows.

'It's half past five. We'll get to Godstow in time for dinner, drink at the Trout, leave Hardcastle's motor-car, and walk back by the river. Wouldn't that be best?'

That is the full account of my first brief visit to Brideshead; could I have known then that it would one day be remembered with tears by a middle-aged captain of infantry?

CHAPTER II

Towards the end of that summer term I received the last visit and Grand Remonstrance of my cousin Jasper. I was just free of the schools, having taken the last paper of History Previous on the afternoon before; Jasper's subfusc suit and white tie proclaimed him still in the thick of it; he had, too, the exhausted but resentful air of one who fears he has failed to do himself full justice on the subject of Pindar's Orphism. Duty alone had brought him to my rooms that afternoon at great inconvenience to himself and, as it happened, to me, who, when he caught me in the door, was on my way to make final arrangements about a dinner I was giving that evening. It was one of several parties designed to comfort Hardcastle – one of the tasks that had lately fallen to Sebastian and me since, by leaving his car out, we had got him into grave trouble with the proctors.

Jasper would not sit down; this was to be no cosy chat; he stood with his back to the fireplace and, in his own phrase, talked to me 'like an uncle'.

'... I've tried to get in touch with you several times in the last week or two. In fact, I have the impression you are avoiding me. If that is so, Charles, I can't say I'm surprised.

'You may think it none of my business, but I feel a sense of responsibility. You know as well as I do that since your – well, since the war, your father has not been really in touch with things – lives in his own world. I don't want to sit back and see you making mistakes which a word in season might save you from.

'I expected you to make mistakes your first year. We all do. I got in with some thoroughly objectionable O.S.C.U. men who ran a mission to hop-pickers during the long vac. But you, my dear Charles, whether you realize it or not, have gone straight, hook line and sinker, into the *very worst set in the University*. You may think that, living in digs, I don't know what goes on in college; but I hear things. In fact, I hear all too much. I find that I've become a figure of mockery on your account at the Dining Club. There's that chap Sebastian Flyte you seem inseparable from. He may be all right, I don't know. His brother Brideshead was a very sound fellow. But this friend of yours looks odd to me and he gets himself talked about. Of course, they're an odd family. The Marchmains have lived apart since the war, you know. An extraordinary thing; everyone thought they were a devoted couple. Then he went off to France with his Yeomanry and just never came back. It was as if he'd been killed. She's a Roman Catholic, so she can't get a divorce – or *won't*, I expect. You can do anything at Rome with money, and they're enormously rich. Flyte *may* be all right, but *Anthony Blanche* – now there's a man there's absolutely no excuse for.'

'I don't particularly like him myself,' I said.

'Well, he's always hanging round here, and the stiffer element in college don't like it. They can't stand him at the House. He was in Mercury again last night. None of these people you go about with pull any weight in their own colleges, and that's the real test. They think because they've got a lot of money to throw about, they can do anything.

'And that's another thing. I don't know what allowance my uncle makes you, but I don't mind betting you're spending double. All *this*,' he said, including in a wide sweep of his hand the evidence of profligacy about him. It was true; my room had cast its austere winter garments, and, by not very slow stages, assumed a richer wardrobe. 'Is *that* paid for?' (the box of a hundred cabinet Partagas on the sideboard) 'or *those*?' (a dozen frivolous, new books on the table) 'or those?' (a Lalique decanter and glasses) 'or *that* peculiarly noisome object?' (a human skull lately purchased from the School of Medicine, which, resting in a bowl of roses, formed, at the moment, the chief decoration of my table. It bore the motto '*Et in Arcadia ego*' inscribed on its forehead.)

'Yes,' I said, glad to be clear of one charge. 'I had to pay cash for the skull.'

'You can't be doing any work. Not that that matters, particularly if you're making something of your career else-where – but are you? Have you spoken at the Union or at any of the clubs? Are you connected with any of the magazines? Are you even making a position in the O.U.D.S.? And *your clothes*!' continued my cousin. 'When you came up I remember advising you to dress as you would in a country house. Your present get-up seems an unhappy compromise between the correct wear for a theatrical party at Maidenhead and a glee-singing competi-tion in a garden suburb.

'And drink – no one minds a man getting tight once or twice a term. In fact, he ought to, on certain occasions. But I hear you're constantly seen drunk in the middle of the afternoon.'

He paused, his duty discharged. Already the perplexities of

the examination school were beginning to reassert themselves in his mind.

'I'm sorry, Jasper,' I said. 'I know it must be embarrassing for you, but I happen to *like* this bad set. I *like* getting drunk at luncheon, and though I haven't yet spent quite double my allowance, I undoubtedly shall before the end of term. I usually have a glass of champagne about this time. Will you join me?'

So my cousin Jasper despaired and, I learned later, wrote to his father on the subject of my excesses who, in his turn, wrote to *my* father, who took no action or particular thought in the matter, partly because he had disliked my uncle for nearly sixty years and partly because, as Jasper had said, he lived in his own world now, since my mother's death.

Thus, in broad outline, Jasper sketched the more prominent features of my first year; some detail may be added on the same scale.

I had committed myself earlier to spend the Easter vacation with Collins and, though I would have broken my word without compunction, and left my former friend friendless, had Sebastian made a sign, no sign was made; accordingly Collins and I spent several economical and instructive weeks together in Ravenna. A bleak wind blew from the Adriatic among those mighty tombs. In an hotel bedroom designed for a warmer season, I wrote long letters to Sebastian and called daily at the post office for his answers. There were two, each from a different address, neither giving any plain news of himself, for he wrote in a style of remote fantasy – ... '*Mummy and two attendant poets have three bad colds in the head, so I have come here. It is the feast of S. Nichodemus of Thyatira, who was martyred by having goatskin nailed to his pate, and is accordingly the patron of bald heads. Tell Collins, who I am sure will be bald before us. There are too many people here, but one, praise heaven! has an ear-trumpet, and that keeps me in good humour. And now I must try to catch a fish. It is too far to send it to you so I will keep the backbone ...*' – which left me fretful. Collins made notes for a little thesis pointing out the inferiority of the original mosaics to their photographs. Here was planted the seed of what became his life's harvest. When, many years later, there appeared the first massive volume of his still unfinished work on Byzantine Art, I was touched to find among two pages of polite, preliminary acknowledgements of debt, my own name: '... *to Charles Ryder, with the aid of whose all-seeing eyes I first saw the Mausoleum of Galla Placidia and San Vitale* ...'

I sometimes wonder whether, had it not been for Sebastian, I might have trodden the same path as Collins round the cultural water-wheel. My father in his youth sat for All Souls and, in a year of hot competition, failed; other successes and honours came his way later, but that early failure impressed itself on him, and through him on me, so that I came up with an ill-considered sense that there lay the proper and natural goal of the life of reason. I, too, should doubtless have failed, but, having failed, I might perhaps have slipped into a less august academic life elsewhere. It is conceivable, but not, I believe, likely, for the hot spring of anarchy rose from depths where was no solid earth, and burst into the sunlight – a rainbow in its cooling vapours – with a power the rocks could not repress.

In the event, that Easter vacation formed a short stretch of level road in the precipitous descent of which Jasper warned me. Descent or ascent? It seems to me that I grew younger daily with each adult habit that I acquired. I had lived a lonely childhood and a boyhood straitened by war and overshadowed by bereavement; to the hard bachelordom of English adolescence, the premature dignity and authority of the school system, I had added a sad and grim strain of my own. Now, that summer term with Sebastian, it seemed as though I was being given a brief spell of what I had never known, a happy childhood, and though its toys were silk shirts and liqueurs and cigars and its naughtiness high in the catalogue of grave sins, there was something of nursery freshness about us that fell little short of the joy of innocence. At the end of the term I took my first schools; it was necessary to pass, if I was to remain at Oxford, and pass I did, after a week in which I forbade Sebastian my rooms and sat up to a late hour, with iced black coffee and charcoal biscuits, cramming myself with the neglected texts. I remember no syllable of them now, but the other, more ancient lore which I acquired that term will be with me in one shape or another to my last hour.

'I like this bad set and I like getting drunk at luncheon'; that was enough then. Is more needed now?

Looking back, now, after twenty years, there is little I would have left undone or done otherwise. I could match my cousin Jasper's game-cock maturity with a sturdier fowl. I could tell him that all the wickedness of that time was like the spirit they mix with the pure grape of the Douro, heady stuff full of dark ingredients; it at once enriched and retarded the whole process of adolescence as the spirit checks the fermentation of the wine, renders it undrinkable, so that it must lie in the dark, year in, year out, until it is brought up at last fit for the table.

I could tell him, too, that to know and love one other human being is the root of all wisdom. But I felt no need for these sophistries as I sat before my cousin, saw him, freed from his inconclusive struggle with Pindar, in his dark grey suit, his white tie, his scholar's gown; heard his grave tones and, all the time, savoured the gillyflowers in full bloom under my windows. I had my secret and sure defence, like a talisman worn in the bosom, felt for in the moment of danger, found and firmly grasped. So I told him what was not in fact the truth, that I usually had a glass of champagne about that time, and asked him to join me.

On the day after Jasper's Grand Remonstrance I received another, in different terms and from an unexpected source.

All the term I had been seeing rather more of Anthony Blanche than my liking for him warranted. I lived now among his friends, but our frequent meetings were more of his choosing than mine, for I held him in considerable awe.

In years, he was barely my senior, but he seemed then to be burdened with the experience of the Wandering Jew. He was indeed a nomad of no nationality.

An attempt had been made in his childhood to make an Englishman of him; he was two years at Eton; then in the middle of the war he had defied the submarines, rejoined his mother in the Argentine, and a clever and audacious schoolboy was added to the valet, the maid, the two chauffeurs, the pekinese, and the second husband. Criss-cross about the world he travelled with them, waxing in wickedness like a Hogarthian page boy. When peace came they returned to Europe, to hotels and furnished villas, spas, casinos, and bathing beaches. At the age of fifteen, for a wager, he was disguised as a girl and taken to play at the big table in the Jockey Club at Buenos Aires; he dined with Proust and Gide and was on closer terms with Cocteau and Diaghilev; Firbank sent him his novels with fervent inscriptions; he had aroused three irreconcilable feuds in Capri; by his own account he had practised black art in Cefalù and had been cured of drug-taking in California and of an Oedipus complex in Vienna.

At times we all seemed children beside him – at most times, but not always, for there was a bluster and zest in Anthony which the rest of us had shed somewhere in our more leisured adolescence, on the playing field or in the school-room; his vices flourished less in the pursuit of pleasure than in the wish to shock, and in the midst of his polished exhibitions I was often reminded of an urchin I had once seen in Naples, capering derisively, with obscene, unambiguous gestures, before a party of English tourists; as he told the tale of his evening at the gaming table, one could see in the roll of his eye just how he had glanced, covertly, over the dwindling pile of chips at his step-father's party; while we had been rolling one another in the mud at football and gorging ourselves with crumpets, Anthony had helped oil fading beauties on sub-tropical sands and had sipped his apéritif in smart little bars, so that the savage we had tamed was still rampant in him. He was cruel, too, in the wanton, insect-maiming manner of the very young, and fearless like a little boy, charging, head down, small fists whirling, at the school prefects.

He asked me to dinner, and I was a little disconcerted to find that we were to dine alone. 'We are going to Thame,' he said. 'There is a delightful hotel there, which luckily doesn't appeal to the Bullingdon. We will drink Rhine wine and imagine ourselves ... where? Not on a j-j-jaunt with J-J-Jorrocks, anyway. But first we will have our apéritif.'

At the George bar he ordered 'Four Alexandra cocktails, please,' ranged them before him with a loud 'Yum-yum' which drew every eye, outraged, upon him. 'I expect you would prefer sherry, but, my dear Charles, you are not going to *have* sherry. Isn't this a delicious concoction? You don't like it? Then I will drink it for you. One, two, three, four, down the red lane they go. *How* the students stare!' And he led me out to the waiting motor-car.

'I hope we shall find no undergraduates there. I am a little out of sympathy with them for the moment. You heard about their treatment of me on Thursday? It was too naughty. Luckily I was wearing my *oldest* pyjamas and it was an evening of oppressive heat, or I might have been seriously cross.' Anthony had a habit of putting his face near one when he spoke; the sweet and creamy cocktail had tainted his breath. I leaned away from him in the corner of the hired car.

'Picture me, my dear, alone and studious. I had just bought a rather forbidding book called *Antic Hay*, which I knew I must read before going to Garsington on Sunday, because everyone was bound to talk about it, and it's so banal saying you have not read the book of the moment, if you haven't. The solution I suppose is not to go to Garsington, but that didn't occur to me until this moment. *So*, my dear, I had an omelet and a peach and a bottle of Vichy water and put on my pyjamas and settled down to read. I must say my thoughts wandered, but I kept turning the pages and watching the light fade, which in Peckwater, my dear, is quite an experience – as darkness falls the stone seems positively to decay under one's eyes. I was reminded of some of those leprous façades in the *vieux port* at Marseille, until suddenly I was disturbed by such a bawling and caterwauling as you never heard, and there, down in the little piazza, I saw a mob of about twenty terrible young men, and do you know what they were chanting? "*We want Blanche. We want Blanche*," in a kind of litany. Such a *public* declaration! Well, I saw it was all up with Mr Huxley for the evening, and I must say I had reached a point of tedium when any interruption was welcome. I was stirred by the bellows, but, do you know, the louder they shouted, the shyer they seemed? They kept saying "Where's Boy?" "He's Boy Mulcaster's friend," "Boy must bring him down." Of course you've met Boy? He's always popping in and out of dear Sebastian's rooms. He's everything we dagos expect of an English lord. A great *parti* I can assure you. All the young ladies in London are after him. He's very hoity-toity with them, I'm told. My dear, he's scared stiff. A great oaf – that's Mulcaster – and what's more, my dear, a *cad*. He came to le Touquet at Easter and, in some extraordinary way, I seemed to have asked him to stay. He lost some infinitesimal sum at cards, and as a result expected me to pay for all his treats – well, Mulcaster was in this party; I could see his ungainly form shuffling about below and hear him saying: "It's no good. He's out. Let's go back and have a drink?" So then I put my head out of the window and called to him; "Good evening, Mulcaster, old sponge and toady, are you lurking among the hobbledehoys? Have you come to repay me the three hundred francs I lent you for the poor drab you picked up in the Casino? It was a niggardly sum for her trouble, and *what* a trouble, Mulcaster. Come up and pay me, poor hooligan!"

'That, my dear, seemed to put a little life into them, and up the stairs they came, clattering. About six of them came into my room, the rest stood mouthing outside. My dear, they looked *too* extraordinary. They had been having one of their ridiculous club dinners, and they were all wearing coloured tail-coats – a sort of livery. "My dears," I said to them, "you look like a lot of most disorderly footmen." Then one of them, rather a juicy little piece, accused me of unnatural vices. "My dear," I said, "I may be inverted but I am not insatiable. Come back when you are *alone*." Then they began to blaspheme in a very shocking manner, and suddenly I, too, began to be annoyed. "Really," I thought, "when I think of all the hullabaloo there was when I was seventeen, and the Duc de Vincennes (old Armand, of course, not Philippe) challenged me to a duel for an affair of the heart, and very much *more* than the heart, I assure you, with the duchess (Stefanie, of course, not old Poppy) – now, to submit to impertinence from these pimply, tipsy virgins ...'' Well, I gave up the light, bantering tone and let myself be just a *little* offensive.

'Then they began saying, "Get hold of him. Put him in Mercury." Now as you know I have two sculptures by Brancusi and several pretty things and I did not want them to start getting rough, so I said, pacifically, "Dear sweet clodhoppers, if you knew anything of sexual psychology you would know that nothing could give me keener pleasure than to be manhandled by you meaty boys. It would be an ecstasy of the very naughtiest kind. So if any of you wishes to be my partner in joy come and seize me. If, on the other hand, you simply wish to satisfy some obscure and less easily classified libido and see me bathe, come with me quietly, dear louts, to the fountain.''

'Do you know, they all looked a little foolish at that? I walked down with them and no one came within a yard of me. Then I got into the fountain and, you know, it was really most refreshing, so I sported there a little and struck some attitudes, until they turned about and walked sulkily home, and I heard Boy Mulcaster saying, "Anyway, we *did* put him in Mercury." You know, Charles, that is just what they'll be saying in thirty years' time. When they're all married to scraggy little women like hens and have cretinous porcine sons like themselves getting drunk at the same club dinner in the same coloured coats, they'll still say, when my name is mentioned, "We put him in Mercury one night," and their barnyard daughters will snigger and think their father was quite a dog in his day, and what a pity he's grown so dull. Oh, *la fatigue du Nord!*'

It was not, I knew, the first time Anthony had been ducked, but the incident seemed much on his mind, for he reverted to it again at dinner.

'Now you can't imagine an *unpleasantness* like that happening to Sebastian, can you?'

'No,' I said; I could not.

'No, Sebastian has charm'; he held up his glass of hock to the candle-light and repeated, '*such* charm. Do you know, I went round to call on Sebastian next day? I thought the tale of my evening's adventures might amuse him. And what do you think I found – besides, of course, his *amusing* toy bear? Mulcaster and two of his cronies of the night before. *They* looked *very* foolish and Sebastian, as composed as Mrs P-p-ponsonby-de-Tomkyns in *P-p-punch*, said, "You know Lord Mulcaster, of course," and the oafs said, "Oh, we just came to see how Aloysius was," for they find the toy bear just as amusing as we do – or, shall I hint, just a *teeny* bit more? So off they went. And I said, "S-s-sebastian, do you realize that those s-sycophantic s-slugs insulted me last night, and but for the warmth of the weather might have given me a s-s-severe cold," and he said, "Poor things. I expect they were drunk." He has a kind word for everyone, you see; he has such charm.

'I can see he has completely captivated you, my dear Charles. Well, I'm not surprised. Of course, you haven't known him as long as I have. I was at school with him. You wouldn't believe it, but in those days people used to say he was a little *bitch*; just a few unkind boys who knew him well. Everyone in pop liked him, of course, and all the masters. I expect it was really that they were jealous of him. He never seemed to get into trouble. The rest of us were constantly being beaten in the most savage way, on the most frivolous pretexts, but never Sebastian. He was the only boy in my house who was never beaten at all. I can see him now, at the age of fifteen. He never had spots you know; all the other boys were spotty. Boy Mulcaster was positively scrofulous. But not Sebastian. Or did he have one, rather a stubborn one at the back of his neck? I think, now, that he did. Narcissus, with one pustule. He and I were both Catholics, so we used to go to mass together. He used to spend *such* a time in the confessional, I used to wonder what he had to say, because he never did anything wrong; never *quite*; at least, he never got punished. Perhaps he was just being charming through the grille. I left under what is called a cloud, you know – I can't think why it is called that; it seemed to me a glare of unwelcome light; the process involved a series of harrowing interviews with m' tutor. It was disconcerting to find how observant that mild old man proved to be. The *things* he knew about me, which I thought no one – except possibly Sebastian – knew. It was a lesson never to trust mild old men – or charming schoolboys; which?

'Shall we have another bottle of this wine, or of something different? Something different, some bloody, old Burgundy, eh? You see, Charles, I understand *all* your tastes. You must come to France with me and drink the wine. We will go at the vintage. I will take you to stay at the Vincennes. It is all made up with them now, and he has the finest wine in France; he and the Prince de Portallon – I will take you there, too. I think they would amuse you, and of course they would *love* you. I want to introduce you to a lot of my friends. I have told Cocteau about you. He is all agog. You see, my dear Charles, you are that very rare thing, An Artist. Oh yes, you must not look bashful. Behind that cold, English, phlegmatic exterior you are An Artist. I have seen those little drawings you keep hidden away in your room. They are *exquisite*. And you, dear Charles, if you will understand me, are *not* exquisite; but not at all. Artists are not exquisite. I am; Sebastian, in a kind of way, is exquisite, but the artist is an eternal type, solid, purposeful, observant – and, beneath it all, p-p-passionate, eh, Charles?

'But who recognizes you? The other day I was speaking to Sebastian about you, and I said, "But you know Charles is *an artist*. He draws like a young Ingres," and do you know what Sebastian said? – "Yes, Aloysius draws very prettily, too, but of course he's rather more modern." *So* charming; *so* amusing.

'Of course those that have charm don't really need brains. Stefanie de Vincennes really tickled me four years ago. My dear, I even used the same coloured varnish for my toe-nails. I used her words and lit my cigarette in the same way and spoke with her tone on the telephone so that the duke used to carry on long and intimate conversations with me, thinking that I was her. It was largely that which put his mind on pistol and sabres in such an old-fashioned manner. My step-father thought it an excellent education for me. He thought it would make me grow out of what he calls my "English habits". Poor man, he is very South American. ... I never heard anyone speak an ill word of Stefanie, except the Duke: and *she*, my dear, is positively cretinous.'

Anthony had lost his stammer in the deep waters of his old romance. It came floating back to him, momentarily, with the coffee and liqueurs. 'Real G-g-green Chartreuse, made before the expulsion of the monks. There are five distinct tastes as it trickles over the tongue. It is like swallowing a sp-spectrum. Do you wish Sebastian was with us? Of course you do. Do I? I wonder. How our thoughts do run on that little bundle of charm to be sure. I think you must be mesmerizing me, Charles. I bring you here, at very considerable expense, my dear, simply to talk about myself, and I find I talk of no one except Sebastian. It's odd because there's really no mystery about him except how he came to be born of such a *very sinister* family.

'I forget if you know his family. I don't suppose he'll ever let you meet them. He's far too clever. They're quite, quite *gruesome*. Do you ever feel there is something a *teeny* bit gruesome about Sebastian? No? Perhaps I imagine it; it's simply that he *looks* so like the rest of them, sometimes.

'There's Brideshead who's something archaic, out of a cave that's been sealed for centuries. He has the face as though an Aztec sculptor had attempted a portrait of Sebastian; he's a learned bigot, a ceremonious barbarian, a snow-bound lama. ... Well, anything you like. And Julia, you know what *she* looks like. Who could help it? Her photograph appears as regularly in the illustrated papers as the advertisements for Beecham's Pills. A face of flawless Florentine *quattrocento* beauty; almost anyone else with those looks would have been tempted to become artistic; not Lady Julia; she's as smart as – well, as smart as Stefanie. Nothing greenery-yallery about her. So gay, so correct, so unaffected. I wonder if she's incestuous. I doubt it; all she wants is power. There ought to be an Inquisition especially set up to burn her. There's another sister, too, I believe, in the schoolroom. Nothing is known of her *yet* except that her governess went mad and drowned herself not long ago. I'm sure she's abominable. So you see there was really very little left for poor Sebastian to do except be sweet and charming.

'It's when one gets to the parents that a bottomless pit opens. My dear, *such* a pair. *How does Lady Marchmain manage it?* It is one of the questions of the age. You have seen her? Very, very beautiful; no artifice, her hair just turning grey in elegant silvery streaks, no rouge, very pale, huge-eyed – it is extraordinary how large those eyes look and how the lids are veined blue where anyone else would have touched them with a finger-tip of paint; pearls and a few great starlike jewels, heirlooms, in ancient settings, a voice as quiet as a prayer, and as powerful. And Lord Marchmain, well, a little fleshy perhaps, but *very* handsome, a magnifico, a voluptuary, Byronic, bored, infectiously slothful, not at all the sort of man you would expect to see easily put down. And that Reinhardt nun, my dear, has destroyed him – but utterly. He daren't show his great purple face anywhere. He is the last, historic, authentic case of someone being hounded out of society. Brideshead won't see him, the girls mayn't, Sebastian does, of course, because he's so charming. No one else goes near him. Why, last September Lady Marchmain was in Venice staying at the Palazzo Fogliere. To tell you the truth she was just a teeny bit ridiculous in Venice. She never went near the Lido, of course, but she was always drifting about the canals in a gondola with Sir Adrian Porson – such attitudes, my dear, like Madame Récamier; once I passed them and I caught the eye of the Fogliere gondolier, whom, of course, I knew, and, my dear, he gave me *such* a wink. She came to all the parties in a sort of cocoon of gossamer, my dear, as though she were part of some Celtic play or a heroine from Maeterlinck; and she *would* go to church. Well, as you know, Venice is the *one* town in Italy where *no one* ever *has* gone to church. Anyway, she was rather a figure of fun that year, and then who should turn up, in the Maltons' yacht, but poor Lord Marchmain. He'd taken a little palace there, but was he allowed in? Lord Malton put him and his valet into a dinghy, my dear, and transhipped him there and then into the steamer for Trieste. He hadn't even his mistress with him. It was her

yearly holiday. No one ever knew how they heard Lady
Marchmain was there. And, do you know, for a week Lord
Malton slunk about as if *he* was in disgrace? And he *was* in
disgrace. The Principessa Fogliere gave a ball and Lord Malton
was not asked nor anyone from his yacht – even the de Pañoses.
How does Lady Marchmain do it? She has convinced the world that
Lord Marchmain is a monster. And what is the truth? They
were married for fifteen years or so and then Lord Marchmain
went to the war; he never came back but formed a connexion
with a highly talented dancer. There are a thousand such cases.
She refuses to divorce him because she is so pious. Well, there
have been cases of that before. Usually, it arouses sympathy for
the adulterer; not for Lord Marchmain though. You would
think that the old reprobate had tortured her, stolen her
patrimony, flung her out of doors, roasted, stuffed, and eaten his
children, and gone frolicking about wreathed in all the flowers
of Sodom and Gomorrah; instead of what? Begetting four
splendid children by her, handing over to her Brideshead and
Marchmain House in St James's and all the money she can
possibly want to spend, while he sits with a snowy shirt front at
Larue's with a personable, middle-aged lady of the theatre, in
most conventional Edwardian style. And she meanwhile keeps a
small gang of enslaved and emaciated prisoners for her exclusive
enjoyment. *She sucks their blood.* You can see the tooth marks all
over Adrian Porson's shoulders when he is bathing. And he, my
dear, was the greatest, the *only*, poet of our time. He's bled dry;
there's nothing left of him. There are five or six others of all ages
and sexes, like wraiths following her around. They never escape
once she's had her teeth into them. It is witchcraft. There's no
other explanation.

    'So you see we mustn't blame Sebastian if at times he seems a
little insipid – but then you don't blame him, do you, Charles?
With that very murky background, what could he do except set
up as being simple and charming, particularly as he isn't very
well endowed in the Top Storey. We couldn't claim *that* for him,
could we, much as we love him?

    'Tell me candidly, have you ever heard Sebastian say

anything you have remembered for five minutes? You know, when I hear him talk, I am reminded of that in some ways nauseating picture of "*Bubbles*". Conversation should be like juggling; up go the balls and the plates, up and over, in and out, good solid objects that glitter in the footlights and fall with a bang if you miss them. But when dear Sebastian speaks it is like a little sphere of soapsud drifting off the end of an old clay pipe, anywhere, full of rainbow light for a second and then – phut! vanished, with nothing left at all, nothing.'

And then Anthony spoke of the proper experiences of an artist, of the appreciation and criticism and stimulus he should expect from his friends, of the hazards he should take in the pursuit of emotion, of one thing and another while I fell drowsy and let my mind wander a little. So we drove home, but his words, as we swung over Magdalen Bridge, recalled the central theme of our dinner. 'Well, my dear, I've no doubt that first thing tomorrow you'll trot round to Sebastian and tell him *everything* I've said about him. And I will tell you two things; one, that it will not make the slightest difference to Sebastian's feeling for me and secondly, my dear – and I beg you to remember this though I have plainly bored you into a condition of coma – that he will immediately start talking about that amusing bear of his. Good night. Sleep innocently.'

But I slept ill. Within an hour of tumbling drowsily to bed I was awake again, thirsty, restless, hot and cold by turns, and unnaturally excited. I had drunk a lot, but neither the mixture, nor the Chartreuse, nor the Mavrodaphne Trifle, nor even the fact that I had sat immobile and almost silent throughout the evening instead of clearing the fumes, as we normally did, in puppyish romps and tumbles, explains the distress of that hag-ridden night. No dream distorted the images of the evening into horrific shapes. I lay awake and clear-headed. I repeated to myself Anthony's words, catching his accent, soundlessly, and the stress and cadence of his speech, while under my closed lids I saw his pale, candle-lit face as it had fronted me across the dinner table. Once during the hours of darkness I brought to light the drawings in my sitting-room and sat at the open window, turning them over. Everything was black and dead-still in the quadrangle; only at the quarter-hours the bells awoke and sang over the gables. I drank soda-water and smoked and fretted, until light began to break and the rustle of a rising breeze turned me back to my bed.

When I awoke Lunt was at the open door. 'I let you lie,' he said. 'I didn't think you'd be going to the Corporate Communion.'

'You were quite right.'

'Most of the freshmen went and quite a few second and third year men. It's all on account of the new chaplain. There was never Corporate Communion before – just Holy Communion for those that wanted it and Chapel and Evening Chapel.'

It was the last Sunday of term; the last of the year. As I went to my bath, the quad filled with gowned and surpliced under-graduates drifting from chapel to hall. As I came back they were standing in groups, smoking; Jasper had bicycled in from his digs to be among them.

I walked down the empty Broad to breakfast, as I often did on Sundays, at a tea-shop opposite Balliol. The air was full of bells from the surrounding spires and the sun, casting long shadows across the open spaces, dispelled the fears of night. The tea-shop was hushed as a library; a few solitary men in bedroom slippers from Balliol and Trinity looked up as I entered, then turned back to their Sunday newspapers. I ate my scrambled eggs and bitter marmalade with the zest which in youth follows a restless night. I lit a cigarette and sat on, while one by one the Balliol and Trinity men paid their bills and shuffled away, slip-slop, across the street to their colleges. It was nearly eleven when I left, and during my walk I heard the change-ringing cease and, all over the town, give place to the single chime which warned the city that service was about to start.

None but church-goers seemed abroad that morning; under-graduates and graduates and wives and trades-people, walking with that unmistakable English church-going pace which eschewed equally both haste and idle sauntering; holding, bound in black lamb-skin and white celluloid, the liturgies of half a dozen conflicting sects; on their way to St Barnabas, St Columba, St Aloysius, St Mary's, Pusey House, Blackfriars, and heaven knows where besides; to restored Norman and revived Gothic, to travesties of Venice and Athens; all in the summer sunshine going to the temples of their race. Four proud infidels alone proclaimed their dissent; four Indians from the gates of Balliol, in freshly-laundered white flannels and neatly pressed blazers, with snow-white turbans on their heads, and in their plump, brown hands bright cushions, a picnic basket and the *Plays Unpleasant* of Bernard Shaw, making for the river.

In the Cornmarket a party of tourists stood on the steps of the Clarendon Hotel discussing a road map with their chauffeur, while opposite, through the venerable arch of the Golden Cross, I greeted a group of undergraduates from my college who had breakfasted there and now lingered with their pipes in the creeper-hung courtyard. A troop of boy scouts, church-bound, too, bright with coloured ribbons and badges, loped past in unmilitary array, and at Carfax I met the Mayor and corporation, in scarlet gowns and gold chains, preceded by wand-bearers and followed by no curious glances, in procession to the preaching at the City Church. In St Aldates I passed a crocodile of choir-boys, in starched collars and peculiar caps, on their way to Tom Gate and the Cathedral. So through a world of piety I made my way to Sebastian.

He was out. I read the letters, none of them very revealing, that littered his writing table and scrutinized the invitation cards on his chimney-piece – there were no new additions. Then I read *Lady into Fox* until he returned.

'I've been to mass at the Old Palace,' he said. 'I haven't been all this term, and Monsignor Bell asked me to dinner twice last week, and I know what that means. Mummy's been writing to him. So I sat bang in front where he couldn't help seeing me and absolutely shouted the Hail Marys at the end; so that's over. How was dinner with Antoine? What did you talk about?'

'Well, he did most of the talking. Tell me, did you know him at Eton?'

'He was sacked my first half. I remember seeing him about. He always has been a noticeable figure.'

'Did he go to church with you?'

'I don't think so, why?'

'Has he met any of your family?'

'Charles, how very peculiar you're being today. No. I don't suppose so.'

'Not your mother at Venice?'

'I believe she did say something about it. I forget what. I think she was staying with some Italian cousins of ours, the Foglieres, and Anthony turned up with his family at the hotel, and there was some party the Foglieres gave that they weren't asked to. I know Mummy said something about it when I told her he was a friend of mine. I can't think why he should want to go to a party at the Foglieres – the princess is so proud of her English blood that she talks of nothing else. Anyway, no one objected to Antoine – *much*, I gather. It was his mother they thought difficult.'

'And who is the Duchesse of Vincennes?'

'Poppy?'

'Stefanie.'

'You must ask Antoine that. He claims to have had an affair with her.'

'Did he?'

'I dare say. I think it's more or less compulsory at Cannes. Why all this interest?'

'I just wanted to find out how much truth there was in what Anthony said last night.'

'I shouldn't think a word. That's his great charm.'

'You may think it charming. I think it's devilish. Do you know he spent the whole of yesterday evening trying to turn me against you, and almost succeeded?'

'Did he? How silly. Aloysius wouldn't approve of that at all, would you, you pompous old bear?'

And then Boy Mulcaster came into the room.

CHAPTER III

I RETURNED home for the Long Vacation without plans and without money. To cover end-of-term expenses I had sold my Omega screen to Collins for ten pounds, of which I now kept four; my last cheque overdrew my account by a few shillings, and I had been told that, without my father's authority, I must draw no more. My next allowance was not due until October. I was thus faced with a bleak prospect and, turning the matter over in my mind, I felt something not far off remorse for the prodigality of the preceding weeks.

I had started the term with my battels paid and over a hundred pounds in hand. All that had gone, and not a penny paid out where I could get credit. There had been no reason for it, no great pleasure unattainable else; it had gone in ducks and drakes. Sebastian used to tease me – 'You spend money like a bookie' – but all of it went on and with him. His own finances were perpetually, vaguely distressed. 'It's all done by lawyers,' he said helplessly, 'and I suppose they embezzle a lot. Anyway, I never seem to get much. Of course, mummy would give me anything I asked for.'

'Then why don't you ask her for a proper allowance?'

'Oh, mummy likes everything to be a present. She's so sweet,' he said, adding one more line to the picture I was forming of her.

Now Sebastian had disappeared into that other life of his where I was not asked to follow, and I was left, instead, forlorn and regretful.

How ungenerously in later life we disclaim the virtuous moods of our youth, living in retrospect long, summer days of unreflecting dissipation. There is no candour in a story of early manhood which leaves out of account the home-sickness for nursery morality, the regrets and resolutions of amendment, the black hours which, like zero on the roulette table, turn up with roughly calculable regularity.

Thus I spent the first afternoon at home, wandering from

53

room to room, looking from the plate-glass windows in turn on the garden and the street, in a mood of vehement self-reproach.

My father, I knew, was in the house, but his library was inviolable, and it was not until just before dinner that he appeared to greet me. He was then in his late fifties, but it was his idiosyncrasy to seem much older than his years; to see him one might have put him at seventy, to hear him speak at nearly eighty. He came to me now, with the shuffling, mandarin-tread which he affected, and a shy smile of welcome. When he dined at home – and he seldom dined elsewhere – he wore a frogged velvet smoking-suit of the kind which had been fashionable many years before and was to be so again, but, at that time, was a deliberate archaism.

'My dear boy, they never told me you were here. Did you have a very exhausting journey? They gave you tea? You are well? I have just made a somewhat audacious purchase from Sonerscheins – a terra-cotta bull of the fifth century. I was examining it and forgot your arrival. Was the carriage *very* full? You had a corner seat?' (He travelled so rarely himself that to hear of others doing so always excited his solicitude.) 'Hayter brought you the evening paper? There is no news, of course – such a lot of nonsense.'

Dinner was announced. My father from long habit took a book with him to the table and then, remembering my presence, furtively dropped it under his chair. 'What do you like to drink? Hayter, what have we for Mr Charles to drink?'

'There's some whisky.'

'There's whisky. Perhaps you like something else? What else have we?'

'There isn't anything else in the house, sir.'

'There's nothing else. You must tell Hayter what you would like and he will get it in. I never keep any wine now. I am forbidden it and no one comes to see me. But while you are here, you must have what you like. You are here for long?'

'I'm not quite sure, father.'

'It's a *very* long vacation,' he said wistfully. 'In my day we used to go on what were called reading parties, always in mountainous areas. Why? Why', he repeated petulantly, 'should alpine scenery be thought conducive to study?'

'I thought of putting in some time at an art school – in the life class.'

'My dear boy, you'll find them all shut. The students go to Barbizon or such places and paint in the open air. There was an institution in my day called a "sketching club" – mixed sexes' (snuffle), 'bicycles' (snuffle), 'pepper-and-salt knickerbockers, holland umbrellas, and, it was popularly thought, free love' (snuffle), '*such* a lot of nonsense. I expect they still go on. You might try that.'

'One of the problems of the vacation is money, father.'

'Oh, I shouldn't worry about a thing like that at your age.'

'You see, I've run rather short.'

'Yes?' said my father without any sound of interest.

'In fact I don't quite know how I'm going to get through the next two months.'

'Well, I'm the worst person to come to for advice. I've never been "short" as you so painfully call it. And yet what else could you say? Hard up? Penurious? Distressed? Embarrassed? Stony-broke?' (snuffle). 'On the rocks? In Queer Street? Let us say you are in Queer Street and leave it at that. Your grandfather once said to me, "Live within your means, but if you do get into difficulties, come to me. Don't go to the Jews." Such a lot of nonsense. You try. Go to those gentlemen in Jermyn Street who offer advances on note of hand only. My dear boy, they won't give you a sovereign.'

'Then what do you suggest my doing?'

'Your cousin Melchior was imprudent with his investments and got into a very queer street. *He* went to Australia.'

I had not seen my father so gleeful since he found two pages of second-century papyrus between the leaves of a Lombardic breviary.

'Hayter, I've dropped my book.'

It was recovered for him from under his feet and propped against the épergne. For the rest of dinner he was silent save for an occasional snuffle of merriment which could not, I thought, be provoked by the work he read.

Presently we left the table and sat in the garden-room; and there, plainly, he put me out of his mind; his thoughts, I knew, were far away, in those distant ages where he moved at ease, where time passed in centuries and all the figures were defaced and the names of his companions were corrupt readings of words of quite other meaning. He sat in an attitude which to anyone else would have been one of extreme discomfort, askew in his upright armchair, with his book held high and obliquely to the light. Now and then he took a gold pencil-case from his watch-chain and made an entry in the margin. The windows were open to the summer night; the ticking of the clocks, the distant murmur of traffic on the Bayswater Road, and my father's regular turning of the pages were the only sounds. I had thought it impolitic to smoke a cigar while pleading poverty; now in desperation I went to my room and fetched one. My father did not look up. I pierced it, lit it, and with renewed confidence said, 'Father, you surely don't want me to spend the whole vacation here with you?'

'Eh?'

'Won't you find it rather a bore having me at home for so long?'

'I trust I should not betray such an emotion even if I felt it,' said my father mildly and turned back to his book.

The evening passed. Eventually all over the room clocks of diverse pattern musically chimed eleven. My father closed his book and removed his spectacles. 'You are very welcome, my dear boy,' he said. 'Stay as long as you find it convenient.' At the door he paused and turned back. 'Your cousin Melchior worked his passage to Australia *before the mast*.' (Snuffle.) 'What, I wonder, is "before the mast"?'

During the sultry week that followed, my relations with my father deteriorated sharply. I saw little of him during the day; he spent hours on end in the library; now and then he emerged and I would hear him calling over the banisters: 'Hayter, get me a cab.' Then he would be away, sometimes for half an hour or less, sometimes for a whole day; his errands were never explained. Often I saw trays going up to him at odd hours, laden with meagre nursery snacks – rusks, glasses of milk, bananas, and so forth. If we met in a passage or on the stairs he would look at me vacantly and say 'Ah-ha,' or 'Very warm,' or 'Splendid, splendid,' but in the evening, when he came to the garden-room in his velvet smoking suit, he always greeted me formally.

The dinner table was our battlefield.

On the second evening I took my book with me to the dining-room. His mild and wandering eye fastened on it with sudden attention, and as we passed through the hall he surreptitiously left his own on a side table. When we sat down, he said plaintively: 'I do think, Charles, you might talk to me. I've had a very exhausting day. I was looking forward to a little conversation.'

'Of course, father. What shall we talk about?'

'Cheer me up. Take me out of myself,' petulantly, 'tell me all about the new plays.'

'But I haven't been to any.'

'You should, you know, you really should. It's not natural in a young man to spend all his evenings at home.'

'Well, father, as I told you, I haven't much money to spare for theatre-going.'

'My dear boy, you must not let money become your master in this way. Why, at your age, your cousin Melchior was part-owner of a musical piece. It was one of his few happy ventures. You should go to the play as part of your education. If you read the lives of eminent men you will find that quite half of them made their first acquaintance with drama from the gallery. I am told there is no pleasure like it. It is there that you find the real critics and devotees. It is called "sitting with the gods". The expense is nugatory, and even while you wait for admission in the street you are diverted by "buskers". We will sit with the gods together one night. How do you find Mrs Abel's cooking?'

'Unchanged.'

'It was inspired by your Aunt Philippa. She gave Mrs Abel ten menus, and they have never been varied. When I am alone I do not notice what I eat, but now that you are here, we must have a change. What would you like? What is in season? Are you fond of lobsters? Hayter, tell Mrs Abel to give us lobsters tomorrow night.'

Dinner that evening consisted of a white, tasteless soup, over-fried fillets of sole with a pink sauce, lamb cutlets propped against a cone of mashed potato, stewed pears in jelly standing on a kind of sponge cake.

'It is purely out of respect for your Aunt Philippa that I dine at this length. She laid it down that a three-course dinner was middle-class. "If you once let the servants get their way," she said, "you will find yourself dining nightly off a single chop." There is nothing I should like more. In fact, that is exactly what I do when I go to my club on Mrs Abel's evening out. But your aunt ordained that at home I must have soup and three courses; some nights it is fish, meat, and savoury, on others it is meat, sweet, savoury – there are a number of possible permutations.

'It is remarkable how some people are able to put their opinions in lapidary form; your aunt had that gift.

'It is odd to think that she and I once dined together nightly – just as you and I do, my boy. Now *she* made unremitting efforts to take me out of myself. She used to tell me about her reading. It was in *her* mind to make a home with me, you know. She thought I should get into funny ways if I was left on my own. Perhaps I *have* got into funny ways. Have I? But it didn't do. I got her out in the end.'

There was an unmistakable note of menace in his voice as he said this.

It was largely by reason of my Aunt Philippa that I now found myself so much a stranger in my father's house. After my mother's death she came to live with my father and me, no doubt, as he said, with the idea of making her home with us. I knew nothing, then, of the nightly agonies at the dinner table. My aunt made herself my companion, and I accepted her without question. That was for a year. The first change was that she reopened her house in Surrey which she had meant to sell, and lived there during my school terms, coming to London only for a few days' shopping and entertainment. In the summer we went to lodgings together at the seaside. Then in my last year at school she left England. '*I got her out in the end,*' he said with derision and triumph of that kindly lady, and he knew that I heard in the words a challenge to myself.

As we left the dining-room my father said, 'Hayter, have you yet said anything to Mrs Abel about the lobsters I ordered for tomorrow?'

'No, sir.'

'Do not do so.'

'Very good, sir.'

And when we reached our chairs in the garden-room he said:

'I wonder whether Hayter had any intention of mentioning lobsters. I rather think not. Do you know, I believe he thought I was *joking*?'

Next day, by chance, a weapon came to hand. I met an old acquaintance of school-days, a contemporary of mine named Jorkins. I never had much liking for Jorkins. Once, in my Aunt Philippa's day, he had come to tea, and she had condemned him as being probably charming at heart, but unattractive at first sight. Now I greeted him with enthusiasm and asked him to dinner. He came and showed little alteration. My father must have been warned by Hayter that there was a guest, for instead of his velvet suit he wore a tail-coat; this, with a black waistcoat, very high collar, and very narrow white tie, was his evening dress; he wore it with an air of melancholy as though it were court mourning, which he had assumed in early youth and, finding the style sympathetic, had retained. He never possessed a dinner jacket.

'Good evening, good evening. So nice of you to come all this way.'

'Oh, it wasn't far,' said Jorkins, who lived in Sussex Square.

'Science annihilates distance,' said my father disconcertingly. 'You are over here on business?'

'Well, I'm *in* business, if that's what you mean.'

'I had a cousin who was in business – you wouldn't know him; it was before your time. I was telling Charles about him only the other night. He has been much in my mind. He came', my father paused to give full weight to the bizarre word – 'a *cropper*.'

Jorkins giggled nervously. My father fixed him with a look of reproach.

'You find his misfortune the subject of mirth? Or perhaps the word I used was unfamiliar; *you* no doubt would say that he "folded up".'

My father was master of the situation. He had made a little fantasy for himself, that Jorkins should be an American, and throughout the evening he played a delicate, one-sided parlour-game with him, explaining any peculiarly English terms that occurred in the conversation, translating pounds into dollars, and courteously deferring to him with such phrases as 'Of course, by *your* standards . . .'; 'All this must seem very parochial to Mr Jorkins'; 'In the vast spaces to which *you* are accustomed . . .' so that my guest was left with the vague sense that there was a misconception somewhere as to his identity, which he never got the chance of explaining. Again and again during dinner he sought my father's eye, thinking to read there the simple statement that this form of address was an elaborate joke, but met instead a look of such mild benignity that he was left baffled.

Once I thought my father had gone too far, when he said: 'I am afraid that, living in London, you must sadly miss your national game.'

'My national game?' asked Jorkins, slow in the uptake, but scenting that here, at last, was the opportunity for clearing the matter up.

My father glanced from him to me and his expression changed from kindness to malice; then back to kindness again as he turned once more to Jorkins. It was the look of a gambler who lays down fours against a full house. 'Your national game,' he said gently, '*cricket*,' and he snuffled uncontrollably, shaking all over and wiping his eyes with his napkin. 'Surely, working in the City, you find your time on the cricket-field greatly curtailed?'

At the door of the dining-room he left us. 'Good night, Mr Jorkins,' he said. 'I hope you will pay us another visit when you next "cross the herring pond".'

'I say, what did your governor mean by that? He seemed almost to think I was American.'

'He's rather odd at times.'

'I mean all that about advising me to visit Westminster Abbey. It seemed rum.'

'Yes. I can't quite explain.'

'I almost thought he was pulling my leg,' said Jorkins in puzzled tones.

My father's counter-attack was delivered a few days later. He sought me out and said, 'Mr Jorkins is still here?'

'No, father, of course not. He only came to dinner.'

'Oh, I hoped he was staying with us. Such a *versatile* young man. But you will be dining in?'

'Yes.'

'I am giving a little dinner party to diversify the rather monotonous series of your evenings at home. You think Mrs Abel is up to it? No. But our guests are not exacting. Sir Cuthbert and Lady Orme-Herrick are what might be called the nucleus. I hope for a little music afterwards. I have included in the invitations some young people for you.'

My presentiments of my father's plan were surpassed by the actuality. As the guests assembled in the room which my father, without self-consciousness, called 'the Gallery', it was plain to me that they had been carefully chosen for my discomfort. The 'young people' were Miss Gloria Orme-Herrick, a student of the cello; her fiancé, a bald young man from the British Museum; and a monoglot Munich publisher. I saw my father snuffling at me from behind a case of ceramics as he stood with them. That evening he wore, like a chivalric badge of battle, a small red rose in his button-hole.

Dinner was long and chosen, like the guests, in a spirit of

careful mockery. It was not of Aunt Philippa's choosing, but
had been reconstructed from a much earlier period, long before
he was of an age to dine downstairs. The dishes were ornamental in appearance and regularly alternated in colour between
red and white. They and the wine were equally tasteless. After
dinner my father led the German publisher to the piano and
then, while he played, left the drawing-room to show Sir
Cuthbert Orme-Herrick the Etruscan bull in the gallery.

It was a gruesome evening, and I was astonished to find,
when at last the party broke up, that it was only a few minutes
after eleven. My father helped himself to a glass of barley-water
and said: 'What very dull friends I have! You know, without the
spur of your presence I should never have roused myself to
invite them. I have been very negligent about entertaining
lately. Now that you are paying me such a long visit, I will have
many such evenings. You liked Miss Gloria Orme-Herrick?'

'No.'

'No? Was it her little moustache you objected to or her very
large feet? Do you think she enjoyed herself?'

'No.'

'That was my impression also. I doubt if any of our guests
will count this as one of their happiest evenings. That young
foreigner played atrociously, I thought. Where can I have met
him? And Miss Constantia Smethwick – where can I have met
her? But the obligations of hospitality must be observed. As long
as you are here, you shall not be dull.'

Strife was internecine during the next fortnight, but I
suffered the more, for my father had greater reserves to draw on
and a wider territory for manoeuvre, while I was pinned to my
bridgehead between the uplands and the sea. He never declared
his war aims, and I do not to this day know whether they were
purely punitive – whether he had really at the back of his mind
some geopolitical idea of getting me out of the country, as my
Aunt Philippa had been driven to Bordighera and cousin
Melchior to Darwin, or whether, as seems most likely, he fought
for the sheer love of a battle in which indeed he shone.

I received one letter from Sebastian, a conspicuous object

which was brought to me in my father's presence one day when he was lunching at home; I saw him look curiously at it and bore it away to read in solitude. It was written on, and enveloped in, heavy late-Victorian mourning paper, black-coroneted and black-bordered. I read it eagerly:

> *Brideshead Castle,*
> *Wiltshire.*
> *I wonder what the date is*
>
> Dearest Charles,
>
> *I found a box of this paper at the back of a bureau so I must write to you as I am mourning for my lost innocence. It never looked like living. The doctors despaired of it from the start.*
>
> *Soon I am off to Venice to stay with my papa in his palace of sin. I wish you were coming. I wish you were here.*
>
> *I am never quite alone. Members of my family keep turning up and collecting luggage and going away again but the white raspberries are ripe.*
>
> *I have a good mind not to take Aloysius to Venice. I don't want him to meet a lot of horrid Italian bears and pick up bad habits.*
>
> *Love or what you will.*
>
> S.

I knew his letters of old; I had had them at Ravenna; I should not have been disappointed; but that day, as I tore the stiff sheet across and let it fall into the basket, and gazed resentfully across the grimy gardens and irregular backs of Bayswater, at the jumble of soil-pipes and fire-escapes and protuberant little conservatories, I saw, in my mind's eye, the pale face of Anthony Blanche, peering through the straggling leaves as it had peered through the candle flames at Thame, and heard, above the murmur of traffic, his clear tones ... 'You mustn't blame Sebastian if at times he seems a little insipid. ... When I hear him talk I am reminded of that in some ways nauseating picture of *"Bubbles"*.'

For days after that I thought I hated Sebastian; then one Sunday afternoon a telegram came from him, which dispelled that shadow, adding a new and darker one of its own.

My father was out and returned to find me in a condition of feverish anxiety. He stood in the hall with his panama hat still on his head and beamed at me.

'You'll never guess how I have spent the day; I have been to the Zoo. It was most agreeable; the animals seem to enjoy the sunshine so much.'

'Father, I've got to leave at once.'

'Yes?'

'A great friend of mine – he's had a terrible accident. I must go to him at once. Hayter's packing for me, now. There's a train in half an hour.'

I showed him the telegram, which read simply: '*Gravely injured come at once Sebastian.*'

'Well,' said my father. 'I'm sorry you are upset. Reading this message I should not say that the accident was as serious as you seem to think – otherwise it would hardly be signed by the victim himself. Still, of course, he may well be fully conscious but blind or paralysed with a broken back. Why exactly is your presence so necessary? You have no medical knowledge. You are not in holy orders. Do you hope for a legacy?'

'I told you, he is a great friend.'

'Well, Orme-Herrick is a great friend of mine, but I should not go tearing off to his death-bed on a warm Sunday afternoon. I should doubt whether Lady Orme-Herrick would welcome me. However, I see you have no such doubts. I shall miss you, my dear boy, but do not hurry back on my account.'

Paddington Station on that August Sunday evening, with the sun streaming through the obscure panes of its roof, the bookstalls shut, and the few passengers strolling unhurried beside their porters, would have soothed a mind less agitated than mine. The train was nearly empty. I had my suitcase put in the corner of a third-class carriage and took a seat in the dining-car. 'First dinner after Reading, sir; about seven o'clock. Can I get you anything now?' I ordered gin and vermouth; it was brought to me as we pulled out of the station. The knives and forks set up their regular jingle; the bright landscape rolled past the windows. But I had no mind for these smooth things;

instead, fear worked like yeast in my thoughts, and the fermentation brought to the surface, in great gobs of scum, the images of disaster; a loaded gun held carelessly at a stile, a horse rearing and rolling over, a shaded pool with a submerged stake, an elm bough falling suddenly on a still morning, a car at a blind corner; all the catalogue of threats to civilized life rose and haunted me; I even pictured a homicidal maniac mouthing in the shadows, swinging a length of lead pipe. The cornfields and heavy woodland sped past, deep in the golden evening, and the throb of the wheels repeated monotonously in my ears, 'You've come too late. You've come too late. He's dead. He's dead. He's dead.'

I dined and changed trains to the local line, and in twilight came to Melstead Carbury, which was my destination.

'Brideshead, sir? Yes, Lady Julia's in the yard.'

She was sitting at the wheel of an open car. I recognized her at once; I could not have failed to do so.

'You're Mr Ryder? Jump in.' Her voice was Sebastian's and his her way of speaking.

'How is he?'

'Sebastian? Oh, he's fine. Have you had dinner? Well, I expect it was beastly. There's some more at home. Sebastian and I are alone, so we thought we'd wait for you.'

'What's happened to him?'

'Didn't he say? I expect he thought you wouldn't come if you knew. He's cracked a bone in his ankle so small that it hasn't a name. But they X-rayed it yesterday, and told him to keep it up for a month. It's a great bore to him, putting out all his plans; he's been making the most enormous fuss. ... Everyone else has gone. He tried to make me stay back with him. Well, I expect you know how maddeningly pathetic he can be. I almost gave in, and then I said: "Surely there must be *someone* you can get hold of," and he said everybody was away or busy and, anyway, no one else would do. But at last he agreed to try you, and I promised I'd stay if you failed him, so you can imagine how popular you are with me. I must say it's noble of you to come all this way at a moment's notice.' But as she said it, I heard, or thought I heard, a tiny note of contempt in her voice that I should be so readily available.

'How did he do it?'

'Believe it or not, playing croquet. He lost his temper and tripped over a hoop. *Not* a very honourable scar.'

She so much resembled Sebastian that, sitting beside her in the gathering dusk, I was confused by the double illusion of familiarity and strangeness. Thus, looking through strong lenses, one may watch a man approaching from afar, study every detail of his face and clothes, believe one has only to put out a hand to touch him, marvel that he does not hear one and look up as one moves, and then, seeing him with the naked eye, suddenly remember that one is to him a distant speck, doubtfully human. I knew her and she did not know me. Her dark hair was scarcely longer than Sebastian's, and it blew back from her forehead as his did; her eyes on the darkling road were his, but larger; her painted mouth was less friendly to the world. She wore a bangle of charms on her wrist and in her ears little gold rings. Her light coat revealed an inch or two of flowered silk; skirts were short in those days, and her legs, stretched forward to the controls of the car, were spindly, as was also the fashion. Because her sex was the palpable difference between the familiar and the strange, it seemed to fill the space between us, so that I felt her to be especially female, as I had felt of no woman before.

'I'm terrified of driving at this time of the evening,' she said. 'There doesn't seem anyone left at home who can drive a car. Sebastian and I are practically camping out here. I hope you haven't come expecting a pompous party.' She leaned forward to the locker for a box of cigarettes.

'No thanks.'

'Light one for me, will you?'

It was the first time in my life that anyone had asked this of me, and as I took the cigarette from my lips and put it in hers, I caught a thin bat's squeak of sexuality, inaudible to any but me.

'Thanks. You've been here before. Nanny reported it. We both thought it very odd of you not to stay to tea with me.'

'That was Sebastian.'

'You seem to let him boss you about a good deal. You shouldn't. It's very bad for him.'

We had turned the corner of the drive now; the colour had died in the woods and sky, and the house seemed painted in *grisaille*, save for the central golden square at the open doors. A man was waiting to take my luggage.

'Here we are.'

She led me up the steps and into the hall, flung her coat on a marble table, and stooped to fondle a dog which came to greet her. 'I wouldn't put it past Sebastian to have started dinner.'

At that moment he appeared between the pillars at the further end, propelling himself in a wheel-chair. He was in pyjamas and dressing gown, with one foot heavily bandaged.

'Well, darling, I've collected your chum,' she said, again with a barely perceptible note of contempt.

'I thought you were dying,' I said, conscious then, as I had been ever since I arrived, of the predominating emotion of vexation, rather than of relief, that I had been bilked of my expectations of a grand tragedy.

'I thought I was, too. The pain was excruciating. Julia, do you think, if *you* asked him, Wilcox would give us champagne tonight?'

'I hate champagne and Mr Ryder has had dinner.'

'*Mister* Ryder? *Mister* Ryder? Charles drinks champagne at all hours. Do you know, seeing this great swaddled foot of mine, I can't get it out of my mind that I have gout, and that gives me a craving for champagne.'

We dined in a room they called 'the Painted Parlour'. It was a spacious octagon, later in design than the rest of the house; its walls were adorned with wreathed medallions, and across its dome prim Pompeian figures stood in pastoral groups. They and the satin-wood and ormolu furniture, the carpet, the hanging bronze candelabrum, the mirrors and sconces, were all a single composition, the design of one illustrious hand. 'We usually eat here when we're alone,' said Sebastian, 'it's so cosy.'

While they dined I ate a peach and told them of the war with my father.

'He sounds a perfect poppet,' said Julia. 'And now I'm going to leave you boys.'

'Where are you off to?'

'The nursery. I promised nanny a last game of halma.' She kissed the top of Sebastian's head. I opened the door for her. 'Good night, Mr Ryder, and good-bye. I don't suppose we'll meet tomorrow. I'm leaving early. I can't tell you how grateful I am to you for relieving me at the sick-bed.'

'My sister's very pompous tonight,' said Sebastian, when she was gone.

'I don't think she cares for me,' I said.

'I don't think she cares for anyone much. I love her. She's so like me.'

'*Do you? Is she?*'

'In looks I mean and the way she talks. I wouldn't love anyone with a character like mine.'

When we had drunk our port, I walked beside Sebastian's chair through the pillared hall to the library, where we sat that night and nearly every night of the ensuing month. It lay on the side of the house that overlooked the lakes; the windows were open to the stars and the scented air, to the indigo and silver, moonlit landscape of the valley and the sound of water falling in the fountain.

'We'll have a heavenly time alone,' said Sebastian, and when next morning, while I was shaving, I saw from my bathroom window Julia, with luggage at her back, drive from the fore-court and disappear at the hill's crest, without a backward glance, I felt a sense of liberation and peace such as I was to know years later when, after a night of unrest, the sirens sounded the 'All Clear'.

CHAPTER IV

THE languor of Youth – how unique and quintessential it is! How quickly, how irrecoverably, lost! The zest, the generous affections, the illusions, the despair, all the traditional attributes of Youth – all save this – come and go with us through life. These things are a part of life itself; but languor – the relaxation of yet unwearied sinews, the mind sequestered and self-regarding – that belongs to Youth alone and dies with it. Perhaps in the mansions of Limbo the heroes enjoy some such compensation for their loss of the Beatific Vision; perhaps the Beatific Vision itself has some remote kinship with this lowly experience; I, at any rate, believed myself very near heaven, during those languid days at Brideshead.

'Why is this house called a "Castle"?'
'It used to be one until they moved it.'
'What can you mean?'
'Just that. We had a castle a mile away, down by the village. Then we took a fancy to the valley and pulled the castle down, carted the stones up here, and built a new house. I'm glad they did, aren't you?'
'If it was mine I'd never live anywhere else.'
'But you see, Charles, it isn't mine. Just at the moment it is, but usually it's full of ravening beasts. If it could only be like this always – always summer, always alone, the fruit always ripe, and Aloysius in a good temper. ...'
It is thus I like to remember Sebastian, as he was that summer, when we wandered alone together through that enchanted palace; Sebastian in his wheel-chair spinning down the box-edged walks of the kitchen gardens in search of alpine strawberries and warm figs, propelling himself through the succession of hot-houses, from scent to scent and climate to climate, to cut the muscat grapes and choose orchids for our button-holes; Sebastian hobbling with a pantomime of difficulty to the old nurseries, sitting beside me on the threadbare,

flowered carpet with the toy-cupboard empty about us and Nanny Hawkins stitching complacently in the corner, saying, 'You're one as bad as the other; a pair of children the two of you. Is that what they teach you at College?' Sebastian supine on the sunny seat in the colonnade, as he was now, and I in a hard chair beside him, trying to draw the fountain.

'Is the dome by Inigo Jones, too? It looks later.'

'Oh, Charles, don't be such a tourist. What does it matter when it was built, if it's pretty?'

'It's the sort of thing I like to know.'

'Oh dear, I thought I'd cured you of all that – the terrible Mr Collins.'

It was an aesthetic education to live within those walls, to wander from room to room, from the Soanesque library to the Chinese drawing-room, adazzle with gilt pagodas and nodding mandarins, painted paper and Chippendale fretwork, from the Pompeian parlour to the great tapestry-hung hall which stood unchanged, as it had been designed two hundred and fifty years before; to sit, hour after hour, in the shade looking out on the terrace.

This terrace was the final consummation of the house's plan; it stood on massive stone ramparts above the lakes, so that from the hall steps it seemed to overhang them, as though, standing by the balustrade, one could have dropped a pebble into the first of them immediately below one's feet. It was embraced by the two arms of the colonnade; beyond the pavilions groves of lime led to the wooded hillsides. Part of the terrace was paved, part planted with flower-beds and arabesques of dwarf box; taller box grew in a dense hedge, making a wide oval, cut into niches and interspersed with statuary, and, in the centre, dominating the whole splendid space rose the fountain; such a fountain as one might expect to find in a piazza of southern Italy; such a fountain as was, indeed, found there a century ago by one of Sebastian's ancestors; found, purchased, imported, and re-erected in an alien but welcoming climate.

Sebastian set me to draw it. It was an ambitious subject for an amateur – an oval basin with an island of sculptured rocks at its centre; on the rocks grew, in stone, formal tropical vegetation and wild English fern in its natural fronds; through them ran a dozen streams that counterfeited springs, and round them sported fantastic tropical animals, camels and camelopards and an ebullient lion, all vomiting water; on the rocks, to the height of the pediment, stood an Egyptian obelisk of red sandstone – but, by some odd chance, for the thing was far beyond me, I brought it off and, by judicious omissions and some stylish tricks, produced a very passable echo of Piranesi. 'Shall I give it to your mother?' I asked.

'Why? You don't know her.'

'It seems polite. I'm staying in her house.'

'Give it to nanny,' said Sebastian.

I did so, and she put it among the collection on the top of her chest of drawers, remarking that it had quite a look of the thing, which she had often heard admired but could never see the beauty of, herself.

For me the beauty was new-found.

Since the days when, as a schoolboy, I used to bicycle round the neighbouring parishes, rubbing brasses and photographing fonts, I had nursed a love of architecture, but, though in opinion I had made that easy leap, characteristic of my generation, from the puritanism of Ruskin to the puritanism of Roger Fry, my sentiments at heart were insular and medieval.

This was my conversion to the Baroque. Here under that high and insolent dome, under those coffered ceilings; here, as I passed through those arches and broken pediments to the pillared shade beyond and sat, hour by hour, before the fountain, probing its shadows, tracing its lingering echoes, rejoicing in all its clustered feats of daring and invention, I felt a whole new system of nerves alive within me, as though the water that spurted and bubbled among its stones, was indeed a life-giving spring.

One day in a cupboard we found a large japanned-tin box of oil-paints still in workable condition.

'Mummy bought them a year or two ago. Someone told her

that you could only appreciate the beauty of the world by trying to paint it. We laughed at her a great deal about it. She couldn't draw at all, and however bright the colours were in the tubes, by the time mummy had mixed them up, they came out a kind of khaki.' Various dry, muddy smears on the palette confirmed this statement. 'Cordelia was always made to wash the brushes. In the end we all protested and made mummy stop.'

The paints gave us the idea of decorating the office; this was a small room opening on the colonnade; it had once been used for estate business, but was now derelict, holding only some garden games and a tub of dead aloes; it had plainly been designed for a softer use, perhaps as a tea-room or study, for the plaster walls were decorated with delicate Rococo panels and the roof was prettily groined. Here, in one of the smaller oval frames, I sketched a romantic landscape, and in the days that followed filled it out in colour, and, by luck and the happy mood of the moment, made a success of it. The brush seemed somehow to do what was wanted of it. It was a landscape without figures, a summer scene of white cloud and blue distances, with an ivy-clad ruin in the foreground, rocks and a waterfall affording a rugged introduction to the receding park-land behind. I knew little of oil-painting and learned its ways as I worked. When, in a week, it was finished, Sebastian was eager for me to start on one of the larger panels. I made some sketches. He called for a *fête champêtre* with a ribboned swing and a Negro page and a shepherd playing the pipes, but the thing languished. I knew it was good chance that had made my landscape, and that this elaborate pastiche was too much for me.

One day we went down to the cellars with Wilcox and saw the empty bays which had once held a vast store of wine; one transept only was used now; there the bins were well stocked, some of them with vintages fifty years old.

'There's been nothing added since his Lordship went abroad,' said Wilcox. 'A lot of the old wine wants drinking up. We ought to have laid down the eighteens and twenties. I've had several letters about it from the wine merchants, but her Ladyship says to ask Lord Brideshead, and he says to ask his Lordship, and his Lordship says to ask the lawyers. That's how we get low. There's enough here for ten years at the rate it's going, but how shall we be then?'

Wilcox welcomed our interest; we had bottles brought up from every bin, and it was during those tranquil evenings with Sebastian that I first made a serious acquaintance with wine and sowed the seed of that rich harvest which was to be my stay in many barren years. We would sit, he and I, in the Painted Parlour with three bottles open on the table and three glasses before each of us; Sebastian had found a book on wine-tasting, and we followed its instructions in detail. We warmed the glass slightly at a candle, filled it a third high, swirled the wine round, nursed it in our hands, held it to the light, breathed it, sipped it, filled our mouths with it, and rolled it over the tongue, ringing it on the palate like a coin on a counter, tilted our heads back and let it trickle down the throat. Then we talked of it and nibbled Bath Oliver biscuits, and passed on to another wine; then back to the first, then on to another, until all three were in circulation and the order of glasses got confused, and we fell out over which was which, and we passed the glasses to and fro between us until there were six glasses, some of them with mixed wines in them which we had filled from the wrong bottle, till we were obliged to start again with three clean glasses each, and the bottles were empty and our praise of them wilder and more exotic.

'... It is a little, shy wine like a gazelle.'

'Like a leprechaun.'

'Dappled, in a tapestry meadow.'

'Like a flute by still water.'

'... And this is a wise old wine.'

'A prophet in a cave.'

'... And this is a necklace of pearls on a white neck.'

'Like a swan.'

'Like the last unicorn.'

And we would leave the golden candle-light of the dining-room for the starlight outside and sit on the edge of the fountain, cooling our hands in the water and listening drunkenly to its splash and gurgle over the rocks.

'Ought we to be drunk *every* night?' Sebastian asked one morning.

'Yes, I think so.'

'I think so too.'

We saw few strangers. There was the agent, a lean and pouchy colonel, who crossed our path occasionally and once came to tea. Usually we managed to hide from him. On Sundays a monk was fetched from a neighbouring monastery to say mass and breakfast with us. He was the first priest I ever met; I noticed how unlike he was to a parson, but Brideshead was a place of such enchantment to me that I expected everything and everyone to be unique; Father Phipps was in fact a bland, bun-faced man with an interest in county cricket which he obstinately believed us to share.

'You know, father, Charles and I simply don't *know* about cricket.'

'I wish I'd seen Tennyson make that fifty-eight last Thursday. That must have been an innings. The account in *The Times* was excellent. Did you see him against the South Africans?'

'I've never seen him.'

'Neither have I. I haven't seen a first-class match for years – not since Father Graves took me when we were passing through Leeds, after we'd been to the induction of the Abbot at Ampleforth. Father Graves managed to look up a train which gave us three hours to wait on the afternoon of the match against Lancashire. That *was* an afternoon. I remember every ball of it. Since then I've had to go by the papers. You seldom go to see cricket?'

'Never,' I said, and he looked at me with the expression I have seen since in the religious, of innocent wonder that those who expose themselves to the dangers of the world should avail themselves so little of its varied solace.

Sebastian always heard his mass, which was ill-attended.

Brideshead was not an old-established centre of Catholicism. Lady Marchmain had introduced a few Catholic servants, but the majority of them, and all the cottagers, prayed, if anywhere, among the Flyte tombs in the little grey church at the gates.

Sebastian's faith was an enigma to me at that time, but not one which I felt particularly concerned to solve. I had no religion. I was taken to church weekly as a child, and at school attended chapel daily, but, as though in compensation, from the time I went to my public school I was excused church in the holidays. The masters who taught me Divinity told me that biblical texts were highly untrustworthy. They never suggested I should try to pray. My father did not go to church except on family occasions and then with derision. My mother, I think, was devout. It once seemed odd to me that she should have thought it her duty to leave my father and me and go off with an ambulance, to Serbia, to die of exhaustion in the snow in Bosnia. But later I recognized some such spirit in myself. Later, too, I have come to accept claims which then, in 1923, I never troubled to examine, and to accept the supernatural as the real. I was aware of no such needs that summer at Brideshead.

Often, almost daily, since I had known Sebastian, some chance word in his conversation had reminded me that he was a Catholic, but I took it as a foible, like his teddy-bear. We never discussed the matter until on the second Sunday at Brideshead, when Father Phipps had left us and we sat in the colonnade with the papers, he surprised me by saying: 'Oh dear, it's very difficult being a Catholic.'

'Does it make much difference to you?'

'Of course. All the time.'

'Well, I can't say I've noticed it. Are you struggling against temptation? You don't seem much more virtuous than me.'

'I'm very, very much wickeder,' said Sebastian indignantly.

'Well then?'

'Who was it used to pray, "O God, make me good, but not yet"?'

'I don't know. You, I should think.'

'Why, yes, *I* do, every day. But it isn't that.' He turned back to the pages of the *News of the World* and said, 'Another naughty scout-master.'

'I suppose they try and make you believe an awful lot of nonsense?'

'Is it nonsense? I wish it were. It sometimes sounds terribly sensible to me.'

'But my dear Sebastian, you can't seriously *believe* it all.'

'Can't I?'

'I mean about Christmas and the star and the three kings and the ox and the ass.'

'Oh yes, I believe that. It's a lovely idea.'

'But you can't *believe* things because they're a lovely idea.'

'But I *do*. That's how I believe.'

'And in prayers? Do you think you can kneel down in front of a statue and say a few words, not even out loud, just in your mind, and change the weather; or that some saints are more influential than others, and you must get hold of the right one to help you on the right problem?'

'Oh yes. Don't you remember last term when I took Aloysius and left him behind I didn't know where. I prayed like mad to St Anthony of Padua that morning, and immediately after lunch there was Mr Nichols at Canterbury Gate with Aloysius in his arms, saying I'd left him in his cab.'

'Well,' I said, 'If you can believe all that and you don't want to be good, where's the difficulty about your religion?'

'If you can't see, you can't.'

'Well, where?'

'Oh, don't be a *bore*, Charles. I want to read about a woman in Hull who's been using an instrument.'

'You started the subject. I was just getting interested.'

'I'll never mention it again ... thirty-eight other cases were taken into consideration in sentencing her to six months – golly!'

But he did mention it again, some ten days later, as we were lying on the roof of the house, sunbathing and watching through a telescope the Agricultural Show which was in progress in the park below us. It was a modest two-day show serving the neighbouring parishes, and surviving more as a fair and social gathering than as a centre of serious competition. A ring was marked out in flags, and round it had been pitched half a dozen tents of varying size; there was a judges' box and some pens for livestock; the largest marquee was for refreshments, and there the farmers congregated in numbers. Preparations had been going on for a week. 'We shall have to hide,' said Sebastian as the day approached. 'My brother will be here. He's a big part of the Agricultural Show.' So we lay on the roof under the balustrade.

Brideshead came down by train in the morning and lunched with Colonel Fender, the agent. I met him for five minutes on his arrival. Anthony Blanche's description was peculiarly apt; he had the Flyte face, carved by an Aztec. We could see him now, through the telescope, moving awkwardly among the tenants, stopping to greet the judges in their box, leaning over a pen gazing seriously at the cattle.

'Queer fellow, my brother,' said Sebastian.

'He looks normal enough.'

'Oh, but he's not. If you only knew, he's much the craziest of us, only it doesn't come out at all. He's all twisted inside. He wanted to be a priest, you know.'

'I didn't.'

'I think he still does. He nearly became a Jesuit, straight from Stonyhurst. It was awful for mummy. She couldn't exactly try and stop him, but of course it was the last thing she wanted. Think what people would have said – the eldest son; it's not as if it had been me. And poor papa. The Church has been enough trouble to him without that happening. There was a frightful to-do – monks and monsignori running round the house like mice, and Brideshead just sitting glum and talking about the will of God. He was the most upset, you see, when papa went abroad – much more than mummy really. Finally they persuaded him to go to Oxford and think it over for three years. Now he's trying to make up his mind. He talks of going into the Guards and into the House of Commons and of marrying. He doesn't know what he wants. I wonder if I should have been like that, if I'd gone to Stonyhurst. I should have gone, only papa went abroad before I was old enough, and the first thing he insisted on was my going to Eton.'

'Has your father given up religion?'

'Well, he's had to in a way; he only took to it when he married mummy. When he went off, he left that behind with the rest of us. You must meet him. He's a very nice man.'

Sebastian had never spoken seriously of his father before.

I said: 'It must have upset you all when your father went away.'

'All but Cordelia. She was too young. It upset *me* at the time. Mummy tried to explain it to the three eldest of us so that we wouldn't hate papa. I was the only one who didn't. I believe she wishes I did. I was always his favourite. I should be staying with him now, if it wasn't for this foot. I'm the only one who goes. Why don't you come too? You'd like him.'

A man with a megaphone was shouting the results of the last event in the field below; his voice came faintly to us.

'So you see we're a mixed family religiously. Brideshead and Cordelia are both fervent Catholics; he's miserable, she's bird-happy; Julia and I are half-heathen; I am happy, I rather think Julia isn't; mummy is popularly believed to be a saint and papa is excommunicated – and I wouldn't know which of them was happy. Anyway, however you look at it, happiness doesn't seem to have much to do with it, and that's all I want. ... I wish I liked Catholics more.'

'They seem just like other people.'

'My dear Charles, that's exactly what they're not – particularly in this country, where they're so few. It's not just that they're a clique – as a matter of fact, they're at least four cliques all blackguarding each other half the time – but they've got an entirely different outlook on life; everything they think important is different from other people. They try and hide it as much as they can, but it comes out all the time. It's quite natural, really, that they should. But you see it's difficult for semi-heathens like Julia and me.'

We were interrupted in this unusually grave conversation by

loud, childish cries from beyond the chimney-stacks, 'Sebastian, Sebastian.'

'Good heavens!' said Sebastian, reaching for a blanket. 'That sounds like my sister Cordelia. Cover yourself up.'

'Where are you?'

There came into view a robust child of ten or eleven; she had the unmistakable family characteristics, but had them ill-arranged in a frank and chubby plainness; two thick old-fashioned pigtails hung down her back.

'Go away, Cordelia. We've got no clothes on.'

'Why? You're quite decent. I guessed you were here. You didn't know I was about, did you? I came down with Bridey and stopped to see Francis Xavier.' (To me) 'He's my pig. Then we had lunch with Colonel Fender and then the show. Francis Xavier got a special mention. That beast Randal got first with a mangy animal. *Darling* Sebastian, I am pleased to see you again. How's your poor foot?'

'Say how-d'you-do to Mr Ryder.'

'Oh, sorry. How d'you do?' All the family charm was in her smile. 'They're all getting pretty boozy down there, so I came away. I say, who's been painting the office? I went in to look for a shooting-stick and saw it.'

'Be careful what you say. It's Mr Ryder.'

'But it's *lovely*. I say, did you really? You *are* clever. Why don't you both dress and come down? There's no one about.'

'Bridey's sure to bring the judges in.'

'But he won't. I heard him making plans not to. He's very sour today. He didn't want me to have dinner with you, but I fixed that. Come on. I'll be in the nursery when you're fit to be seen.'

We were a sombre little party that evening. Only Cordelia was perfectly at ease, rejoicing in the food, the lateness of the hour, and her brothers' company. Brideshead was three years older than Sebastian and I, but he seemed of another gener-ation. He had the physical tricks of his family, and his smile, when it rarely came, was as lovely as theirs; he spoke, in their voice, with a gravity and restraint which in my cousin Jasper would have sounded pompous and false, but in him was plainly unassumed and unconscious.

'I am so sorry to miss so much of your visit,' he said to me. 'You are being looked after properly? I hope Sebastian is seeing to the wine. Wilcox is apt to be rather grudging when he is on his own.'

'He's treated us very liberally.'

'I am delighted to hear it. You are fond of wine?'

'Very.'

'I wish I were. It is such a bond with other men. At Magdalen I tried to get drunk more than once, but I did not enjoy it. Beer and whisky I find even less appetizing. Events like this afternoon's are a torment to me in consequence.'

'I like wine,' said Cordelia.

'My sister Cordelia's last report said that she was not only the worst girl in the school, but the worst there had ever been in the memory of the oldest nun.'

'That's because I refused to be an Enfant de Marie. Reverend Mother said that if I didn't keep my room tidier I couldn't be one, so I said, well, I won't be one, and I don't believe our Blessed Lady cares two hoots whether I put my gym shoes on the left or the right of my dancing shoes. Reverend Mother was livid.'

'Our Lady cares about obedience.'

'Bridey, you mustn't be pious,' said Sebastian. 'We've got an atheist with us.'

'Agnostic,' I said.

'Really? Is there much of that at your college? There was a certain amount at Magdalen.'

'I really don't know. I was one long before I went to Oxford.'

'It's everywhere,' said Brideshead.

Religion seemed an inevitable topic that day. For some time we talked about the Agricultural Show. Then Brideshead said, 'I saw the Bishop in London last week. You know, he wants to close our chapel.'

'Oh, he couldn't,' said Cordelia.

'I don't think mummy will let him,' said Sebastian.

'It's too far away,' said Brideshead. 'There are a dozen families round Melstead who can't get here. He wants to open a mass centre there.'

'But what about us?' said Sebastian. 'Do we have to drive out on winter mornings?'

'We must have the Blessed Sacrament here,' said Cordelia. 'I like popping in at odd times; so does mummy.'

'So do I,' said Brideshead, 'but there are so few of us. It's not as though we were old Catholics with everyone on the estate coming to mass. It'll have to go sooner or later, perhaps after mummy's time. The point is whether it wouldn't be better to let it go now. You are an artist, Ryder, what do you think of it aesthetically?'

'I think it's *beautiful*,' said Cordelia with tears in her eyes.

'Is it Good Art?'

'Well, I don't quite know what you mean,' I said warily. 'I think it's a remarkable example of its period. Probably in eighty years it will be greatly admired.'

'But surely it can't be good twenty years ago and good in eighty years, and not good now?'

'Well, it may be *good* now. All I mean is that I don't happen to like it much.'

'But is there a difference between liking a thing and thinking it good?'

'Bridey, don't be so Jesuitical,' said Sebastian, but I knew that this disagreement was not a matter of words only, but expressed a deep and impassable division between us; neither had any understanding of the other, nor ever could.

'Isn't that just the distinction you made about wine?'

'No. I like and think good the end to which wine is sometimes the means – the promotion of sympathy between man and man. But in my own case it does not achieve that end, so I neither like it nor think it good for me.'

'Bridey, do stop.'

'I'm sorry,' he said, 'I thought it rather an interesting point.'

'Thank God I went to Eton,' said Sebastian.

After dinner Brideshead said: 'I'm afraid I must take Sebastian away for half an hour. I shall be busy all day tomorrow, and I'm off immediately after the show. I've a lot of papers for father to sign. Sebastian must take them out and explain them to him. It's time you were in bed, Cordelia.'

'Must digest first,' she said. 'I'm not used to gorging like this at night. I'll talk to Charles.'

' "*Charles*"?' said Sebastian. ' "*Charles*"? "Mr Ryder" to you, child.'

'Come on, Charles.'

When we were alone she said: 'Are you really an agnostic?'

'Does your family always talk about religion all the time?'

'Not all the time. It's a subject that just comes up naturally, doesn't it?'

'Does it? It never has with me before.'

'Then perhaps you *are* an agnostic. I'll pray for you.'

'That's very kind of you.'

'I can't spare you a whole rosary you know. Just a decade. I've got such a long list of people. I take them in order and they get a decade about once a week.'

'I'm sure it's more than I deserve.'

'Oh, I've got some harder cases than you. Lloyd George and the Kaiser and Olive Banks.'

'Who is she?'

'She was bunked from the convent last term. I don't quite know what for. Reverend Mother found something she'd been writing. D'you know, if you weren't an agnostic, I should ask you for five shillings to buy a black god-daughter.'

'Nothing will surprise me about your religion.'

'It's a new thing a missionary priest started last term. You send five bob to some nuns in Africa and they christen a baby and name her after you. I've got six black Cordelias already. Isn't it lovely?'

When Brideshead and Sebastian returned, Cordelia was sent to bed. Brideshead began again on our discussion.

'Of course, you are right really,' he said. 'You take art as a means not as an end. That is strict theology, but it's unusual to find an agnostic believing it.'

'Cordelia has promised to pray for me,' I said.

'She made a novena for her pig,' said Sebastian.

'You know all this is very puzzling to me,' I said.

'I think we're causing scandal,' said Brideshead.

That night I began to realize how little I really knew of Sebastian, and to understand why he had always sought to keep me apart from the rest of his life. He was like a friend made on board ship, on the high seas; now we had come to his home port.

Brideshead and Cordelia went away; the tents were struck on the show ground, the flags uprooted; the trampled grass began to regain its colour; the month that had started in leisurely fashion came swiftly to its end. Sebastian walked without a stick now and had forgotten his injury.

'I think you'd better come with me to Venice,' he said.

'No money.'

'I thought of that. We live on papa when we get there. The lawyers pay my fare – first class and sleeper. We can both travel third for that.'

And so we went; first by the long, cheap sea-crossing to Dunkirk, sitting all night on deck under a clear sky, watching the grey dawn break over the sand dunes; then to Paris, on wooden seats, where we drove to the Lotti, had baths and shaved, lunched at Foyot's, which was hot and half-empty, loitered sleepily among the shops, and sat long in a café waiting till the time of our train; then in the warm, dusty evening to the Gare de Lyon, to the slow train south, again the wooden seats, a carriage full of the poor, visiting their families – travelling, as the poor do in Northern countries, with a multitude of small bundles and an air of patient submission to authority – and sailors returning from leave. We slept fitfully, jolting and stopping, changed once in the night, slept again and awoke in an empty carriage, with pine woods passing the windows and the distant view of mountain peaks. New uniforms at the frontier, coffee and bread at the station buffet, people round us of Southern grace and gaiety; on again into the plains, conifers changing to vine and olive, a change of trains at Milan; garlic sausage, bread, and a flask of Orvieto bought from a trolley (we had spent all our money save for a few francs, in Paris); the sun mounted high and the country glowed with heat; the carriage filled with peasants, ebbing and flowing at each station, the smell of garlic was overwhelming in the hot carriage. At last in the evening we arrived at Venice.

A sombre figure was there to meet us. 'Papa's valet, Plender.'

'I met the express,' said Plender. 'His Lordship thought you must have looked up the train wrong. This seemed only to come from Milan.'

'We travelled third.'

Plender tittered politely. 'I have the gondola here. I shall follow with the luggage in the *vaporetto*. His Lordship had gone to the Lido. He was not sure he would be home before you – that was when we expected you on the Express. He should be there by now.'

He led us to the waiting boat. The gondoliers wore green and white livery and silver plaques on their chests; they smiled and bowed.

'*Palazzo. Pronto.*'

'*Sì, signore Plender.*'

And we floated away.

'You've been here before?'

'No.'

'I came once before – from the sea. This is the way to arrive.'

'*Ecco ci siamo, signori.*'

The palace was a little less than it sounded, a narrow Palladian façade, mossy steps, a dark archway of rusticated stone. One boatman leapt ashore, made fast to the post, rang the bell; the other stood on the prow keeping the craft in to the steps. The doors opened; a man in rather raffish summer livery of striped linen led us up the stairs from shadow into light; the *piano nobile* was in full sunshine, ablaze with frescoes of the school of Tintoretto.

Our rooms were on the floor above, reached by a precipitous

marble staircase; they were shuttered against the afternoon sun; the butler threw them open and we looked out on the Grand Canal; the beds had mosquito nets.

'*Mostica* not now.'

There was a little bulbous press in each room, a misty, gilt-framed mirror, and no other furniture. The floor was of bare marble slabs.

'A bit bleak?' asked Sebastian.

'Bleak? Look at that.' I led him again to the window and the incomparable pageant below and about us.

'No, you couldn't call it bleak.'

A tremendous explosion drew us next door. We found a bathroom which seemed to have been built in a chimney. There was no ceiling; instead the walls ran straight through the floor above to the open sky. The butler was almost invisible in the steam of an antiquated geyser. There was an overpowering smell of gas and a tiny trickle of cold water.

'No good.'

'*Sì, Sì, subito, signori.*'

The butler ran to the top of the staircase and began to shout down it; a female voice, more strident than his, answered. Sebastian and I returned to the spectacle below our windows. Presently the argument came to an end and a woman and child appeared, who smiled at us, scowled at the butler, and put on Sebastian's press a silver basin and ewer of boiling water. The butler meanwhile unpacked and folded our clothes and, lapsing into Italian, told us of the unrecognized merits of the geyser, until suddenly cocking his head sideways he became alert, said '*Il marchese*,' and darted downstairs.

'We'd better look respectable before meeting papa,' said Sebastian. 'We needn't dress. I gather he's alone at the moment.'

I was full of curiosity to meet Lord Marchmain. When I did so I was first struck by his normality, which, as I saw more of him, I found to be studied. It was as though he were conscious of a Byronic aura, which he considered to be in bad taste and was at pains to suppress. He was standing on the balcony of the saloon and, as he turned to greet us, his face was in deep shadow. I was aware only of a tall and upright figure.

'Darling papa,' said Sebastian, 'how young you are looking!'

He kissed Lord Marchmain on the cheek and I, who had not kissed my father since I left the nursery, stood shyly behind him.

'This is Charles. Don't you think my father very handsome, Charles?'

Lord Marchmain shook my hand.

'Whoever looked up your train,' he said – and his voice also was Sebastian's – 'made a *bêtise*. There's no such one.'

'We came on it.'

'You can't have. There was only a slow train from Milan at that time. I was at the Lido. I have taken to playing tennis there with the professional in the early evening. It is the only time of day when it is not too hot. I hope you boys will be fairly comfortable upstairs. This house seems to have been designed for the comfort of only one person, and I am that one. I have a room the size of this and a very decent dressing-room. Cara has taken possession of the other sizeable room.'

I was fascinated to hear him speak of his mistress so simply and casually; later I suspected that it was done for effect, for me.

'How is she?'

'Cara? Well, I hope. She will be back with us tomorrow. She is visiting some American friends at a villa on the Brenta canal. Where shall we dine? We might go to the Luna, but it is filling up with English now. Would you be too dull at home? Cara is sure to want to go out tomorrow, and the cook here is really quite excellent.'

He had moved away from the window and now stood in the full evening sunlight, with the red damask of the walls behind him. It was a noble face, a controlled one, just, it seemed, as he planned it to be; slightly weary, slightly sardonic, slightly voluptuous. He seemed in the prime of life; it was odd to think that he was only a few years younger than my father.

We dined at a marble table in the windows; everything was either of marble, or velvet, or dull, gilt *gesso*, in this house. Lord

Marchmain said, 'And how do you plan your time here? Bathing or sight-seeing?'

'*Some* sight-seeing, anyway,' I said.

'Cara will like that – she, as Sebastian will have told you, is your hostess here. You can't do both, you know. Once you go to the Lido there is no escaping – you play backgammon, you get caught at the bar, you get stupefied by the sun. Stick to the churches.'

'Charles is very keen on painting,' said Sebastian.

'Yes?' I noticed the hint of deep boredom which I knew so well in my own father. 'Yes? Any particular Venetian painter?'

'Bellini,' I answered rather wildly.

'Yes? Which?'

'I'm afraid I didn't know there were two of them.'

'Three to be precise. You will find that in the great ages painting was very much a family business. How did you leave England?'

'It has been lovely,' said Sebastian.

'Was it? *Was* it? It has been my tragedy that I abominate the English countryside. I suppose it is a disgraceful thing to inherit great responsibilities and to be entirely indifferent to them. I am all the Socialists would have me be, and a great stumbling-block to my own party. Well, my elder son will change all that, I've no doubt, if they leave him anything to inherit. . . . Why, I wonder, are Italian sweets always thought to be so good? There was always an Italian pastry-cook at Brideshead until my father's day. He had an Austrian, so much better. And now I suppose there is some British matron with beefy forearms.'

After dinner we left the palace by the street door and walked through a maze of bridges and squares and alleys, to Florian's for coffee, and watched the grave crowds crossing and recrossing under the campanile. 'There is nothing quite like a Venetian crowd,' said Lord Marchmain. 'The city is crawling with Anarchists, but an American woman tried to sit here the other night with bare shoulders and they drove her away by coming to stare at her, quite silently; they were like circling gulls coming back and back to her, until she left. Our countrymen are much less dignified when they attempt to express moral disapproval.'

An English party had just then come from the waterfront, made for a table near us, and then suddenly moved to the other side, where they looked askance at us and talked with their heads close together. 'That is a man and his wife I used to know when I was in politics. A prominent member of your church, Sebastian.'

As we went up to bed that night Sebastian said: 'He's rather a poppet, isn't he?'

Lord Marchmain's mistress arrived next day. I was nineteen years old and completely ignorant of women. I could not with any certainty recognize a prostitute in the streets. I was therefore not indifferent to the fact of living under the roof of an adulterous couple, but I was old enough to hide my interest. Lord Marchmain's mistress, therefore, found me with a multitude of conflicting expectations about her, all of which were, for the moment, disappointed by her appearance. She was not a voluptuous Toulouse-Lautrec odalisque; she was not a 'little bit of fluff'; she was a middle-aged, well-preserved, well-dressed, well-mannered woman such as I had seen in countless public places and occasionally met. Nor did she seem marked by any social stigma. On the day of her arrival we lunched at the Lido, where she was greeted at almost every table.

'Vittoria Corombona has asked us all to her ball on Saturday.'

'It is very kind of her. You know I do not dance,' said Lord Marchmain.

'But for the boys? It is a thing to be seen – the Corombona palace lit up for the ball. One does not know how many such balls there will be in the future.'

'The boys can do as they like. We must refuse.'

'And I have asked Mrs Hacking Brunner to luncheon. She has a charming daughter. Sebastian and his friend will like her.'

'Sebastian and his friend are more interested in Bellini than heiresses.'

'But that is what I have always wished,' said Cara, changing her point of attack adroitly. 'I have been here more times than I can count and Alex has not once let me inside San Marco even. We will become *tourists*, yes?'

We became tourists; Cara enlisted as guide a midget Venetian nobleman to whom all doors were open, and with him at her side and a guide book in her hand, she came with us, flagging sometimes but never giving up, a neat, prosaic figure amid the immense splendours of the place.

The fortnight at Venice passed quickly and sweetly – perhaps too sweetly; I was drowning in honey, stingless. On some days life kept pace with the gondola, as we nosed through the side-canals and the boatman uttered his plaintive musical bird-cry of warning; on other days with the speed-boat bouncing over the lagoon in a stream of sun-lit foam; it left a confused memory of fierce sunlight on the sands and cool, marble interiors; of water everywhere, lapping on smooth stone, reflected in a dapple of light on painted ceilings; of a night at the Corombona palace such as Byron might have known, and another Byronic night fishing for scampi in the shallows of Chioggia, the phosphorescent wake of the little ship, the lantern swinging in the prow, and the net coming up full of weed and sand and floundering fishes; of melon and *prosciutto* on the balcony in the cool of the morning; of hot cheese sandwiches and champagne cocktails at Harry's bar.

I remember Sebastian looking up at the Colleoni statue and saying, 'It's rather sad to think that whatever happens you and I can never possibly get involved in a war.'

I remember most particularly one conversation towards the end of my visit.

Sebastian had gone to play tennis with his father and Cara at last admitted to fatigue. We sat in the late afternoon at the windows overlooking the Grand Canal, she on the sofa with a piece of needlework, I in an armchair, idle. It was the first time we had been alone together.

'I think you are very fond of Sebastian,' she said.

'Why, certainly.'

'I know of these romantic friendships of the English and the

Germans. They are not Latin. I think they are very good if they
do not go on too long.'

She was so composed and matter-of-fact that I could not
take her amiss, but I failed to find an answer. She seemed not to
expect one but continued stitching, pausing sometimes to match
the silk from a work-bag at her side.

'It is a kind of love that comes to children before they know
its meaning. In England it comes when you are almost men; I
think I like that. It is better to have that kind of love for another
boy than for a girl. Alex you see had it for a girl, for his wife. Do
you think he loves *me*?'

'Really, Cara, you ask the most embarrassing questions.
How should I know? I assume ...'

'He does not. But not the littlest piece. Then why does he
stay with me? I will tell you; because I protect him from Lady
Marchmain. He hates her; but you can have no conception how
he hates her. You would think him so calm and English – the
milord, rather blasé, all passion dead, wishing to be comfortable
and not to be worried, following the sun, with me to look after
that one thing that no man can do for himself. My friend, he is a
volcano of hate. He cannot breathe the same air as she. He will
not set foot in England because it is her home; he can scarcely be
happy with Sebastian because he is her son. But Sebastian hates
her too.'

'I'm sure you're wrong there.'

'He may not admit it to you. He may not admit it to himself;
they are full of hate – hate of themselves. Alex and his family. . . .
Why do you think he will never go into Society?'

'I always thought people had turned against him.'

'My dear boy, you are very young. People turn against a
handsome, clever, wealthy man like Alex? Never in your life. It
is he who has driven them away. Even now they come back
again and again to be snubbed and laughed at. And all for
Lady Marchmain. He will not touch a hand which may have
touched hers. When we have guests I see him thinking, "Have
they perhaps just come from Brideshead? Are they on their way
to Marchmain House? Will they speak of me to my wife? Are

they a link between me and her whom I hate?" But, seriously, with my heart, that is how he thinks. He is mad. And how has she deserved all this hate? She has done nothing except to be loved by someone who was not grown up. I have never met Lady Marchmain; I have seen her once only; but if you live with a man you come to know the other woman he has loved. I know Lady Marchmain very well. She is a good and simple woman who has been loved in the wrong way.

'When people hate with all that energy, it is something in themselves they are hating. Alex is hating all the illusions of boyhood – innocence, God, hope. Poor Lady Marchmain has to bear all that. A woman has not all these ways of loving.

'Now Alex is very fond of me and I protect him from his own innocence. We are comfortable.

'Sebastian is in love with his own childhood. That will make him very unhappy. His teddy-bear, his nanny ... and he is nineteen years old. ...'

She stirred on her sofa, shifting her weight so that she could look down at the passing boats, and said in fond, mocking tones: 'How good it is to sit in the shade and talk of love,' and then added with a sudden swoop to earth, 'Sebastian drinks too much.'

'I suppose we both do.'

'With you it does not matter. I have watched you together. With Sebastian it is different. He will be a drunkard if someone does not come to stop him. I have known so many. Alex was nearly a drunkard when he met me; it is in the blood. I see it in the *way* Sebastian drinks. It is not your way.'

We arrived in London on the day before term began. On the way from Charing Cross I dropped Sebastian in the forecourt of his mother's house; 'Here is "Marchers",' he said with a sigh which meant the end of a holiday. 'I won't ask you in, the place is probably full of my family. We'll meet at Oxford'; I drove across the park to my home.

My father greeted me with his usual air of mild regret.

'Here today,' he said; 'gone tomorrow. I seem to see very

little of you. Perhaps it is dull for you here. How could it be otherwise? You have enjoyed yourself?'

'Very much. I went to Venice.'

'Yes. Yes. I suppose so. The weather was fine?'

When he went to bed after an evening of silent study, he paused to ask: 'The friend you were so much concerned about, did he die?'

'No.'

'I am very thankful. You should have written to tell me. I worried about him so much.'

CHAPTER V

'IT is typical of Oxford,' I said, 'to start the new year in autumn.'

Everywhere, on cobble and gravel and lawn, the leaves were falling and in the college gardens the smoke of the bonfires joined the wet river mist, drifting across the grey walls; the flags were oily underfoot and as, one by one, the lamps were lit in the windows round the quad, the golden lights were diffuse and remote, new figures in new gowns wandered through the twilight under the arches and the familiar bells now spoke of a year's memories.

The autumnal mood possessed us both – as though the riotous exuberance of June had died with the gillyflowers, whose scent at my windows now yielded to the damp leaves, smouldering in a corner of the quad.

It was the first Sunday evening of term.

'I feel precisely one hundred years old,' said Sebastian.

He had come up the night before, a day earlier than I, and this was our first meeting since we parted in the taxi.

'I've had a talking-to from Mgr Bell this afternoon. That makes the fourth since I came up – my tutor, the junior dean, Mr Samgrass of All Souls, and now Mgr Bell.'

'Who is Mr Samgrass of All Souls?'

'Just someone of mummy's. They all say that I made a very bad start last year, that I have been *noticed*, and that if I don't mend my ways I shall get sent down. How does one mend one's ways? I suppose one joins the League of Nations Union, and reads the *Isis* every week, and drinks coffee in the morning at the Cadena café, and smokes a great pipe and plays hockey and goes out to tea on Boar's Hill and to lectures at Keble, and rides a bicycle with a little tray full of note-books and drinks cocoa in the evening and discusses sex seriously. Oh, Charles, what has happened since last term? I feel so old.'

'I feel middle-aged. That is infinitely worse. I believe we have had all the fun we can expect here.'

We sat silent in the firelight as darkness fell.

'Anthony Blanche has gone down.'

'Why?'

'He wrote to me. Apparently he's taken a flat in Munich – he has formed an attachment to a policeman there.'

'I shall miss him.'

'I suppose I shall, too, in a way.'

We fell silent again and sat so still in the firelight that a man who came in to see me, stood for a moment in the door and then went away thinking the room empty.

'This is no way to start a new year,' said Sebastian; but this sombre October evening seemed to breathe its chill, moist air over the succeeding weeks. All that term and all that year Sebastian and I lived more and more in the shadows and, like a fetish, hidden first from the missionary and at length forgotten, the toy bear, Aloysius, sat unregarded on the chest-of-drawers in Sebastian's bedroom.

There was a change in both of us. We had lost the sense of discovery which had infused the anarchy of our first year. I began to settle down.

Unexpectedly, I missed my cousin Jasper, who had got his first in Greats and was now cumbrously setting about a life of public mischief in London; I needed him to shock; without that massive presence the college seemed to lack solidity; it no longer provoked and gave point to outrage as it had done in the summer. Moreover, I had come back glutted and a little chastened; with the resolve to go slow. Never again would I expose myself to my father's humour; his whimsical persecution had convinced me, as no rebuke could have done, of the folly of living beyond my means. I had had no talking-to this term; my success in History Previous and a beta minus in one of my Collections papers had put me on easy terms with my tutor which I managed to maintain without undue effort.

I kept a tenuous connexion with the History School, wrote my two essays a week, and attended an occasional lecture. Besides this I started my second year by joining the Ruskin School of Art; two or three mornings a week we met, about a dozen of us – half, at least, the daughters of north Oxford – among the casts from the antique at the Ashmolean Museum; twice a week we drew from the nude in a small room over a teashop; some pains were taken by the authorities to exclude any hint of lubricity on these evenings, and the young woman who sat to us was brought from London for the day and not allowed to reside in the University city; one flank, that nearer the oil stove, I remember, was always rosy and the other mottled and puckered as though it had been plucked. There, in the smell of the oil lamp, we sat astride the donkey stools and evoked a barely visible wraith of Trilby. My drawings were worthless; in my own rooms I designed elaborate little pastiches, some of which, preserved by friends of the period, come to light occasionally to embarrass me.

We were instructed by a man of about my age, who treated us with defensive hostility; he wore very dark blue shirts, a lemon-yellow tie, and horn-rimmed glasses, and it was largely by reason of this warning that I modified my own style of dress until it approximated to what my cousin Jasper would have thought suitable for country-house visiting. Thus soberly dressed and happily employed I became a fairly respectable member of my college.

With Sebastian it was different. His year of anarchy had filled a deep, interior need of his, the escape from reality, and as he found himself increasingly hemmed in, where he once felt himself free, he became at times listless and morose, even with me.

We kept very much to our own company that term, each so much bound up in the other that we did not look elsewhere for friends. My cousin Jasper had told me that it was normal to spend one's second year shaking off the friends of one's first, and it happened as he said. Most of my friends were those I had made through Sebastian; together we shed them and made no others. There was no renunciation. At first we seemed to see them as often as ever; we went to parties but gave few of our own. I was not concerned to impress the new freshmen who, like their London sisters, were here being launched in Society; there were strange faces now at every party and I, who a few months back had been voracious of new acquaintances, now felt surfeited; even our small circle of intimates, so lively in the summer sunshine, seemed dimmed and muted now in the pervading fog, the river-borne twilight that softened and obscured all that year for me. Anthony Blanche had taken something away with him when he went; he had locked a door and hung the key on his chain; and all his friends, among whom he had always been a stranger, needed him now.

The Charity matinée was over, I felt; the impresario had buttoned his astrakhan coat and taken his fee and the disconsolate ladies of the company were without a leader. Without him they forgot their cues and garbled their lines; they needed him to ring the curtain up at the right moment; they needed him to direct the lime-lights; they needed his whisper in the wings, and his imperious eye on the leader of the band; without him there were no photographers from the weekly press, no prearranged goodwill and expectation of pleasure. No stronger bond held them together than common service; now the gold lace and velvet were packed away and returned to the costumier and the drab uniform of the day put on in its stead. For a few happy hours of rehearsal, for a few ecstatic minutes of performance, they had played splendid parts, their own great ancestors, the famous paintings they were thought to resemble; now it was over and in the bleak light of day they must go back to their homes; to the husband who came to London too often, to the lover who lost at cards, and to the child who grew too fast.

Anthony Blanche's set broke up and became a bare dozen lethargic, adolescent Englishmen. Sometimes in later life they would say: 'Do you remember that extraordinary fellow we used all to know at Oxford – Anthony Blanche? I wonder what became of him.' They lumbered back into the herd from which they had been so capriciously chosen and grew less and less individually recognizable. The change was not so apparent to them as to us, and they still congregated on occasions in our rooms; but we gave up seeking them. Instead we formed the taste for lower company and spent our evenings, as often as not, in Hogarthian little inns in St Ebb's and St Clement's and the streets between the old market and the canal, where we managed to be gay and were, I believe, well liked by the company. The Gardener's Arms and the Nag's Head, the Druid's Head near the theatre, and the Turf in Hell Passage knew us well; but in the last of these we were liable to meet other undergraduates – pub-crawling hearties from BNC – and Sebastian became possessed by a kind of phobia, like that which sometimes comes over men in uniform against their own service, so that many an evening was spoilt by their intrusion, and he would leave his glass half empty and turn sulkily back to college.

It was thus that Lady Marchmain found us when, early in that Michaelmas term, she came for a week to Oxford. She found Sebastian subdued, with all his host of friends reduced to one, myself. She accepted me as Sebastian's friend and sought to make me hers also, and in doing so, unwittingly struck at the roots of our friendship. That is the single reproach I have to set against her abundant kindness to me.

Her business in Oxford was with Mr Samgrass of All Souls, who now began to play an increasingly large part in our lives. Lady Marchmain was engaged in making a memorial book for circulation among her friends, about her brother, Ned, the eldest of three legendary heroes all killed between Mons and Passchendaele; he had left a quantity of papers – poems, letters, speeches, articles; to edit them, even for a restricted circle, needed tact and countless decisions in which the judgement of an adoring sister was liable to err. Acknowledging this, she had sought outside advice, and Mr Samgrass had been found to help her.

He was a young history don, a short, plump man, dapper in dress, with sparse hair brushed flat on an over-large head, neat hands, small feet, and the general appearance of being too often bathed. His manner was genial and his speech idiosyncratic. We came to know him well.

It was Mr Samgrass's particular aptitude to help others with their work, but he was himself the author of several stylish little books. He was a great delver in muniment-rooms and had a sharp nose for the picturesque. Sebastian spoke less than the truth when he described him as 'someone of mummy's'; he was someone of almost everyone's who possessed anything to attract him.

Mr Samgrass was a genealogist and a legitimist; he loved dispossessed royalty and knew the exact validity of the rival claims of the pretenders to many thrones; he was not a man of religious habit, but he knew more than most Catholics about their Church; he had friends in the Vatican and could talk at length of policy and appointments, saying which contemporary ecclesiastics were in good favour, which in bad, what recent theological hypothesis was suspect, and how this or that Jesuit or Dominican had skated on thin ice or sailed near the wind in his Lenten discourses; he had everything except the Faith, and later liked to attend benediction in the chapel of Brideshead and see the ladies of the family with their necks arched in devotion under their black lace mantillas; he loved forgotten scandals in high life and was an expert in putative parentage; he claimed to love the past, but I always felt that he thought all the splendid company, living or dead, with whom he associated slightly absurd; it was Mr Samgrass who was real, the rest were an insubstantial pageant. He was the Victorian tourist, solid and patronizing, for whose amusement these foreign things were paraded. And there was something a little too brisk about his literary manners; I suspected the existence of a dictaphone somewhere in his panelled rooms.

He was with Lady Marchmain when I first met them, and I thought then that she could not have found a greater contrast to herself than this intellectual-on-the-make, nor a better foil to her own charm. It was not her way to make a conspicuous entry into anyone's life, but towards the end of that week Sebastian said rather sourly: 'You and mummy seem very thick,' and I realized that in fact I was being drawn into intimacy by swift, imperceptible stages, for she was impatient of any human relationship that fell short of it. By the time that she left I had promised to spend all next vacation, except Christmas itself, at Brideshead.

One Monday morning a week or two later I was in Sebastian's room waiting for him to return from a tutorial, when Julia walked in, followed by a large man whom she introduced as 'Mr Mottram' and addressed as 'Rex'. They were motoring up from a house where they had spent the week-end, they explained. Rex Mottram was warm and confident in a check ulster; Julia cold and rather shy in furs; she made straight for the fire and crouched over it shivering.

'We hoped Sebastian might give us luncheon,' she said. 'Failing him we can always try Boy Mulcaster, but I somehow thought we should eat better with Sebastian, and we're very hungry. We've been literally starved all the week-end at the Chasms.'

'He and Sebastian are both lunching with me. Come too.'

So, without demur, they joined the party in my rooms, one of the last of the old kind that I gave. Rex Mottram exerted himself to make an impression. He was a handsome fellow with dark hair growing low on his forehead and heavy black eyebrows. He spoke with an engaging Canadian accent. One quickly learned all that he wished one to know about him, that he was a lucky man with money, a member of parliament, a gambler, a good fellow; that he played golf regularly with the Prince of Wales and was on easy terms with 'Max' and 'F.E.' and 'Gertie' Lawrence and Augustus John and Carpentier – with anyone, it seemed, who happened to be mentioned. Of the University he said: 'No, I was never here. It just means you start life three years behind the other fellow.'

His life, so far as he made it known, began in the war, where he had got a good M.C. serving with the Canadians and had ended as A.D.C. to a popular general.

He cannot have been more than thirty at the time we met him, but he seemed very old to us in Oxford. Julia treated him, as she seemed to treat all the world, with mild disdain, but with an air of possession. During luncheon she sent him to the car for her cigarettes, and once or twice when he was talking very big, she apologized for him, saying: 'Remember he's a colonial,' to which he replied with boisterous laughter.

When he had gone I asked who he was.

'Oh, just someone of Julia's,' said Sebastian.

We were slightly surprised a week later to get a telegram from him asking us and Boy Mulcaster to dinner in London on the following night for 'a party of Julia's'.

'I don't think he knows anyone young,' said Sebastian; 'all his friends are leathery old sharks in the City and the House of Commons. Shall we go?'

We discussed it, and because our life at Oxford was now so much in the shadows, we decided that we would.

'Why does he want Boy?'

'Julia and I have known him all our lives. I suppose, finding him at lunch with you, he thought he was a chum.'

We had no great liking for Mulcaster, but the three of us were in high spirits when, having got leave for the night from our colleges, we drove off on the London road in Hardcastle's car.

We were to spend the night at Marchmain House. We went there to dress and, while we dressed, drank a bottle of champagne, going in and out of one another's rooms which were together three floors up and rather shabby compared with the splendours below. As we came downstairs Julia passed us going up to her room still in her day clothes.

'I'm going to be late,' she said; 'you boys had better go on to Rex's. It's heavenly of you to come.'

'What is this party?'

'A ghastly charity ball I'm involved with. Rex insisted on giving a dinner party for it. See you there.'

Rex Mottram lived within walking distance of Marchmain House.

'Julia's going to be late,' we said, 'she's only just gone up to dress.'

'That means an hour. We'd better have some wine.'

A woman who was introduced as 'Mrs Champion' said: 'I'm sure she'd sooner we started, Rex.'

'Well, let's have some wine first anyway.'

'Why a Jeroboam, Rex?' she said peevishly. 'You always want to have everything too big.'

'Won't be too big for us,' he said, taking the bottle in his own hands and easing the cork.

There were two girls there, contemporaries of Julia's; they all seemed involved in the management of the ball. Mulcaster knew them of old and they, without much relish I thought, knew him. Mrs Champion talked to Rex. Sebastian and I found ourselves drinking alone together as we always did.

At length Julia arrived, unhurried, exquisite, unrepentant. 'You shouldn't have let him wait,' she said. 'It's his Canadian courtesy.'

Rex Mottram was a liberal host, and by the end of dinner the three of us who had come from Oxford were rather drunk. While we were standing in the hall waiting for the girls to come down and Rex and Mrs Champion had drawn away from us, talking, acrimoniously, in low voices, Mulcaster said, 'I say, let's slip away from this ghastly dance and go to Ma Mayfield's.'

'Who is Ma Mayfield?'

'You know Ma Mayfield. Everyone knows Ma Mayfield of the Old Hundredth. I've got a regular there – a sweet little thing called Effie. There'd be the devil to pay if Effie heard I'd been to London and hadn't been in to see her. Come and meet Effie at Ma Mayfield's.'

'All right,' said Sebastian, 'let's meet Effie at Ma Mayfield's.'

'We'll take another bottle of pop off the good Mottram and then leave the bloody dance and go to the Old Hundredth. How about that?'

It was not a difficult matter to leave the ball; the girls whom

Rex Mottram had collected had many friends there and, after we had danced together once or twice, our table began to fill up; Rex Mottram ordered more and more wine; presently the three of us were together on the pavement.

'D'you know where this place is?'

'Of course I do. A hundred Sink Street.'

'Where's that?'

'Just off Leicester Square. Better take the car.'

'Why?'

'Always better to have one's own car on an occasion like this.'

We did not question this reasoning, and there lay our mistake. The car was in the forecourt of Marchmain House within a hundred yards of the hotel where we had been dancing. Mulcaster drove and, after some wandering, brought us safely to Sink Street. A commissionaire at one side of a dark doorway and a middle-aged man in evening dress on the other side of it, standing with his face to the wall cooling his forehead on the bricks, indicated our destination.

'Keep out, you'll be poisoned,' said the middle-aged man.

'Members?' said the commissionaire.

'The name is Mulcaster,' said Mulcaster. 'Viscount Mulcaster.'

'Well, try inside,' said the commissionaire.

'You'll be robbed, poisoned and infected and robbed,' said the middle-aged man.

Inside the dark doorway was a bright hatch.

'Members?' asked a stout woman, in evening dress.

'I like that,' said Mulcaster. 'You ought to know me by now.'

'Yes, dearie,' said the woman without interest. 'Ten bob each.'

'Oh, look here, I've never paid before.'

'Daresay not, dearie. We're full up tonight so it's ten bob. Anyone who comes after you will have to pay a quid. You're lucky.'

'Let me speak to Mrs Mayfield.'

'I'm Mrs Mayfield. Ten bob each.'

'Why, Ma, I didn't recognize you in your finery. You know me, don't you? Boy Mulcaster.'

'Yes, duckie. Ten bob each.'

We paid, and the man who had been standing between us and the inner door now made way for us. Inside it was hot and crowded, for the Old Hundredth was then at the height of its success. We found a table and ordered a bottle; the waiter took payment before he opened it.

'Where's Effie tonight?' asked Mulcaster.

'Effie 'oo?'

'Effie, one of the girls who's always here. The pretty dark one.'

'There's lots of girls works here. Some of them's dark and some of them's fair. You might call some of them pretty. I haven't the time to know them by name.'

'I'll go and look for her,' said Mulcaster.

While he was away two girls stopped near our table and looked at us curiously. 'Come on,' said one to the other, 'we're wasting our time. They're only fairies.'

Presently Mulcaster returned in triumph with Effie to whom, without its being ordered, the waiter immediately brought a plate of eggs and bacon.

'First bite I've had all the evening,' she said. 'Only thing that's any good here is the breakfast; makes you fair peckish hanging about.'

'That's another six bob,' said the waiter.

When her hunger was appeased, Effie dabbed her mouth and looked at us.

'I've seen you here before, often, haven't I?' she said to me.

'I'm afraid not.'

'But I've seen *you*?' to Mulcaster.

'Well, I should rather hope so. You haven't forgotten our little evening in September?'

'No, darling, of course not. You were the boy in the Guards who cut your toe, weren't you?'

'Now, Effie, don't be a tease.'

'No, that was another night, wasn't it? I know – you were

with Bunty the time the police were in and we all hid in the place they keep the dust-bins.'

'Effie loves pulling my leg, don't you, Effie? She's annoyed with me for staying away so long, aren't you?'

'Whatever you say, I know I *have* seen you before somewhere.'

'Stop teasing.'

'I wasn't meaning to tease. Honest. Want to dance?'

'Not at the minute.'

'Thank the Lord. My shoes pinch something terrible tonight.'

Soon she and Mulcaster were deep in conversation. Sebastian leaned back and said to me: 'I'm going to ask that pair to join us.'

The two unattached women who had considered us earlier, were again circling towards us. Sebastian smiled and rose to greet them: soon they, too, were eating heartily. One had the face of a skull, the other of a sickly child. The Death's Head seemed destined for me. 'How about a little party,' she said, 'just the six of us over at my place?'

'Certainly,' said Sebastian.

'We thought you were fairies when you came in.'

'That was our extreme youth.'

Death's Head giggled. 'You're a good sport,' she said.

'You're very sweet really,' said the Sickly Child. 'I must just tell Mrs Mayfield we're going out.'

It was still early, not long after midnight, when we regained the street. The commissionaire tried to persuade us to take a taxi. 'I'll look after your car, sir, I wouldn't drive yourself, sir, really I wouldn't.'

But Sebastian took the wheel and the two women sat one on the other beside him, to show him the way. Effie and Mulcaster and I sat in the back. I think we cheered a little as we drove off.

We did not drive far. We turned into Shaftesbury Avenue and were making for Piccadilly when we narrowly escaped a head-on collision with a taxi-cab.

'For Christ's sake,' said Effie, 'look where you're going. D'you want to murder us all?'

'Careless fellow that,' said Sebastian.

'It isn't safe the way you're driving,' said Death's Head. 'Besides, we ought to be on the other side of the road.'

'So we should,' said Sebastian, swinging abruptly across.

'Here, stop. I'd sooner walk.'

'Stop? Certainly.'

He put on the brakes and we came abruptly to a halt broadside across the road. Two policemen quickened their stride and approached us.

'Let me out of this,' said Effie, and made her escape with a leap and a scamper.

The rest of us were caught.

'I'm sorry if I am impeding the traffic, officer,' said Sebastian with care, 'but the lady insisted on my stopping for her to get out. She would take no denial. As you will have observed, she was pressed for time. A matter of nerves you know.'

'Let me talk to him,' said Death's Head. 'Be a sport, handsome; no one's seen anything but you. The boys don't mean any harm. I'll get them into a taxi and see them home quiet.'

The policemen looked us over, deliberately, forming their own judgement. Even then everything might have been well had not Mulcaster joined in. 'Look here, my good man,' he said. 'There's no need for you to notice anything. We've just come from Ma Mayfield's. I reckon she pays you a nice retainer to keep your eyes shut. Well, you can keep 'em shut on us too, and you won't be the losers by it.'

That resolved any doubts which the policemen may have felt. In a short time we were in the cells.

I remember little of the journey there or the process of admission. Mulcaster, I think, protested vigorously and, when we were made to empty our pockets, accused his gaolers of theft. Then we were locked in, and my first clear memory is of tiled walls with a lamp set high up under thick glass, a bunk, and a door which had no handle on my side. Somewhere to the left of me Sebastian and Mulcaster were raising Cain. Sebastian had been steady on his legs and fairly composed on the way to the station; now, shut in, he seemed in a frenzy and was pounding the door, and shouting: 'Damn you, I'm not drunk. Open this door. I insist on seeing the doctor. I tell you I'm not drunk,' while Mulcaster, beyond, cried: 'My God, you'll pay for this! You're making a great mistake, I can tell you. Telephone the Home Secretary. Send for my solicitors. I will have *habeas corpus*.'

Groans of protest rose from the other cells where various tramps and pickpockets were trying to get some sleep: 'Aw, pipe down!' 'Give a man some peace, can't yer?' ... 'Is this a blinking lock-up or a looney-house?' – and the sergeant, going his rounds, admonished them through the grille. 'You'll be here all night if you don't sober up.'

I sat on the bunk in low spirits and dozed a little. Presently the racket subsided and Sebastian called: 'I say, Charles, are you there?'

'Here I am.'

'This is the hell of a business.'

'Can't we get bail or something?'

Mulcaster seemed to have fallen asleep.

'I tell you the man – Rex Mottram. He'd be in his element here.'

We had some difficulty in getting in touch with him; it was half an hour before the policeman in charge answered my bell. At last he consented, rather sceptically, to send a telephone message to the hotel where the ball was being held. There was another long delay and then our prison doors were opened.

Seeping through the squalid air of the police station, the sour smell of dirt and disinfectant, came the sweet, rich smoke of a Havana cigar – of two Havana cigars, for the sergeant in charge was smoking also.

Rex stood in the charge-room looking the embodiment – indeed, the burlesque – of power and prosperity; he wore a fur-lined overcoat with broad astrakhan lapels and a silk hat. The police were deferential and eager to help.

'We had to do our duty,' they said. 'Took the young gentlemen into custody for their own protection.'

Mulcaster looked crapulous and began a confused complaint that he had been denied legal representation and civil rights. Rex said: 'Better leave all the talking to me.'

I was clear-headed now and watched and listened with fascination while Rex settled our business. He examined the charge sheets, spoke affably to the men who had made the arrest; with the slightest perceptible nuance he opened the way for bribery and quickly covered it when he saw that things had now lasted too long and the knowledge had been too widely shared; he undertook to deliver us at the magistrate's court at ten next morning, and then led us away. His car was outside.

'It's no use discussing things tonight. Where are you sleeping?'

'Marchers,' said Sebastian.

'You'd better come to me. I can fix you up for tonight. Leave everything to me.'

It was plain that he rejoiced in his efficiency.

Next morning the display was even more impressive. I awoke with the startled and puzzled sense of being in a strange room, and in the first seconds of consciousness the memory of the evening before returned, first as though of a nightmare, then of reality. Rex's valet was unpacking a suitcase. On seeing me move he went to the wash-hand stand and poured something from a bottle. 'I think I have everything from Marchmain House,' he said. 'Mr Mottram sent round to Heppell's for this.'

I took the draught and felt better.

A man was there from Trumper's to shave us.

Rex joined us at breakfast. 'It's important to make a good appearance at the court,' he said. 'Luckily none of you look much the worse for wear.'

After breakfast the barrister arrived and Rex delivered a summary of the case.

'Sebastian's in a jam,' he said. 'He's liable to anything up to six months' imprisonment for being drunk in charge of a car. You'll come up before Grigg unfortunately. He takes rather a

grim view of cases of this sort. All that will happen this morning
is that we shall ask to have Sebastian held over for a week to
prepare the defence. You two will plead guilty, say you're sorry,
and pay your five bob fine. I'll see what can be done about
squaring the evening papers. The *Star* may be difficult.

'Remember, the important thing is to keep out all mention of
the Old Hundredth. Luckily the tarts were sober and aren't
being charged, but their names have been taken as witnesses. If
we try and break down the police evidence, they'll be called.
We've got to avoid that at all costs, so we shall have to swallow
the police story whole and appeal to the magistrate's good
nature not to wreck a young man's career for a single boyish
indiscretion. It'll work all right. We shall need a don to give
evidence of good character. Julia tells me you have a tame one
called Samgrass. He'll do. Meanwhile *your* story is simply that
you came up from Oxford for a perfectly respectable dance,
weren't used to wine, had too much, and lost the way driving
home.

'After that we shall have to see about fixing things with your
authorities at Oxford.'

'I told them to call my solicitors,' said Mulcaster, 'and they
refused. They've put themselves hopelessly in the wrong, and I
don't see why they should get away with it.'

'For heaven's sake don't start any kind of argument. Just
plead guilty and pay up. Understand?'

Mulcaster grumbled but submitted.

Everything happened at court as Rex had predicted. At half
past ten we stood in Bow Street, Mulcaster and I free men,
Sebastian bound over to appear in a week's time. Mulcaster
had kept silent about his grievance; he and I were admonished
and fined five shillings each and fifteen shillings costs. Mulcaster
was becoming rather irksome to us, and it was with relief that
we heard his plea of other business in London. The barrister
bustled off and Sebastian and I were left alone and disconsolate.

'I suppose mummy's got to hear about it,' he said. 'Damn,
damn, damn! It's cold. I won't go home. I've nowhere to go.
Let's just slip back to Oxford and wait for *them* to bother *us*.'

The raffish habitués of the police court came and went, up and down the steps; still we stood on the windy corner, undecided.

'Why not get hold of Julia?'

'I might go abroad.'

'My dear Sebastian, you'll only be given a talking-to and fined a few pounds.'

'Yes, but it's all the *bother* – mummy and Bridey and all the family and the dons. I'd sooner go to prison. If I just slip away abroad they can't get me back, can they? That's what people do when the police are after them. I know mummy will make it seem she has to bear the whole brunt of the business.'

'Let's telephone Julia and get her to meet us somewhere and talk it over.'

We met at Gunter's in Berkeley Square. Julia, like most women then, wore a green hat pulled down to her eyes with a diamond arrow in it; she had a small dog under her arm, three-quarters buried in the fur of her coat. She greeted us with an unusual show of interest.

'Well, you are a pair of pickles; I must say you look remarkably well on it. The only time I got tight I was paralysed all the next day. I do think you might have taken me with you. The ball was positively lethal, and I've always longed to go to the Old Hundredth. No one will ever take me. Is it heaven?'

'So you know all about that, too?'

'Rex telephoned me this morning and told me everything. What were your girl friends like?'

'Don't be prurient,' said Sebastian.

'Mine was like a skull.'

'Mine was like a consumptive.'

'*Goodness.*' It had clearly raised us in Julia's estimation that we had been out with women; to her they were the point of interest.

'Does mummy know?'

'Not about your skulls and consumptives. She knows you were in the clink. I told her. She was divine about it, of course. You know anything Uncle Ned did was always perfect, and he got locked up once for taking a bear into one of Lloyd George's meetings, so she really feels quite human about the whole thing. She wants you both to lunch with her.'

'Oh God!'

'The only trouble is the papers and the family. Have you got an awful family, Charles?'

'Only a father. He'll never hear about it.'

'Ours are awful. Poor mummy is in for a ghastly time with them. They'll be writing letters and paying visits of sympathy, and all the time at the back of their minds one half will be saying, "That's what comes of bringing the boy up a Catholic," and the other half will say, "That's what comes of sending him to Eton instead of Stonyhurst." Poor mummy can't get it right.'

We lunched with Lady Marchmain. She accepted the whole thing with humorous resignation. Her only reproach was: 'I can't think why you went off and stayed with Mr Mottram. You might have come and told me about it first.'

'How am I going to explain it to all the family?' she asked. 'They will be so shocked to find that they're more upset about it than I am. Do you know my sister-in-law, Fanny Rosscommon? She has always thought I brought the children up badly. Now I am beginning to think she must be right.'

When we left I said: 'She couldn't have been more charming. What were you so worried about?'

'I can't explain,' said Sebastian miserably.

A week later when Sebastian came up for trial he was fined ten pounds. The newspapers reported it with painful prominence, one of them under the ironic headline: '*Marquis's son unused to wine*'. The magistrate said that it was only through the prompt action of the police that he was not up on a grave charge ... 'It is purely by good fortune that you do not bear the responsibility of a serious accident. ...' Mr Samgrass gave evidence that Sebastian bore an irreproachable character and that a brilliant future at the University was in jeopardy. The papers took hold of this too – '*Model Student's Career at Stake*'. But for Mr Samgrass's evidence, said the magistrate, he would have been disposed to give an exemplary sentence; the law was the same for an Oxford undergraduate as for any young hooligan; indeed the better the home the more shameful the offence. ...

It was not only at Bow Street that Mr Samgrass was of value. At Oxford he showed all the zeal and acumen which were Rex Mottram's in London. He interviewed the college authorities, the proctors, the Vice-Chancellor; he induced Mgr Bell to call on the Dean of Christ Church; he arranged for Lady March-main to talk to the Chancellor himself; and, as a result of all this, the three of us were gated for the rest of the term. Hardcastle, for no very clear reason, was again deprived of the use of his car, and the affair blew over. The most lasting penalty we suffered was our intimacy with Rex Mottram and Mr Samgrass, but since Rex's life was in London in a world of politics and high finance and Mr Samgrass's nearer to our own at Oxford, it was from him we suffered the more.

For the rest of that term he haunted us. Now that we were 'gated' we could not spend our evenings together, and from nine o'clock onwards were alone and at Mr Samgrass's mercy. Hardly an evening seemed to pass but he called on one or the other of us. He spoke of 'our little escapade' as though he, too, had been in the cells, and had that bond with us. ... Once I climbed out of college and Mr Samgrass found me in Sebas-tian's rooms after the gate was shut and that, too, he made into a bond. It did not surprise me, therefore, when I arrived at Brideshead, after Christmas, to find Mr Samgrass, as though in wait for me, sitting alone before the fire in the room they called the 'Tapestry Hall'.

'You find me in solitary possession,' he said, and indeed he seemed to possess the hall and the sombre scenes of venery that hung round it, to possess the caryatids on either side of the fireplace, to possess me, as he rose to take my hand and greet me like a host: 'This morning,' he continued, 'we had a lawn meet of the Marchmain Hounds – a deliciously archaic spectacle – and all our young friends are foxhunting, even Sebastian who, you will not be surprised to hear, looked remarkably elegant in his pink coat. Brideshead was impressive rather than elegant; he is Joint-master with a local figure of fun named Sir Walter Strickland-Venables. I wish the two of them could be included in these rather humdrum tapestries – they would give a note of fantasy.

'Our hostess remained at home; also a convalescent Dominican who has read too much Maritain and too little Hegel; Sir Adrian Porson, of course, and two rather forbidding Magyar cousins – I have tried them in German and in French, but in neither tongue are they diverting. All these have now driven off to visit a neighbour. I have been spending a cosy afternoon before the fire with the incomparable Charlus. Your arrival emboldens me to ring for some tea. How can I prepare you for the party? Alas, it breaks up tomorrow. Lady Julia departs to celebrate the New Year elsewhere, and takes the *beau-monde* with her. I shall miss the pretty creatures about the house – particularly one Celia; she is the sister of our old companion in adversity, Boy Mulcaster, and wonderfully unlike him. She has a birdlike style of conversation, pecking away at the subject in a way I find most engaging, and a school-monitor style of dress which I can only call "saucy". I shall miss her, for I do not go tomorrow. Tomorrow I start work in earnest on our hostess's book – which, believe me, is a treasure-house of period gems; pure authentic 1914.'

Tea was brought and, soon after it, Sebastian returned; he had lost the hunt early, he said, and hacked home; the others were not long after him, having been fetched by car at the end of the day; Brideshead was absent; he had business at the kennels and Cordelia had gone with him. The rest filled the hall and were soon eating scrambled eggs and crumpets; and Mr Samgrass, who had lunched at home and dozed all the afternoon before the fire, ate eggs and crumpets with them. Presently Lady Marchmain's party returned, and when, before we went upstairs to dress for dinner, she said 'Who's coming to chapel for the Rosary?' and Sebastian and Julia said they must have their baths at once, Mr Samgrass went with her and the friar.

'I wish Mr Samgrass would go,' said Sebastian, in his bath; 'I'm sick of being grateful to him.'

In the course of the next fortnight distaste for Mr Samgrass came to be a little unspoken secret throughout the house; in his presence Sir Adrian Porson's fine old eyes seemed to search a distant horizon and his lips set in classic pessimism. Only the Hungarian cousins who, mistaking the status of tutor, took him for an unusually privileged upper servant, were unaffected by his presence.

Mr Samgrass, Sir Adrian Porson, the Hungarians, the friar, Brideshead, Sebastian, Cordelia were all who remained of the Christmas party.

Religion predominated in the house; not only in its practices – the daily mass and Rosary, morning and evening in the chapel – but in all its intercourse. 'We must make a Catholic of Charles,' Lady Marchmain said, and we had many little talks together during my visits when she delicately steered the subject into a holy quarter. After the first of these Sebastian said: 'Has mummy been having one of her "little talks" with you? She's always doing it. I wish to hell she wouldn't.'

One was never summoned for a little talk, or consciously led to it; it merely happened, when she wished to speak intimately, that one found oneself alone with her, if it was summer, in a secluded walk by the lakes or in a corner of the walled rose-gardens; if it was winter, in her sitting-room on the first floor.

This room was all her own; she had taken it for herself and changed it so that, entering, one seemed to be in another house. She had lowered the ceiling and the elaborate cornice which, in one form or another, graced every room was lost to view; the walls, one panelled in brocade, were stripped and washed blue and spotted with innumerable little water-colours of fond association; the air was sweet with the fresh scent of flowers and musty potpourri; her library in soft leather covers, well-read works of poetry and piety, filled a small rosewood bookcase; the chimney-piece was covered with small personal treasures – an ivory Madonna, a plaster St Joseph, posthumous miniatures of her three soldier brothers. When Sebastian and I lived alone at

Brideshead during that brilliant August we had kept out of his mother's room.

Scraps of conversation come back to me with the memory of her room. I remember her saying: 'When I was a girl we were comparatively poor, but still much richer than most of the world, and when I married I became very rich. It used to worry me, and I thought it wrong to have so many beautiful things when others had nothing. Now I realize that it is possible for the rich to sin by coveting the privileges of the poor. The poor have always been the favourites of God and his saints, but I believe that it is one of the special achievements of Grace to sanctify the whole of life, riches included. Wealth in pagan Rome was necessarily something cruel; it's not any more.'

I said something about a camel and the eye of a needle and she rose happily to the point.

'But of *course*,' she said, 'it's very unexpected for a camel to go through the eye of a needle, but the gospel is simply a catalogue of unexpected things. It's not to be *expected* that an ox and an ass should worship at the crib. Animals are always doing the oddest things in the lives of the saints. It's all part of the poetry, the Alice-in-Wonderland side, of religion.'

But I was as untouched by her faith as I was by her charm: or, rather, I was touched by both alike. I had no mind then for anything except Sebastian, and I saw him already as being threatened, though I did not yet know how black was the threat. His constant, despairing prayer was to be let alone. By the blue waters and rustling palms of his own mind he was happy and harmless as a Polynesian; only when the big ship dropped anchor beyond the coral reef, and the cutter beached in the lagoon, and, up the slope that had never known the print of a boot, there trod the grim invasion of trader, administrator, missionary, and tourist – only then was it time to disinter the archaic weapons of the tribe and sound the drums in the hills; or, more easily, to turn from the sunlit door and lie alone in the darkness, where the impotent, painted deities paraded the walls in vain, and cough his heart out among the rum bottles.

And since Sebastian counted among the intruders his own

conscience and all claims of human affection, his days in Arcadia were numbered. For in this, to me, tranquil time Sebastian took fright. I knew him well in that mood of alertness and suspicion, like a deer suddenly lifting his head at the far notes of the hunt; I had seen him grow wary at the thought of his family or his religion, now I found I, too, was suspect. He did not fail in love, but he lost his joy of it, for I was no longer part of his solitude. As my intimacy with his family grew, I became part of the world which he sought to escape; I became one of the bonds which held him. That was the part for which his mother, in all our little talks, was seeking to fit me. Everything was left unsaid. It was only dimly and at rare moments that I suspected what was afoot.

Outwardly Mr Samgrass was the only enemy. For a fortnight Sebastian and I remained at Brideshead, leading our own life. His brother was engaged in sport and estate management; Mr Samgrass was at work in the library on Lady Marchmain's book; Sir Adrian Porson demanded most of Lady Marchmain's time. We saw little of them except in the evenings; there was room under that domed roof for a wide variety of independent lives.

After a fortnight Sebastian said: 'I can't stand Mr Samgrass any more. Let's go to London,' so he came to stay with me and now began to use my home in preference to 'Marchers'. My father liked him. 'I think your friend very amusing,' he said. 'Ask him *often*.'

Then, back at Oxford, we took up again the life that seemed to be shrinking in the cold air. The sadness that had been strong in Sebastian the term before gave place to a kind of sullenness even towards me. He was sick at heart somewhere, I did not know how, and I grieved for him, unable to help.

When he was gay now it was usually because he was drunk, and when drunk he developed an obsession of 'mocking Mr Samgrass'. He composed a ditty of which the refrain was, 'Green arse, Samgrass – Samgrass green arse', sung to the tune of St Mary's chime, and he would thus serenade him, perhaps once a week, under his windows. Mr Samgrass was distinguished as being the first don to have a private telephone installed in his rooms. Sebastian in his cups used to ring him up and sing him this simple song. And all this Mr Samgrass took in good part, as it is called, smiling obsequiously when we met, but with growing confidence, as though each outrage in some way strengthened his hold on Sebastian.

It was during this term that I began to realize that Sebastian was a drunkard in quite a different sense to myself. I got drunk often, but through an excess of high spirits, in the love of the moment, and the wish to prolong and enhance it; Sebastian drank to escape. As we together grew older and more serious I drank less, he more. I found that sometimes after I had gone back to my college, he sat up late and alone, soaking. A succession of disasters came on him so swiftly and with such unexpected violence that it is hard to say when exactly I recognized that my friend was in deep trouble. I knew it well enough in the Easter vacation.

Julia used to say, 'Poor Sebastian. It's something chemical in him.'

That was the cant phrase of the time, derived from heaven knows what misconception of popular science. 'There's something chemical between them' was used to explain the overmastering hate or love of any two people. It was the old concept of determinism in a new form. I do not believe there was anything chemical in my friend.

The Easter party at Brideshead was a bitter time, culminating in a small but unforgettably painful incident. Sebastian got very drunk before dinner in his mother's house, and thus marked the beginning of a new epoch in his melancholy record, another stride in the flight from his family which brought him to ruin.

It was at the end of the day when the large Easter party left Brideshead. It was called the Easter party, though in fact it began on the Tuesday of Easter Week, for the Flytes all went into retreat at the guest-house of a monastery from Maundy Thursday until Easter. This year Sebastian had said he would not go, but at the last moment had yielded, and came home in a state of acute depression from which I totally failed to raise him.

He had been drinking very hard for a week – only I knew how hard – and drinking in a nervous, surreptitious way, totally unlike his old habit. During the party there was always a grog tray in the library, and Sebastian took to slipping in there at odd moments during the day without saying anything even to me. The house was largely deserted during the day. I was at work painting another panel in the little garden-room in the colonnade. Sebastian complained of a cold, stayed in, and during all that time was never quite sober; he escaped attention by being silent. Now and then I noticed him attract curious glances, but most of the party knew him too slightly to see the change in him, while his own family were occupied, each with their particular guests.

When I remonstrated he said, 'I can't stand all these people about,' but it was when they finally left and he had to face his family at close quarters that he broke down.

The normal practice was for a cocktail tray to be brought into the drawing-room at six; we mixed our own drinks and the bottles were removed when we went to dress; later, just before dinner, cocktails appeared again, this time handed round by the footmen.

Sebastian disappeared after tea; the light had gone and I spent the next hour playing mah-jong with Cordelia. At six I was alone in the drawing-room, when he returned; he was frowning in a way I knew all too well, and when he spoke I recognized the drunken thickening in his voice.

'Haven't they brought the cocktails yet?' He pulled clumsily on the bell-rope.

I said, 'Where have you been?'

'Up with nanny.'

'I don't believe it. You've been drinking somewhere.'

'I've been reading in my room. My cold's worse today.'

When the tray arrived he slopped gin and vermouth into a tumbler and carried it out of the room with him. I followed him upstairs, where he shut his bedroom door in my face and turned the key.

I returned to the drawing-room full of dismay and foreboding.

The family assembled. Lady Marchmain said: 'What's become of Sebastian?'

'He's gone to lie down. His cold is worse.'

'Oh dear, I hope he isn't getting flu. I thought he had a feverish look once or twice lately. Is there anything he wants?'

'No, he particularly asked not to be disturbed.'

I wondered whether I ought to speak to Brideshead, but that grim, rock-crystal mask forbade all confidence. Instead, on the way upstairs to dress, I told Julia.

'Sebastian's drunk.'

'He can't be. He didn't even come for a cocktail.'

'He's been drinking in his room all the afternoon.'

'How very peculiar! What a bore he is! Will he be all right for dinner?'

'No.'

'Well, *you* must deal with him. It's no business of mine. Does he often do this?'

'He has lately.'

'How very boring.'

I tried Sebastian's door, found it locked, and hoped he was sleeping, but, when I came back from my bath, I found him sitting in the chair before my fire; he was dressed for dinner, all but his shoes, but his tie was awry and his hair on end; he was very red in the face and squinting slightly. He spoke indistinctly.

'Charles, what you said was quite true. Not with nanny. Been drinking whisky up here. None in the library now party's gone. Now party's gone and only mummy. Feeling rather drunk. Think I'd better have something-on-a-tray up here. Not dinner with mummy.'

'Go to bed,' I told him. 'I'll say your cold's worse.'

'Much worse.'

I took him to his room which was next to mine and tried to

get him to bed, but he sat in front of his dressing table squinnying at himself in the glass, trying to remake his bow-tie. On the writing table by the fire was a half-empty decanter of whisky. I took it up, thinking he would not see, but he spun round from the mirror and said: 'You put that down.'

'Don't be an ass, Sebastian. You've had enough.'

'What the devil's it got to do with you? You're only a guest here – *my* guest. I drink what I want to in my own house.'

He would have fought me for it at that moment.

'Very well,' I said, putting the decanter back, 'only for God's sake keep out of sight.'

'Oh, mind your own business. You came here as my friend; now you're spying on me for my mother, I know. Well, you can get out, and tell her from me that I'll choose my friends and she her spies in future.'

So I left him and went down to dinner.

'I've been in to Sebastian,' I said. 'His cold has come on rather badly. He's gone to bed and says he doesn't want anything.'

'Poor Sebastian,' said Lady Marchmain. 'He'd better have a glass of hot whisky. I'll go and have a look at him.'

'Don't, mummy, I'll go,' said Julia rising.

'*I'll* go,' said Cordelia, who was dining down that night, for a treat to celebrate the departure of the guests. She was at the door and through it before anyone could stop her.

Julia caught my eye and gave a tiny, sad shrug.

In a few minutes Cordelia was back, looking grave. 'No, he doesn't seem to want anything,' she said.

'How was he?'

'Well, I don't *know*, but I *think* he's very drunk,' she said.

'*Cordelia.*'

Suddenly the child began to giggle. ' "Marquis's Son Unused to Wine",' she quoted. ' "Model Student's Career Threatened".'

'Charles, is this true?' asked Lady Marchmain.

'Yes.'

Then dinner was announced, and we went to the dining-room where the subject was not mentioned.

When Brideshead and I were left alone he said: 'Did you say Sebastian was drunk?'

'Yes.'

'Extraordinary time to choose. Couldn't you stop him?'

'No.'

'No,' said Brideshead, 'I don't suppose you could. I once saw my father drunk, in this room. I wasn't more than about ten at the time. You can't stop people if they want to get drunk. My mother couldn't stop my father, you know.'

He spoke in his odd, impersonal way. The more I saw of this family, I reflected, the more singular I found them. 'I shall ask my mother to read to us tonight.'

It was the custom, I learned later, always to ask Lady Marchmain to read aloud on evenings of family tension. She had a beautiful voice and great humour of expression. That night she read part of *The Wisdom of Father Brown*. Julia sat with a stool covered with manicure things and carefully revarnished her nails; Cordelia nursed Julia's Pekinese; Brideshead played patience; I sat unoccupied studying the pretty group they made, and mourning my friend upstairs.

But the horrors of that evening were not yet over.

It was sometimes Lady Marchmain's practice, when the family were alone, to visit the chapel before going to bed. She had just closed her book and proposed going there when the door opened and Sebastian appeared. He was dressed as I had last seen him, but now instead of being flushed he was deathly pale.

'Come to apologize,' he said.

'Sebastian, dear, do go back to your room,' said Lady Marchmain. 'We can talk about it in the morning.'

'Not to you. Come to apologize to Charles. I was bloody to him and he's my guest. He's my guest and my only friend and I was bloody to him.'

A chill spread over us. I led him back to his room; his family went to their prayers. I noticed when we got upstairs that the decanter was now empty. 'It's time you were in bed,' I said.

Sebastian began to weep. 'Why do you take their side

against me? I knew you would if I let you meet them. Why do you spy on me?'

He said more than I can bear to remember, even at twenty years' distance. At last I got him to sleep and very sadly went to bed myself.

Next morning, he came to my room very early, while the house still slept; he drew the curtains and the sound of it woke me, to find him there fully dressed, smoking, with his back to me, looking out of the windows to where the long dawn-shadows lay across the dew and the first birds were chattering in the budding tree-tops. When I spoke he turned a face which showed no ravages of the evening before, but was fresh and sullen as a disappointed child's.

'Well,' I said. 'How do you feel?'

'Rather odd. I think perhaps I'm still a little drunk. I've just been down to the stables trying to get a car but everything was locked. We're off.'

He drank from the water-bottle by my pillow, threw his cigarette from the window, and lit another with hands which trembled like an old man's.

'Where are you going?'

'I don't know. London, I suppose. Can I come and stay with you?'

'Of course.'

'Well, get dressed. They can send our luggage on by train.'

'We can't just go like this.'

'We can't stay.'

He sat on the window seat looking away from me, out of the window. Presently he said: 'There's smoke coming from some of the chimneys. They must have opened the stables now. Come on.'

'I can't go,' I said. 'I must say good-bye to your mother.'

'Sweet bulldog.'

'Well, I don't happen to like running away.'

'And I couldn't care less. And I shall go on running away, as far and as fast as I can. You can hatch up any plot you like with my mother; I shan't come back.'

'That's how you talked last night.'

'I know. I'm sorry, Charles. I told you I was still drunk. If it's any comfort to you, I absolutely detest myself.'

'It's no comfort at all.'

'It must be a little, I should have thought. Well, if you won't come, give my love to nanny.'

'You're really going?'

'Of course.'

'Shall I see you in London?'

'Yes, I'm coming to stay with you.'

He left me but I did not sleep again; nearly two hours later a footman came with tea and bread and butter and set my clothes out for a new day.

Later that morning I sought Lady Marchmain; the wind had freshened and we stayed indoors; I sat near her before the fire in her room, while she bent over her needlework and the budding creeper rattled on the window-panes.

'I wish I had not *seen* him,' she said. 'That was cruel. I do not mind the *idea* of his being drunk. It is a thing all men do when they are young. I am used to the *idea* of it. My brothers were wild at his age. What hurt last night was that there was nothing *happy* about him.'

'I know,' I said. 'I've never seen him like that before.'

'And last night of all nights . . . when everyone had gone and there were only ourselves here – you see, Charles, I look on you very much as one of ourselves. Sebastian loves you – when there was no need for him to make an effort to be gay. And he wasn't gay. I slept very little last night, and all the time I kept coming back to that one thing; he was so unhappy.'

It was impossible for me to explain to her what I only half understood myself; even then I felt, 'She will learn it soon enough. Perhaps she knows it now.'

'It was horrible,' I said. 'But please don't think that's his usual way.'

'Mr Samgrass told me he was drinking too much all last term.'

'Yes, but not like that – never before.'

'Then why now? here? with us? All night I have been thinking and praying and wondering what I was to say to him, and now, this morning, he isn't here at all. That was cruel of him, leaving without a word. I don't want him to be ashamed – it's being ashamed that makes it all so wrong of him.'

'He's ashamed of being unhappy,' I said.

'Mr Samgrass says he is noisy and high-spirited. I believe,' she said, with a faint light of humour streaking the clouds, 'I believe you and he tease Mr Samgrass rather. It's naughty of you. I'm very fond of Mr Samgrass, and you should be too, after all he's done for you. But I think perhaps if I were your age and a man, I might be just a little inclined to tease Mr Samgrass myself. No, I don't mind that, but last night and this morning are something quite different. You see, *it's all happened before.*'

'I can only say I've seen him drunk often and I've been drunk with him often, but last night was quite new to me.'

'Oh, I don't mean with Sebastian. I mean years ago. I've been through it all before with someone else whom I loved. Well, you must know what I mean – with his father. He used to be drunk in just that way. Someone told me he is not like that now. I pray God it's true and thank God for it with all my heart, if it is. But the *running away – he* ran away, too, you know. It was as you said just now, he was ashamed of being unhappy. Both of them unhappy, ashamed, and running away. It's too pitiful. The men I grew up with' – and her great eyes moved from the embroidery to the three miniatures in the folding leather case on the chimney-piece – 'were not like that. I simply don't understand it. Do you, Charles?'

'Only very little.'

'And yet Sebastian is fonder of you than of any of us, you know. You've got to help him. I can't.'

I have here compressed into a few sentences what, there, required many. Lady Marchmain was not diffuse, but she took hold of her subject in a feminine, flirtatious way, circling, approaching, retreating, feinting; she hovered over it like a butterfly; she played 'grandmother's steps' with it, getting nearer the real point imperceptibly while one's back was turned, standing rooted when she was observed. The unhappiness, the running away – these made up her sorrow, and in her own way she exposed the whole of it, before she was done. It was an hour before she had said all she meant to say. Then, as I rose to leave her, she added as though in an afterthought: 'I wonder have you seen my brothers' book? It has just come out.'

I told her I had looked through it in Sebastian's rooms.

'I should like you to have a copy. May I give you one? They were three splendid men; Ned was the best of them. He was the last to be killed, and when the telegram came, as I knew it would come, I thought: 'Now it's my son's turn to do what Ned can never do now.' I was alone then. He was just going to Eton. If you read Ned's book you'll understand.'

She had a copy lying ready on her bureau. I thought at the time, 'She planned this parting before ever I came in. Had she rehearsed all the interview? If things had gone differently would she have put the book back in the drawer?'

She wrote her name and mine on the fly leaf, the date and place.

'I prayed for you, too, in the night,' she said.

I closed the door behind me, shutting out the *bondieuserie*, the low ceiling, the chintz, the lambskin bindings, the views of Florence, the bowls of hyacinth and potpourri, the *petit-point*, the intimate feminine, modern world, and was back under the coved and coffered roof, the columns and entablature of the central hall, in the august, masculine atmosphere of a better age.

I was no fool; I was old enough to know that an attempt had been made to suborn me and young enough to have found the experience agreeable.

I did not see Julia that morning, but just as I was leaving Cordelia ran to the door of the car and said: 'Will you be seeing Sebastian? Please give him my special love. Will you remember – my *special* love?'

In the train to London I read the book Lady Marchmain

had given me. The frontispiece reproduced the photograph of a young man in Grenadier uniform, and I saw plainly revealed there the origin of that grim mask which, in Brideshead, overlaid the gracious features of his father's family; this was a man of the woods and caves, a hunter, a judge of the tribal council, the repository of the harsh traditions of a people at war with their environment. There were other illustrations in the book, snapshots of the three brothers on holiday, and in each I traced the same archaic lines; and remembering Lady March-main, starry and delicate, I could find no likeness to her in these sombre men.

She appeared seldom in the book; she was older than the eldest of them by nine years and had married and left home while they were schoolboys; between her and them stood two other sisters; after the birth of the third daughter there had been pilgrimages and pious benefactions in request for a son, for theirs was a wide property and an ancient name; male heirs had come late and, when they came, in a profusion which at the time seemed to promise continuity to the line which, in the tragic event, ended abruptly with them.

The family history was typical of the Catholic squires of England; from Elizabeth's reign till Victoria's they lived seques-tered lives, among their tenantry and kinsmen, sending their sons to school abroad, often marrying there, inter-marrying, if not, with a score of families like themselves, debarred from all preferment, and learning, in those lost generations, lessons which could still be read in the lives of the last three men of the house.

Mr Samgrass's deft editorship had assembled and arranged a curiously homogeneous little body of writing – poetry, letters, scraps of a journal, an unpublished essay or two, which all exhaled the same high-spirited, serious, chivalrous, other-worldly air; and the letters from their contemporaries, written after their deaths, all in varying degrees of articulateness, told the same tale of men who were, in all the full flood of academic and athletic success, of popularity and the promise of great rewards ahead, seen somehow as set apart from their fellows, garlanded victims, devoted to the sacrifice. These men must die to make a world for Hooper; they were the aborigines, vermin by right of law, to be shot off at leisure so that things might be safe for the travelling salesman, with his polygonal pince-nez, his fat wet hand-shake, his grinning dentures. I wondered, as the train carried me farther and farther from Lady Marchmain, whether perhaps there was not on her, too, the same blaze, marking her and hers for destruction by other ways than war. Did she see a sign in the red centre of her cosy grate and hear it in the rattle of creeper on the window-pane, this whisper of doom?

Then I reached Paddington and, returning home, found Sebastian there, and the sense of tragedy vanished, for he was gay and free as when I first met him.

'Cordelia sent you her special love.'

'Did you have a "little talk" with mummy?'

'Yes.'

'Have you gone over to her side?'

The day before I would have said: 'There aren't two sides'; that day I said, 'No, I'm with you, "Sebastian *contra mundum*".'

And that was all the conversation we had on the subject, then or ever.

But the shadows were closing round Sebastian. We returned to Oxford and once again the gillyflowers bloomed under my windows and the chestnut lit the streets and the warm stones strewed their flakes upon the cobble; but it was not as it had been; there was mid-winter in Sebastian's heart.

The weeks went by; we looked for lodgings for the coming term and found them in Merton Street, a secluded, expensive little house near the tennis court.

Meeting Mr Samgrass, whom we had seen less often of late, I told him of our choice. He was standing at the table in Blackwell's where recent German books were displayed, setting aside a little heap of purchases.

'You're sharing digs with Sebastian?' he said. 'So he *is* coming up next term?'

'I suppose so. Why shouldn't he be?'

'I don't know why; I somehow thought perhaps he wasn't. I'm always wrong about things like that. I like Merton Street.'

He showed me the books he was buying, which, since I knew no German, were not of interest to me. As I left him he said: 'Don't think me interfering, you know, but I shouldn't make any *definite* arrangement in Merton Street until you're sure.'

I told Sebastian of this conversation and he said: 'Yes, there's a plot on. Mummy wants me to go and live with Mgr Bell.'

'Why didn't you tell me about it?'

'Because I'm *not* going to live with Mgr Bell.'

'I still think you might have told me. When did it start?'

'Oh, it's been going on. Mummy's very clever, you know. She saw she'd failed with you. I expect it was the letter you wrote after reading Uncle Ned's book.'

'I hardly said anything.'

'That was it. If you were going to be any help to her, you would have said a lot. Uncle Ned is the test, you know.'

But it seemed she had not quite despaired, for a few days later I got a note from her which said: '*I shall be passing through Oxford on Tuesday and hope to see you and Sebastian. I would like to see you alone for five minutes before I see him. Is that too much to ask? I will come to your rooms at about twelve.*'

She came; she admired my rooms. ... 'My brothers Simon and Ned were here, you know. Ned had rooms on the garden front. I wanted Sebastian to come here, too, but my husband was at Christ Church and, as you know, he took charge of Sebastian's education'; she admired my drawings ... '*everyone* loves your paintings in the garden-room. We shall never forgive you if you don't finish them.' Finally, she came to her point.

'I expect you've guessed already what I have come to ask. Quite simply, is Sebastian drinking too much this term?'

I had guessed; I answered: 'If he were, I shouldn't answer. As it is, I can say, "No".'

She said: 'I believe you. Thank God!' and we went together to luncheon at Christ Church.

That night Sebastian had his third disaster and was found by the junior dean at one o'clock, wandering round Tom Quad hopelessly drunk.

I had left him morose but completely sober at a few minutes before twelve. In the succeeding hour he had drunk half a bottle of whisky alone. He did not remember much about it when he came to tell me next morning.

'Have you been doing that a lot,' I asked, 'drinking by yourself after I've gone?'

'About twice; perhaps four times. It's only when they start bothering me. I'd be all right if they'd only leave me alone.'

'They won't now,' I said.

'I know.'

We both knew that this was a crisis. I had no love for Sebastian that morning; he needed it, but I had none to give.

'Really,' I said, 'if you are going to embark on a solitary bout of drinking every time you see a member of your family, it's perfectly hopeless.'

'Oh, yes,' said Sebastian with great sadness. 'I *know*. It's hopeless.'

But my pride was stung because I had been made to look a liar and I could not respond to his need.

'Well, what do you propose to do?'

'I shan't do anything. They'll do it all.'

And I let him go without comfort.

Then the machinery began to move again, and I saw it all repeated as it had happened in December; Mr Samgrass and Mgr Bell saw the Dean of Christ Church; Brideshead came up for a night; the heavy wheels stirred and the small wheels spun. Everyone was exceedingly sorry for Lady Marchmain, whose brothers' names stood in letters of gold on the war memorial, whose brothers' memory was fresh in many breasts.

She came to see me and, again, I must reduce to a few words a conversation which took us from Holywell to the Parks, through Mesopotamia, and over the ferry to north Oxford, where she was staying the night with a houseful of nuns who were in some way under her protection.

'You *must* believe', I said, 'that when I told you Sebastian was not drinking, I was telling you the truth, as I knew it.'

'I know you wish to be a good friend to him.'

'That is not what I mean. I believed what I told you. I still believe it to some extent. I believe he has been drunk two or three times before, not more.'

'It's no good, Charles,' she said. 'All you can mean is that you have not as much influence or knowledge of him as I thought. It is no good either of us trying to believe him. I've known drunkards before. One of the most terrible things about them is their deceit. Love of truth is the first thing that goes.

'After that happy luncheon together. When you left he was so sweet to me, just as he used to be as a little boy, and I agreed to all he wanted. You know I had been doubtful about his sharing rooms with you. I know you'll understand me when I say that. You know that we are all fond of you apart from your being Sebastian's friend. We should miss you so much if you ever stopped coming to stay with us. But I want Sebastian to have all sorts of friends, not just one. Mgr Bell tells me he never mixes with the other Catholics, never goes to the Newman, very rarely goes to mass even. Heaven forbid that he should only know Catholics, but he must know *some*. It needs a very strong faith to stand entirely alone and Sebastian's isn't strong.

'But I was so happy at luncheon on Tuesday that I gave up all my objections; I went round with him and saw the rooms you had chosen. They are charming. And we decided on some furniture you could have from London to make them nicer. And then, on the very night after I had seen him! – No, Charles, it is not in the Logic of the Thing.'

As she said it I thought, 'That's a phrase she's picked up from one of her intellectual hangers-on.'

'Well,' I said, 'have you a remedy?'

'The college are being extraordinarily kind. They say they will not send him down provided he goes to live with Mgr Bell. It's not a thing I could have suggested myself, but it was the Monsignor's own idea. He specially sent a message to you to say how welcome you would always be. There's not room for you actually in the Old Palace, but I daresay you wouldn't want that yourself.'

'Lady Marchmain, if you want to make him a drunkard that's the way to do it. Don't you see that any idea of his being *watched* would be fatal?'

'Oh, dear, it's no good trying to explain. Protestants always think Catholic priests are spies.'

'I don't mean that.' I tried to explain but made a poor business of it. 'He must feel free.'

'But he's been free, always, up till now, and look at the result.'

We had reached the ferry; we had reached a deadlock. With scarcely another word I saw her to the convent, then took the bus back to Carfax.

Sebastian was in my rooms waiting for me. 'I'm going to cable to papa,' he said. 'He won't let them force me into this priest's house.'

'But if they make it a condition of your coming up?'

'I shan't come up. Can you imagine me – serving mass twice a week, helping at tea parties for shy Catholic freshmen, dining with the visiting lecturer at the Newman, drinking a glass of port when we have guests, with Mgr Bell's eye on me to see I don't get too much, being explained, when I was out of the room, as the rather embarrassing local inebriate who's being taken in because his mother is so charming?'

'I told her it wouldn't do,' I said.

'Shall we get really drunk tonight?'

'It's the one time it could do no conceivable harm,' I said.

'*Contra mundum?*'

'*Contra mundum.*'

'Bless you, Charles. There aren't many evenings left to us.'

And that night, the first time for many weeks, we got deliriously drunk together; I saw him to the gate as all the bells were striking midnight, and reeled back to my rooms under a starry heaven which swam dizzily among the towers, and fell asleep in my clothes as I had not done for a year.

Next day Lady Marchmain left Oxford, taking Sebastian with her. Brideshead and I went to his rooms to sort out what he would have sent on and what leave behind.

Brideshead was as grave and impersonal as ever. 'It's a pity Sebastian doesn't know Mgr Bell better,' he said. 'He'd find him a charming man to live with. I was there my last year. My mother believes Sebastian is a confirmed drunkard. Is he?'

'He's in danger of becoming one.'

'I believe God prefers drunkards to a lot of respectable people.'

'For God's sake,' I said, for I was near to tears that morning, 'why bring God into everything?'

'I'm sorry. I forgot. But you know that's an extremely funny question.'

'Is it?'

'To me. Not to you.'

'No, not to me. It seems to me that without your religion Sebastian would have the chance to be a happy and healthy man.'

'It's arguable,' said Brideshead. 'Do you think he will need this elephant's foot again?'

That evening I went across the quad to visit Collins. He was alone with his texts, working by the failing light at his open window. 'Hullo,' he said. 'Come in. I haven't seen you all the term. I'm afraid I've nothing to offer you. Why have you deserted the smart set?'

'I'm the loneliest man in Oxford,' I said. 'Sebastian Flyte's been sent down.'

Presently I asked him what he was doing in the long vacation. He told me; it sounded excruciatingly dull. Then I asked him if he had got digs for next term. Yes, he told me, rather far out but very comfortable. He was sharing with Tyngate, the secretary of the college Essay Society.

'There's one room we haven't filled yet. Barker was coming, but he feels, now he's standing for president of the Union, he ought to be nearer in.'

It was in both our minds that perhaps I might take that room.

'Where are you going?'

'I *was* going to Merton Street with Sebastian Flyte. That's no use now.'

Still neither of us made the suggestion and the moment passed. When I left he said: 'I hope you find someone for Merton Street,' and I said, 'I hope you find someone for the Iffley Road,' and I never spoke to him again.

There was only ten days of term to go; I got through them somehow and returned to London as I had done in such different circumstances the year before, with no plans made.

'That very good-looking friend of yours,' asked my father. 'Is he not with you?'

'No.'

'I quite thought he had taken this over as his home. I'm sorry, I liked him.'

'Father, do you particularly want me to take my degree?'

'*I* want you to? Good gracious, why should *I* want such a thing? No use to me. Not much use to you either, as far as I've seen.'

'That's exactly what I've been thinking. I thought perhaps it was rather a waste of time going back to Oxford.'

Until then my father had taken only a limited interest in what I was saying: now he put down his book, took off his spectacles, and looked at me hard. 'You've been sent down,' he said. 'My brother warned me of this.'

'No, I've not.'

'Well, then, what's all the talk about?' he asked testily, resuming his spectacles, searching for his place on the page. 'Everyone stays up at least three years. I knew one man who took seven to get a pass degree in theology.'

'I only thought that if I was not going to take up one of the professions where a degree is necessary, it might be best to start now on what I intend doing. I intend to be a painter.'

But to this my father made no answer at the time.

The idea, however, seemed to take root in his mind; by the time we spoke of the matter again it was firmly established.

'When you're a painter,' he said at Sunday luncheon, 'you'll need a studio.'

'Yes.'

'Well, there isn't a studio here. There isn't even a room you could use decently as a studio. I'm not going to have you painting in the gallery.'

'No. I never meant to.'

'Nor will I have undraped models all over the house, nor critics with their horrible jargon. And I don't like the smell of turpentine. I presume you intend to do the thing thoroughly and use oil-paint?' My father belonged to a generation which divided painters into the serious and the amateur, according as they used oil or water.

'I don't suppose I should do much painting the first year. Anyway, I should be working at a school.'

'Abroad?' asked my father hopefully. 'There are some excellent schools abroad, I believe.'

It was all happening rather faster than I intended.

'Abroad or here. I should have to look round first.'

'Look round abroad,' he said.

'Then you agree to my leaving Oxford?'

'Agree? Agree? My dear boy, you're twenty-two.'

'Twenty,' I said, 'twenty-one in October.'

'Is that all? It seems *much* longer.'

A letter from Lady Marchmain completes this episode.

'*My dear Charles*,' she wrote, '*Sebastian left me this morning to join his father abroad. Before he went I asked him if he had written to you. He said no, so I must write, tho' I can hardly hope to say in a letter what I could not say on our last walk. But you must not be left in silence.*

'*The college has sent Sebastian down for a term only, and will take him back after Christmas on condition he goes to live with Mgr Bell. It is for him to decide. Meanwhile Mr Samgrass has very kindly consented to take charge of him. As soon as his visit to his father is over Mr Samgrass will pick him up and they will go together to the Levant, where Mr*

Samgrass has long been anxious to investigate a number of orthodox monasteries. He hopes this may be a new interest for Sebastian.

'*Sebastian's stay here has not been happy.*

'*When they come home at Christmas I know Sebastian will want to see you, and so shall we all. I hope your arrangements for next term have not been too much upset and that everything will go well with you.*

Yours sincerely,

Teresa Marchmain.

'*I went to the garden-room this morning and was so very sorry.*'

BOOK TWO

BRIDESHEAD DESERTED

CHAPTER I

'AND when we reached the top of the pass,' said Mr Samgrass, 'we heard the galloping horses behind, and two soldiers rode up to the head of the caravan and turned us back. The General had sent them, and they reached us only just in time. There was a Band, not a mile ahead.'

He paused, and his small audience sat silent, conscious that he had sought to impress them but in doubt as to how they could politely show their interest.

'*A Band?*' said Julia. '*Goodness!*'

Still he seemed to expect more. At last Lady Marchmain said, 'I suppose the sort of folk-music you get in those parts *is* very monotonous.'

'Dear Lady Marchmain, a Band of *Brigands*.' Cordelia, beside me on the sofa, began to giggle noiselessly. 'The mountains are full of them. Stragglers from Kemal's army; Greeks who got cut off in the retreat. Very desperate fellows, I assure you.'

'Do pinch me,' whispered Cordelia.

I pinched her and the agitation of the sofa-springs ceased. 'Thanks,' she said, wiping her eyes with the back of her hand.

'So you never got to wherever-it-was,' said Julia. 'Weren't you terribly disappointed, Sebastian?'

'Me?' said Sebastian from the shadows beyond the lamp-light, beyond the warmth of the burning logs, beyond the family circle, and the photographs spread out on the card-table. 'Me? Oh, I don't think I was there that day, was I, Sammy?'

'That was the day you were ill.'

'I was ill,' he repeated like an echo, 'so I never should have got to wherever-it-was, should I, Sammy?'

'Now *this*, Lady Marchmain, is the caravan at Aleppo in the courtyard of the inn. That's our Armenian cook, Begedbian; that's me on the pony; that's the tent folded up; that's a rather tiresome Kurd who would follow us about at the time. ... Here I am in Pontus, Ephesus, Trebizond, Krak-des-chevaliers, Samothrace, Batum – of course, I haven't got them in chronological order yet.'

'All guides and ruins and mules,' said Cordelia. 'Where's Sebastian?'

'He,' said Mr Samgrass, with a hint of triumph in his voice, as though he had expected the question and prepared the answer, 'he held the camera. He became quite an expert as soon as he learned not to put his hand over the lens, didn't you, Sebastian?'

There was no answer from the shadows. Mr Samgrass delved again into his pigskin satchel.

'Here,' he said, 'is a group taken by a street photographer on the terrace of the St George Hotel at Beirut. There's Sebastian.'

'Why,' I said, 'there's Anthony Blanche, surely?'

'Yes, we saw quite a lot of him; met him by chance at Constantinople. A delightful companion. I can't think how I missed knowing him. He came with us all the way to Beirut.'

Tea had been cleared away and the curtains drawn. It was two days after Christmas, the first evening of my visit; the first, too, of Sebastian's and Mr Samgrass's, whom to my surprise I had found on the platform when I arrived.

Lady Marchmain had written three weeks before: '*I have just heard from Mr Samgrass that he and Sebastian will be home for Christmas as we hoped. I had not heard from them for so long that I was afraid they were lost and did not want to make any arrangements until I knew. Sebastian will be longing to see you. Do come to us for Christmas if you can manage it, or as soon after as you can.*'

Christmas with my uncle was an engagement I could not break, so I travelled across country and joined the local train midway, expecting to find Sebastian already established; there he was, however, in the next carriage to mine, and when I asked him what he was doing, Mr Samgrass replied with such glibness and at such length, telling me of mislaid luggage and of Cook's being shut over the holidays, that I was at once aware of some other explanation which was being withheld.

Mr Samgrass was not at ease; he maintained all the physical habits of self-confidence, but guilt hung about him like stale cigar smoke, and in Lady Marchmain's greeting of him I caught a note of anticipation. He kept up a lively account of his tour during tea, and then Lady Marchmain drew him away with her, upstairs, for a 'little talk'. I watched him go with something near compassion; it was plain to anyone with a poker sense that Mr Samgrass held a very imperfect hand and, as I watched him at tea, I began to suspect that he was not only bluffing but cheating. There was something he must say, did not want to say, and did not quite know how to say to Lady Marchmain about his doings over Christmas, but, more than that, I guessed, there was a great deal he ought to say and had no intention at all of saying, about the whole Levantine tour.

'Come and see nanny,' said Sebastian.

'Please, can I come, too?' said Cordelia.

'Come on.'

We climbed to the nursery in the dome. On the way Cordelia said: 'Aren't you at all pleased to be home?'

'Of course I'm pleased,' said Sebastian.

'Well, you might show it a bit. I've been looking forward to it so much.'

Nanny did not particularly wish to be talked to; she liked visitors best when they paid no attention to her and let her knit away, and watch their faces and think of them as she had known them as small children; their present goings-on did not signify much beside those early illnesses and crimes.

'Well,' she said, 'you *are* looking peaky. I expect it's all that foreign food doesn't agree with you. You must fatten up now you're back. Looks as though you'd been having some late nights, too, by the look of your eyes – dancing, I suppose.' (It was ever Nanny Hawkins's belief that the upper classes spent most of their leisure evenings in the ballroom.) 'And that shirt wants darning. Bring it to me before it goes to the wash.'

Sebastian certainly did look ill; five months had wrought the change of years in him. He was paler, thinner, pouchy under the eyes, drooping in the corners of his mouth, and he showed the scars of a boil on the side of his chin; his voice seemed flatter and his movements alternately listless and jumpy; he looked down-at-heel, too, with clothes and hair, which formerly had been happily negligent, now unkempt; worst of all, there was a wariness in his eye which I had surprised there at Easter, and which now seemed habitual to him.

Restrained by this wariness I asked him nothing of himself, but told him instead about my autumn and winter. I told him about my rooms in the Île Saint-Louis and the art school, and how good the old teachers were and how bad the students.

'They never go near the Louvre,' I said, 'or, if they do, it's only because one of their absurd reviews has suddenly "discovered" a master who fits in with that month's aesthetic theory. Half of them are out to make a popular splash like Picabia; the other half quite simply want to earn their living doing advertisements for *Vogue* and decorating night clubs. And the teachers still go on trying to make them paint like Delacroix.'

'Charles,' said Cordelia, 'Modern Art is all bosh, isn't it?'

'Great bosh.'

'Oh, I'm so glad. I had an argument with one of our nuns and she said we shouldn't try and criticize what we didn't understand. Now I shall tell her I have had it straight from a real artist, and snubs to her.'

Presently it was time for Cordelia to go to her supper, and for Sebastian and me to go down to the drawing-room for our cocktails. Brideshead was there alone, but Wilcox followed on our heels to say to him: 'Her Ladyship would like to speak to you upstairs, my Lord.'

'That's unlike mummy, sending for anyone. She usually lures them up herself.'

There was no sign of the cocktail tray. After a few minutes Sebastian rang the bell. A footman answered. 'Mr Wilcox is upstairs with her Ladyship.'

'Well, never mind, bring in the cocktail things.'

'Mr Wilcox has the keys, my Lord.'

'Oh ... well, send him in with them when he comes down.'

We talked a little about Anthony Blanche – 'He had a beard in Istanbul, but I made him take it off' – and after ten minutes Sebastian said: 'Well, I don't want a cocktail, anyway; I'm off to my bath,' and left the room.

It was half past seven; I supposed the others had gone to dress, but, as I was going to follow them, I met Brideshead coming down.

'Just a moment, Charles, there's something I've got to explain. My mother has given orders that no drinks are to be left in any of the rooms. You'll understand why. If you want anything, ring and ask Wilcox – only better wait until you're alone. I'm sorry, but there it is.'

'Is that necessary?'

'I gather very necessary. You may or may not have heard, Sebastian had another outbreak as soon as he got back to England. He was lost over Christmas. Mr Samgrass only found him yesterday evening.'

'I guessed something of the kind had happened. Are you sure this is the best way of dealing with it?'

'It's my mother's way. Will you have a cocktail, now that he's gone upstairs?'

'It would choke me.'

I was always given the room I had on my first visit; it was next to Sebastian's, and we shared what had once been a dressing-room and had been changed to a bathroom twenty years back by the substitution for the bed of a deep, copper, mahogany-framed bath, that was filled by pulling a brass lever heavy as a piece of marine engineering; the rest of the room remained unchanged; a coal fire always burned there in winter. I often think of that bathroom – the water-colours dimmed by steam and the huge towel warming on the back of the chintz armchair – and contrast it with the uniform, clinical, little chambers, glittering with chromium-plate and looking-glass, which pass for luxury in the modern world.

I lay in the bath and then dried slowly by the fire, thinking all the time of my friend's black home-coming. Then I put on my dressing gown and went to Sebastian's room, entering, as I always did, without knocking. He was sitting by his fire half-dressed, and he started angrily when he heard me and put down a tooth glass.

'Oh, it's you. You gave me a fright.'

'So you got a drink,' I said.

'I don't know what you mean.'

'For Christ's sake,' I said, 'you don't have to pretend with me! You might offer me some.'

'It's just something I had in my flask. I've finished it now.'

'What's going on?'

'Nothing. A lot. I'll tell you some time.'

I dressed and called in for Sebastian, but found him still sitting as I had left him, half-dressed over his fire.

Julia was alone in the drawing-room.

'Well,' I asked, 'what's going on?'

'Oh, just another boring family *potin*. Sebastian got tight again, so we've all got to keep an eye on him. It's too tedious.'

'It's pretty boring for him, too.'

'Well, it's his fault. Why can't he behave like anyone else? Talking of keeping an eye on people, what about Mr Samgrass? Charles, do you notice anything at all fishy about that man?'

'Very fishy. Do you think your mother saw it?'

'Mummy only sees what suits her. She can't have the whole household under surveillance. *I'm* causing anxiety, too, you know.'

'I didn't know,' I said, adding humbly, 'I've only just come from Paris,' so as to avoid giving the impression that any trouble she might be in was not widely notorious.

It was an evening of peculiar gloom. We dined in the Painted Parlour. Sebastian was late, and so painfully excited were we that I think it was in all our minds that he would make some sort of low-comedy entrance, reeling and hiccuping. When he came it was, of course, with perfect propriety; he apologized, sat in the empty place, and allowed Mr Samgrass to resume his mono-logue, uninterrupted and, it seemed, unheard. Druses, patri-

archs, icons, bed-bugs, Romanesque remains, curious dishes of
goat and sheeps' eyes, French and Turkish officials – all the catalogue of Near Eastern travel was provided for our amusement.

I watched the champagne go round the table. When it came
to Sebastian he said: 'I'll have whisky, please,' and I saw Wilcox
glance over his head to Lady Marchmain and saw her give a
tiny, hardly perceptible nod. At Brideshead they used small
individual spirit decanters which held about a quarter of a
bottle, and were always placed, full, before anyone who asked
for it; the decanter which Wilcox put before Sebastian was half-
empty. Sebastian raised it very deliberately, tilted it, looked at
it, and then in silence poured the liquor into his glass, where it
covered two fingers. We all began talking at once, all except
Sebastian, so that for a moment Mr Samgrass found himself
talking to no one, telling the candlesticks about the Maronites;
but soon we fell silent again, and he had the table until Lady
Marchmain and Julia left the room.

'Don't be long, Bridey,' she said, at the door, as she always
said, and that evening we had no inclination to delay. Our
glasses were filled with port and the decanter was at once taken
from the room. We drank quickly and went to the drawing-
room, where Brideshead asked his mother to read, and she read
The Diary of a Nobody with great spirit until ten o'clock, when
she closed the book and said she was unaccountably tired, so
tired that she would not visit the chapel that night.

'Who's hunting tomorrow?' she asked.

'Cordelia,' said Brideshead. 'I'm taking that young horse of
Julia's, just to show him the hounds; I shan't keep him out more
than a couple of hours.'

'Rex is arriving some time,' said Julia. 'I'd better stay in to
greet him.'

'Where's the meet?' said Sebastian suddenly.

'Just here at Flyte St Mary.'

'Then I'd like to hunt, please, if there's anything for me.'

'Of course. That's delightful. I'd have asked you, only you
always used to complain so of being made to go out. You can
have Tinkerbell. She's been going very nicely this season.'

Everyone was suddenly pleased that Sebastian wanted to hunt; it seemed to undo some of the mischief of the evening. Brideshead rang the bell for whisky.

'Anyone else want any?'

'Bring me some, too,' said Sebastian, and, though it was a footman this time and not Wilcox, I saw the same exchange of glance and nod between the servant and Lady Marchmain. Everyone had been warned. The two drinks were brought in, poured out already in the glasses, like 'doubles' at a bar, and all our eyes followed the tray, as though we were dogs in a dining-room smelling game.

The good humour engendered by Sebastian's wish to hunt persisted, however; Brideshead wrote out a note for the stables, and we all went to bed quite cheerfully.

Sebastian got straight to bed; I sat by his fire and smoked a pipe. I said: 'I rather wish I was coming out with you tomorrow.'

'Well,' he said, 'you wouldn't see much sport. I can tell you exactly what I'm going to do. I shall leave Bridey at the first covert, hack over to the nearest good pub, and spend the entire day quietly soaking in the bar parlour. If they treat me like a dipsomaniac, they can bloody well have a dipsomaniac. I hate hunting, anyway.'

'Well, I can't stop you.'

'You can, as a matter of fact – by not giving me any money. They stopped my banking account, you know, in the summer. It's been one of my chief difficulties. I pawned my watch and cigarette case to ensure a happy Christmas, so I shall have to come to you tomorrow for my day's expenses.'

'I won't. You know perfectly well I can't.'

'Won't you, Charles? Well, I daresay I shall manage on my own somehow. I've got rather clever at that lately – managing on my own. I've had to.'

'Sebastian, what *have* you and Mr Samgrass been up to?'

'He told you at dinner – ruins and guides and mules, that's what Sammy's been up to. We decided to go our own ways, that's all. Poor Sammy's really behaved rather well so far. I hoped he would keep it up, but he seems to have been very indiscreet about my happy Christmas. I suppose he thought if he gave too good an account of me, he might lose his job as keeper.

'He makes quite a good thing out of it, you know. I don't mean that he steals. I should think he's fairly honest about money. He certainly keeps an embarrassing little note-book in which he puts down all the travellers' cheques he cashes and what he spends it on, for mummy and the lawyer to see. But he wanted to go to all these places, and it's very convenient for him to have me to take him in comfort, instead of going as dons usually do. The only disadvantage was having to put up with my company, and we soon solved that for him.

'We began very much on a Grand Tour, you know, with letters to all the chief people everywhere, and stayed with the Military Governor at Rhodes and the Ambassador at Constantinople. That was what Sammy had signed on for in the first place. Of course, he had his work cut out keeping his eye on me, but he warned all our hosts beforehand that I was not responsible.'

'Sebastian.'

'Not *quite* responsible – and as I had no money to spend I couldn't get away very much. He even did the tipping for me, put the note into the man's hand and jotted the amount down then and there in his note-book. My lucky time was at Constantinople. I managed to make some money at cards one evening when Sammy wasn't looking. Next day I gave him the slip and was having a very happy hour in the bar at the Tokatlian when who should come in but Anthony Blanche with a beard and a Jew boy. Anthony lent me a tenner just before Sammy came panting in and recaptured me. After that I didn't get a minute out of sight; the Embassy staff put us in the boat to Piraeus and watched us sail away. But in Athens it was easy. I simply walked out of the Legation one day after lunch, changed my money at Cook's, and asked about sailings to Alexandria just to fox Sammy, then went down to the port in a bus, found a sailor who spoke American, lay up with him till his ship sailed, and popped back to Constantinople, and that was that.

'Anthony and the Jew boy shared a very nice, tumble-down house near the bazaars. I stayed there till it got too cold, then Anthony and I drifted south till we met Sammy by appointment in Syria three weeks ago.'

'Didn't Sammy mind?'

'Oh, I think he quite enjoyed himself in his own ghastly way – only of course there was no more high life for him. I think he was a bit anxious at first. I didn't want him to get the whole Mediterranean Fleet out, so I cabled him from Constantinople that I was quite well and would he send money to the Ottoman Bank. He came hopping over as soon as he got my cable. Of course he was in a difficult position, because I'm of age and not certified yet, so he couldn't have me arrested. He couldn't leave me to starve while he was living on my money, and he couldn't tell mummy without looking pretty silly. I had him all ways, poor Sammy. My original idea had been to leave him flat, but Anthony was very helpful about that, and said it was far better to arrange things amicably; and he *did* arrange things very amicably. So here I am.'

'After Christmas.'

'Yes, I was determined to have a happy Christmas.'

'Did you?'

'I think so. I don't remember it much, and that's always a good sign, isn't it?'

Next morning at breakfast Brideshead wore scarlet; Cordelia, very smart herself, with her chin held high over her white stock, wailed when Sebastian appeared in a tweed coat: '*Oh, Sebastian*, you can't come out like that. Do go and change. You look so lovely in hunting clothes.'

'Locked away somewhere. Gibbs couldn't find them.'

'That's a fib. I helped get them out myself before you were called.'

'Half the things are missing.'

'It just encourages the Strickland-Venableses. They're behaving rottenly. They've even taken their grooms out of top hats.'

It was a quarter to eleven before the horses were brought round, but no one else appeared downstairs; it was as though they were in hiding, listening for Sebastian's retreating hooves before showing themselves.

Just as he was about to start, when the others were already mounted, Sebastian beckoned me into the hall. On the table beside his hat, gloves, whip, and sandwiches, lay the flask he had put out to be filled. He picked it up and shook it; it was empty.

'You see,' he said, 'I can't even be trusted that far. It's they who are mad, not me. Now you can't refuse me money.'

I gave him a pound.

'More,' he said.

I gave him another and watched him mount and trot after his brother and sister.

Then, as though it were his cue on the stage, Mr Samgrass came to my elbow, put an arm in mine, and led me back to the fire. He warmed his neat little hands and then turned to warm his seat.

'So Sebastian is in pursuit of the fox,' he said, 'and our little problem is shelved for an hour or two?'

I was not going to stand this from Mr Samgrass.

'I heard all about your Grand Tour, last night,' I said.

'Ah, I rather supposed you might have.' Mr Samgrass was undismayed, relieved, it seemed, to have someone else in the know. 'I did not harrow our hostess with all that. After all, it turned out far better than one had any right to expect. I did feel, however, that some explanation was due to her of Sebastian's Christmas festivities. You may have observed last night that there were certain precautions.'

'I did.'

'You thought them excessive? I am with you, particularly as they tend to compromise the comfort of our own little visit. I have seen Lady Marchmain this morning. You must not suppose I am just out of bed. I have had a little talk upstairs with our hostess. I think we may hope for some relaxation tonight. Yesterday was *not* an evening that any of us would wish to have repeated. I earned less gratitude than I deserved, I think, for my efforts to distract you.'

It was repugnant to me to talk about Sebastian to Mr Samgrass, but I was compelled to say: 'I'm not sure that tonight would be the best time to start the relaxation.'

'But surely? Why not tonight, after a day in the field under Brideshead's inquisitorial eye? Could one choose better?'

'Oh, I suppose it's none of my business really.'

'Nor mine, strictly, now that he is safely home. Lady Marchmain did me the honour of consulting me. But it is less Sebastian's welfare than our own I have at heart at the moment. I need my third glass of port; I need that hospitable tray in the library. And yet you specifically advise against it *tonight*. I wonder why. Sebastian can come to no mischief today. For one thing, he has no money. I happen to know. I saw to it. I even have his watch and cigarette case upstairs. He will be quite harmless . . . as long as no one is so wicked as to give him any. . . . Ah, Lady Julia, good morning to you, good morning. And how is the peke this hunting morning?'

'Oh, the peke's all right. Listen. I've got Rex Mottram coming here today. We simply can't have another evening like last night. Someone must speak to mummy.'

'Someone *has*. I spoke. I think it will be all right.'

'Thank God for that. Are you painting today, Charles?'

It had been the custom that on every visit to Brideshead I painted a medallion on the walls of the garden-room. The custom suited me well, for it gave me a good reason to detach myself from the rest of the party; when the house was full, the garden-room became a rival to the nursery, where from time to time people took refuge to complain about the others; thus without effort I kept in touch with the gossip of the place. There were three finished medallions now, each rather pretty in its way, but unhappily each in a different way, for my tastes had changed and I had become more dexterous in the eighteen months since the series was begun. As a decorative scheme, they were a failure. That morning was typical of the many mornings when I had found the garden-room a sanctuary. There I went and was soon at work. Julia came with me to see me started and we talked, inevitably, of Sebastian.

'Don't you get bored with the subject?' she asked. 'Why must everyone make such a Thing about it?'

'Just because we're fond of him.'

'Well, I'm fond of him too, in a way, I suppose, only I wish he'd behave like anybody else. I've grown up with one family skeleton, you know – papa. Not to be talked of before the servants, not to be talked of before us when we were children. If mummy is going to start making a skeleton out of Sebastian, it's *too* much. If he wants to be always tight, why doesn't he go to Kenya or somewhere where it doesn't matter?'

'Why does it matter less being unhappy in Kenya than anywhere else?'

'Don't pretend to be stupid, Charles. You understand perfectly.'

'You mean there won't be so many embarrassing situations for you? Well, all I was trying to say was that I'm afraid there may be an embarrassing situation tonight if Sebastian gets the chance. He's in a bad mood.'

'Oh, a day's hunting will put that all right.'

It was touching to see the faith which everybody put in the value of a day's hunting. Lady Marchmain, who looked in on me during the morning, mocked herself for it with that delicate irony for which she was famous.

'I've always detested hunting,' she said, 'because it seems to produce a particularly gross kind of caddishness in the nicest people. I don't know what it is, but the moment they dress up and get on a horse they become like a lot of Prussians. And so boastful after it. The evenings I've sat at dinner appalled at seeing the men and women I know, transformed into half-awake, self-opinionated, monomaniac louts! ... and yet, you know, – it must be something derived from centuries ago – my heart is quite light today to think of Sebastian out with them. "There's nothing wrong with him really," I say, "he's gone hunting" – as though it were an answer to prayer.'

She asked me about my life in Paris. I told her of my rooms

with their view of the river and the towers of Notre Dame. 'I'm hoping Sebastian will come and stay with me when I go back.'

'It would have been lovely,' said Lady Marchmain, sighing as though for the unattainable.

'I hope he's coming to stay with me in London.'

'Charles, you know it isn't possible. London's the worst place. Even Mr Samgrass couldn't hold him there. We have no secrets in this house. He was *lost*, you know, all through Christmas. Mr Samgrass only found him because he couldn't pay his bill in the place where he was, so they telephoned our house. It's too horrible. No, London is impossible; if he can't behave himself here, with us ... We must keep him happy and healthy here for a bit, hunting, and then send him abroad again with Mr Samgrass. ... You see, I've been through all this before.'

The retort was there, unspoken, well-understood by both of us – 'You couldn't keep *him*; *he* ran away. So will Sebastian. Because they both hate you.'

A horn and the huntsman's cry sounded in the valley below us.

'There they go now, drawing the home woods. I hope he's having a good day.'

Thus with Julia and Lady Marchmain I reached deadlock, not because we failed to understand one another, but because we understood too well. With Brideshead, who came home to luncheon and talked to me on the subject – for the subject was everywhere in the house like a fire deep in the hold of a ship, below the water-line, black and red in the darkness, coming to light in acrid wisps of smoke that oozed under hatches and billowed suddenly from the scuttles and air pipes – with Brideshead, I was in a strange world, a dead world to me, in a moon-landscape of barren lava, a high place of toiling lungs.

He said: 'I hope it is dipsomania. That is simply a great misfortune that we must all help him bear. What I used to fear was that he just got drunk deliberately when he liked and because he liked.'

'That's exactly what he did – what we both did. It's what he does with me now. I can keep him to that, if only your mother would trust me. If you worry him with keepers and cures he'll be a physical wreck in a few years.'

'There's nothing *wrong* in being a physical wreck, you know. There's no moral obligation to be Postmaster-General or Master of Foxhounds or to live to walk ten miles at eighty.'

'*Wrong*,' I said. '*Moral obligation* – now you're back on religion again.'

'I never left it,' said Brideshead.

'D'you know, Bridey, if I ever felt for a moment like becoming a Catholic, I should only have to talk to you for five minutes to be cured. You manage to reduce what seem quite sensible propositions to stark nonsense.'

'It's odd you should say that. I've heard it before from other people. It's one of the many reasons why I don't think I should make a good priest. It's something in the way my mind works, I suppose.'

At luncheon Julia had no thoughts except for her guest who was coming that day. She drove to the station to meet him and brought him home to tea.

'Mummy, do look at Rex's Christmas present.'

It was a small tortoise with Julia's initials set in diamonds in the living shell, and this slightly obscene object, now slipping impotently on the polished boards, now striding across the card-table, now lumbering over a rug, now withdrawn at a touch, now stretching its neck and swaying its withered, antediluvian head, became a memorable part of the evening, one of those needle-hooks of experience which catch the attention when larger matters are at stake.

'Dear me,' said Lady Marchmain. 'I wonder if it eats the same sort of things as an ordinary tortoise.'

'What will you do when it's dead?' asked Mr Samgrass. 'Can you have another tortoise fitted into the shell?'

Rex had been told about the problem of Sebastian – he could scarcely have endured in that atmosphere without – and had a solution pat. He propounded it cheerfully and openly at tea, and after a day of whispering it was a relief to hear the thing discussed. 'Send him to Borethus at Zürich. Borethus is the man. He works miracles every day at that sanatorium of his. You know how Charlie Kilcartney used to drink.'

'No,' said Lady Marchmain, with that sweet irony of hers. 'No, I'm afraid I don't know how Charlie Kilcartney drank.'

Julia, hearing her lover mocked, frowned at the tortoise, but Rex Mottram was impervious to such delicate mischief.

'Two wives despaired of him,' he said. 'When he got engaged to Sylvia, she made it a condition that he should take the cure at Zürich. And it worked. He came back in three months a different man. And he hasn't touched a drop since, even though Sylvia walked out on him.'

'Why did she do that?'

'Well, poor Charlie got rather a bore when he stopped drinking. But that's not really the point of the story.'

'No, I suppose not. In fact, I suppose, really, it's meant to be an encouraging story.'

Julia scowled at her jewelled tortoise.

'He takes sex cases, too, you know.'

'Oh dear, what very peculiar friends poor Sebastian will make in Zürich.'

'He's booked up for months ahead, but I think he'd find room if I asked him. I could telephone him from here tonight.'

(In his kindest moments Rex displayed a kind of hectoring zeal as if he were thrusting a vacuum cleaner on an unwilling housewife.)

'We'll think about it.'

And we were thinking about it when Cordelia returned from hunting.

'Oh, Julia, *what's* that? How *beastly*.'

'It's Rex's Christmas present.'

'Oh, sorry. I'm always putting my foot in it. But how cruel! It must have hurt frightfully.'

'They can't feel.'

'How d'you know? Bet they can.'

She kissed her mother, whom she had not seen that day, shook hands with Rex, and rang for eggs.

'I had one tea at Mrs Barney's, where I telephoned for the car, but I'm still hungry. It was a spiffing day. Jean Strickland-Venables fell in the mud. We ran from Bengers to Upper Eastrey without a check. I reckon that's five miles, don't you, Bridey?'

'Three.'

'Not as he ran. . . .' Between mouthfuls of scrambled egg she told us about the hunt. '. . . You should have seen Jean when she came out of the mud.'

'Where's Sebastian?'

'He's in disgrace.' The words, in that clear, child's voice had the ring of a bell tolling, but she went on: 'Coming out in that beastly rat-catcher coat and mean little tie like something from Captain Morvin's Riding Academy. I just didn't recognize him at the meet, and I hope nobody else did. Isn't he back? I expect he got lost.'

When Wilcox came to clear the tea, Lady Marchmain asked: 'No sign of Lord Sebastian?'

'No, my Lady.'

'He must have stopped for tea with someone. How very unlike him.'

Half an hour later, when Wilcox brought in the cocktail tray, he said: 'Lord Sebastian has just rung up to be fetched from South Twining.'

'South Twining? Who lives there?'

'He was speaking from the hotel, my Lady.'

'South Twining?' said Cordelia. 'Goodness, he *did* get lost!'

When he arrived he was flushed and his eyes were feverishly bright; I saw that he was two-thirds drunk.

'Dear boy,' said Lady Marchmain. 'How nice to see you looking so well again. Your day in the open has done you good. The drinks are on the table; do help yourself.'

There was nothing unusual in her speech but the fact of her saying it. Six months ago it would not have been said.

'Thanks,' said Sebastian. 'I will.'

A blow, expected, repeated, falling on a bruise, with no smart or shock of surprise, only a dull and sickening pain and the doubt whether another like it could be borne – that was how it felt, sitting opposite Sebastian at dinner that night, seeing his clouded eye and groping movements, hearing his thickened voice breaking in, ineptly, after long brutish silences. When at length Lady Marchmain and Julia and the servants left us, Brideshead said: 'You'd best go to bed, Sebastian.'

'Have some port first.'

'Yes, have some port if you want it. But don't come into the drawing-room.'

'Too bloody drunk,' said Sebastian nodding heavily. 'Like olden times. Gentlemen always too drunk join ladies in olden times.'

('And yet, you know, it *wasn't*,' said Mr Samgrass, trying to be chatty with me about it afterwards, 'it wasn't at all like olden times. I wonder where the difference lies. The lack of good humour? The lack of companionship? You know I think he must have been drinking by himself today. Where did he get the money?')

'Sebastian's gone up,' said Brideshead when we reached the drawing-room.

'Yes? Shall I read?'

Julia and Rex played bezique; the tortoise, teased by the pekinese, withdrew into his shell; Lady Marchmain read *The Diary of a Nobody* aloud until, quite early, she said it was time for bed.

'Can't I stay up and play a little longer, mummy? Just three games?'

'Very well, darling. Come in and see me before you go to bed. I shan't be asleep.'

It was plain to Mr Samgrass and me that Julia and Rex wanted to be left alone, so we went, too; it was not plain to Brideshead, who settled down to read *The Times*, which he had not yet seen that day. Then, going to our side of the house, Mr Samgrass said: 'It wasn't at all like olden times.'

Next morning I said to Sebastian: 'Tell me honestly, do you want me to stay on here?'

'No, Charles, I don't believe I do.'

'I'm no help?'

'No help.'

So I went to make my excuses to his mother.

'There's something I must ask you, Charles. Did you give Sebastian money yesterday?'

'Yes.'

'Knowing how he was likely to spend it?'

'Yes.'

'I don't understand it,' she said. 'I simply don't understand how anyone can be so callously wicked.'

She paused, but I do not think she expected any answer; there was nothing I could say unless I were to start all over again on that familiar, endless argument.

'I'm not going to reproach you,' she said. 'God knows it's not for me to reproach anyone. Any failure in my children is my failure. But I don't understand it. I don't understand how you can have been so nice in so many ways, and then do something so wantonly cruel. I don't understand how we all liked you so much. Did you hate us all the time? I don't understand how we deserved it.'

I was unmoved; there was no part of me remotely touched by her distress. It was as I had often imagined being expelled from school. I almost expected to hear her say: 'I have already written to inform your unhappy father.' But as I drove away and turned back in the car to take what promised to be my last view of the house, I felt that I was leaving part of myself behind, and that wherever I went afterwards I should feel the lack of it, and search for it hopelessly, as ghosts are said to do, frequenting the spots where they buried material treasures without which they cannot pay their way to the nether world.

'I shall never go back,' I said to myself.

A door had shut, the low door in the wall I had sought and found in Oxford; open it now and I should find no enchanted garden.

I had come to the surface, into the light of common day and the fresh sea-air, after long captivity in the sunless coral palaces and waving forests of the ocean bed.

I had left behind me – what? Youth? Adolescence? Romance? The conjuring stuff of these things, 'the Young Magician's Compendium', that neat cabinet where the ebony wand had its place beside the delusive billiard balls, the penny that folded double, and the feather flowers that could be drawn into a hollow candle.

'I have left behind illusion,' I said to myself. 'Henceforth I live in a world of three dimensions – with the aid of my five senses.'

I have since learned that there is no such world, but then, as the car turned out of sight of the house, I thought it took no finding, but lay all about me at the end of the avenue.

Thus I returned to Paris, and to the friends I had found there and the habits I had formed. I thought I should hear no more of Brideshead, but life has few separations as sharp as that. It was not three weeks before I received a letter in Cordelia's Frenchified convent hand:

'*Darling Charles,*' she said. '*I was so very miserable when you went. You might have come and said good-bye!*

'*I heard all about your disgrace, and I am writing to say that I am in disgrace, too. I sneaked Wilcox's keys and got whisky for Sebastian and got caught. He did seem to want it so. And there was (and is) an awful row.*

'*Mr Samgrass has gone (good!), and I think he is a bit in disgrace, too, but I don't know why.*

'*Mr Mottram is very popular with Julia (bad!) and is taking Sebastian away (bad! bad!) to a German doctor.*

'*Julia's tortoise disappeared. We think it buried itself, as they do, so there goes a packet (expression of Mr Mottram's).*

'*I am very well.*

'*With love from*
                Cordelia.'

It must have been about a week after receiving this letter that I returned to my rooms one afternoon to find Rex waiting for me.

It was about four, for the light began to fail early in the studio at that time of year. I could see by the expression on the concierge's face, when she told me I had a visitor waiting, that there was something impressive upstairs; she had a vivid gift of expressing differences of age or attraction; this was the expression which meant someone of the first consequence, and Rex indeed seemed to justify it, as I found him in his big travelling coat, filling the window that looked over the river.

'Well,' I said. 'Well.'

'I came this morning. They told me where you usually lunched but I couldn't see you there. Have you got him?'

I did not need to ask whom. 'So he's given you the slip, too?'

'We got here last night and were going on to Zürich today. I left him at the Lotti after dinner, as he said he was tired, and went round to the Travellers' for a game.'

I noticed how, even with me, he was making excuses, as though rehearsing his story for retelling elsewhere. 'As he said he was tired' was good. I could not well imagine Rex letting a half-tipsy boy interfere with his cards.

'So you came back and found him gone?'

'Not at all. I wish I had. I found him sitting up for me. I had a run of luck at the Travellers' and cleaned up a packet. Sebastian pinched the lot while I was asleep. All he left me was two first-class tickets to Zürich stuck in the edge of the looking-glass. I had nearly three hundred quid, blast him!'

'And now he may be almost anywhere.'

'Anywhere. You're *not* hiding him by any chance?'

'No. My dealings with that family are over.'

'I think mine are just beginning,' said Rex. 'I say, I've got a lot to talk about, and I promised a chap at the Travellers' I'd give him his revenge this afternoon. Won't you dine with me?'

'Yes. Where?'

'I usually go to Ciro's.'

'Why not Paillard's?'

'Never heard of it. I'm paying you know.'

'I know you are. Let me order dinner.'

'Well, all right. What's the place again?' I wrote it down for him. 'Is it the sort of place you see native life?'

'Yes, you might call it that.'

'Well, it'll be an experience. Order something good.'

'That's my intention.'

I was there twenty minutes before Rex. If I had to spend an evening with him, it should, at any rate, be in my own way. I remember the dinner well – soup of *oseille*, a sole quite simply cooked in a white-wine sauce, a *caneton à la presse*, a lemon soufflé. At the last minute, fearing that the whole thing was too simple for Rex, I added *caviar aux blinis*. And for wine I let him give me a bottle of 1906 Montrachet, then at its prime, and, with the duck, a Clos de Bèze of 1904.

Living was easy in France then; with the exchange as it was, my allowance went a long way and I did not live frugally. It was very seldom, however, that I had a dinner like this, and I felt well disposed to Rex, when at last he arrived and gave up his hat and coat with the air of not expecting to see them again. He looked round the sombre little place with suspicion as though hoping to see apaches or a drinking party of students. All he saw was four senators with napkins tucked under their beards eating in absolute silence. I could imagine him telling his commercial friends later: '... interesting fellow I know; an art student living in Paris. Took me to a funny little restaurant – sort of place you'd pass without looking at – where there was some of the best food I ever ate. There were half a dozen senators there, too, which shows you it was the right place. Wasn't at all cheap, either.'

'Any sign of Sebastian?' he asked.

'There won't be,' I said, 'until he needs money.'

'It's a bit thick, going off like that. I was rather hoping that if I made a good job of him, it might do me a bit of good in another direction.'

He plainly wished to talk of his own affairs; they could wait, I thought, for the hour of tolerance and repletion, for the cognac; they could wait until the attention was blunted and one could listen with half the mind only; now in the keen moment when the *maître d'hôtel* was turning the blinis over in the pan, and, in the background, two humbler men were preparing the press, we would talk of myself.

'Did you stay long at Brideshead? Was my name mentioned after I left?'

'Was it mentioned? I got sick of the sound of it, old boy. The Marchioness got what she called a 'bad conscience' about you. She piled it on pretty thick, I gather, at your last meeting.'

' "Callously wicked", "wantonly cruel".'

'Hard words.'

' "It doesn't matter what people call you unless they call you pigeon pie and eat you up." '

'Eh?'

'A saying.'

'Ah.' The cream and hot butter mingled and overflowed, separating each glaucous bead of caviar from its fellows, capping it in white and gold.

'I like a bit of chopped onion with mine,' said Rex. 'Chap-who-knew told me it brought out the flavour.'

'Try it without first,' I said. 'And tell me more news of myself.'

'Well, of course, Greenacre, or whatever he was called – the snooty don – he came a cropper. That was well received by all. He was the blue-eyed boy for a day or two after you left. Shouldn't wonder if he hadn't put the old girl up to pitching you out. He was always being pushed down our throats, so in the end Julia couldn't bear it any more and gave him away.'

'*Julia* did?'

'Well, he'd begun to stick his nose into *our* affairs, you see. Julia spotted he was a fake, and one afternoon when Sebastian was tight – he was tight most of the time – she got the whole story of the Grand Tour out of him. And that was the end of Mr Samgrass. After that the Marchioness began to think she might have been a bit rough with you.'

'And what about the row with Cordelia?'

'That eclipsed everything. That kid's a walking marvel – she'd been feeding Sebastian whisky right under our noses for a week. We couldn't think where he was getting it. That's when the Marchioness finally crumbled.'

The soup was delicious after the rich blinis – hot, thin, bitter, frothy.

'I'll tell you a thing, Charles, that Ma Marchmain hasn't let on to anyone. She's a very sick woman. Might peg out any minute. George Anstruther saw her in the autumn and put it at two years.'

'How on earth do you know?'

'It's the kind of thing I hear. With the way her family are going on at the moment, I wouldn't give her a year. I know just the man for her in Vienna. He put Sonia Bamfshire on her feet when everyone including Anstruther had despaired of her. But Ma Marchmain won't do anything about it. I suppose it's something to do with her crack-brain religion, not to take care of the body.'

The sole was so simple and unobtrusive that Rex failed to notice it. We ate to the music of the press – the crunch of the bones, the drip of blood and marrow, the tap of the spoon basting the thin slices of breast. There was a pause here of a quarter of an hour, while I drank the first glass of the Clos de Bèze and Rex smoked his first cigarette. He leaned back, blew a cloud of smoke across the table, and remarked, 'You know, the food here isn't half bad; someone ought to take this place up and make something of it.'

Presently he began again on the Marchmains:

'I'll tell you another thing, too – they'll get a jolt financially soon if they don't look out.'

'I thought they were enormously rich.'

'Well, they are rich in the way people are who just let their money sit quiet. Everyone of that sort is poorer than they were in 1914, and the Flytes don't seem to realize it. I reckon those lawyers who manage their affairs find it convenient to give them all the cash they want and no questions asked. Look at the way they live – Brideshead and Marchmain House both going full blast, pack of foxhounds, no rents raised, nobody sacked, dozens of old servants doing damn all, being waited on by other servants, and then besides all that there's the old boy setting up a separate establishment – and setting it up on no humble scale either. D'you know how much they're overdrawn?'

'Of course I don't.'

'Jolly near a hundred thousand in London. I don't know what they owe elsewhere. Well, that's quite a packet, you know, for people who aren't *using* their money. Ninety-eight thousand last November. It's the kind of thing I hear.'

Those were the kind of things he heard, mortal illness and debt, I thought.

I rejoiced in the Burgundy. It seemed a reminder that the world was an older and better place than Rex knew, that mankind in its long passion had learned another wisdom than his. By chance I met this same wine again, lunching with my wine merchant in St James's Street, in the first autumn of the war; it had softened and faded in the intervening years, but it still spoke in the pure, authentic accent of its prime, the same words of hope.

'I don't mean that they'll be paupers; the old boy will always be good for an odd thirty thousand a year, but there'll be a shake-up coming soon, and when the upper classes get the wind up, their first idea is usually to cut down on the girls. I'd like to get the little matter of a marriage settlement through, before it comes.'

We had by no means reached the cognac, but here we were on the subject of himself. In twenty minutes I should have been ready for all he had to tell. I closed my mind to him as best I could and gave myself to the food before me, but sentences came breaking in on my happiness, recalling me to the harsh, acquisitive world which Rex inhabited. He wanted a woman; he wanted the best on the market, and he wanted her at his own price; that was what it amounted to.

'. . . Ma Marchmain doesn't like me. Well, I'm not asking her to. It's not her I want to marry. She hasn't the guts to say openly: "You're not a gentleman. You're an adventurer from the Colonies." She says we live in different atmospheres. That's all right, but Julia happens to fancy my atmosphere. . . . Then she brings up religion. I've nothing against her Church; we don't take much account of Catholics in Canada, but that's different; in Europe you've got some very posh Catholics. All right, Julia can go to church whenever she wants to. I shan't try and stop her. It doesn't mean two pins to her, as a matter of fact, but I like a girl to have religion. What's more, she can bring the children up Catholic. I'll make all the "promises" they want. . . . Then there's my past. "We know so little about you." She knows a sight too much. You may know I've been tied up with someone else for a year or two.'

I knew; everyone who had ever met Rex knew of his affair with Brenda Champion; knew also that it was from this affair that he derived everything which distinguished him from every other stock-jobber; his golf with the Prince of Wales, his membership of Bratt's, even his smoking-room comradeship at the House of Commons, for, when he first appeared there, his party chiefs did not say of him, 'Look, there is the promising young member for north Gridley who spoke so well on Rent Restrictions.' They said: 'There's Brenda Champion's latest'; it had done him a great deal of good with men; women he could usually charm.

'Well, that's all washed up. Ma Marchmain was too delicate to mention the subject; all she said was that I had "notoriety". Well, what does she expect as a son-in-law – a sort of half-baked monk like Brideshead? Julia knows all about the other thing; if she doesn't care, I don't see it's anyone else's business.'

After the duck came a salad of watercress and chicory in a faint mist of chives. I tried to think only of the salad. I succeeded for a time in thinking only of the soufflé. Then came the cognac and the proper hour for these confidences. '. . . Julia's just rising twenty. I don't want to wait till she's of age. Anyway, I don't want to marry without doing the thing properly . . . nothing hole-in-corner. . . . I have to see she isn't jockeyed out of her proper settlement. So as the Marchioness won't play ball I'm off to see the old man and square him. I gather he's likely to agree to anything he knows will upset her. He's at Monte Carlo at the moment. I'd planned to go there after dropping Sebastian off at Zürich. That's why it's such a bloody bore having lost him.'

The cognac was not to Rex's taste. It was clear and pale and it came to us in a bottle free from grime and Napoleonic cyphers. It was only a year or two older than Rex and lately bottled. They gave it to us in very thin tulip-shaped glasses of modest size.

'Brandy's one of the things I do know a bit about,' said Rex. 'This is a bad colour. What's more, I can't taste it in this thimble.'

They brought him a balloon the size of his head. He made them warm it over the spirit lamp. Then he rolled the splendid spirit round, buried his face in the fumes, and pronounced it the sort of stuff he put soda in at home.

So, shamefacedly, they wheeled out of its hiding place the vast and mouldy bottle they kept for people of Rex's sort.

'That's the stuff,' he said, tilting the treacly concoction till it left dark rings round the sides of his glass. 'They've always got some tucked away, but they won't bring it out unless you make a fuss. Have some.'

'I'm quite happy with this.'

'Well, it's a crime to drink it, if you don't really appreciate it.'

He lit his cigar and sat back at peace with the world; I, too, was at peace in another world than his. We both were happy. He talked of Julia and I heard his voice, unintelligible at a great distance, like a dog's barking miles away on a still night.

At the beginning of May the engagement was announced. I saw the notice in the *Continental Daily Mail* and assumed that Rex had 'squared the old man'. But things did not go as were expected. The next news I had of them was in the middle of June, when I read that they had been married very quietly at the Savoy Chapel. No royalty was present; nor was the Prime Minister; nor were any of Julia's family. It sounded like a 'hole-in-the-corner' affair, but it was not for several years that I heard the full story.

CHAPTER II

It is time to speak of Julia, who till now has played an intermittent and somewhat enigmatic part in Sebastian's drama. It was thus she appeared to me at the time, and I to her. We pursued separate aims which brought us near to one another, but we remained strangers. She told me later that she had made a kind of note of me in her mind, as, scanning the shelf for a particular book, one will sometimes have one's attention caught by another, take it down, glance at the title page and, saying 'I must read that, too, when I've the time,' replace it, and continue the search. On my side the interest was keener, for there was always the physical likeness between brother and sister, which, caught repeatedly in different poses, under different lights, each time pierced me anew; and, as Sebastian in his sharp decline seemed daily to fade and crumble, so much the more did Julia stand out clear and firm.

She was thin in those days, flat-chested, leggy; she seemed all limbs and neck, bodiless, spidery; thus far she conformed to the fashion, but the hair-cut and the hats of the period, and the blank stare and gape of the period, and the clownish dabs of rouge high on the cheekbones, could not reduce her to type.

When I first met her, when she met me in the station yard and drove me home through the twilight, that high summer of 1923, she was just eighteen and fresh from her first London season.

Some said it was the most brilliant season since the war, that things were getting into their stride again. Julia was at the centre of it. There were then remaining perhaps half a dozen London houses which could be called 'historic'; Marchmain House in St James's was one of them, and the ball given for Julia, in spite of the ignoble costume of the time, was by all accounts a splendid spectacle. Sebastian went down for it and half-heartedly suggested my coming with him; I refused and came to regret my refusal, for it was the last ball of its kind given there; the last of a splendid series.

How could I have known? There seemed time for everything in those days; the world was open to be explored at leisure. I was so full of Oxford that summer; London could wait, I thought.

The other great houses belonged to kinsmen or to childhood friends of Julia's, and besides them there were countless substantial houses in the squares of Mayfair and Belgravia, alight and thronged, one or other of them, night after night. Foreigners returning on post from their own waste lands wrote home that here they seemed to catch a glimpse of the world they had believed lost for ever among the mud and wire, and through those halcyon weeks Julia darted and shone, part of the sunshine between the trees, part of the candle-light in the mirror's spectrum, so that elderly men and women, sitting aside with their memories, saw her as herself the blue-bird. ' "Bridey" Marchmain's eldest girl,' they said. 'Pity he can't see her tonight.'

That night and the night after and the night after, wherever she went, always in her own little circle of intimates, she brought a moment of joy, such as strikes deep to the heart on the river's bank when the kingfisher suddenly flares across the water.

This was the creature, neither child nor woman, that drove me through the dusk that summer evening, untroubled by love, taken aback by the power of her own beauty, hesitating on the cool edge of life; one who had suddenly found herself armed, unawares; the heroine of a fairy story turning over in her hands the magic ring; she had only to stroke it with her fingertips and whisper the charmed word, for the earth to open at her feet and belch forth her titanic servant, the fawning monster who would bring her whatever she asked, but bring it, perhaps, in unwelcome shape.

She had no interest in me that evening; the jinn rumbled below us uncalled; she lived apart in a little world, within a little world, the innermost of a system of concentric spheres, like the ivory balls laboriously carved in China; a little problem troubling her mind – little, as she saw it, in abstract terms and symbols. She was wondering, dispassionately and leagues distant from reality, whom she should marry. Thus strategists hesitate over the map, the few pins and lines of coloured chalk, contemplating a change in the pins and lines, a matter of inches, which outside the room, out of sight of the studious officers, may engulf past, present, and future in ruin or life. She was a symbol to herself then, lacking the life of both child and woman; victory and defeat were changes of pin and line; she knew nothing of war.

'If only one lived abroad,' she thought, 'where these things are arranged between parents and lawyers.'

To be married, soon and splendidly, was the aim of all her friends. If she looked further than the wedding, it was to see marriage as the beginning of individual existence; the skirmish where one gained one's spurs, from which one set out on the true quests of life.

She outshone by far all the girls of her age, but she knew that, in that little world within a world which she inhabited, there were certain grave disabilities from which she suffered. On the sofas against the wall where the old people counted up the points, there were things against her. There was the scandal of her father; that slight, inherited stain upon her brightness that seemed deepened by something in her own way of life – waywardness and wilfulness, a less disciplined habit than most of her contemporaries'; but for that, who knows? ...

One subject eclipsed all others in importance for the ladies along the wall; who would the young princes marry? They could not hope for purer lineage or a more gracious presence than Julia's; but there was this faint shadow on her that unfitted her for the highest honours; there was also her religion.

Nothing could have been further from Julia's ambitions than a royal marriage. She knew, or thought she knew, what she wanted and it was not that. But wherever she turned, it seemed, her religion stood as a barrier between her and her natural goal.

As it seemed to her, the thing was a dead loss. If she apostatized now, having been brought up in the Church, she would go to hell, while the Protestant girls of her acquaintance, schooled in happy ignorance, could marry eldest sons, live at peace with their world, and get to heaven before her. There could be no eldest son for her, and younger sons were indelicate things, necessary, but not to be much spoken of. Younger sons had none of the privileges of obscurity; it was their plain duty to remain hidden until some disaster perchance promoted them to their brothers' places, and, since this was their function, it was desirable that they should keep themselves wholly suitable for succession. Perhaps in a family of three or four boys, a Catholic might get the youngest without opposition. There were of course the Catholics themselves, but these came seldom into the little world Julia had made for herself; those who did were her mother's kinsmen, who, to her, seemed grim and eccentric. Of the dozen or so rich and noble Catholic families, none at that time had an heir of the right age. Foreigners – there were many among her mother's family – were tricky about money, odd in their ways, and a sure mark of failure in the English girl who wed them. What was there left?

This was Julia's problem after her weeks of triumph in London. She knew it was not insurmountable. There must, she thought, be a number of people outside her own world who were well qualified to be drawn into it; the shame was that she must seek them. Not for her the cruel, delicate luxury of choice, the indolent, cat-and-mouse pastimes of the hearth-rug. No Penelope she; she must hunt in the forest.

She had made a preposterous little picture of the kind of man who would do: he was an English diplomat of great but not very virile beauty, now abroad, with a house smaller than Brideshead, nearer to London; he was old, thirty-two or -three, and had been recently and tragically widowed; Julia thought she would prefer a man a little subdued by earlier grief. He had a great career before him but had grown listless in his loneliness; she was not sure he was not in danger of falling into the hands of an unscrupulous foreign adventuress; he needed a new infusion of young life to carry him to the Embassy at Paris. While professing a mild agnosticism himself, he had a liking for the shows of religion and was perfectly agreeable to having his children brought up Catholic; he believed, however, in the prudent restriction of his family to two boys and a girl, comfortably spaced over twelve years, and did not demand, as a Catholic husband might, yearly pregnancies. He had twelve thousand a year above his pay, and no near relations. Someone like that would do, Julia thought, and she was in search of him when she met me at the railway station. I was not her man. She told me as much, without a word, when she took the cigarette from my lips.

All this I learned about Julia, bit by bit, as one does learn the former – as it seems at the time, the preparatory – life of a woman one loves, so that one thinks of oneself as having been part of it, directing it by devious ways, towards oneself.

Julia left Sebastian and me at Brideshead and went to stay with an aunt, Lady Rosscommon, in her villa at Cap Ferrat. All the way she pondered her problem. She had given a name to her widower-diplomat; she called him 'Eustace', and from that moment he became a figure of fun to her, a little interior, incommunicable joke, so that when at last such a man did cross her path – though he was not a diplomat but a wistful major in the Life Guards – and fall in love with her and offer her just those gifts she had chosen, she sent him away moodier and more wistful than ever; for by that time she had met Rex Mottram.

Rex's age was greatly in his favour, for among Julia's friends there was a kind of gerontophilic snobbery; young men were held to be gauche and pimply; it was thought very much more chic to be seen lunching alone at the Ritz – a thing, in any case, allowed to few girls of that day, to the tiny circle of Julia's intimates; a thing looked at askance by the elders who kept the score, chatting pleasantly against the walls of the ballrooms – at the table on the left as you came in, with a starched and wrinkled old roué whom your mother had been warned of as a girl, than in the centre of the room with a party of exuberant young bloods. Rex, indeed, was neither starched nor wrinkled; his seniors thought him a pushful young cad, but Julia recognized the unmistakable chic – the flavour of 'Max' and 'F.E.'

and the Prince of Wales, of the big table in the Sporting Club, the second magnum, and the fourth cigar, of the chauffeur kept waiting hour after hour without compunction – which her friends would envy. His social position was unique; it had an air of mystery, even of crime, about it; people said Rex went about armed. Julia and her friends had a fascinated abhorrence of what they called 'Pont Street'; they collected phrases that damned their user, and among themselves – and often, disconcertingly, in public – talked a language made up of them. It was 'Pont Street' to wear a signet ring and to give chocolates at the theatre; it was 'Pont Street' at a dance to say, 'Can I forage for you?' Whatever Rex might be, he was definitely not 'Pont Street'. He had stepped straight from the underworld into the world of Brenda Champion who was herself the innermost of a number of concentric ivory spheres. Perhaps Julia recognized in Brenda Champion an intimation of what she and her friends might be in twelve years' time; there was an antagonism between the girl and the woman that was hard to explain otherwise. Certainly the fact of his being Brenda Champion's property sharpened Julia's appetite for Rex.

Rex and Brenda Champion were staying at the next villa on Cap Ferrat, taken that year by a newspaper magnate and frequented by politicians. They would not normally have come within Lady Rosscommon's ambit, but, living so close, the parties mingled and at once Rex began warily to pay his court.

All that summer he had been feeling restless. Mrs Champion had proved a dead end; it had all been intensely exciting at first, but now the bonds had begun to chafe. Mrs Champion lived as, he found, the English seemed apt to do, in a little world within a little world; Rex demanded a wider horizon. He wanted to consolidate his gains; to strike the black ensign, go ashore, hang the cutlass up over the chimney, and think about the crops. It was time he married; he, too, was in search of a 'Eustace', but, living as he did, he met few girls. He knew of Julia; she was by all accounts top débutante, a suitable prize.

With Mrs Champion's cold eyes watching behind her sunglasses, there was little Rex could do at Cap Ferrat except establish a friendliness which could be widened later. He was never entirely alone with Julia, but he saw to it that she was included in most things they did; he taught her chemin-de-fer, he arranged that it was always in his car that they drove to Monte Carlo or Nice; he did enough to make Lady Rosscommon write to Lady Marchmain, and Mrs Champion move him, sooner than they had planned, to Antibes.

Julia went to Salzburg to join her mother.

'Aunt Fanny tells me you made great friends with Mr Mottram. I'm sure he can't be very nice.'

'I don't think he is,' said Julia. 'I don't know that I like nice people.'

There is proverbially a mystery among most men of new wealth, how they made their first ten thousand; it is the qualities they showed then, before they became bullies, when every man was someone to be placated, when only hope sustained them and they could count on nothing from the world but what could be charmed from it, that make them, if they survive their triumph, successful with women. Rex, in the comparative freedom of London, became abject to Julia; he planned his life about hers, going where he would meet her, ingratiating himself with those who could report well of him to her; he sat on a number of charitable committees in order to be near Lady Marchmain; he offered his services to Brideshead in getting him a seat in Parliament (but was there rebuffed); he expressed a keen interest in the Catholic Church until he found that this was no way to Julia's heart. He was always ready to drive her in his Hispano wherever she wanted to go; he took her and parties of her friends to ring-side seats at prize-fights and introduced them afterwards to the pugilists; and all the time he never once made love to her. From being agreeable, he became indispensable to her; from having been proud of him in public she became a little ashamed, but by that time, between Christmas and Easter, he had become indispensable. And then, without in the least expecting it, she suddenly found herself in love.

It came to her, this disturbing and unsought revelation, one evening in May, when Rex had told her he would be busy at the

House, and, driving by chance down Charles Street, she saw him leaving what she knew to be Brenda Champion's house. She was so hurt and angry that she could barely keep up appearances through dinner; as soon as she could, she went home and cried bitterly for ten minutes; then she felt hungry, wished she had eaten more at dinner, ordered some bread-and-milk, and went to bed saying: 'When Mr Mottram telephones in the morning, whatever time it is, say I am not to be disturbed.'

Next day she breakfasted in bed as usual, read the papers, telephoned to her friends. Finally she asked: 'Did Mr Mottram ring up by any chance?'

'Oh yes, my lady, four times. Shall I put him through when he rings again?'

'Yes. No. Say I've gone out.'

When she came downstairs there was a message for her on the hall table. *Mr Mottram expects Lady Julia at the Ritz at 1.30.* 'I shall lunch at home today,' she said.

That afternoon she went shopping with her mother; they had tea with an aunt and returned at six.

'Mr Mottram is waiting, my Lady. I've shown him into the library.'

'Oh, mummy, I can't be bothered with him. Do tell him to go home.'

'That's not at all kind, Julia. I've often said he's not my favourite among your friends, but I have grown quite used to him, almost to like him. You really mustn't take people up and drop them like this – particularly people like Mr Mottram.'

'Oh, mummy, *must* I see him? There'll be a scene if I do.'

'Nonsense, Julia, you twist that poor man round your finger.'

So Julia went into the library and came out an hour later engaged to be married.

'Oh, mummy, I warned you this would happen if I went in there.'

'You did nothing of the kind. You merely said there would be a scene. I never conceived of a scene of *this* kind.'

'Anyway, you do like him, mummy. You said so.'

'He has been very kind in a number of ways. I regard him as entirely unsuitable as your husband. So will everyone.'

'Damn everybody.'

'We know nothing about him. He may have black blood – in fact he is suspiciously dark. Darling, the whole thing's impossible. I can't see how you can have been so foolish.'

'Well, what right have I got otherwise to be angry with him if he goes with that horrible old woman? You make a great thing about rescuing fallen women. Well, I'm rescuing a fallen man for a change. I'm saving Rex from mortal sin.'

'Don't be irreverent, Julia.'

'Well, isn't it mortal sin to sleep with Brenda Champion?'

'Or indecent.'

'He's promised never to see her again. I couldn't ask him to do that unless I admitted I was in love with him could I?'

'Mrs Champion's morals, thank God, are not my business. Your happiness is. If you must know, I think Mr Mottram a kind and useful friend, but I wouldn't trust him an inch, and I'm sure he'll have very unpleasant children. They always revert. I've no doubt you'll regret the whole thing in a few days. Meanwhile *nothing is to be done*. No one must be told anything or allowed to suspect. You must stop lunching with him. You may see him here, of course, but nowhere in public. You had better send him to me and I will have a little talk to him about it.'

Thus began a year's secret engagement for Julia; a time of great stress, for Rex made love to her that afternoon for the first time; not, as had happened to her once or twice before with sentimental and uncertain boys, but with a passion that disclosed the corner of something like it in her. Their passion frightened her, and she came back from the confessional one day determined to put an end to it.

'Otherwise I must stop seeing you,' she said.

Rex was humble at once, just as he had been in the winter, day after day, when he used to wait for her in the cold in his big car.

'If only we could be married immediately,' she said.

For six weeks they remained at arm's length, kissing when they met and parted, sitting meantime at a distance, talking of what they would do and where they would live and of Rex's chances of an under-secretaryship. Julia was content, deep in love, living in the future. Then, just before the end of the session, she learned that Rex had been staying the week-end with a stockbroker at Sunningdale, when he said he was at his constituency, and that Mrs Champion had been there, too.

On the evening she heard of this, when Rex came as usual to Marchmain House, they re-enacted the scene of two months before.

'What do you expect?' he said. 'What right have you to ask so much, when you give so little?'

She took her problem to Farm Street and propounded it in general terms, not in the confessional, but in a dark little parlour kept for such interviews.

'Surely, Father, it can't be wrong to commit a small sin myself in order to keep him from a much worse one?'

But the gentle old Jesuit was unyielding. She barely listened to him; he was refusing her what she wanted, that was all she needed to know.

When he had finished he said, 'Now you had better make your confession.'

'No, thank you,' she said, as though refusing the offer of something in a shop. 'I don't think I want to today,' and walked angrily home.

From that moment she shut her mind against her religion.

And Lady Marchmain saw this and added it to her new grief for Sebastian and her old grief for her husband and to the deadly sickness in her body, and took all these sorrows with her daily to church; it seemed her heart was transfixed with the swords of her dolours, a living heart to match the plaster and paint; what comfort she took home with her, God knows.

So the year wore on and the secret of the engagement spread from Julia's confidantes to their confidantes, until, like ripples at last breaking on the mud-verge, there were hints of it in the

Press, and Lady Rosscommon as Lady-in-Waiting was closely questioned about it, and something had to be done. Then, after Julia had refused to make her Christmas communion and Lady Marchmain had found herself betrayed first by me, then by Mr Samgrass, then by Cordelia, in the first grey days of 1925, she decided to act. She forbade all talk of an engagement; she forbade Julia and Rex ever to meet; she made plans for shutting Marchmain House for six months and taking Julia on a tour of visits to their foreign kinsmen. It was characteristic of an old, atavistic callousness that went with her delicacy that, even at this crisis, she did not think it unreasonable to put Sebastian in Rex's charge on the journey to Dr Borethus, and Rex, having failed her in that matter, went on to Monte Carlo, where he completed her rout. Lord Marchmain did not concern himself with the finer points of Rex's character; those, he believed, were his daughter's business. Rex seemed a rough, healthy, prosperous fellow whose name was already familiar to him from reading the political reports; he gambled in an open-handed but sensible manner; he seemed to keep reasonably good company; he had a future; Lady Marchmain disliked him. Lord Marchmain was, on the whole, relieved that Julia should have chosen so well, and gave his consent to an immediate marriage.

Rex gave himself to the preparations with gusto. He bought her a ring, not, as she expected, from a tray at Cartier's, but in a back room in Hatton Garden from a man who brought stones out of a safe in little bags and displayed them for her on a writing-desk; then another man in another back room made designs for the setting with a stub of pencil on a sheet of note-paper, and the result excited the admiration of all her friends.

'How d'you know about these things, Rex?' she asked.

She was daily surprised by the things he knew and the things he did not know; both, at the time, added to his attraction.

His present house in Hertford Street was large enough for them both, and had lately been furnished and decorated by the most expensive firm. Julia said she did not want a house in the country yet; they could always take places furnished when they wanted to go away.

There was trouble about the marriage settlement with which Julia refused to interest herself. The lawyers were in despair. Rex absolutely refused to settle any capital. 'What do I want with trustee stock?' he asked.

'I don't know, darling.'

'I make money work for me,' he said. 'I expect fifteen, twenty per cent and I get it. It's pure waste tying up capital at three and a half.'

'I'm sure it is, darling.'

'These fellows talk as though I were trying to rob you. It's *they* who are doing the robbing. They want to rob you of two-thirds of the income I can make you.'

'Does it matter, Rex? We've got heaps, haven't we?'

Rex hoped to have the whole of Julia's dowry in his hands, to make it work for him. The lawyers insisted on tying it up, but they could not get, as they asked, a like sum from him. Finally, grudgingly, he agreed to insure his life, after explaining at length to the lawyers that this was merely a device for putting part of his legitimate profits into other people's pockets; but he had some connexion with an insurance office which made the arrangement slightly less painful to him, by which he took for himself the agent's commission which the lawyers were them-selves expecting.

Last and least came the question of Rex's religion. He had once attended a royal wedding in Madrid, and he wanted something of the kind for himself.

'That's one thing your Church can do,' he said, 'put on a good show. You never saw anything to equal the cardinals. How many do you have in England?'

'Only one, darling.'

'Only *one*? Can we hire some others from abroad?'

It was then explained to him that a mixed marriage was a very unostentatious affair.

'How d'you mean "mixed"? I'm not a nigger or anything.'

'No, darling, between a Catholic and a Protestant.'

'Oh, *that*? Well, if that's all, it's soon unmixed. I'll become a Catholic. What does one have to do?'

Lady Marchmain was dismayed and perplexed by this new development; it was no good her telling herself that in charity she must assume his good faith; it brought back memories of another courtship and another conversion.

'Rex,' she said. 'I sometimes wonder if you realize how big a thing you are taking on in the Faith. It would be very wicked to take a step like this without believing sincerely.'

He was masterly in his treatment of her.

'I don't pretend to be a very devout man,' he said, 'nor much of a theologian, but I know it's a bad plan to have two religions in one house. A man needs a religion. If your Church is good enough for Julia, it's good enough for me.'

'Very well,' she said, 'I will see about having you instructed.'

'Look, Lady Marchmain, I haven't the time. Instruction will be wasted on me. Just you give me the form and I'll sign on the dotted line.'

'It usually takes some months – often a lifetime.'

'Well, I'm a quick learner. Try me.'

So Rex was sent to Farm Street to Father Mowbray, a priest renowned for his triumphs with obdurate catechumens. After the third interview he came to tea with Lady Marchmain.

'Well, how do you find my future son-in-law?'

'He's the most difficult convert I have ever met.'

'Oh dear, I thought he was going to make it so easy.'

'That's exactly it. I can't get anywhere near him. He doesn't seem to have the least intellectual curiosity or natural piety.

'The first day I wanted to find out what sort of religious life he had till now, so I asked him what he meant by prayer. He said: "*I* don't mean anything. *You tell me*." I tried to, in a few words, and he said: "Right. So much for prayer. What's the next thing?" I gave him the catechism to take away. Yesterday I asked him whether Our Lord had more than one nature. He said: "Just as many as you say, Father."

'Then again I asked him: "Supposing the Pope looked up and saw a cloud and said 'It's going to rain', would that be bound to happen?" "Oh, yes, Father." "But supposing it didn't?" He thought a moment and said, "I suppose it would be sort of raining spiritually, only we were too sinful to see it."

'Lady Marchmain, he doesn't correspond to any degree of paganism known to the missionaries.'

'Julia,' said Lady Marchmain, when the priest had gone, 'are you sure that Rex isn't doing this thing purely with the idea of pleasing us?'

'I don't think it enters his head,' said Julia.

'He's really sincere in his conversion?'

'He's absolutely determined to become a Catholic, mummy,' and to herself she said: 'In her long history the Church must have had some pretty queer converts. I don't suppose all Clovis's army were exactly Catholic-minded. One more won't hurt.'

Next week the Jesuit came to tea again. It was the Easter holidays and Cordelia was there, too.

'Lady Marchmain,' he said. 'You should have chosen one of the younger fathers for this task. I shall be dead long before Rex is a Catholic.'

'Oh dear, I thought it was going so well.'

'It was, in a sense. He was exceptionally docile, said he accepted everything I told him, remembered bits of it, asked no questions. I wasn't happy about him. He seemed to have no sense of reality, but I knew he was coming under a steady Catholic influence, so I was willing to receive him. One has to take a chance sometimes – with semi-imbeciles, for instance. You never know quite how much they have understood. As long as you know there's someone to keep an eye on them, you *do* take the chance.'

'How I wish Rex could hear this!' said Cordelia.

'But yesterday I got a regular eye-opener. The trouble with modern education is you never know how ignorant people are. With anyone over fifty you can be fairly confident what's been taught and what's been left out. But these young people have such an intelligent, knowledgeable surface, and then the crust suddenly breaks and you look down into the depths of confusion you didn't know existed. Take yesterday. He seemed to be doing very well. He learned large bits of the catechism by heart, and the Lord's Prayer, and the Hail Mary. Then I asked him as usual if there was anything troubling him, and he looked at me in a crafty way and said, "Look, Father, I don't think you're being straight with me. I want to join your Church and I'm going to join your Church, but you're holding too much back." I asked what he meant, and he said: "I've had a long talk with a Catholic – a very pious, well-educated one, and I've learned a thing or two. For instance, that you have to sleep with your feet pointing East because that's the direction of heaven, and if you die in the night you can walk there. Now I'll sleep with my feet pointing any way that suits Julia, but d'you expect a grown man to believe about walking to heaven? And what about the Pope who made one of his horses a Cardinal? And what about the box you keep in the church porch, and if you put in a pound note with someone's name on it, they get sent to hell. I don't say there mayn't be a good reason for all this," he said, "but you ought to tell me about it and not let me find out for myself." '

'What *can* the poor man have meant?' said Lady Marchmain.

'You see he's a long way from the Church yet,' said Father Mowbray.

'But who can he have been talking to? Did he dream it all? Cordelia, what's the matter?'

'What a chump! Oh, mummy, what a glorious chump!'

'Cordelia, it was *you*.'

'Oh, mummy, who could have dreamed he'd swallow it? I told him such a lot besides. About the sacred monkeys in the Vatican – all kinds of things.'

'Well, you've very considerably increased *my* work,' said Father Mowbray.

'Poor Rex,' said Lady Marchmain. 'You know, I think it makes him rather lovable. You must treat him like an idiot child, Father Mowbray.'

So the instruction was continued, and Father Mowbray at length consented to receive Rex a week before his wedding.

'You'd think they'd be all over themselves to have me in,' Rex complained. 'I can be a lot of help to them one way and another; instead they're like the chaps who issue cards for a casino. What's more,' he added, 'Cordelia's got me so muddled I don't know what's in the catechism and what she's invented.'

Thus things stood three weeks before the wedding; the cards had gone out, presents were coming in fast, the bridesmaids were delighted with their dresses. Then came what Julia called 'Bridey's bombshell'.

With characteristic ruthlessness he tossed his load of explosive without warning into what, till then, had been a happy family party. The library at Marchmain House was being devoted to wedding presents; Lady Marchmain, Julia, Cordelia, and Rex were busy unpacking and listing them. Brideshead came in and watched them for a moment.

'Chinky vases from Aunt Betty,' said Cordelia. 'Old stuff. I remember them on the stairs at Buckborne.'

'What's all this?' asked Brideshead.

'Mr, Mrs, *and* Miss Pendle-Garthwaite, one early morning tea set. Goode's, thirty shillings, jolly mean.'

'You'd better pack all that stuff up again.'

'Bridey, what *do* you mean?'

'Only that the wedding's off.'

'*Bridey.*'

'I thought I'd better make some inquiries about my prospective brother-in-law, as no one else seemed interested,' said Brideshead. 'I got the final answer tonight. He was married in Montreal in 1915 to a Miss Sarah Evangeline Cutler, who is still living there.'

'Rex, is this true?'

Rex stood with a jade dragon in his hand looking at it critically; then he set it carefully on its ebony stand and smiled openly and innocently at them all.

'Sure it's true,' he said. 'What about it? What are you all looking so het up about? She isn't a thing to me. She never meant any good. I was only a kid, anyhow. The sort of mistake anyone might make. I got my divorce back in 1919. I didn't even know where she was living till Bridey here told me. What's all the rumpus?'

'You might have told me,' said Julia.

'You never asked. Honest, I've not given her a thought in years.'

His sincerity was so plain that they had to sit down and talk about it calmly.

'Don't you realize, you poor sweet oaf,' said Julia, 'that you can't get married as a Catholic when you've another wife alive?'

'But I *haven't*. Didn't I just tell you we were divorced six years ago.'

'But you *can't* be divorced as a Catholic.'

'I wasn't a Catholic and I was divorced. I've got the papers somewhere.'

'But didn't Father Mowbray explain to you about marriage?'

'He said I wasn't to be divorced from you. Well, I don't want to be. I can't remember all he told me – sacred monkeys, plenary indulgences, four last things – if I remembered all he told me I shouldn't have time for anything else. Anyhow, what about your Italian cousin, Francesca? – she married twice.'

'She had an annulment.'

'All right then, I'll get an annulment. What does it cost? Who do I get it from? Has Father Mowbray got one? I only want to do what's right. Nobody told me.'

It was a long time before Rex could be convinced of the existence of a serious impediment to his marriage. The discussion took them to dinner, lay dormant in the presence of the servants, started again as soon as they were alone, and lasted long after midnight. Up, down, and round the argument circled and swooped like a gull, now out to sea, out of sight, cloud-bound, among irrelevances and repetitions, now right on the patch where the offal floated.

'What d'you want me to do? Who should I see?' Rex kept asking. 'Don't tell me there isn't someone who can fix this.'

'There's nothing to do, Rex,' said Brideshead. 'It simply means your marriage can't take place. I'm sorry from every-one's point of view that it's come so suddenly. You ought to have told us yourself.'

'Look,' said Rex. 'Maybe what you say is right; maybe strictly by law I shouldn't get married in your cathedral. But the cathedral is booked; no one there is asking any questions; the Cardinal knows nothing about it; Father Mowbray knows nothing about it. Nobody except us knows a thing. So why make a lot of trouble? Just stay mum and let the thing go through, as if nothing had happened. Who loses anything by that? Maybe I risk going to hell. Well, I'll risk it. What's it got to do with anyone else?'

'Why not?' said Julia. 'I don't believe these priests know everything. I don't believe in hell for things like that. I don't know that I believe in it for anything. Anyway, that's our look out. We're not asking you to risk your souls. Just keep away.'

'Julia, I hate you,' said Cordelia, and left the room.

'We're all tired,' said Lady Marchmain. 'If there was anything to say, I'd suggest our discussing it in the morning.'

'But there's nothing to discuss,' said Brideshead, 'except what is the least offensive way we can close the whole incident. Mother and I will decide that. We must put a notice in *The Times* and the *Morning Post*; the presents will have to go back. I don't know what is usual about the bridesmaids' dresses.'

'Just a moment,' said Rex. 'Just a moment. Maybe you can stop us marrying in your Cathedral. All right, to hell, we'll be married in a Protestant church.'

'I can stop that, too,' said Lady Marchmain.

'But I don't think you will, mummy,' said Julia. 'You see, I've been Rex's mistress for some time now, and I shall go on being, married or not.'

'Rex, is this true?'

'No damn it, it's not,' said Rex. 'I wish it were.'

'I see we *shall* have to discuss it all again in the morning,' said Lady Marchmain faintly. 'I can't go on any more now.'

And she needed her son's help up the stairs.

'What on earth made you tell your mother that?' I asked, when, years later, Julia described the scene to me.

'That's exactly what Rex wanted to know. I suppose because

I thought it was true. Not literally – though you must remember I was only twenty, and no one really knows the "facts of life" by being told them – but, of course, I didn't mean it was true literally. I didn't know how else to express it. I meant I was much too deep with Rex just to be able to say "the marriage arranged will not now take place", and leave it at that. I wanted to be made an honest woman. I've been wanting it ever since – come to think of it.'

'And then?'

'And then the talks went on and on. Poor mummy. And priests came into it and aunts came into it. There were all kinds of suggestions – that Rex should go to Canada, that Father Mowbray should go to Rome and see if there were any possible grounds for an annulment; that I should go abroad for a year. In the middle of it Rex just telegraphed to papa: "Julia and I prefer wedding ceremony take place by Protestant rites. Have you any objection?" He answered, "Delighted", and that settled the matter as far as mummy stopping us legally went. There was a lot of personal appeal after that. I was sent to talk to priests and nuns and aunts. Rex just went on quietly – or fairly quietly – with the plans.

'Oh, Charles, what a squalid wedding! The Savoy Chapel was the place where divorced couples got married in those days – a poky little place not at all what Rex had intended. I wanted just to slip into a registry office one morning and get the thing over with a couple of charwomen as witnesses, but nothing else would do but Rex had to have bridesmaids and orange-blossom and the Wedding March. It was gruesome.

'Poor mummy behaved like a martyr and insisted on my having her lace in spite of everything. Well, she more or less had to – the dress had been planned round it. My own friends came, of course, and the curious accomplices Rex called *his* friends; the rest of the party were very oddly assorted. None of mummy's family came, of course; one or two of papa's. All the stuffy people stayed away – you know, the Anchorages and Chasms and Vanbrughs – and I thought, "Thank God for that, they always look down their noses at me, anyhow," but Rex was furious, because it was just them he wanted apparently.

'I hoped at one moment there'd be no party at all. Mummy said we couldn't use Marchers, and Rex wanted to telegraph papa and invade the place with an army of caterers headed by the family solicitor. In the end it was decided to have a party the evening before at home to see the presents – apparently that was all right according to Father Mowbray. Well, no one can ever resist going to see her own present, so that was quite a success, but the reception Rex gave next day at the Savoy for the wedding guests was very squalid.

'There was great awkwardness about the tenants. In the end Bridey went down and gave them a dinner and bonfire there which wasn't at all what they expected in return for their silver soup tureen.

'Poor Cordelia took it hardest. She had looked forward so much to being my bridesmaid – it was a thing we used to talk about long before I came out – and of course she was a very pious child, too. At first she wouldn't speak to me. Then on the morning of the wedding – I'd moved to Aunt Fanny Rosscommon's the evening before; it was thought more suitable – she came bursting in before I was up, straight from Farm Street, in floods of tears, begged me not to marry, then hugged me, gave me a dear little brooch she'd bought, and said she prayed I'd always be happy. *Always happy*, Charles!

'It was an awfully unpopular wedding, you know. Everyone took mummy's side, as everyone always did – not that she got any benefit from it. All through her life mummy had all the sympathy of everyone except those she loved. They all said I'd behaved abominably to her. In fact, poor Rex found he'd married an outcast, which was exactly the opposite of all he'd wanted.

'So you see things never looked like going right. There was a hoodoo on us from the start. But I was still nuts about Rex.

'Funny to think of, isn't it?

'You know Father Mowbray hit on the truth about Rex at once, that it took me a year of marriage to see. He simply wasn't all there. He wasn't a complete human being at all. He was a tiny bit of one, unnaturally developed; something in a bottle, an organ kept alive in a laboratory. I thought he was a sort of primitive savage, but he was something absolutely modern and up-to-date that only this ghastly age could produce. A tiny bit of a man pretending he was the whole.

'Well, it's all over now.'

It was ten years later that she said this to me in a storm in the Atlantic.

CHAPTER III

I RETURNED to London in the spring of 1926 for the General Strike.

It was the topic of Paris. The French, exultant as always at the discomfiture of their former friends, and transposing into their own precise terms our mistier notions from across the Channel, foretold revolution and civil war. Every evening the kiosks displayed texts of doom, and, in the cafés, acquaintances greeted one half-derisively with: 'Ha, my friend, you are better off here than at home, are you not?' until I and several friends in circumstances like my own came seriously to believe that our country was in danger and that our duty lay there. We were joined by a Belgian Futurist, who lived under the, I think, assumed name of Jean de Brissac la Motte, and claimed the right to bear arms in any battle anywhere against the lower classes.

We crossed together, in a high-spirited, male party, expecting to find unfolding before us at Dover the history so often repeated of late, with so few variations, from all parts of Europe, that I, at any rate, had formed in my mind a clear, composite picture of 'Revolution' – the red flag on the post office, the overturned tram, the drunken N.C.O.s, the gaol open and gangs of released criminals prowling the streets, the train from the capital that did not arrive. One had read it in the papers, seen it in the films, heard it at café tables again and again for six or seven years now, till it had become part of one's experience, at second hand, like the mud of Flanders and the flies of Mesopotamia.

Then we landed and met the old routine of the customs-
sheds, the punctual boat-train, the porters lining the platform
at Victoria and converging on the first-class carriages; the long
line of waiting taxis.

'We'll separate,' we said, 'and see what's happening. We'll
meet and compare notes at dinner,' but we knew already in our
hearts that nothing was happening; nothing, at any rate, which
needed our presence.

'Oh dear,' said my father, meeting me by chance on the
stairs, 'how delightful to see you again so soon.' (I had been
abroad fifteen months.) 'You've come at a very awkward time,
you know. They're having another of those strikes in two days –
such a lot of nonsense – and I don't know when you'll be able to
get away.'

I thought of the evening I was forgoing, with the lights
coming out along the banks of the Seine, and the company I
should have had there – for I was at the time concerned with
two emancipated American girls who shared a *garçonnière* in
Auteuil – and wished I had not come.

We dined that night at the Café Royal. There things were a
little more warlike, for the Café was full of undergraduates who
had come down for 'National Service'. One group, from
Cambridge, had that afternoon signed on to run messages for
Transport House, and their table backed on another group's,
who were enrolled as special constables. Now and then one or
other party would shout provocatively over the shoulder, but it
is hard to come into serious conflict back to back, and the affair
ended with their giving each other tall glasses of lager beer.

'You should have been in Budapest when Horthy marched
in,' said Jean. '*That* was politics.'

A party was being given that night in Regent's Park for the
'Black Birds' who had newly arrived in England. One of us had
been asked and thither we all went.

To us, who frequented Bricktop's and the Bal Nègre in the
Rue Blomet, there was nothing particularly remarkable in the
spectacle; I was scarcely inside the door when I heard an unmistakable voice, an echo from what now seemed a distant past.

'*No*,' it said, 'they are not animals in a *zoo*, Mulcaster, to be *goggled at*. They are *artists*, my dear, very great artists, to be *revered*.'

Anthony Blanche and Boy Mulcaster were at the table where the wine stood.

'Thank God here's someone I know,' said Mulcaster, as I joined them. 'Girl brought me. Can't see her anywhere.'

'She's given you the *slip*, my dear, and do you know why? Because you look ridiculously *out of place*, Mulcaster. It isn't your kind of party at all; you ought not to be here; you ought to go away, you know, to the Old Hundredth or some lugubrious dance in Belgrave Square.'

'Just come from one,' said Mulcaster. 'Too early for the Old Hundredth. I'll stay on a bit. Things may cheer up.'

'I spit on you,' said Anthony. 'Let me talk to *you*, Charles.'

We took a bottle and our glasses and found a corner in another room. At our feet five members of the 'Black Birds' orchestra squatted on their heels and threw dice.

'*That* one,' said Anthony, 'the rather *pale* one, my dear, conked Mrs Arnold Frickheimer the other morning on the *nut*, my dear, with a bottle of milk.'

Almost immediately, inevitably, we began to talk of Sebastian.

'My dear, he's such a *sot*. He came to live with me in Marseille last year when you threw him over, and really it was as much as I could stand. Sip, sip, sip like a dowager all day long. And so *sly*. I was always missing little things, my dear, things I rather liked; once I lost two suits that had arrived from Lesley and Roberts that morning. Of course, I didn't *know* it was Sebastian – there were some rather queer fish, my dear, in and out of my little apartment. Who knows better than you my taste for queer fish? Well, eventually, my dear, we found the pawnshop where Sebastian was p-p-popping them and *then* he hadn't got the tickets; there was a market for them, too, at the bistro.

'I can see that puritanical, disapproving look in your eye, dear Charles, as though you thought I had led the boy on. It's

one of Sebastian's less lovable qualities that he always gives the
impression of being l-l-led on – like a little horse at a circus. But
I assure you I did everything. I said to him again and again,
"Why drink? If you want to be intoxicated there are so many
much more delicious things." I took him to quite the best man;
well, you know him as well as I do, Nada Alopov and Jean
Luxmore and *everyone we know* has been to him for years – he's
always in the Regina Bar – and then we had trouble over that
because Sebastian gave him a bad cheque – a *s-s-stumer*, my dear
– and a whole lot of very menacing men came round to the flat –
thugs, my dear – and Sebastian was making no sense at the time
and it was all most unpleasant.'

Boy Mulcaster wandered towards us and sat down, without
encouragement, by my side.

'Drink running short in there,' he said, helping himself from
our bottle and emptying it. 'Not a soul in the place I ever set
eyes on before – all black fellows.'

Anthony ignored him and continued: 'So then we left
Marseille and went to Tangier, and *there*, my dear, Sebastian
took up with his *new* friend. How can I describe him? He is like
the footman in *Warning Shadows* – a great clod of a German
who'd been in the Foreign Legion. He got out by shooting off
his great toe. It hadn't healed yet. Sebastian found him,
starving as tout to one of the houses in the Kasbah, and brought
him to stay with us. It was *too* macabre. So back I came, my
dear, to good old England – *Good old England*,' he repeated,
embracing with a flourish of his hand the Negroes gambling at
our feet, Mulcaster staring blankly before him, and our hostess
who, in pyjamas, now introduced herself to us.

'Never seen you before,' she said. 'Never asked you. Who are
all this white trash, anyway? Seems to me I must be in the
wrong house.'

'A time of national emergency,' said Mulcaster. 'Anything
may happen.'

'Is the party going well?' she asked anxiously. 'D'you think
Florence Mills would sing? We've met before,' she added to
Anthony.

'Often, my dear, but you never asked me tonight.'

'Oh dear, perhaps I don't like you. I thought I liked everyone.'

'Do you think,' asked Mulcaster, when our hostess had left us, 'that it might be witty to give the fire alarm?'

'Yes, Boy, run away and ring it.'

'Might cheer things up, I mean.'

'Exactly.'

So Mulcaster left us in search of the telephone.

'I think Sebastian and his lame chum went to French Morocco,' continued Anthony. 'They were in trouble with the Tangier police when I left them. The Marchioness has been a positive pest ever since I came to London, trying to make me get into touch with them. What a time that poor woman's having! It only shows there's some justice in life.'

Presently Miss Mills began to sing and everyone, except the crap players, crowded to the next room.

'That's my girl,' said Mulcaster. 'Over there with that black fellow. That's the girl who brought me.'

'She seems to have forgotten you now.'

'Yes. I wish I hadn't come. Let's go somewhere.'

Two fire engines drove up as we left and a host of helmeted figures joined the throng upstairs.

'That chap, Blanche,' said Mulcaster, '*not* a good fellow. I put him in Mercury once.'

We went to a number of night clubs. In two years Mulcaster seemed to have attained his simple ambition of being known and liked in such places. At the last of them he and I were kindled by a great flame of patriotism.

'You and I,' he said, 'were too young to fight in the war. Other chaps fought, millions of them dead. Not us. We'll show them. We'll show the dead chaps we can fight, too.'

'That's why I'm here,' I said. 'Come from overseas, rallying to old country in hour of need.'

'Like Australians.'

'Like the poor dead Australians.'

'What you in?'

'Nothing yet. War not ready.'

'Only one thing to join – Bill Meadows' show – Defence Corps. All good chaps. Being fixed in Bratt's.'

'I'll join.'

'You remember Bratt's?'

'No. I'll join that, too.'

'That's right. All good chaps like the dead chaps.'

So I joined Bill Meadows' show, which was a flying squad, protecting food deliveries in the poorest parts of London. First I was enrolled in the Defence Corps, took an oath of loyalty, and was given a helmet and truncheon; then I was put up for Bratt's Club and, with a number of other recruits, elected at a committee meeting specially called for the occasion. For a week we sat under orders in Bratt's, and thrice a day we drove out in a lorry at the head of a convoy of milk vans. We were jeered at and sometimes pelted with muck, but only once did we go into action.

We were sitting round after luncheon that day when Bill Meadows came back from the telephone in high spirits.

'Come on,' he said. 'There's a perfectly good battle in the Commercial Road.'

We drove at great speed and arrived to find a steel hawser stretched between lamp posts, an overturned truck and a policeman, alone on the pavement, being kicked by half a dozen youths. On either side of this centre of disturbance, and at a little distance from it, two opposing parties had formed. Near us, as we disembarked, a second policeman was sitting on the pavement, dazed, with his head in his hands and blood running through his fingers; two or three sympathizers were standing over him; on the other side of the hawser was a hostile knot of young dockers. We charged in cheerfully, relieved the police-man, and were just falling upon the main body of the enemy when we came into collision with a party of local clergy and town councillors who arrived simultaneously by another route to try persuasion. They were our only victims, for just as they went down there was a cry of 'Look out. The coppers,' and a lorry-load of police drew up in our rear.

The crowd broke and disappeared. We picked up the peacemakers (only one of whom was seriously hurt), patrolled some of the side streets looking for trouble and finding none, and at length returned to Bratt's. Next day the General Strike was called off and the country everywhere, except in the coal fields, returned to normal. It was as though a beast long fabled for its ferocity had emerged for an hour, scented danger, and slunk back to its lair. It had not been worth leaving Paris.

Jean, who joined another company, had a pot of ferns dropped on his head by an elderly widow in Camden Town and was in hospital for a week.

It was through my membership of Bill Meadows' squad that Julia learned I was in England. She telephoned to say her mother was anxious to see me.

'You'll find her terribly ill,' she said.

I went to Marchmain House on the first morning of peace. Sir Adrian Porson passed me in the hall, leaving, as I arrived; he held a bandanna handkerchief to his face and felt blindly for his hat and stick; he was in tears.

I was shown into the library and in less than a minute Julia joined me. She shook hands with a gentleness and gravity that were unfamiliar; in the gloom of that room she seemed a ghost.

'It's sweet of you to come. Mummy has kept asking for you, but I don't know if she'll be able to see you now, after all. She's just said "good-bye" to Adrian Porson and it's tired her.'

'Good-bye?'

'Yes. She's dying. She may live a week or two or she may go at any minute. She's so weak. I'll go and ask nurse.'

The stillness of death seemed in the house already. No one ever sat in the library at Marchmain House. It was the one ugly room in either of their houses. The bookcases of Victorian oak held volumes of Hansard and obsolete encyclopedias that were never opened; the bare mahogany table seemed set for the meeting of a committee; the place had the air of being both public and unfrequented; outside lay the forecourt, the railings, the quiet cul-de-sac.

Presently Julia returned.

'No, I'm afraid you can't see her. She's asleep. She may lie like that for hours; I can tell you what she wanted. Let's go somewhere else. I hate this room.'

We went across the hall to the small drawing-room where luncheon parties used to assemble, and sat on either side of the fireplace. Julia seemed to reflect the crimson and gold of the walls and lose some of her warmness.

'First, I know, mummy wanted to say how sorry she is she was so beastly to you last time you met. She's spoken of it often. She knows now she was wrong about you. I'm quite sure you understood and put it out of your mind immediately, but it's the kind of thing mummy can never forgive *herself* – it's the kind of thing she so seldom did.'

'Do tell her I understood completely.'

'The other thing, of course, you have guessed – Sebastian. She wants him. I don't know if that's possible. Is it?'

'I hear he's in a very bad way.'

'We heard that, too. We cabled to the last address we had, but there was no answer. There still may be time for him to see her. I thought of you as the only hope, as soon as I heard you were in England. Will you try and get him? It's an awful lot to ask, but I think Sebastian would want it, too, if he realized.'

'I'll try.'

'There's no one else we can ask. Rex is so busy.'

'Yes. I heard reports of all he's been doing organizing the gas works.'

'Oh yes,' Julia said with a touch of her old dryness. 'He's made a lot of kudos out of the strike.'

Then we talked for a few minutes about the Bratt's squad. She told me Brideshead had refused to take any public service because he was not satisfied with the justice of the cause; Cordelia was in London, in bed now, as she had been watching by her mother all night. I told her I had taken up architectural painting and that I enjoyed it. All this talk was nothing; we had said all we had to say in the first two minutes; I stayed for tea and then left her.

Air France ran a service of a kind to Casablanca; there I took
the bus to Fez, starting at dawn and arriving in the new town at
evening. I telephoned from the hotel to the British Consul and
dined with him that evening, in his charming house by the walls
of the old town. He was a kind, serious man.

'I'm delighted someone has come to look after young Flyte at
last,' he said. 'He's been something of a thorn in our sides here.
This is no place for a remittance man. The French don't
understand him at all. They think everyone who's not engaged
in trade is a spy. It's not as though he lived like a Milord.
Things aren't easy here. There's war going on not thirty miles
from this house, though you might not think it. We had some
young fools on bicycles only last week who'd come to volunteer
for Abdul Krim's army.

'Then the Moors are a tricky lot; they don't hold with drink
and our young friend, as you may know, spends most of his day
drinking. What does he want to come here for? There's plenty of
room for him at Rabat or Tangier, where they cater for tourists.
He's taken a house in the native town, you know. I tried to stop
him, but he got it from a Frenchman in the Department of Arts.
I don't say there's any harm in him, but he's an anxiety. There's
an awful fellow sponging on him – a German out of the Foreign
Legion. A thoroughly bad hat by all accounts. There's bound to
be trouble.

'Mind you, I *like* Flyte. I don't see much of him. He used to
come here for baths until he got fixed up at his house. He was
always perfectly charming, and my wife took a great fancy to
him. What he needs is occupation.'

I explained my errand.

'You'll probably find him at home now. Goodness knows
there's nowhere to go in the evenings in the old town. If you like
I'll send the porter to show you the way.'

So I set out after dinner, with the consular porter going
ahead lantern in hand. Morocco was a new and strange country
to me. Driving that day, mile after mile, up the smooth,
strategic road, past the vineyards and military posts and the
new, white settlements and the early crops already standing

high in the vast, open fields, and the hoardings advertising the
staples of France – Dubonnet, Michelin, Magasin du Louvre – I
had thought it all very suburban and up-to-date; now, under
the stars, in the walled city, whose streets were gentle, dusty
stairways, and whose walls rose windowless on either side,
closed overhead, then opened again to the stars; where the dust
lay thick among the smooth paving-stones and figures passed
silently, robed in white, on soft slippers or hard, bare soles;
where the air was scented with cloves and incense and wood
smoke – now I knew what had drawn Sebastian here and held
him so long.

The consular porter strode arrogantly ahead with his light
swinging and his tall cane banging; sometimes an open doorway
revealed a silent group seated in golden lamplight round a
brazier.

'Very dirty peoples,' the porter said scornfully, over his
shoulder. 'No education. French leave them dirty. Not like
British peoples. My peoples,' he said, 'always very British
peoples.'

For he was from the Sudan Police, and regarded this ancient
centre of his culture as a New Zealander might regard Rome.

At length we came to the last of many studded doors, and the
porter beat on it with his stick.

'British Lord's house,' he said.

Lamplight and a dark face appeared at the grating. The
consular porter spoke peremptorily; bolts were withdrawn and
we entered a small courtyard with a well in its centre and a vine
trained overhead.

'I wait here,' said the porter. 'You go with this native fellow.'

I entered the house; down a step and into the living-room I
found a gramophone, an oil-stove and, between them, a young
man. Later, when I looked about me, I noticed other, more
agreeable things – the rugs on the floor, the embroidered silk on
the walls, the carved and painted beams of the ceiling, the
heavy, pierced lamp that hung from a chain and cast soft
shadows of its own tracery about the room. But on first entering
these three things, the gramophone for its noise – it was playing

a French record of a jazz band – the stove for its smell, and the young man for his wolfish look, struck my senses. He was lolling in a basket chair, with a bandaged foot stuck forward on a box; he was dressed in a kind of thin, mid-European imitation tweed with a tennis shirt open at the neck; the unwounded foot wore a brown canvas shoe. There was a brass tray by his side on wooden legs, and on it were two beer bottles, a dirty plate, and a saucer full of cigarette ends; he held a glass of beer in his hand and a cigarette lay on his lower lip and stuck there when he spoke. He had long fair hair combed back without a parting and a face that was unnaturally lined for a man of his obvious youth; one of his front teeth was missing, so that his sibilants came sometimes with a lisp, sometimes with a disconcerting whistle, which he covered with a giggle; the teeth he had were stained with tobacco and set far apart.

This was plainly the 'thoroughly bad hat' of the consul's description, the film footman of Anthony's.

'I'm looking for Sebastian Flyte. This is his house, is it not?' I spoke loudly to make myself heard above the dance music, but he answered softly in English fluent enough to suggest that it was now habitual to him.

'Yeth. But he isn't here. There's no one but me.'

'I've come from England to see him on important business. Can you tell me where I can find him?'

The record came to its end. The German turned it over, wound up the machine, and started it playing again before answering.

'Sebastian's sick. The brothers took him away to the Infirmary. Maybe they'll let you thee him, maybe not. I got to go there myself one day thoon to have my foot dressed. I'll ask them then. When he's better they'll let you thee him, maybe.'

There was another chair and I sat down on it. Seeing that I meant to stay, the German offered me some beer.

'You're not Thebastian's brother?' he said. 'Cousin maybe? Maybe you married hith thister?'

'I'm only a friend. We were at the university together.'

'I had a friend at the university. We studied History. My

friend was cleverer than me; a little weak fellow – I used to pick him up and shake him when I was angry – but *tho* clever. Then one day we said: "What the hell? There is no work in Germany. Germany is down the drain," so we said good-bye to our professors, and they said: "Yes, Germany is down the drain. There is nothing for a student to do here now," and we went away and walked and walked and at last we came here. Then we said, "There is no army in Germany now, but we must be tholdiers," so we joined the Legion. My friend died of dysentery last year, campaigning in the Atlas. When he was dead, I said, "What the hell?" so I shot my foot. It is now full of pus, though I have done it one year.'

'Yes,' I said. 'That's very interesting. But my immediate concern is with Sebastian. Perhaps you would tell me about him.'

'He is a very good fellow, Sebastian. He is all right for me. Tangier was a stinking place. He brought me here – nice house, nice food, nice servant – everything is all right for me here, I reckon. I like it all right.'

'His mother is very ill,' I said. 'I have come to tell him.'

'She rich?'

'Yes.'

'Why don't she give him more money? Then we could live at Casablanca, maybe, in a nice flat. You know her well? You could make her give him more money?'

'What's the matter with him?'

'I don't know. I reckon maybe he drink too much. The brothers will look after him. It's all right for him there. The brothers are good fellows. Very cheap there.'

He clapped his hands and ordered more beer.

'You thee? A nice thervant to look after me. It is all right.'

When I had got the name of the hospital I left.

'Tell Thebastian I am still here and all right. I reckon he's worrying about me, maybe.'

The hospital, where I went next morning, was a collection of bungalows between the old and the new towns. It was kept by

Franciscans. I made my way through a crowd of diseased Moors to the doctor's room. He was a layman, clean shaven, dressed in white, starched overalls. We spoke in French, and he told me Sebastian was in no danger, but quite unfit to travel. He had had the grippe, with one lung slightly affected; he was very weak; he lacked resistance; what could one expect? He was an alcoholic. The doctor spoke dispassionately, almost brutally, with the relish men of science sometimes have for limiting themselves to inessentials, for pruning back their work to the point of sterility; but the bearded, barefooted brother in whose charge he put me, the man of no scientific pretensions who did the dirty jobs of the ward, had a different story.

'He's so patient. Not like a young man at all. He lies there and never complains – and there is much to complain of. We have no facilities. The Government give us what they can spare from the soldiers. And he is so kind. There is a poor German boy with a foot that will not heal and secondary syphilis, who comes here for treatment. Lord Flyte found him starving in Tangier and took him in and gave him a home. A real Samaritan.'

'Poor simple monk,' I thought, 'poor booby.' God forgive me!

Sebastian was in the wing kept for Europeans, where the beds were divided by low partitions into cubicles with some air of privacy. He was lying with his hands on the quilt staring at the wall, where the only ornament was a religious oleograph.

'Your friend,' said the brother.

He looked round slowly.

'Oh, I thought he meant Kurt. What are *you* doing here, Charles?'

He was more than ever emaciated; drink, which made others fat and red, seemed to wither Sebastian. The brother left us, and I sat by his bed and talked about his illness.

'I was out of my mind for a day or two,' he said. 'I kept thinking I was back in Oxford. You went to my house? Did you like it? Is Kurt still there? I won't ask you if you liked Kurt; no one does. It's funny – I couldn't get on without him, you know.'

Then I told him about his mother. He said nothing for some

time, but lay gazing at the oleograph of the Seven Dolours. Then:

'Poor mummy. She really was a *femme fatale*, wasn't she? She killed at a touch.'

I telegraphed to Julia that Sebastian was unable to travel, and stayed a week at Fez, visiting the hospital daily until he was well enough to move. His first sign of returning strength, on the second day of my visit, was to ask for brandy. By next day he had got some, somehow, and kept it under the bedclothes.

The doctor said: 'Your friend is drinking again. It is forbidden here. What can I do? This is not a reformatory school. I cannot police the wards. I am here to cure people, not to protect them from vicious habits, or teach them self-control. Cognac will not hurt him now. It will make him weaker for the next time he is ill, and then one day some little trouble will carry him off, pouff. This is not a home for inebriates. He must go at the end of the week.'

The lay brother said: 'Your friend is so much happier today, it is like one transfigured.'

'Poor simple monk,' I thought, 'poor booby'; but he added, 'You know why? He has a bottle of cognac in bed with him. It is the second I have found. No sooner do I take one away than he gets another. He is so naughty. It is the Arab boys who fetch it for him. But it is good to see him happy again when he has been so sad.'

On my last afternoon I said, 'Sebastian, now your mother's dead' – for the news had reached us that morning – 'do you think of going back to England?'

'It *would* be lovely, in some ways,' he said, 'but do you think Kurt would like it?'

'For God's sake,' I said, 'you don't mean to spend your life with Kurt, do you?'

'I don't know. He seems to mean to spend it with me. "It'th all right for him, I reckon, maybe,"' he said, mimicking Kurt's accent, and then he added what, if I had paid more attention, should have given me the key I lacked; at the time I heard and remembered it, without taking notice. 'You know, Charles,' he said, 'it's rather a pleasant change when all your life you've had people looking after you, to have someone to look after yourself. Only of course it has to be someone pretty hopeless to need looking after by *me*.'

I was able to straighten his money affairs before I left. He had lived till then by getting into difficulties and then tele-graphing for odd sums to his lawyers. I saw the branch manager of the bank and arranged for him, if funds were forthcoming from London, to receive Sebastian's quarterly allowance and pay him a weekly sum of pocket money with a reserve to be drawn in emergencies. This sum was only to be given to Sebastian personally, and only when the manager was satisfied that he had a proper use for it. Sebastian agreed readily to all this.

'Otherwise,' he said, 'Kurt will get me to sign a cheque for the whole lot when I'm tight and then he'll go off and get into all kinds of trouble.'

I saw Sebastian home from the hospital. He seemed weaker in his basket chair than he had been in bed. The two sick men, he and Kurt, sat opposite one another with the gramophone between them.

'It was time you came back,' said Kurt. 'I need you.'

'Do you, Kurt?'

'I reckon so. It's not so good being alone when you're sick. That boy's a lazy fellow – always slipping off when I want him. Once he stayed out all night and there was no one to make my coffee when I woke up. It's no good having a foot full of pus. Times I can't sleep good. Maybe another time I shall slip off, too, and go where I can be looked after.' He clapped his hands but no servant came. 'You see?' he said.

'What d'you want?'

'Cigarettes. I got some in the bag under my bed.'

Sebastian began painfully to rise from his chair.

'I'll get them,' I said. 'Where's his bed?'

'No, that's my job,' said Sebastian.

'Yeth,' said Kurt, 'I reckon that's Sebastian's job.'

So I left him with his friend in the little enclosed house at the end of the alley. There was nothing more I could do for Sebastian.

I had meant to return direct to Paris, but this business of Sebastian's allowance meant that I must go to London and see Brideshead. I travelled by sea, taking the P. & O. from Tangier, and was home in early June.

'Do you consider,' asked Brideshead, 'that there is anything vicious in my brother's connexion with this German?'

'No. I'm sure not. It's simply a case of two waifs coming together.'

'You say he is a criminal?'

'I said "a criminal type". He's been in the military prison and was dishonourably discharged.'

'And the doctor says Sebastian is killing himself with drink?'

'Weakening himself. He hasn't D.T.s or cirrhosis.'

'He's not insane?'

'Certainly not. He's found a companion he happens to like and a place where he happens to like living.'

'Then he must have his allowance as you suggest. The thing is quite clear.'

In some ways Brideshead was an easy man to deal with. He had a kind of mad certainty about everything which made his decisions swift and easy.

'Would you like to paint this house?' he asked suddenly. 'A picture of the front, another of the back on the park, another of the staircase, another of the big drawing-room? Four small oils; that is what my father wants done for a record, to keep at Brideshead. I don't know any painters. Julia said you specialized in architecture.'

'Yes,' I said. 'I should like to very much.'

'You know it's being pulled down? My father's selling it. They are going to put up a block of flats here. They're keeping the name – we can't stop them apparently.'

'What a sad thing.'

'Well, I'm sorry of course. But you think it good architecturally?'

'One of the most beautiful houses I know.'

'Can't see it. I've always thought it rather ugly. Perhaps your pictures will make me see it differently.'

This was my first commission; I had to work against time, for the contractors were only waiting for the final signature to start their work of destruction. In spite, or perhaps, because, of that – for it is my vice to spend too long on a canvas, never content to leave well alone – those four paintings are particular favourites of mine, and it was their success, both with myself and others, that confirmed me in what has since been my career.

I began in the long drawing-room, for they were anxious to shift the furniture, which had stood there since it was built. It was a long, elaborate, symmetrical Adam room, with two bays of windows opening into Green Park. The light, streaming in from the west on the afternoon when I began to paint there, was fresh green from the young trees outside.

I had the perspective set out in pencil and the detail carefully placed. I held back from painting, like a diver on the water's edge; once in I found myself buoyed and exhilarated. I was normally a slow and deliberate painter; that afternoon and all next day, and the day after, I worked fast. I could do nothing wrong. At the end of each passage I paused, tense, afraid to start the next, fearing, like a gambler, that luck must turn and the pile be lost. Bit by bit, minute by minute, the thing came into being. There were no difficulties; the intricate multiplicity of light and colour became a whole; the right colour was where I wanted it on the palette; each brush stroke, as soon as it was complete, seemed to have been there always.

Presently on the last afternoon I heard a voice behind me say: 'May I stay here and watch?'

I turned and found Cordelia.

'Yes,' I said, 'if you don't talk,' and I worked on, oblivious of her, until the failing sun made me put up my brushes.

'It must be lovely to be able to do that.'

I had forgotten she was there.

'It is.'

I could not even now leave my picture, although the sun was

down and the room fading to monochrome. I took it from the easel and held it up to the windows, put it back and lightened a shadow. Then, suddenly weary in head and eyes and back and arm, I gave it up for the evening and turned to Cordelia.

She was now fifteen and had grown tall, nearly to her full height, in the last eighteen months. She had not the promise of Julia's full *quattrocento* loveliness; there was a touch of Brideshead already in her length of nose and high cheekbone; she was in black, mourning for her mother.

'I'm tired,' I said.

'I bet you are. Is it finished?'

'Practically. I must go over it again tomorrow.'

'D'you know it's long past dinner time? There's no one here to cook anything now. I only came up today, and didn't realize how far the decay had gone. You wouldn't like to take me out to dinner, would you?'

We left by the garden door, into the park, and walked in the twilight to the Ritz Grill.

'You've seen Sebastian? He won't come home, even now?'

I did not realize till then that she had understood so much. I said so.

'Well, I love him more than anyone,' she said. 'It's sad about Marchers, isn't it? Do you know they're going to build a block of flats, and that Rex wanted to take what he called a "penthouse" at the top. Isn't it like him? Poor Julia. That was too much for her. He couldn't understand at all; he thought she would like to keep up with her old home. Things have all come to an end very quickly, haven't they? Apparently papa has been terribly in debt for a long time. Selling Marchers has put him straight again and saved I don't know how much a year in rates. But it seems a shame to pull it down. Julia says she'd sooner that than to have someone else live there.'

'What's going to happen to you?'

'What, indeed? There are all kinds of suggestions. Aunt Fanny Rosscommon wants me to live with her. Then Rex and Julia talk of taking over half Brideshead and living there. Papa won't come back. We thought he might, but no.

'They've closed the chapel at Brideshead, Bridey and the Bishop; mummy's Requiem was the last mass said there. After she was buried the priest came in – I was there alone. I don't think he saw me – and took out the altar stone and put it in his bag; then he burned the wads of wool with the holy oil on them and threw the ash outside; he emptied the holy-water stoop and blew out the lamp in the sanctuary, and left the tabernacle open and empty, as though from now on it was always to be Good Friday. I suppose none of this makes any sense to you, Charles, poor agnostic. I stayed there till he was gone, and then, suddenly, there wasn't any chapel there any more, just an oddly decorated room. I can't tell you what it felt like. You've never been to Tenebrae, I suppose?'

'Never.'

'Well, if you had you'd know what the Jews felt about their temple. *Quomodo sedet sola civitas* ... it's a beautiful chant. You ought to go once, just to hear it.'

'Still trying to convert me, Cordelia?'

'Oh, no. That's all over, too. D'you know what papa said when he became a Catholic? Mummy told me once. He said to her: "You have brought back my family to the faith of their ancestors." Pompous, you know. It takes people different ways. Anyhow, the family haven't been very constant, have they? There's him gone and Sebastian gone and Julia gone. But God won't let them go for long, you know. I wonder if you remember the story mummy read us the evening Sebastian first got drunk – I mean the *bad* evening. "Father Brown" said something like "I caught him" (the thief) "with an unseen hook and an invisible line which is long enough to let him wander to the ends of the world and still to bring him back with a twitch upon the thread." '

We scarcely mentioned her mother. All the time we talked, she ate voraciously. Once she said:

'Did you see Sir Adrian Porson's poem in *The Times*? It's funny: he knew her best of anyone – he loved her all his life, you know – and yet it doesn't seem to have anything to do with her at all.

'I got on best with her of any of us, but I don't believe I ever really loved her. Not as she wanted or deserved. It's odd I didn't, because I'm full of natural affections.'

'I never really knew your Mother,' I said.

'You didn't like her. I sometimes think when people wanted to hate God they hated mummy.'

'What do you mean by that, Cordelia?'

'Well, you see, she was saintly but she wasn't a saint. No one could really hate a saint, could they? They can't really hate God either. When they want to hate him and his saints they have to find something like themselves and pretend it's God and hate that. I suppose you think that's all bosh.'

'I heard almost the same thing once before – from someone very different.'

'Oh, I'm quite serious. I've thought about it a lot. It seems to explain poor mummy.'

Then this odd child tucked into her dinner with renewed relish. 'First time I've ever been taken out to dinner alone at a restaurant,' she said.

Later: 'When Julia heard they were selling Marchers she said: "Poor Cordelia. She won't have her coming-out ball there after all." It's a thing we used to talk about – like my being her bridesmaid. That didn't come off either. When Julia had her ball I was allowed down for an hour, to sit in the corner with Aunt Fanny, and she said, "In six years' time you'll have all this." ... I hope I've got a vocation.'

'I don't know what that means.'

'It means you can be a nun. If you haven't a vocation it's no good however much you want to be; and if you have a vocation, you can't get away from it, however much you hate it. Bridey thinks he has a vocation and hasn't. I used to think Sebastian had and hated it – but I don't know now. Everything has changed so much suddenly.'

But I had no patience with this convent chatter. I had felt the brush take life in my hand that afternoon; I had had my finger in the great, succulent pie of creation. I was a man of the Renaissance that evening – of Browning's renaissance. I, who had walked the streets of Rome in Genoa velvet and had seen the stars through Galileo's tube, spurned the friars, with their dusty tomes and their sunken, jealous eyes and their crabbed hair-splitting speech.

'You'll fall in love,' I said.

'Oh, pray not. I say, do you think I could have another of those scrumptious meringues?'

BOOK THREE

A TWITCH UPON THE THREAD

CHAPTER I

My theme is memory, that winged host that soared about me one grey morning of war-time.

These memories, which are my life – for we possess nothing certainly except the past – were always with me. Like the pigeons of St Mark's, they were everywhere, under my feet, singly, in pairs, in little honey-voiced congregations, nodding, strutting, winking, rolling the tender feathers of their necks, perching sometimes, if I stood still, on my shoulder; until, suddenly, the noon gun boomed and in a moment, with a flutter and sweep of wings, the pavement was bare and the whole sky above dark with a tumult of fowl. Thus it was that morning of war-time.

For nearly ten dead years after that evening with Cordelia I was borne along a road outwardly full of change and incident, but never during that time, except sometimes in my painting – and that at longer and longer intervals – did I come alive as I had been during the time of my friendship with Sebastian. I took it to be youth, not life, that I was losing. My work upheld me, for I had chosen to do what I could do well, did better daily, and liked doing; incidentally it was something which no one else at that time was attempting to do. I became an architectural painter.

More even than the work of the great architects, I loved buildings that grew silently with the centuries, catching and keeping the best of each generation, while time curbed the artist's pride and the Philistine's vulgarity, and repaired the clumsiness of the dull workman. In such buildings England abounded, and, in the last decade of their grandeur, Englishmen seemed for the first time to become conscious of what before was taken for granted, and to salute their achievement at the moment of extinction. Hence my prosperity, far beyond my merits; my work had nothing to recommend it except my growing technical skill, enthusiasm for my subject, and independence of popular notions.

The financial slump of the period, which left many painters without employment, served to enhance my success, which was, indeed, itself a symptom of the decline. When the water-holes were dry people sought to drink at the mirage. After my first exhibition I was called to all parts of the country to make portraits of houses that were soon to be deserted or debased; indeed, my arrival seemed often to be only a few paces ahead of the auctioneer's, a presage of doom.

I published three splendid folios – *Ryder's Country Seats*, *Ryder's English Homes*, and *Ryder's Village and Provincial Architecture*, which each sold its thousand copies at five guineas apiece. I seldom failed to please, for there was no conflict between myself and my patrons; we both wanted the same thing. But, as the years passed, I began to mourn the loss of something I had known in the drawing-room of Marchmain House and once or twice since, the intensity and singleness and the belief that it was not all done by hand – in a word, the inspiration.

In quest of this fading light I went abroad, in the augustan manner, laden with the apparatus of my trade, for two years' refreshment among alien styles. I did not go to Europe; her treasures were safe, too safe, swaddled in expert care, obscured by reverence. Europe could wait. There would be a time for Europe, I thought; all too soon the days would come when I should need a man at my side to put up my easel and carry my paints; when I could not venture more than an hour's journey from a good hotel; when I should need soft breezes and mellow sunshine all day long; then I would take my old eyes to Germany and Italy. Now while I had the strength I would go to the wild lands where man had deserted his post and the jungle was creeping back to its old strongholds.

Accordingly, by slow but not easy stages, I travelled through Mexico and Central America in a world which had all I needed, and the change from parkland and hall should have quickened me and set me right with myself. I sought inspiration among gutted palaces and cloisters embowered in weed, derelict churches where the vampire-bats hung in the dome like dry seed-pods and only the ants were ceaselessly astir tunnelling in the rich stalls; cities where no road led, and mausoleums where a single, agued family of Indians sheltered from the rains. There in great labour, sickness, and occasionally in some danger, I made the first drawings for *Ryder's Latin America*. Every few weeks I came to rest, finding myself once more in the zone of trade or tourism, recuperated, set up my studio, transcribed my sketches, anxiously packed the complete canvases, dispatched them to my New York agent, and then set out again, with my small retinue, into the wastes.

I was in no great pains to keep in touch with England. I followed local advice for my itinerary and had no settled route, so that much of my mail never reached me, and the rest accumulated until there was more than could be read at a sitting. I used to stuff a bundle of letters into my bag and read them when I felt inclined, which was in circumstances so incongruous – swinging in my hammock, under the net, by the light of a storm-lantern; drifting down river, amidships in the canoe, with the boys astern of me lazily keeping our nose out of the bank, with the dark water keeping pace with us, in the green shade, with the great trees towering above us and the monkeys screeching in the sunlight, high overhead among the flowers on the roof of the forest; on the veranda of a hospitable ranch, where the ice and the dice clicked, and a tiger cat played with its chain on the mown grass – that they seemed voices so distant as to be meaningless; their matter passed clean through the mind, and out, leaving no mark, like the facts about themselves which fellow travellers distribute so freely in American railway trains.

But despite this isolation and this long sojourn in a strange world, I remained unchanged, still a small part of myself pretending to be whole. I discarded the experiences of those two years with my tropical kit and returned to New York as I had set out. I had a fine haul – eleven paintings and fifty odd drawings – and when eventually I exhibited them in London, the art critics, many of whom hitherto had been patronizing in tone, as my success invited, acclaimed a new and richer note in my work. *Mr Ryder*, the most respected of them wrote, *rises like a fresh young trout to the hypodermic injection of a new culture and discloses a powerful facet in the vista of his potentialities ... By focusing the frankly traditional battery of his elegance and erudition on the maelstrom of barbarism, Mr Ryder has at last found himself.*

Grateful words, but, alas, not true by a long chalk. My wife, who crossed to New York to meet me and saw the fruits of our separation displayed in my agent's office, summed the thing up better by saying: 'Of course, I can see they're perfectly brilliant and really rather beautiful in a sinister way, but somehow I don't feel they are quite *you*.'

In Europe my wife was sometimes taken for an American because of her dapper and jaunty way of dressing, and the curiously hygienic quality of her prettiness; in America she assumed an English softness and reticence. She arrived a day or two before me, and was on the pier when my ship docked.

'It has been a long time,' she said fondly when we met.

She had not joined the expedition; she explained to our friends that the country was unsuitable and she had her son at home. There was also a daughter now, she remarked, and it came back to me that there had been talk of this before I started, as an additional reason for her staying behind. There had been some mention of it, too, in her letters.

'I don't believe you read my letters,' she said that night, when at last, late, after a dinner party and some hours at a cabaret, we found ourselves alone in our hotel bedroom.

'Some went astray. I remember distinctly your telling me that the daffodils in the orchard were a dream, that the nursery-maid was a jewel, that the Regency four-poster was a find, but frankly I do not remember hearing that your new baby was called Caroline. Why did you call it that?'

'After Charles, of course.'

'Ah!'

'I made Bertha Van Halt godmother. I thought she was safe for a good present. What do you think she gave?'

'Bertha Van Halt is a well-known trap. What?'

'A fifteen shilling book-token. Now that Johnjohn has a companion –'

'Who?'

'Your son, darling. You haven't forgotten him, too?'

'For Christ's sake,' I said, 'why do you call him that?'

'It's the name he invented for himself. Don't you think it sweet? Now that Johnjohn has a companion I think we'd better not have any more for some time, don't you?'

'Just as you please.'

'Johnjohn talks of you such a lot. He prays every night for your safe return.'

She talked in this way while she undressed, with an effort to appear at ease; then she sat at the dressing table, ran a comb through her hair, and with her bare back towards me, looking at herself in the glass, said: 'Shall I put my face to bed?'

It was a familiar phrase, one that I did not like; she meant, should she remove her make-up, cover herself with grease and put her hair in a net.

'No,' I said, 'not at once.'

Then she knew what was wanted. She had neat, hygienic ways for that too, but there were both relief and triumph in her smile of welcome; later we parted and lay in our twin beds a yard or two distant, smoking. I looked at my watch; it was four o'clock, but neither of us was ready to sleep, for in that city there is neurosis in the air which the inhabitants mistake for energy.

'I don't believe you've changed at all, Charles.'

'No, I'm afraid not.'

'D'you want to change?'

'It's the only evidence of life.'

'But you might change so that you didn't love me any more.'

'There is that risk.'

'Charles, you haven't stopped loving me?'

'You said yourself I hadn't changed.'

'Well, I'm beginning to think you have. I haven't.'

'No,' I said, 'no; I can see that.'

'Were you at all frightened at meeting me today?'

'Not the least.'

'You didn't wonder if I should have fallen in love with someone else in the meantime?'

'No. Have you?'

'You know I haven't. Have you?'

'No. I'm not in love.'

My wife seemed content with this answer. She had married me six years ago at the time of my first exhibition, and had done much since then to push our interests. People said she had 'made' me, but she herself took credit only for supplying me with a congenial background; she had firm faith in my genius and in the 'artistic temperament', and in the principle that things done on the sly are not really done at all.

Presently she said: 'Looking forward to getting home?' (My father gave me as a wedding present the price of a house, and I bought an old rectory in my wife's part of the country.) 'I've got a surprise for you.'

'Yes?'

'I've turned the old barn into a studio for you, so that you needn't be disturbed by the children or when we have people to stay. I got Emden to do it. Everyone thinks it a great success. There was an article on it in *Country Life*; I brought it for you to see.'

She showed me the article: '... *happy example of architectural good manners. ... Sir Joseph Emden's tactful adaptation of traditional material to modern needs ...*'; there were some photographs; wide oak boards now covered the earthen floor; a high, stone-mullioned bay-window had been built in the north wall, and the great timbered roof, which before had been lost in shadow, now stood out stark, well lit, with clean white plaster between the beams; it looked like a village hall. I remembered the smell of the place, which would now be lost.

'I rather liked that barn,' I said.

'But you'll be able to work there, won't you?'

'After squatting in a cloud of sting-fly,' I said, 'under a sun which scorched the paper off the block as I drew, I could work on the top of an omnibus. I expect the vicar would like to borrow the place for whist drives.'

'There's a lot of work waiting for you. I promised Lady Anchorage you would do Anchorage House as soon as you got back. That's coming down, too, you know – shops underneath and two-roomed flats above. You don't think, do you, Charles, that all this exotic work you've been doing, is going to spoil you for that sort of thing?'

'Why should it?'

'Well, it's so different. Don't be cross.'

'It's just another jungle closing in.'

'I know just how you feel, darling. The Georgian Society made such a fuss, but we couldn't do anything. . . . Did you ever get my letter about Boy?'

'Did I? What did it say?'

('Boy' Mulcaster was her brother.)

'About his engagement. It doesn't matter now because it's all off, but father and mother were terribly upset. She was an awful girl. They had to give her money in the end.'

'No, I heard nothing of Boy.'

'He and Johnjohn are tremendous friends, now. It's so sweet to see them together. Whenever he comes the first thing he does is to drive straight to the Old Rectory. He just walks into the house, pays no attention to anyone else, and hollers out: "Where's my chum Johnjohn?" and Johnjohn comes tumbling downstairs and off they go into the spinney together and play for hours. You'd think, to hear them talk to each other, they were the same age. It was really Johnjohn who made him see reason about that girl; seriously, you know, he's frightfully sharp. He must have heard mother and me talking because next time Boy came he said: "Uncle Boy shan't marry horrid girl and leave Johnjohn," and that was the very day he settled for two thousand pounds out of court. Johnjohn admires Boy so tremendously and imitates him in everything. It's so good for them both.'

I crossed the room and tried once more, ineffectively, to moderate the heat of the radiators; I drank some iced water and opened the window, but, besides the sharp night air, music was borne in from the next room where they were playing the wireless. I shut it and turned back towards my wife.

At length she began talking again, more drowsily. . . .

'The garden's come on a lot. . . . The box hedges you planted grew five inches last year. . . . I had some men down from London to put the tennis court right . . . first-class cook at the moment . . .'

As the city below us began to wake, we both fell asleep, but not for long; the telephone rang and a voice of hermaphroditic gaiety said: 'Savoy-Carlton-Hotel-goodmorning. It is now a quarter to eight.'

'I didn't ask to be called, you know.'

'Pardon me?'

'Oh, it doesn't matter.'

'You're welcome.'

As I was shaving, my wife from the bath said: 'Just like old times. I'm not worrying any more, Charles.'

'Good.'

'I was so terribly afraid that two years might have made a difference. Now I know we can start again exactly where we left off.'

'When?' I asked. 'What? When we left off what?'

'When you went away, of course.'

'You are not thinking of something else, a little time before?'

'Oh, Charles, that's old history. That was nothing. It was never anything. It's all over and forgotten.'

'I just wanted to know,' I said. 'We're back as we were the day I went abroad, is that it?'

So we started that day exactly where we left off two years before, with my wife in tears.

My wife's softness and English reticence, her very white, small regular teeth, her neat rosy finger-nails, her schoolgirl air of innocent mischief and her schoolgirl dress, her modern jewellery, which was made at great expense to give the impression, at a distance, of having been mass produced, her ready, rewarding smile, her deference to me and her zeal in my interests, her motherly heart which made her cable daily to the nanny at home – in short, her peculiar charm – made her popular among the Americans, and our cabin on the day of departure was full of cellophane packages – flowers, fruit, sweets, books, toys for the children – from friends she had known for a week. Stewards, like sisters in a nursing home, used to judge their passengers' importance by the number and value of these trophies; we therefore started the voyage in high esteem.

My wife's first thought on coming aboard was of the passenger list.

'Such a lot of friends,' she said. 'It's going to be a lovely trip. Let's have a cocktail party this evening.'

The companion-ways were no sooner cast off than she was busy with the telephone.

'Julia. This is Celia – Celia Ryder. It's lovely to find you on board. What have you been up to? Come and have a cocktail this evening and tell me all about it.'

'Julia who?'

'Mottram. I haven't seen her for years.'

Nor had I; not, in fact, since my wedding day, not to speak to for any time, since the private view of my exhibition where the four canvases of Marchmain House, lent by Brideshead, had hung together attracting much attention. Those pictures were my last contact with the Flytes; our lives, so close for a year or two, had drawn apart. Sebastian, I knew, was still abroad; Rex and Julia, I sometimes heard said, were unhappy together. Rex was not prospering quite as well as had been predicted; he remained on the fringe of the Government, prominent but vaguely suspect. He lived among the very rich, and in his speeches seemed to incline to revolutionary policies, flirting, with Communists and Fascists. I heard the Mottrams' names in conversation; I saw their faces now and again peeping from the *Tatler*, as I turned the pages impatiently waiting for someone to come, but they and I had fallen apart, as one could in England

and only there, into separate worlds, little spinning planets of personal relationship; there is probably a perfect metaphor for the process to be found in physics, from the way in which, I dimly apprehend, particles of energy group and regroup themselves in separate magnetic systems; a metaphor ready to hand for the man who can speak of these things with assurance; not for me, who can only say that England abounded in these small companies of intimate friends, so that, as in this case of Julia and myself, we could live in the same street in London, see at times, a few miles distant, the same rural horizon, could have a liking one for the other, a mild curiosity about the other's fortunes, a regret, even, that we should be separated, and the knowledge that either of us had only to pick up the telephone and speak by the other's pillow, enjoy the intimacies of the levee, coming in, as it were, with the morning orange juice and the sun, yet be restrained from doing so by the centripetal force of our own worlds, and the cold, interstellar space between them.

My wife, perched on the back of the sofa in a litter of cellophane and silk ribbons, continued telephoning, working brightly through the passenger list ... 'Yes, do of course bring him, I'm told he's sweet. ... Yes, I've got Charles back from the wilds at last; isn't it lovely. ... What a treat seeing your name in the list! It's made my trip ... darling, we were at the Savoy-Carlton, too; how can we have missed you?' ... Sometimes she turned to me and said: 'I have to make sure you're still really there. I haven't got used to it yet.'

I went up and out as we steamed slowly down the river to one of the great glass cases where the passengers stood to watch the land slip by. 'Such a lot of friends,' my wife had said. They looked a strange crowd to me; the emotions of leave-taking were just beginning to subside; some of them, who had been drinking till the last moment with those who were seeing them off, were still boisterous; others were planning where they would have their deck chairs; the band played unnoticed – all were as restless as ants.

I turned into some of the halls of the ship, which were huge without any splendour, as though they had been designed for a railway coach and preposterously magnified. I passed through vast bronze gates on which paper-thin Assyrian animals cavorted; I trod carpets the colour of blotting paper; the painted panels of the walls were like blotting paper, too – kindergarten work in flat, drab colours – and between the walls were yards and yards of biscuit-coloured wood which no carpenter's tool had ever touched, wood that had been bent round corners, invisibly joined strip to strip, steamed and squeezed and polished; all over the blotting-paper carpet were strewn tables designed perhaps by a sanitary engineer, square blocks of stuffing, with square holes for sitting in, and uphol-stered, it seemed, in blotting paper also; the light of the hall was suffused from scores of hollows, giving an even glow, casting no shadows – the whole place hummed from its hundred ventila-tors and vibrated with the turn of the great engines below.

'Here I am,' I thought, 'back from the jungle, back from the ruins. Here, where wealth is no longer gorgeous and power has no dignity. *Quomodo sedet sola civitas*' (for I had heard that great lament, which Cordelia once quoted to me in the drawing-room of Marchmain House, sung by a half-caste choir in Guatemala, nearly a year ago).

A steward came up to me.

'Can I get you anything, sir?'

'A whisky and soda, not iced.'

'I'm sorry, sir, *all* the soda is iced.'

'Is the water iced, too?'

'Oh yes, sir.'

'Well, it doesn't matter.'

He trotted off, puzzled, soundless in the pervading hum.

'Charles.'

I looked behind me. Julia was sitting in a cube of blotting paper, her hands folded in her lap, so still that I had passed by without noticing her.

'I heard you were here. Celia telephoned to me. It's delightful.'

'What are you doing?'

She opened the empty hands in her lap with a little eloquent gesture. 'Waiting. My maid's unpacking; she's been so disagreeable ever since we left England. She's complaining now about my cabin. I can't think why. It seems a lap to me.'

The steward returned with whisky and two jugs, one of iced water, the other of boiling water; I mixed them to the right temperature. He watched and said: 'I'll remember that's how you take it, sir.'

Most passengers had fads; he was paid to fortify their self-esteem. Julia asked for a cup of hot chocolate. I sat by her in the next cube.

'I never see you now,' she said. 'I never seem to see anyone I like. I don't know why.'

But she spoke as though it were a matter of weeks rather than of years; as though, too, before our parting we had been firm friends. It was dead contrary to the common experience of such encounters, when time is found to have built its own defensive lines, camouflaged vulnerable points, and laid a field of mines across all but a few well-trodden paths, so that, more often than not, we can only signal to one another from either side of the tangle of wire. Here she and I, who were never friends before, met on terms of long and unbroken intimacy.

'What have you been doing in America?'

She looked up slowly from her chocolate and, her splendid, serious eyes in mine, said: 'Don't you know? I'll tell you about it sometime. I've been a mug. I thought I was in love with someone, but it didn't turn out that way.' And my mind went back ten years to the evening at Brideshead, when that lovely, spidery child of nineteen, as though brought in for an hour from the nursery and nettled by lack of attention from the grown-ups, had said: '*I'm* causing anxiety, too, you know,' and I had thought at the time, though scarcely, it now seemed to me, in long trousers myself, 'How important these girls make themselves with their love affairs.'

Now it was different; there was nothing but humility and friendly candour in the way she spoke.

I wished I could respond to her confidence, give some token

of acceptance, but there was nothing in my last, flat, eventful years that I could share with her. I began instead to talk of my time in the jungle, of the comic characters I had met and the lost places I had visited, but in this mood of old friendship the tale faltered and came to an end abruptly.

'I long to see the paintings,' she said.

'Celia wanted me to unpack some and stick them round the cabin for her cocktail party. I couldn't do that.'

'No ... is Celia as pretty as ever? I always thought she had the most delicious looks of any girl of my year.'

'She hasn't changed.'

'You have, Charles. So lean and grim; not at all the pretty boy Sebastian brought home with him. Harder, too.'

'And you're softer.'

'Yes, I think so ... and very patient now.'

She was not yet thirty, but was approaching the zenith of her loveliness, all her rich promise abundantly fulfilled. She had lost that fashionable, spidery look; the head that I used to think *quattrocento*, which had sat a little oddly on her, was now part of herself and not at all Florentine; not connected in any way with painting or the arts or with anything except herself, so that it would be idle to itemize and dissect her beauty, which was her own essence, and could only be known in her and by her authority and in the love I was soon to have for her.

Time had wrought another change, too; not for her the sly, complacent smile of la Gioconda; the years had been more than 'the sound of lyres and flutes', and had saddened her. She seemed to say: 'Look at me. I have done my share. I am beautiful. It is something quite out of the ordinary, this beauty of mine. I am made for delight. But what do *I* get out of it? Where is *my* reward?'

That was the change in her from ten years ago; that, indeed, was her reward, this haunting, magical sadness which spoke straight to the heart and struck silence; it was the completion of her beauty.

'Sadder, too,' I said.

'Oh yes, much sadder.'

My wife was in exuberant spirits when, two hours later, I returned to the cabin.

'I've had to do everything. How does it look?'

We had been given, without paying more for it, a large suite of rooms, one so large, in fact, that it was seldom booked except by directors of the line, and on most voyages, the chief purser admitted, was given to those he wished to honour. (My wife was adept in achieving such small advantages, first impressing the impressionable with her chic and my celebrity and, superiority once firmly established, changing quickly to a pose of almost flirtatious affability.) In token of her appreciation the chief purser had been asked to our party and he, in token of his appreciation, had sent before him the life-size effigy of a swan, moulded in ice and filled with caviar. This chilly piece of magnificence now dominated the room, standing on a table in the centre, thawing gently, dripping at the beak into its silver dish. The flowers of the morning delivery hid as much as possible of the panelling (for this room was a miniature of the monstrous hall above).

'You must get dressed at once. Where have you been all this time?'

'Talking to Julia Mottram.'

'D'you know her? Oh, of course, you were a friend of the dipso brother. Goodness, her glamour!'

'She greatly admires your looks, too.'

'She used to be a girl friend of Boy's.'

'Surely not?'

'He always said so.'

'Have you considered,' I asked, 'how your guests are going to eat this caviar?'

'I have. It's insoluble. But there's all this' – she revealed some trays of glassy titbits – 'and anyway, people always find ways of eating things at parties. D'you remember we once ate potted shrimps with a paper knife?'

'Did we?'

'Darling, it was the night you popped the question.'

'As I remember, you popped.'

'Well, the night we got engaged. But you haven't said how you like the arrangements.'

The arrangements, apart from the swan and the flowers, consisted of a steward already inextricably trapped in the corner behind an improvised bar, and another steward, tray in hand, in comparative freedom.

'A cinema actor's dream,' I said.

'Cinema actors,' said my wife; 'that's what I want to talk about.'

She came with me to my dressing-room and talked while I changed. It had occurred to her that, with my interest in architecture, my true *métier* was designing scenery for the films, and she had asked two Hollywood magnates to the party with whom she wished to ingratiate me.

We returned to the sitting-room.

'Darling, I believe you've taken against my bird. Don't be beastly about it in front of the purser. It was sweet of him to think of it. Besides, you know, if you had read about it in the description of a sixteenth-century banquet in Venice, you would have said those were the days to live.'

'In sixteenth-century Venice it would have been a somewhat different shape.'

'Here is Father Christmas. We were just in raptures over your swan.'

The chief purser came into the room and shook hands, powerfully.

'Dear Lady Celia,' he said, 'if you'll put on your warmest clothes and come on an expedition into the cold storage with me tomorrow, I can show you a whole Noah's Ark of such objects. The toast will be along in a minute. They're keeping it hot.'

'Toast!' said my wife, as though this was something beyond the dreams of gluttony. 'Do you hear that, Charles? *Toast.*'

Soon the guests began to arrive; there was nothing to delay them. 'Celia,' they said, 'what a grand cabin and what a beautiful swan!' and, for all that it was one of the largest in the ship, our room was soon painfully crowded; they began to put out their cigarettes in the little pool of ice-water which now surrounded the swan.

The purser made a sensation, as sailors like to do, by predicting a storm. 'How can you be so beastly?' asked my wife, conveying the flattering suggestion that not only the cabin and the caviar, but the waves, too, were at his command. 'Anyway, storms don't affect a ship like this, do they?'

'Might hold us back a bit.'

'But it wouldn't make us sick?'

'Depends if you're a good sailor. I'm always sick in storms, ever since I was a boy.'

'I don't believe it. He's just being sadistic. Come over here, there's something I want to show you.'

It was the latest photograph of her children. 'Charles hasn't even seen Caroline yet. Isn't it thrilling for him?'

There were no friends of mine there, but I knew about a third of the party, and talked away civilly enough. An elderly woman said to me, 'So you're Charles. I feel I know you, through and through, Celia's talked so much about you.'

'Through and through,' I thought. 'Through and through is a long way, madam. Can you indeed see into those dark places where my own eyes seek in vain to guide me? Can you tell me, dear Mrs Stuyvesant Oglander – if I am correct in thinking that is how I heard my wife speak of you – why it is that at this moment, while I talk to you, here, about my forthcoming exhibition, I am thinking all the time only of when Julia will come? Why can I talk like this to you, but not to her? Why have I already set her apart from humankind, and myself with her? What is going on in those secret places of my spirit with which you make so free? What is cooking, Mrs Stuyvesant Oglander?'

Still Julia did not come, and the noise of twenty people in that tiny room, which was so large that no one hired it, was the noise of a multitude.

Then I saw a curious thing. There was a little red-headed man whom no one seemed to know, a dowdy fellow quite unlike the general run of my wife's guests; he had been standing by the caviar for twenty minutes eating as fast as a rabbit. Now he wiped his mouth with his handkerchief and, on the impulse apparently, leaned forward and dabbed the beak of the swan, removing the drop of water that had been swelling there and would soon have fallen. Then he looked round furtively to see if he had been observed, caught my eye, and giggled nervously.

'Been wanting to do that for a long time,' he said. 'Bet you don't know how many drops to the minute. I do, I counted.'

'I've no idea.'

'Guess. Tanner if you're wrong; half a dollar if you're right. That's fair.'

'Three,' I said.

'Coo, you're a sharp one. Been counting 'em yourself.' But he showed no inclination to pay this debt. Instead he said: 'How d'you figure this out. I'm an Englishman born and bred, but this is my first time on the Atlantic.'

'You flew out perhaps?'

'No, nor over it.'

'Then I presume you went round the world and came across the Pacific.'

'You *are* a sharp one and no mistake. I've made quite a bit getting into arguments over that one.'

'What was your route?' I asked, wishing to be agreeable.

'Ah, that'd be telling. Well, I must skedaddle. So long.'

'Charles,' said my wife, 'this is Mr Kramm, of Interastral Films.'

'So you are Mr Charles Ryder,' said Mr Kramm.

'Yes.'

'Well, well, well,' he paused. I waited. 'The purser here says we're heading for dirty weather. What d'you know about that?'

'Far less than the purser.'

'Pardon me, Mr Ryder, I don't quite get you.'

'I mean I know less than the purser.'

'Is that so? Well, well, well. I've enjoyed our talk very much. I hope that it will be the first of many.'

An Englishwoman said: 'Oh, that swan! Six weeks in America has given me an absolute phobia of ice. Do tell me, how did it feel meeting Celia again after two years? I know I should feel

indecently bridal. But Celia's never quite got the orange
blossom out of her hair, has she?'

Another woman said: 'Isn't it heaven saying good-bye and
knowing we shall meet again in half an hour and go on meeting
every half-hour for days?'

Our guests began to go, and each on leaving informed me of
something my wife had promised to bring me to in the near
future; it was the theme of the evening that we should all be
seeing a lot of each other, that we had formed one of those
molecular systems that physicists can illustrate. At last the swan
was wheeled out, too, and I said to my wife, 'Julia never came.'

'No, she telephoned. I couldn't hear what she said, there was
such a noise going on – something about a dress. Quite lucky
really, there wasn't room for a cat. It was a lovely party, wasn't
it? Did you hate it very much? You behaved beautifully and
looked so distinguished. Who was your red-haired chum?'

'No chum of mine.'

'How *very* peculiar! Did you say anything to Mr Kramm
about working in Hollywood?'

'Of course not.'

'Oh, Charles, you are a worry to me. It's not enough just to
stand about looking distinguished and a martyr for Art. Let's go
to dinner. We're at the Captain's table. I don't suppose he'll
dine down tonight, but it's polite to be fairly punctual.'

By the time that we reached the table the rest of the party
had arranged themselves. On either side of the Captain's empty
chair sat Julia and Mrs Stuyvesant Oglander; besides them
there was an English diplomat and his wife, Senator Stuyvesant
Oglander, and an American clergyman at present totally
isolated between two pairs of empty chairs. This clergyman
later described himself – redundantly it seemed – as an Episco-
palian Bishop. Husbands and wives sat together here. My wife
was confronted with a quick decision, and although the steward
attempted to direct us otherwise, sat so that she had the senator
and I the Bishop. Julia gave us both a little dismal signal of
sympathy.

'I'm miserable about the party,' she said, 'my beastly maid

totally disappeared with every dress I have. She only turned up half an hour ago. She'd been playing ping-pong.'

'I've been telling the Senator what he missed,' said Mrs Stuyvesant Oglander. 'Wherever Celia is, you'll find she knows all the significant people.'

'On my right,' said the Bishop, 'a significant couple are expected. They take all their meals in their cabin except when they have been informed in advance that the Captain will be present.'

We were a gruesome circle; even my wife's high social spirit faltered. At moments I heard bits of her conversation.

'... an extraordinary little red-haired man. Captain Foulenough in person.'

'But I understood you to say, Lady Celia, that you were unacquainted with him.'

'I meant he was *like* Captain Foulenough.'

'I begin to comprehend. He impersonated this friend of yours in order to come to your party.'

'No, no. Captain Foulenough is simply a comic character.'

'There seems to have been nothing very amusing about this other man. Your friend is a comedian?'

'No, no. Captain Foulenough is an imaginary character in an English paper. You know, like your "Popeye".'

The senator laid down knife and fork. 'To recapitulate: an imposter came to your party and you admitted him because of a fancied resemblance to a fictitious character in a cartoon.'

'Yes, I suppose that was it really.'

The senator looked at his wife as much as to say: 'Significant people, huh!'

I heard Julia across the table trying to trace, for the benefit of the diplomat, the marriage-connexions of her Hungarian and Italian cousins. The diamonds flashed in her hair and on her fingers, but her hands were nervously rolling little balls of crumb, and her starry head drooped in despair.

The Bishop told me of the goodwill mission on which he was travelling to Barcelona ... 'a very, very valuable work of clearance has been performed, Mr Ryder. The time has now come to rebuild on broader foundations. I have made it my aim to reconcile the so-called Anarchists and the so-called Communists, and with that in view I and my committee have digested all the available documentation of the subject. Our conclusion, Mr Ryder, is unanimous. There is *no* fundamental diversity between the two ideologies. It is a matter of personalities, Mr Ryder, and what personalities have put asunder personalities can unite. ...'

On the other side I heard: 'And may I make so bold as to ask what institutions sponsored your husband's expedition?'

The diplomat's wife bravely engaged the Bishop across the gulf that separated them.

'And what language will you speak when you get to Barcelona?'

'The language of Reason and Brotherhood, madam,' and, turning back to me, 'The speech of the coming century is in thoughts not in words. Do you not agree, Mr Ryder?'

'Yes,' I said. 'Yes.'

'What are words?' said the Bishop.

'What indeed?'

'Mere conventional symbols, Mr Ryder, and this is an age rightly sceptical of conventional symbols.'

My mind reeled; after the parrot-house fever of my wife's party, and unplumbed emotions of the afternoon, after all the exertions of my wife's pleasures in New York, after the months of solitude in the steaming, green shadows of the jungle, this was too much. I felt like Lear on the heath, like the Duchess of Malfi bayed by madmen. I summoned cataracts and hurricanoes, and as if by conjury the call was immediately answered.

For some time now, though whether it was a mere trick of the nerves I did not then know, I had felt a recurrent and persistently growing motion – a heave and shudder of the large dining-room as of the breast of a man in deep sleep. Now my wife turned to me and said: 'Either I am a little drunk or it's getting rough,' and, even as she spoke we found ourselves leaning sideways in our chairs; there was a crash and tinkle of falling cutlery by the wall, and on our table the wine glasses all together toppled and rolled over, while each of us steadied the plate and forks and looked at the other with expressions that varied between frank horror in the diplomat's wife and relief in Julia.

The gale which, unheard, unseen, unfelt, in our enclosed and insulated world had, for an hour, been mounting over us, had now veered and fallen full on our bows.

Silence followed the crash, then a high, nervous babble of laughter. Stewards laid napkins on the pools of spilt wine. We tried to resume the conversation, but all were waiting, as the little ginger man had watched the drop swell and fall from the swan's beak, for the next great blow; it came, heavier than the last.

'This is where I say good night to you all,' said the diplomat's wife, rising.

Her husband led her to their cabin. The dining-room was emptying fast. Soon only Julia, my wife, and I were left at the table, and, telepathically, Julia said, 'Like King Lear.'

'Only each of us is all three of them.'

'What can you mean?' asked my wife.

'Lear, Kent, Fool.'

'Oh, dear, it's like that agonizing Foulenough conversation over again. Don't try and explain.'

'I doubt if I could,' I said.

Another climb, another vast drop. The stewards were at work making things fast, shutting things up, hustling away unstable ornaments.

'Well, we've finished dinner and set a fine example of British phlegm,' said my wife. 'Let's go and see what's on.'

Once, on our way to the lounge, we had all three to cling to a pillar; when we got there we found it almost deserted; the band played but no one danced; the tables were set for tombola but no one bought a card, and the ship's officer, who made a speciality of calling the numbers with all the patter of the lower deck – 'sweet sixteen and never been kissed – key of the door, twenty-one – clickety-click, sixty-six' – was idly talking to his colleagues; there were a score of scattered novel readers, a few games of bridge, some brandy drinking in the smoking-room, but all our guests of two hours before had disappeared.

The three of us sat for a little by the empty dance floor; my wife was full of schemes by which, without impoliteness, we could move to another table in the dining-room. 'It's crazy to go to the restaurant,' she said, 'and pay extra for exactly the same dinner. Only film people go there, anyway. I don't see why we should be made to.'

Presently she said: 'It's making my head ache and I'm tired, anyway. I'm going to bed.'

Julia went with her. I walked round the ship, on one of the covered decks where the wind howled and the spray leaped up from the darkness and smashed white and brown against the glass screen; men were posted to keep the passengers off the open decks. Then I, too, went below.

In my dressing-room everything breakable had been stowed away, the door to the cabin was hooked open, and my wife called plaintively from within.

'I feel terrible. I didn't know a ship of this size could pitch like this,' she said, and her eyes were full of consternation and resentment, like those of a woman who, at the end of her time, at length realizes that however luxurious the nursing home, and however well paid the doctor, her labour is inevitable; and the lift and fall of the ship came regularly as the pains of childbirth.

I slept next door; or, rather, I lay there between dreaming and waking. In a narrow bunk, on a hard mattress, there might have been rest, but here the beds were broad and buoyant; I collected what cushions I could find and tried to wedge myself firm, but through the night I turned with each swing and twist of the ship – she was rolling now as well as pitching – and my head rang with the creak and thud.

Once, an hour before dawn, my wife appeared like a ghost in the doorway, supporting herself with either hand on the jambs, saying: 'Are you awake? Can't you do something? Can't you get something from the doctor?'

I rang for the night steward, who had a draught ready prepared, which comforted her a little.

And all night between dreaming and waking I thought of Julia; in my brief dreams she took a hundred fantastic and terrible and obscene forms, but in my waking thoughts she returned with her sad, starry head just as I had seen her at dinner.

After first light I slept for an hour or two, then awoke clear-headed, with a joyous sense of anticipation.

The wind had dropped a little, the steward told me, but was still blowing hard and there was a very heavy swell; 'which there's nothing worse than a heavy swell', he said, 'for the enjoyment of the passengers. There's not many breakfasts wanted this morning.'

I looked in at my wife, found her sleeping, and closed the door between us; then I ate salmon kedgeree and cold Braden-ham ham and telephoned for a barber to come and shave me.

'There's a lot of stuff in the sitting-room for the lady,' said the steward; 'shall I leave it for the time?'

I went to see. There was a second delivery of cellophane parcels from the shops on board, some ordered by radio from friends in New York whose secretaries had failed to remind them of our departure in time, some by our guests as they left the cocktail party. It was no day for flower vases; I told him to leave them on the floor and then, struck by the thought, removed the card from Mr Kramm's roses and sent them with my love to Julia.

She telephoned while I was being shaved.

'What a deplorable thing to do, Charles! How unlike you!'

'Don't you like them?'

'What can I do with roses on a day like this?'

'Smell them.'

There was a pause and a rustle of unpacking. 'They've absolutely no smell at all.'

'What have you had for breakfast?'

'Muscat grapes and cantaloup.'

'When shall I see you?'

'Before lunch. I'm busy till then with a masseuse.'

'A masseuse?'

'Yes, isn't it peculiar? I've never had one before, except once when I hurt my shoulder hunting. What is it about being on a boat that makes everyone behave like a film star?'

'I don't.'

'How about these very embarrassing roses?'

The barber did his work with extraordinary dexterity – indeed, with agility, for he stood like a swordsman in a ballet sometimes on the point of one foot, sometimes on the other, lightly flicking the lather off his blade, and swooping back to my chin as the ship righted herself; I should not have dared use a safety razor on myself.

The telephone rang again.

It was my wife.

'How are you, Charles?'

'Tired.'

'Aren't you coming to see me?'

'I came once. I'll be in again.'

I brought her the flowers from the sitting-room; they completed the atmosphere of a maternity ward which she had managed to create in the cabin; the stewardess had the air of a midwife, standing by the bed, a pillar of starched linen and composure. My wife turned her head on the pillow and smiled wanly; she stretched out a bare arm and caressed with the tips of her fingers the cellophane and silk ribbons of the largest bouquet. 'How sweet people are,' she said faintly, as though the gale were a private misfortune of her own for which the world in its love was condoling with her.

'I take it you're not getting up.'

'Oh no, Mrs Clark is being so sweet'; she was always quick to get servants' names. 'Don't bother. Come in sometimes and tell me what's going on.'

'Now, now, dear,' said the stewardess, 'the less we are disturbed today the better.'

My wife seemed to make a sacred, female rite even of seasickness.

Julia's cabin, I knew, was somewhere below ours. I waited

for her by the lift on the main deck; when she came we walked once round the promenade; I held the rail; she took my other arm. It was hard going; through the streaming glass we saw a distorted world of grey sky and black water. When the ship rolled heavily I swung her round so that she could hold the rail with her other hand; the howl of the wind was subdued, but the whole ship creaked with strain. We made the circuit once, then Julia said: 'It's no good. That woman beat hell out of me, and I feel limp, anyway. Let's sit down.'

The great bronze doors of the lounge had torn away from their hooks and were swinging free with the roll of the ship; regularly and, it seemed, irresistibly, first one, then the other, opened and shut; they paused at the completion of each half circle, began to move slowly and finished fast with a resounding clash. There was no real risk in passing them, except of slipping and being caught by that swift, final blow; there was ample time to walk through unhurried but there was something forbidding in the sight of that great weight of uncontrolled metal, flapping to and fro, which might have made a timid man flinch or skip through too quickly; I rejoiced to feel Julia's hand perfectly steady on my arm and know, as I walked beside her, that she was wholly undismayed.

'Bravo,' said a man sitting nearby. 'I confess I went round the other way. I didn't like the look of those doors somehow. They've been trying to fix them all the morning.'

There were few people about that day, and that few seemed bound together by a camaraderie of reciprocal esteem; they did nothing except sit rather glumly in their armchairs, drink occasionally, and exchange congratulations on not being seasick.

'You're the first lady I've seen,' said the man.

'I'm very lucky.'

'*We* are very lucky,' he said, with a movement which began as a bow and ended as a lurch forward to his knees, as the blotting-paper floor dipped steeply between us. The roll carried us away from him, clinging together but still on our feet, and we quickly sat where our dance led us, on the further side, in isolation; a web of life-lines had been stretched across the lounge, and we seemed like boxers, roped into the ring.

The steward approached. 'Your usual, sir? Whisky and tepid water, I think. And for the lady? Might I suggest a nip of champagne?'

'D'you know, the awful thing is I *would* like champagne very much,' said Julia. 'What a life of pleasure – roses, half an hour with a female pugilist, and now champagne!'

'I wish you wouldn't go on about the roses. It wasn't my idea in the first place. Someone sent them to Celia.'

'Oh, that's quite different. It lets you out completely. But it makes my massage worse.'

'I was shaved in bed.'

'I'm glad about the roses,' said Julia. 'Frankly, they were a shock. They made me think we were starting the day on the wrong foot.'

I knew what she meant, and in that moment felt as though I had shaken off some of the dust and grit of ten dry years; then and always, however she spoke to me, in half sentences, single words, stock phrases of contemporary jargon, in scarcely perceptible movements of eyes or lips or hands, however inexpressible her thought, however quick and far it had glanced from the matter in hand, however deep it had plunged, as it often did, straight from the surface to the depths, I knew; even that day when I still stood on the extreme verge of love, I knew what she meant.

We drank our wine and soon our new friend came lurching towards us down the life-line.

'Mind if I join you? Nothing like a bit of rough weather for bringing people together. This is my tenth crossing, and I've never seen anything like it. I can see you are an experienced sailor, young lady.'

'No. As a matter of fact, I've never been at sea before except coming to New York and, of course, crossing the Channel. I don't feel sick, thank God, but I feel tired. I thought at first it was only the massage, but I'm coming to the conclusion it's the ship.'

'My wife's in a terrible way. She's an experienced sailor. Only shows, doesn't it?'

He joined us at luncheon, and I did not mind his being there; he had clearly taken a fancy to Julia, and he thought we were man and wife; this misconception and his gallantry seemed in some way to bring her and me closer together. 'Saw you two last night at the Captain's table,' he said, 'with all the nobs.'

'Very dull nobs.'

'If you ask me, nobs always are. When you get a storm like this you find out what people are really made of.'

'You have a predilection for good sailors?'

'Well, put like that I don't know that I do – what I mean is, it makes for getting together.'

'Yes.'

'Take us for example. But for this we might never have met. I've had some very romantic encounters at sea in my time. If the lady will excuse me, I'd like to tell you about a little adventure I had in the Gulf of Lions when I was younger than I am now.'

We were both weary; lack of sleep, the incessant din, and the strain every movement required, wore us down. We spent that afternoon apart in our cabins. I slept and when I awoke the sea was as high as ever, inky clouds swept over us, and the glass streamed still with water, but I had grown used to the storm in my sleep, had made its rhythm mine, had become part of it, so that I arose strongly and confidently and found Julia already up and in the same temper.

'What d'you think?' she said. 'That man's giving a little "get-together party" tonight in the smoking-room for all the good sailors. He asked me to bring my husband.'

'Are we going?'

'Of course. . . . I wonder if I ought to feel like the lady our friend met on the way to Barcelona. I don't, Charles, not a bit.'

There were eighteen people at the 'get-together party'; we had nothing in common except immunity from seasickness. We drank champagne, and presently our host said: 'Tell you what, I've got a roulette wheel. Trouble is we can't go to my cabin on account of the wife, and we aren't allowed to play in public.'

So the party adjourned to my sitting-room and we played for low stakes until late into the night, when Julia left and our host had drunk too much wine to be surprised that she and I were not in the same quarters. When all but he had gone, he fell asleep in his chair, and I left him there. It was the last I saw of him, for later – so the steward told me when he came from returning the roulette things to the man's cabin – he broke his thigh, falling in the corridor, and was taken to the ship's hospital.

All next day Julia and I spent together without interruption; talking, scarcely moving, held in our chairs by the swell of the sea. After luncheon the last hardy passengers went to rest and we were alone as though the place had been cleared for us, as though tact on a titanic scale had sent everyone tip-toeing out to leave us to one another.

The bronze doors of the lounge had been fixed, but not before two seamen had been badly injured. They had tried various devices, lashing with ropes and, later, when these failed, with steel hawsers, but there was nothing to which they could be made fast; finally, they drove wooden wedges under them, catching them in the brief moment of repose when they were full open, and these held firm.

When, before dinner, she went to her cabin to get ready (no one dressed that night) and I came with her, uninvited, unopposed, expected, and behind closed doors took her in my arms and first kissed her, there was no alteration from the mood of the afternoon. Later, turning it over in my mind, as I turned in my bed with the rise and fall of the ship, through the long, lonely, drowsy night, I recalled the courtships of the past, dead, ten years; how, knotting my tie before setting out, putting the gardenia in my button-hole, I would plan my evening and think at such and such a time, at such and such an opportunity, I shall cross the start-line and open my attack for better or worse; 'this phase of the battle has gone on long enough', I would think; 'a decision must be reached.' With Julia there were no phases, no start-line, no tactics at all.

But later that night when she went to bed and I followed her to her door, she stopped me.

'No, Charles, not yet. Perhaps never. I don't know. I don't know if I want love.'

Then something, some surviving ghost from those dead ten years – for one cannot die, even for a little, without some loss – made me say, 'Love? I'm not asking for love.'

'Oh yes, Charles, you are,' she said, and putting up her hand gently stroked my cheek; then shut her door.

And I reeled back, first on one wall, then on the other, of the long, softly lighted, empty corridor; for the storm, it appeared, had the form of a ring; all day we had been sailing through its still centre; now we were once more in the full fury of the wind – and that night was to be rougher than the one before.

Ten hours of talking: what had we to say? Plain fact mostly, the record of our two lives, so long widely separate, now being knit to one. Through all that storm-tossed night I rehearsed what she had told me; she was no longer the alternate succubus and starry vision of the night before; she had given all that was transferable of her past into my keeping. She told me, as I have already retold, of her courtship and marriage; she told me, as though fondly turning the pages of an old nursery-book, of her childhood, and I lived long, sunny days with her in the meadows, with Nanny Hawkins on her camp stool and Cordelia asleep in the pram, slept quiet nights under the dome with the religious pictures fading round the cot as the nightlight burned low and the embers settled in the grate. She told me of her life with Rex and of the secret, vicious, disastrous escapade that had taken her to New York. She, too, had had her dead years. She told me of her long struggle with Rex as to whether she should have a child; at first she wanted one, but learned after a year that an operation was needed to make it possible; by that time Rex and she were out of love, but he still wanted his child, and when at last she consented, it was born dead.

'Rex has never been unkind to me intentionally,' she said. 'It's just that he isn't a real person at all; he's just a few faculties of a man highly developed; the rest simply isn't there. He couldn't imagine why it hurt me to find two months after we came back to London from our honeymoon, that he was still keeping up with Brenda Champion.'

'I was glad when I found Celia was unfaithful,' I said. 'I felt it was all right for me to dislike her.'

'Is she? Do you? I'm glad. I don't like her either. Why did you marry her?'

'Physical attraction. Ambition. Everyone agrees she's the ideal wife for a painter. Loneliness, missing Sebastian.'

'You loved him, didn't you?'

'Oh yes. He was the forerunner.'

Julia understood.

The ship creaked and shuddered, rose and fell. My wife called to me from the next room: 'Charles, are you there?'

'Yes.'

'I've been asleep such a long while. What time is it?'

'Half past three.'

'It's no better, is it?'

'Worse.'

'I feel a little better, though. D'you think they'd bring me some tea or something if I rang the bell?'

I got her some tea and biscuits from the night steward.

'Did you have an amusing evening?'

'Everyone's seasick.'

'Poor Charles. It was going to have been such a lovely trip, too. It may be better tomorrow.'

I turned out the light and shut the door between us.

Waking and dreaming, through the strain and creak and heave of the long night, firm on my back with my arms and legs spread wide to check the roll, and my eyes open to the darkness, I lay thinking of Julia.

'... We thought papa might come back to England after mummy died, or that he might marry again, but he lives just as he did. Rex and I often go to see him now. I've grown fond of him. ... Sebastian's disappeared completely ... Cordelia's in Spain with an ambulance ... Bridey leads his own extraordinary life. He wanted to shut Brideshead after mummy died, but papa wouldn't have it for some reason, so Rex and I live there now, and Bridey has two rooms up in the dome, next to Nanny Hawkins, part of the old nurseries. He's like a character from Chekhov. One meets him sometimes coming out of the library or on the stairs – I never know when he's at home – and now and then he suddenly comes in to dinner like a ghost quite unexpectedly.

'. . . Oh, Rex's parties! Politics and money. They can't do anything except for money; if they walk round the lake they have to make bets about how many swans they see . . . sitting up till two, amusing Rex's girls, hearing them gossip, rattling away endlessly on the backgammon board while the men play cards and smoke cigars. The cigar smoke. I can smell it in my hair when I wake up in the morning; it's in my clothes when I dress at night. Do I smell of it now? D'you think that woman who rubbed me, felt it in my skin?

'. . . At first I used to stay away with Rex in his friends' houses. He doesn't make me any more. He was ashamed of me when he found I didn't cut the kind of figure he wanted, ashamed of himself for having been taken in. I wasn't at all the article he'd bargained for. He can't see the point of me, but whenever he's made up his mind there isn't a point and he's begun to feel comfortable, he gets a surprise – some man, or even woman, he respects, takes a fancy to me and he suddenly sees that there is a whole world of things we understand and he doesn't . . . he was upset when I went away. He'll be delighted to have me back. I was faithful to him until this last thing came along. There's nothing like a good upbringing. Do you know last year, when I thought I was going to have a child, I'd decided to have it brought up a Catholic? I hadn't thought about religion before; I haven't since; but just at that time, when I was waiting for the birth, I thought, "That's one thing I can give her. It doesn't seem to have done me much good, but my child shall have it." It was odd, wanting to give something one had lost oneself. Then, in the end, I couldn't even give that: I couldn't even give her life. I never saw her; I was too ill to know what was going on, and afterwards, for a long time, until now, I didn't want to speak about her – she was a daughter, so Rex didn't so much mind her being dead.

'I've been punished a little for marrying Rex. You see, I can't get all that sort of thing out of my mind, quite – Death, Judgement, Heaven, Hell, Nanny Hawkins, and the catechism. It becomes part of oneself, if they give it one early enough. And yet I wanted my child to have it ... now I suppose I shall be punished for what I've just done. Perhaps that is why you and I are here together like this ... part of a plan.'

That was almost the last thing she said to me – 'part of a plan' – before we went below and I left her at the cabin door.

Next day the wind had again dropped, and again we were wallowing in the swell. The talk was less of seasickness now than of broken bones; people had been thrown about in the night, and there had been many nasty accidents on bathroom floors.

That day, because we had talked so much the day before and because what we had to say needed few words, we spoke little. We had books; Julia found a game she liked. When after long silences we spoke, our thoughts, we found, had kept pace together side by side.

Once I said, 'You are standing guard over your sadness.'

'It's all I have earned. You said yesterday. My wages.'

'An I.O.U. from life. A promise to pay on demand.'

Rain ceased at midday; at evening the clouds dispersed and the sun, astern of us, suddenly broke into the lounge where we sat, putting all the lights to shame.

'Sunset,' said Julia, 'the end of our day.'

She rose and, though the roll and pitch of the ship seemed unabated, led me up to the boat-deck. She put her arm through mine and her hand into mine, in my great-coat pocket. The deck was dry and empty, swept only by the wind of the ship's speed. As we made our halting, laborious way forward, away from the flying smuts of the smoke stack, we were alternately jostled together, then strained, nearly sundered, arms and fingers interlocked as I held the rail and Julia clung to me, thrust together again, drawn apart; then, in a plunge deeper than the rest, I found myself flung across her, pressing her against the rail, warding myself off her with the arms that held her prisoner on either side, and as the ship paused at the end of its drop as though gathering strength for the ascent, we stood thus embraced, in the open, cheek against cheek, her hair blowing across my eyes; the dark horizon of tumbling water, flashing now with gold, stood still above us, then came sweeping down till I was staring through Julia's dark hair into a wide and golden sky, and she was thrown forward on my heart, held up by my hands on the rail, her face still pressed to mine.

In that minute, with her lips to my ear and her breath warm in the salt wind, Julia said, though I had not spoken, 'Yes, now,' and as the ship righted herself and for the moment ran into calmer waters, Julia led me below.

It was no time for the sweets of luxury; they would come, in their season, with the swallow and the lime flowers. Now on the rough water there was a formality to be observed, no more. It was as though a deed of conveyance of her narrow loins had been drawn and sealed. I was making my first entry as the freeholder of a property I would enjoy and develop at leisure.

We dined that night high up in the ship, in the restaurant, and saw through the bow windows the stars come out and sweep across the sky as once, I remembered, I had seen them sweep above the towers and gables of Oxford. The stewards promised that tomorrow night the band would play again and the place be full. We had better book now, they said, if we wanted a good table.

'Oh dear,' said Julia, 'where can we hide in fair weather, we orphans of the storm?'

I could not leave her that night, but early next morning, as once again I made my way back along the corridor, I found I could walk without difficulty; the ship rode easily on a smooth sea, and I knew that our solitude was broken.

My wife called joyously from her cabin: 'Charles, Charles, I feel so well. What do you think I am having for breakfast?'

I went to see. She was eating a beefsteak.

'I've fixed up for a visit to the hairdresser – do you know they couldn't take me till four o'clock this afternoon, they're so busy suddenly? So I shan't appear till the evening, but lots of people are coming in to see us this morning, and I've asked Miles and Janet to lunch with us in our sitting-room. I'm afraid I've been a worthless wife to you the last two days. What have you been up to?'

'One gay evening', I said, 'we played roulette till two o'clock, next door in the sitting-room, and our host passed out.'

'Goodness. It sounds very disreputable. Have you been behaving, Charles? You haven't been picking up sirens?'

'There was scarcely a woman about. I spent most of the time with Julia.'

'Oh, good. I always wanted to bring you together. She's one of my friends I knew you'd like. I expect you were a godsend to her. She's had rather a gloomy time lately. I don't expect she mentioned it, but ...' my wife proceeded to relate a current version of Julia's journey to New York. 'I'll ask her to cocktails this morning,' she concluded.

Julia came among the others, and it was happiness enough, now merely to be near her.

'I hear you've been looking after my husband for me,' my wife said.

'Yes, we've become very matey. He and I and a man whose name we don't know.'

'Mr Kramm, what have you done to your arm?'

'It was the bathroom floor,' said Mr Kramm, and explained at length how he had fallen.

That night the captain dined at his table and the circle was complete, for claimants came to the chairs on the Bishop's right, two Japanese who expressed deep interest in his projects for world-brotherhood. The captain was full of chaff at Julia's endurance in the storm, offering to engage her as a seaman; years of sea-going had given him jokes for every occasion. My wife, fresh from the beauty parlour, was unmarked by her three days of distress, and in the eyes of many seemed to outshine

Julia, whose sadness had gone and been replaced by an incommunicable content and tranquillity; incommunicable save to me; she and I, separated by the crowd, sat alone together close enwrapped, as we had lain in each other's arms the night before.

There was a gala spirit in the ship that night. Though it meant rising at dawn to pack, everyone was determined that for this one night he would enjoy the luxury the storm had denied him. There was no solitude. Every corner of the ship was thronged; dance music and high, excited chatter, stewards darting everywhere with trays of glasses, the voice of the officer in charge of tombola – 'Kelly's eye – number one; legs, eleven; and we'll Shake the Bag' – Mrs Stuyvesant Oglander in a paper cap, Mr Kramm and his bandages, the two Japanese decorously throwing paper streamers and hissing like geese.

I did not speak to Julia, alone, all that evening.

We met for a minute next day on the starboard side of the ship while everyone else crowded to port to see the officials come aboard and to gaze at the green coastline of Devon.

'What are your plans?'

'London for a bit,' she said.

'Celia's going straight home. She wants to see the children.'

'You, too?'

'No.'

'In London then.'

'Charles, the little red-haired man – Foulenough. Did you see? Two plain clothes police have taken him off.'

'I missed it. There was such a crowd on that side of the ship.'

'I found out the trains and sent a telegram. We shall be home by dinner. The children will be asleep. Perhaps we might wake Johnjohn up, just for once.'

'You go down,' I said. 'I shall have to stay in London.'

'Oh, but Charles, you *must* come. You haven't seen Caroline.'

'Will she change much in a week or two?'

'Darling, she changes every day.'

'Then what's the point of seeing her now? I'm sorry, my dear, but I must get the pictures unpacked and see how they've travelled. I must fix up for the exhibition right away.'

'Must you?' she said, but I knew that her resistance ended when I appealed to the mysteries of my trade. 'It's very disappointing. Besides, I don't know if Andrew and Cynthia will be out of the flat. They took it till the end of the month.'

'I can go to an hotel.'

'But that's so grim. I can't bear you to be alone your first night home. I'll stay and go down tomorrow.'

'You mustn't disappoint the children.'

'No.' Her children, my art, the two mysteries of our trades.

'Will you come for the week-end?'

'If I can.'

'All British passports to the smoking-room, please,' said a steward.

'I've arranged with that sweet Foreign Office man at our table to get us off early with him,' said my wife.

CHAPTER II

It was my wife's idea to hold the private view on Friday.

'We are out to catch the critics this time,' she said. 'It's high time they began to take you seriously, and they know it. This is their chance. If you open on Monday, they'll most of them have just come up from the country, and they'll dash off a few paragraphs before dinner – I'm only worrying about the weeklies of course. If we give them the week-end to think about it, we shall have them in an urbane Sunday-in-the-country mood. They'll settle down after a good luncheon, tuck up their cuffs, and turn out a nice, leisurely full-length essay, which they'll reprint later in a nice little book. Nothing less will do this time.'

She was up and down from the Old Rectory several times during the month of preparation, revising the list of invitations and helping with the hanging.

On the morning of the private view I telephoned to Julia

and said: 'I'm sick of the pictures already and never want to see them again, but I suppose I shall have to put in an appearance.'

'D'you want me to come?'

'I'd much rather you didn't.'

'Celia sent a card with "Bring everyone" written across it in green ink. When do we meet?'

'In the train. You might pick up my luggage.'

'If you'll have it packed soon I'll pick you up, too, and drop you at the gallery. I've got a fitting next door at twelve.'

When I reached the gallery my wife was standing looking through the window to the street. Behind her half a dozen unknown picture-lovers were moving from canvas to canvas, catalogue in hand; they were people who had once bought a wood-cut and were consequently on the gallery's list of patrons.

'No one has come yet,' said my wife. 'I've been here since ten and it's been very dull. Whose car was that you came in?'

'Julia's.'

'Julia's? Why didn't you bring her in? Oddly enough, I've just been talking about Brideshead to a funny little man who seemed to know us very well. He said he was called Mr Samgrass. Apparently he's one of Lord Copper's middle-aged young men on the *Daily Beast*. I tried to feed him some paragraphs, but he seemed to know more about you than I do. He said he'd met me years ago at Brideshead. I wish Julia had come in; then we could have asked her about him.'

'I remember him well. He's a crook.'

'Yes, that stuck out a mile. He's been talking all about what he calls the "Brideshead set". Apparently Rex Mottram has made the place a nest of party mutiny. Did you know? What would Teresa Marchmain have thought?'

'I'm going there tonight.'

'Not tonight, Charles; you can't go there *tonight*. You're expected at home. You promised, as soon as the exhibition was ready, you'd come home. Johnjohn and Nanny have made a banner with "Welcome" on it. And you haven't seen Caroline yet.'

'I'm sorry, it's all settled.'

'Besides, Daddy will think it so odd. And Boy is home for Sunday. And you haven't seen the new studio. You can't go tonight. Did they ask me?'

'Of course; but I knew you wouldn't be able to come.'

'I can't now. I could have, if you'd let me know earlier. I should adore to see the "Brideshead set" at home. I do think you're perfectly beastly, but this is no time for a family rumpus. The Clarences promised to come in before luncheon; they may be here any minute.'

We were interrupted, however, not by royalty, but by a woman reporter from one of the dailies, whom the manager of the gallery now led up to us. She had not come to see the pictures but to get a 'human story' of the dangers of my journey. I left her to my wife, and next day read in her paper: *'Charles "Stately Homes" Ryder steps off the map. That the snakes and vampires of the jungle have nothing on Mayfair is the opinion of socialite artist Ryder, who has abandoned the houses of the great for the ruins of equatorial Africa. ...'*

The rooms began to fill and I was soon busy being civil. My wife was everywhere, greeting people, introducing people, deftly transforming the crowd into a party. I saw her lead friends forward one after another to the subscription list that had been opened for the book of *Ryder's Latin America*; I heard her say: 'No, darling, I'm not at all surprised, but you wouldn't expect *me* to be, would you? You see Charles lives for one thing – Beauty. I think he got bored with finding it ready-made in England; he had to go and create it for himself. He wanted new worlds to conquer. After all, he has said the last word about country houses, hasn't he? Not, I mean, that he's given that up altogether. I'm sure he'll always do one or two more for *friends*.'

A photographer brought us together, flashed a lamp in our faces, and let us part.

Presently there was the slight hush and edging away which follows the entry of a royal party. I saw my wife curtsey and heard her say: 'Oh, sir, you are sweet'; then I was led into the clearing and the Duke of Clarence said: 'Pretty hot out there I should think.'

'It was, sir.'

'Awfully clever the way you've hit off the impression of heat. Makes me feel quite uncomfortable in my great-coat.'

'Ha, ha.'

When they had gone my wife said: 'Goodness, we're late for lunch. Margot's giving a party in your honour,' and in the taxi she said: 'I've just thought of something. Why don't you write and ask the Duchess of Clarence's permission to dedicate *Latin America* to her?'

'Why should I?'

'She'd love it so.'

'I wasn't thinking of dedicating it to anyone.'

'There you are; that's typical of you, Charles. Why miss an opportunity to give pleasure?'

There were a dozen at luncheon, and though it pleased my hostess and my wife to say that they were there in my honour, it was plain to me that half of them did not know of my exhibition and had come because they had been invited and had no other engagement. Throughout luncheon they talked, without stopping, of Mrs Simpson, but they all, or nearly all, came back with us to the gallery.

The hour after luncheon was the busiest time. There were representatives of the Tate Gallery and the National Art Collections Fund, who all promised to return shortly with colleagues and, in the meantime, reserved certain pictures for further consideration. The most influential critic, who in the past had dismissed me with a few wounding commendations, peered out at me from between his slouch hat and woollen muffler, gripped my arm, and said: 'I knew you had it. I saw it there. I've been waiting for it.'

From fashionable and unfashionable lips alike I heard fragments of praise. 'If you'd asked me to guess,' I overheard, 'Ryder's is the last name would have occurred to me. They're so virile, so passionate.'

They all thought they had found something new. It had not been thus at my last exhibition in these same rooms, shortly before my going abroad. Then there had been an unmistakable note of weariness. Then the talk had been less of me than of the houses, anecdotes of their owners. That same woman, it came back to me, who now applauded my virility and passion, had stood quite near me, before a painfully laboured canvas, and said, 'So facile'.

I remembered the exhibition, too, for another reason; it was the week I detected my wife in adultery. Then, as now, she was a tireless hostess, and I heard her say: 'Whenever I see anything lovely nowadays – a building or a piece of scenery – I think to myself, "that's by Charles". I see everything through his eyes. He *is* England to me.'

I heard her say that; it was the sort of thing she had the habit of saying. Throughout our married life, again and again, I had felt my bowels shrivel within me at the things she said. But that day, in this gallery, I heard her unmoved, and suddenly realized that she was powerless to hurt me any more; I was a free man; she had given me my manumission in that brief, sly lapse of hers; my cuckold's horns made me lord of the forest.

At the end of the day my wife said: 'Darling, I must go. It's been a terrific success, hasn't it? I'll think of something to tell them at home, but I wish it hadn't got to happen quite this way.'

'So she knows,' I thought. 'She's a sharp one. She's had her nose down since luncheon and picked up the scent.'

I let her get clear of the place and was about to follow – the rooms were nearly empty – when I heard a voice at the turnstile I had not heard for many years, an unforgettable self-taught stammer, a sharp cadence of remonstration.

'No. I have *not* brought a card of invitation. I do not even know whether I received one. I have not come to a social function; I do not seek to scrape acquaintance with Lady Celia; I do not want my photograph in the *Tatler*; I have not come to exhibit myself. I have come to see the *pictures*. Perhaps you are unaware that there are any pictures here. I happen to have a personal interest in the *artist* – if that word has any meaning for you.'

'Antoine,' I said, 'come in.'

'My dear, there is a g-g-gorgon here who thinks I am g-g-gate-crashing. I only arrived in London yesterday, and heard quite by chance at luncheon that you were having an exhibition, so of course I dashed impetuously to the shrine to pay homage. Have I changed? Would you recognize me? Where are the pictures? Let me explain them to you.'

Anthony Blanche had not changed from when I last saw him; not, indeed, from when I first saw him. He swept lightly across the room to the most prominent canvas – a jungle landscape – paused a moment, his head cocked like a knowing terrier, and asked: 'Where, my dear Charles, did you find this sumptuous greenery? The corner of a hothouse at T-t-trent or T-t-tring? What gorgeous usurer nurtured these fronds for your pleasure?'

Then he made a tour of the two rooms; once or twice he sighed deeply, otherwise he kept silence. When he came to the end he sighed once more, more deeply than ever, and said: 'But they tell me, my dear, you are happy in love. That is everything, is it not, or nearly everything?'

'Are they as bad as that?'

Anthony dropped his voice to a piercing whisper: 'My dear, let us not expose your little imposture before these good, plain people' – he gave a conspiratorial glance to the last remnants of the crowd – 'let us not spoil their innocent pleasure. We know, you and I, that this is all t-t-terrible t-t-tripe. Let us go, before we offend the connoisseurs. I know of a *louche* little bar quite near here. Let us go there and talk of your other c-c-conquests.'

It needed this voice from the past to recall me; the indiscriminate chatter of praise all that crowded day had worked on me like a succession of advertisement hoardings on a long road, kilometre after kilometre between the poplars, commanding one to stay at some new hotel, so that when at the end of the drive, stiff and dusty, one arrives at the destination, it seems inevitable to turn into the yard under the name that had first bored, then angered one, and finally become an inseparable part of one's fatigue.

Anthony led me from the gallery and down a side street to a door between a disreputable newsagent and a disreputable chemist, painted with the words 'Blue Grotto Club. Members only.'

'Not quite your milieu, my dear, but mine, I assure you. After all, you have been in your milieu all day.'

He led me downstairs, from a smell of cats to a smell of gin and cigarette-ends and the sound of a wireless.

'I was given the address by a dirty old man in the Boeuf sur le Toit. I am most grateful to him. I have been out of England so long, and really sympathetic little joints like this change so fast. I presented myself here for the first time yesterday evening, and already I feel *quite* at home. Good evening, Cyril.'

' 'Lo, Toni, back again?' said the youth behind the bar.

'We will take our drinks and sit in a corner. You must remember, my dear, that *here* you are just as conspicuous and, may I say, abnormal, my dear, as I should be in B-b-bratt's.'

The place was painted cobalt; there was cobalt linoleum on the floor. Fishes of silver and gold paper had been pasted haphazard on ceiling and walls. Half a dozen youths were drinking and playing with the slot-machines; an older, natty, crapulous-looking man seemed to be in control; there was some sniggering round the fruit-gum machine; then one of the youths came up to us and said, 'Would your friend care to rhumba?'

'No, Tom, he would *not*, and I'm not going to give you a drink; not yet, anyway. That's a very impudent boy, a regular little gold-digger, my dear.'

'Well,' I said, affecting an ease I was far from feeling in that den, 'what have you been up to all these years?'

'My dear, it is what *you* have been up to that we are here to talk about. I've been watching you, my dear. I'm a faithful old body and I've kept my eye on you.' As he spoke the bar and the bar-tender, the blue wicker furniture, the gambling-machines, the gramophone, the couple of youths dancing on the oilcloth, the youths sniggering round the slots, the purple-veined, stiffly-dressed elderly man drinking in the corner opposite us, the whole drab and furtive joint seemed to fade, and I was back in

Oxford looking out over Christ Church meadow through a window of Ruskin-Gothic. 'I went to your first exhibition,' said Anthony; 'I found it – charming. There was an interior of Marchmain House, very English, very correct, but quite delicious. "Charles has done something," I said; "not all he will do, not all he can do, but something."

'Even then, my dear, I wondered a little. It seemed to me that there was something a little *gentlemanly* about your painting. You must remember I am not English; I cannot understand this keen zest to be well-bred. English snobbery is more macabre to me even than English morals. However, I said, "Charles has done something delicious. What will he do next?"

'The next thing I saw was your very handsome volume – *Village and Provincial Architecture*, was it called? Quite a tome, my dear, and what did I find? Charm again. "Not quite my cup of tea," I thought; "this is too English." I have the fancy for rather spicy things, you know, not for the shade of the cedar tree, the cucumber sandwich, the silver cream-jug, the English girl dressed in whatever English girls do wear for tennis – not that, not Jane Austen, *not* M-m-miss M-m-mitford. Then, to be frank, dear Charles, I despaired of you. "I am a degenerate old d-d-dago," I said "and Charles – I speak of your art, my dear – is a dean's daughter in flowered muslin."

'Imagine then my excitement at luncheon today. Everyone was talking about you. My hostess was a friend of my mother's, a Mrs Stuyvesant Oglander; a friend of yours, too, my dear. Such a frump! Not at all the society I imagined you to keep. However, they had all been to your exhibition, but it was *you* they talked of, how you had broken away, my dear, gone to the tropics, become a Gauguin, a Rimbaud. You can imagine how my old heart leaped.

' "Poor Celia," they said, "after all she's done for him." "He owes everything to her. It's too bad." "And with Julia," they said, "after the way she behaved in America." "Just as she was going back to Rex."

' "But the pictures," I said; "Tell me about *them*."

' "Oh, the pictures," they said; "they're most peculiar."

"Not at all what he usually does." "Very forceful." "Quite barbaric." "I call them downright unhealthy," said Mrs Stuyvesant Oglander.

'My dear, I could hardly keep still in my chair. I wanted to dash out of the house and leap in a taxi and say, "Take me to Charles's unhealthy pictures." Well, I went, but the gallery after luncheon was so full of absurd women in the sort of hats they should be made to *eat*, that I rested a little – I rested here with Cyril and Tom and these saucy boys. Then I came back at the unfashionable time of five o'clock, all agog, my dear; and what did I find? I found, my dear, a very naughty and very successful practical joke. It reminded me of dear Sebastian when he liked so much to dress up in false whiskers. It was charm again, my dear, simple, creamy English charm, playing tigers.'

'You're quite right,' I said.

'My dear, of course I'm right. I was right years ago – more years, I am happy to say, than either of us shows – when I *warned* you. I took you out to dinner to warn you of charm. I warned you expressly and in great detail of the Flyte family. Charm is the great English blight. It does not exist outside these damp islands. It spots and kills anything it touches. It kills love; it kills art; I greatly fear, my dear Charles, it has killed *you*.'

The youth called Tom approached us again. 'Don't be a tease, Toni; buy me a drink.' I remembered my train and left Anthony with him.

As I stood on the platform by the restaurant-car I saw my luggage and Julia's go past with Julia's sour-faced maid strutting beside the porter. They had begun shutting the carriage doors when Julia arrived, unhurried, and took her place in front of me. I had a table for two. This was a very convenient train; there was half an hour before dinner and half an hour after it; then, instead of changing to the branch line, as had been the rule in Lady Marchmain's day, we were met at the junction. It was night as we drew out of Paddington, and the glow of the town gave place first to the scattered lights of the suburbs, then to the darkness of the fields.

'It seems days since I saw you,' I said.

'Six hours; and we were together all yesterday. You look worn out.'

'It's been a day of nightmare – crowds, critics, the Clarences, a luncheon party at Margot's, ending up with half an hour's well-reasoned abuse of my pictures in a pansy bar. ... I think Celia knows about us.'

'Well, she had to know some time.'

'Everyone seems to know. My pansy friend had not been in London twenty-four hours before he'd heard.'

'Damn everybody.'

'What about Rex?'

'Rex isn't anybody at all,' said Julia; 'he just doesn't exist.'

The knives and forks jingled on the tables as we sped through the darkness; the little circle of gin and vermouth in the glasses lengthened to oval, contracted again, with the sway of the carriage, touched the lip, lapped back again, never spilt; I was leaving the day behind me. Julia pulled off her hat and tossed it into the rack above her, and shook her night-dark hair with a little sigh of ease – a sigh fit for the pillow, the sinking firelight, and a bedroom window open to the stars and the whisper of bare trees.

'It's great to have you back, Charles; like the old days.'

'Like the old days?' I thought.

Rex, in his early forties, had grown heavy and ruddy; he had lost his Canadian accent and acquired instead the hoarse, loud tone that was common to all his friends, as though their voices were perpetually strained to make themselves heard above a crowd, as though, with youth forsaking them, there was no time to wait the opportunity to speak, no time to listen, no time to reply; time for a laugh – a throaty mirthless laugh, the base currency of goodwill.

There were half a dozen of these friends in the Tapestry Hall: politicians; 'young Conservatives' in the early forties, with sparse hair and high blood-pressure; a Socialist from the coal-mines who had already caught their clear accents, whose cigars came to pieces on his lips, whose hand shook when he poured himself out a drink; a financier older than the rest, and, one might guess from the way they treated him, richer; a love-sick columnist, who alone was silent, gloating sombrely on the only woman of the party; a woman they called 'Grizel', a knowing rake whom, in their hearts, they all feared a little.

They all feared Julia, too, Grizel included. She greeted them and apologized for not being there to welcome them, with a formality which hushed them for a minute; then she came and sat with me near the fire, and the storm of talk arose once more and whirled about our ears.

'Of course, he can marry her and make her queen tomorrow.'

'We had our chance in October. Why didn't we send the Italian fleet to the bottom of Mare Nostrum? Why didn't we blow Spezia to blazes? Why didn't we land on Pantelleria?'

'Franco's simply a German agent. They tried to put him in to prepare air bases to bomb France. That bluff has been called, anyway.'

'It would make the monarchy stronger than it's been since Tudor times. The people are with him.'

'The Press are with him.'

'I'm with him.'

'Who cares about divorce now except a few old maids who aren't married, anyway?'

'If he has a show-down with the old gang, they'll just disappear like, like ...'

'Why didn't we close the canal? Why didn't we bomb Rome?'

'It wouldn't have been necessary. One firm note ...'

'One firm speech.'

'One show-down.'

'Anyway, Franco will soon be skipping back to Morocco. Chap I saw today just come from Barcelona. ...'

'... Chap just come from Fort Belvedere. ...'

'... Chap just come from the Palazzo Venezia. ...'

'All we want is a show-down.'

'A show-down with Baldwin.'

'A show-down with Hitler.'

'A show-down with the Old Gang.'

'. . . That I should live to see my country, the land of Clive and Nelson. . . .'

'. . . *My* country of Hawkins and Drake.'

'. . . *My* country of Palmerston. . . .'

'Would you very much mind not doing that?' said Grizel to the columnist, who had been attempting in a maudlin manner to twist her wrist; 'I don't happen to enjoy it.'

'I wonder which is the more horrible,' I said, 'Celia's Art and Fashion or Rex's Politics and Money.'

'Why worry about them?'

'Oh, my darling, why is it that love makes me hate the world? It's supposed to have quite the opposite effect. I feel as though all mankind, and God, too, were in a conspiracy against us.'

'They are, they are.'

'But we've got our happiness in spite of them; here and now, we've taken possession of it. They can't hurt us, can they?'

'Not tonight; not now.'

'Not for how many nights?'

CHAPTER III

'Do you remember,' said Julia, in the tranquil, lime-scented evening, 'do you remember the storm?'

'The bronze doors banging.'

'The roses in cellophane.'

'The man who gave the "get-together" party and was never seen again.'

'Do you remember how the sun came out on our last evening just as it has done today?'

It had been an afternoon of low cloud and summer squalls, so overcast that at times I had stopped work and roused Julia from the light trance in which she sat – she had sat so often;

I never tired of painting her, forever finding in her new wealth and delicacy – until at length we had gone early to our baths and, on coming down, dressed for dinner, in the last half-hour of the day, we found the world transformed; the sun had emerged; the wind had fallen to a soft breeze which gently stirred the blossom in the limes and carried its fragrance, fresh from the late rains, to merge with the sweet breath of box and the drying stone. The shadow of the obelisk spanned the terrace.

I had carried two garden cushions from the shelter of the colonnade and put them on the rim of the fountain. There Julia sat, in a tight little gold tunic and a white gown, one hand in the water idly turning an emerald ring to catch the fire of the sunset; the carved animals mounted over her dark head in a cumulus of green moss and glowing stone and dense shadow, and the waters round them flashed and bubbled and broke into scattered flames.

'. . . So much to remember,' she said. 'How many days have there been since then, when we haven't seen each other; a hundred, do you think?'

'Not so many.'

'Two Christmases' – those bleak, annual excursions into propriety. Boughton, home of my family, home of my cousin Jasper, with what glum memories of childhood I revisited its pitch-pine corridors and dripping walls! How querulously my father and I, seated side by side in my uncle's Humber, approached the avenue of Wellingtonias knowing that at the end of the drive we should find my uncle, my aunt, my Aunt Philippa, my cousin Jasper, and, of recent years, Jasper's wife and children; and besides them, perhaps already arrived, perhaps every moment expected, my wife and my children. This annual sacrifice united us; here among the holly and mistletoe and the cut spruce, the parlour games ritually performed, the brandy-butter and the Carlsbad plums, the village choir in the pitch-pine minstrels' gallery, gold twine and sprigged wrapping-paper, she and I were accepted, whatever ugly rumours had been afloat in the past year, as man and wife. 'We must keep it up, whatever it costs us, for the sake of the children,' my wife said.

'Yes, two Christmases. ... And the three days of good taste before I followed you to Capri.'

'Our first summer.'

'Do you remember how I hung about Naples, then followed, how we met by arrangement on the hill path and how flat it fell?'

'I went back to the villa and said, "Papa, who do you think has arrived at the hotel?" and he said, "Charles Ryder, I suppose." I said, "Why did you think of him?" and papa replied, "Cara came back from Paris with the news that you and he were inseparable. He seems to have a penchant for my children. However, bring him here; I think we have the room." '

'There was the time you had jaundice and wouldn't let me see you.'

'And when I had flu and you were afraid to come.'

'Countless visits to Rex's constituency.'

'And Coronation Week, when you ran away from London. Your goodwill mission to your father-in-law. The time you went to Oxford to paint the picture they didn't like. Oh, yes, quite a hundred days.'

'A hundred days wasted out of two years and a bit ... not a day's coldness or mistrust or disappointment.'

'Never that.'

We fell silent; only the birds spoke in a multitude of small, clear voices in the lime trees; only the waters spoke among their carved stones.

Julia took the handkerchief from my breast pocket and dried her hand; then lit a cigarette. I feared to break the spell of memories, but for once our thoughts had not kept pace together, for when at length Julia spoke, she said sadly: 'How many more? Another hundred?'

'A lifetime.'

'I want to marry you, Charles.'

'One day; why now?'

'War,' she said, 'this year, next year, sometime soon. I want a day or two with you of real peace.'

'Isn't this peace?'

The sun had sunk now to the line of woodland beyond the valley; all the opposing slope was already in twilight, but the lakes below us were aflame; the light grew in strength and splendour as it neared death, drawing long shadows across the pasture, falling full on the rich stone spaces of the house, firing the panes in the windows, glowing on cornices and colonnade and dome, spreading out all the stacked merchandise of colour and scent from earth and stone and leaf, glorifying the head and golden shoulders of the woman beside me.

'What do you mean by "peace", if not this?'

'So much more'; and then in a chill, matter-of-fact tone she continued: 'Marriage isn't a thing we can take when the impulse moves us. There must be a divorce – two divorces. We must make plans.'

'Plans, divorce, war – on an evening like this.'

'Sometimes,' said Julia, 'I feel the past and the future pressing so hard on either side that there's no room for the present at all.'

Then Wilcox came down the steps into the sunset to tell us that dinner was ready.

Shutters were up, curtains drawn, candles lit, in the Painted Parlour.

'Hullo, it's laid for three.'

'Lord Brideshead arrived half an hour ago, my lady. He sent a message would you please not wait dinner for him as he may be a little late.'

'It seems months since he was here last,' said Julia. 'What *does* he do in London?'

It was often a matter for speculation between us – giving birth to many fantasies, for Bridey was a mystery; a creature from underground; a hard-snouted, burrowing, hibernating animal who shunned the light. He had been completely without action in all his years of adult life; the talk of his going into the army and into parliament and into a monastery, had all come to nothing. All that he was known with certainty to have done –

and this because in a season of scant news it had formed the subject of a newspaper article entitled '*Peer's Unusual Hobby*' — was to form a collection of match-boxes; he kept them mounted on boards, card-indexed, yearly occupying a larger and larger space in his small house in Westminster. At first he was bashful about the notoriety which the newspaper caused, but later greatly pleased, for he found it the means of his getting into touch with other collectors in all parts of the world with whom he now corresponded and swapped duplicates. Other than this he was not known to have any interests. He remained Joint-Master of the Marchmain and hunted with them dutifully on their two days a week when he was at home; he never hunted with the neighbouring pack, who had the better country. He had no real zest for sport, and had not been out a dozen times that season; he had few friends; he visited his aunts; he went to public dinners held in the Catholic interest. At Brideshead he performed all unavoidable local duties, bringing with him to platform and fête and committee room his own thin mist of clumsiness and aloofness.

'There was a girl found strangled with a piece of barbed wire at Wandsworth last week,' I said, reviving an old fantasy.

'That must be Bridey. He is naughty.'

When we had been a quarter of an hour at the table, he joined us, coming ponderously into the room in the bottle-green velvet smoking suit which he kept at Brideshead and always wore when he was there. At thirty-eight he had grown heavy and bald, and might have been taken for forty-five.

'Well,' he said, 'well, only you two; I hoped to find Rex here.'

I often wondered what he made of me and of my continual presence; he seemed to accept me, without curiosity, as one of the household. Twice in the past two years he had surprised me by what seemed to be acts of friendship; that Christmas he had sent me a photograph of himself in the robes of a Knight of Malta, and shortly afterwards asked me to go with him to a dining club. Both acts had an explanation: he had had more copies of his portrait printed than he knew what to do with; he was proud of his club. It was a surprising association of men quite eminent in their professions who met once a month for an evening of ceremonious buffoonery; each had his sobriquet – Bridey was called 'Brother Grandee' – and a specially designed jewel worn like an order of chivalry, symbolizing it; they had club buttons for their waistcoats and an elaborate ritual for the introduction of guests; after dinner a paper was read and facetious speeches were made. There was plainly some competition to bring guests of distinction, and since Bridey had few friends, and since I was tolerably well known, I was invited. Even on that convivial evening I could feel my host emanating little magnetic waves of social uneasiness, creating, rather, a pool of general embarrassment about himself in which he floated with log-like calm.

He sat down opposite me and bowed his sparse, pink head over his plate.

'Well, Bridey. What's the news?'

'As a matter of fact,' he said, 'I have some news. But it can wait.'

'Tell us now.'

He made a grimace which I took to mean 'not in front of the servants', and said, 'How is the painting, Charles?'

'Which painting?'

'Whatever you have on the stocks.'

'I began a sketch of Julia, but the light was tricky all today.'

'Julia? I thought you'd done her before. I suppose it's a change from architecture, and much more difficult.'

His conversation abounded in long pauses during which his mind seemed to remain motionless; he always brought one back with a start to the exact point where he had stopped. Now after more than a minute he said: 'The world is full of different subjects.'

'Very true, Bridey.'

'If I were a painter,' he said, 'I should choose an entirely different subject every time; subjects with plenty of action in them like ...' Another pause. What, I wondered was coming? The Flying Scotsman? The Charge of the Light Brigade?

Henley Regatta? Then surprisingly he said: '... like Macbeth.'
There was something supremely preposterous in the idea of
Bridey as a painter of action pictures; he was usually preposterous yet somehow achieved a certain dignity by his remoteness
and agelessness; he was still half-child, already half-veteran;
there seemed no spark of contemporary life in him; he had a
kind of massive rectitude and impermeability, an indifference to
the world, which compelled respect. Though we often laughed
at him, he was never wholly ridiculous; at times he was even
formidable.

We talked of the news from central Europe until, suddenly
cutting across this barren topic, Bridey asked: 'Where are
mummy's jewels?'

'This was hers,' said Julia, 'and this. Cordelia and I had all
her own things. The family jewels went to the bank.'

'It's so long since I've seen them – I don't know that I ever
saw them all. What is there? Aren't there some rather famous
rubies, someone was telling me?'

'Yes, a necklace. Mummy used often to wear it, don't you
remember? And there are the pearls – she always had those out.
But most of it stayed in the bank year after year. There are some
hideous diamond fenders, I remember, and a Victorian diamond collar no one could wear now. There's a mass of good
stones. Why?'

'I'd like to have a look at them some day.'

'I say, papa isn't going to pop them, is he? He hasn't got into
debt again?'

'No, no, nothing like that.'

Bridey was a slow and copious eater. Julia and I watched
him between the candles. Presently he said: 'If I was Rex' – his
mind seemed full of such suppositions: 'If I was Archbishop of
Westminster', 'If I was head of the Great Western Railway', 'If
I was an actress', as though it were a mere trick of fate that he
was none of these things, and he might awake any morning to
find the matter adjusted – 'if I was Rex I should want to live in
my constituency.'

'Rex says it saves four days' work a week not to.'

'I'm sorry he's not here. I have a little announcement to make.'

'Bridey, don't be so mysterious. Out with it.'

He made the grimace which seemed to mean 'not before the servants'.

Later when port was on the table and we three were alone Julia said: 'I'm not going till I hear the announcement.'

'Well,' said Bridey, sitting back in his chair and gazing fixedly at his glass. 'You have only to wait until Monday to see it in black and white in the newspapers. I am engaged to be married. I hope you are pleased.'

'Bridey. How ... how very exciting! Who to?'

'Oh, no one you know.'

'Is she pretty?'

'I don't think you would exactly call her pretty; 'comely' is the word I think of in her connexion. She is a big woman.'

'Fat?'

'No, big. She is called Mrs Muspratt; her Christian name is Beryl. I have known her for a long time, but until last year she had a husband; now she is a widow. Why do you laugh?'

'I'm sorry. It isn't the least funny. It's just so unexpected. Is she ... is she about your own age?'

'Just about, I believe. She has three children, the eldest boy has just gone to Ampleforth. She is not at all well off.'

'But, Bridey, where did you find her?'

'Her late husband, Admiral Muspratt, collected match-boxes,' he said with complete gravity.

Julia trembled on the verge of laughter, recovered her self-possession, and asked: 'You're not marrying her for her match-boxes?'

'No, no; the whole collection was left to the Falmouth Town Library. I have a great affection for her. In spite of all her difficulties she is a very cheerful woman, very fond of acting. She is connected with the Catholic Players' Guild.'

'Does papa know?'

'I had a letter from him this morning giving me his approval. He has been urging me to marry for some time.'

It occurred both to Julia and myself simultaneously that we were allowing curiosity and surprise to predominate; now we congratulated him in gentler tones from which mockery was almost excluded.

'Thank you,' he said, 'thank you. I think I am very fortunate.'

'But when are we going to meet her? I do think you might have brought her down with you.'

He said nothing, sipped and gazed.

'Bridey,' said Julia. 'You sly, smug old brute, why haven't you brought her here?'

'Oh, I couldn't do that, you know.'

'Why couldn't you? I'm dying to meet her. Let's ring her up now and invite her. She'll think us most peculiar leaving her alone at a time like this.'

'She has the children,' said Brideshead. 'Besides, you *are* peculiar, aren't you?'

'What can you mean?'

Brideshead raised his head and looked solemnly at his sister, and continued in the same simple way, as though he were saying nothing particularly different from what had gone before, 'I couldn't ask her here, as things are. It wouldn't be suitable. After all, I am a lodger here. This is Rex's house at the moment, so far as it's anybody's. What goes on here is his business. But I couldn't bring Beryl here.'

'I simply don't understand,' said Julia rather sharply. I looked at her. All the gentle mockery had gone; she was alert, almost scared, it seemed. 'Of course, Rex and I want her to come.'

'Oh, yes, I don't doubt that. The difficulty is quite otherwise.' He finished his port, refilled his glass, and pushed the decanter towards me. 'You must understand that Beryl is a woman of strict Catholic principle fortified by the prejudices of the middle class. I couldn't possibly bring her here. It is a matter of indifference whether you choose to live in sin with Rex or Charles or both – I have always avoided inquiry into the details of your *ménage* – but in no case would Beryl consent to be your guest.'

Julia rose. 'Why, you pompous ass . . .' she said, stopped, and turned towards the door.

At first I thought she was overcome by laughter; then, as I opened the door to her, I saw with consternation that she was in tears. I hesitated. She slipped past me without a glance.

'I may have given the impression that this was a marriage of convenience,' Brideshead continued placidly. 'I cannot speak for Beryl; no doubt the security of my position has some influence on her. Indeed, she has said as much. But for myself, let me emphasize, I am ardently attracted.'

'Bridey, what a bloody offensive thing to say to Julia!'

'There was nothing she should object to. I was merely stating a fact well known to her.'

She was not in the library; I mounted to her room, but she was not there. I paused by her laden dressing table wondering if she would come. Then through the open window, as the light streamed out across the terrace into the dusk, to the fountain which in that house seemed always to draw us to itself for comfort and refreshment, I caught the glimpse of a white skirt against the stones. It was nearly night. I found her in the darkest refuge, on a wooden seat, in a bay of the clipped box which encircled the basin. I took her in my arms and she pressed her face to my heart.

'Aren't you cold out here?'

She did not answer, only clung closer to me, and shook with sobs.

'My darling, what is it? Why do you mind? What does it matter what that old booby says?'

'I don't; it doesn't. It's just the shock. Don't laugh at me.'

In the two years of our love, which seemed a lifetime, I had not seen her so moved or felt so powerless to help.

'How dare he speak to you like that?' I said. 'The cold-blooded old humbug . . .' But I was failing her in sympathy.

'No,' she said, 'it's not that. He's quite right. They know all about it, Bridey and his widow; they've got it in black and white; they bought it for a penny at the church door. You can get anything there for a penny, in black and white, and nobody to see that you pay; only an old woman with a broom at the other end, rattling round the confessionals, and a young woman lighting a candle at the Seven Dolours. Put a penny in the box, or not, just as you like; take your tract. There you've got it, in black and white.

'All in one word, too, one little, flat, deadly word that covers a lifetime.

' "Living in Sin"; not just doing wrong, as I did when I went to America; doing wrong, knowing it is wrong, stopping doing it, forgetting. That's not what they mean. That's not Bridey's pennyworth. He means just what it says in black and white.

'*Living in sin*, with sin, always the same, like an idiot child carefully nursed, guarded from the world. "Poor Julia," they say, "she can't go out. She's got to take care of her sin. A pity it ever lived," they say, "but it's so strong. Children like that always are. Julia's so good to her little, mad sin." '

'An hour ago,' I thought, 'under the sunset, she sat turning her ring in the water and counting the days of happiness; now under the first stars and the last grey whisper of day, all this mysterious tumult of sorrow! What had happened to us in the Painted Parlour? What shadow had fallen in the candlelight? Two rough sentences and a trite phrase.' She was beside herself; her voice, now muffled in my breast, now clear and anguished, came to me in single words and broken sentences.

'Past and future; the years when I was trying to be a good wife, in the cigar smoke, while the counters clicked on the backgammon board, and the man who was "dummy" at the men's table filled the glasses; when I was trying to bear his child, torn in pieces by something already dead; putting him away, forgetting him, finding you, the past two years with you, all the future with you, all the future with or without you, war coming, world ending – sin.

'A word from so long ago, from Nanny Hawkins stitching by the hearth and the nightlight burning before the Sacred Heart. Cordelia and me with the catechism, in mummy's room, before luncheon on Sundays. Mummy carrying my sin with her to church, bowed under it and the black lace veil, in the chapel; slipping out with it in London before the fires were lit; taking it with her through the empty streets, where the milkman's ponies stood with their forefeet on the pavement; mummy dying with my sin eating at her, more cruelly than her own deadly illness.

'Mummy dying with it; Christ dying with it, nailed hand and foot; hanging over the bed in the night-nursery; hanging year after year in the dark little study at Farm Street with the shining oilcloth; hanging in the dark church where only the old charwoman raises the dust and one candle burns; hanging at noon, high among the crowds and the soldiers; no comfort except a sponge of vinegar and the kind words of a thief; hanging for ever; never the cool sepulchre and the grave clothes spread on the stone slab, never the oil and spices in the dark cave; always the midday sun and the dice clicking for the seamless coat.

'No way back; the gates barred; all the saints and angels posted along the walls. Thrown away, scrapped, rotting down; the old man with lupus and the forked stick who limps out at nightfall to turn the rubbish, hoping for something to put in his sack, something marketable, turns away with disgust.

'Nameless and dead, like the baby they wrapped up and took away before I had seen her.'

Between her tears she talked herself into silence. I could do nothing; I was adrift in a strange sea; my hands on the metal-spun threads of her tunic were cold and stiff, my eyes dry; I was as far from her in spirit, as she clung to me in the darkness, as when years ago I had lit her cigarette on the way from the station; as far as when she was out of mind, in the dry, empty years at the Old Rectory, and in the jungle.

Tears spring from speech; presently in her silence her weeping stopped. She sat up, away from me, took my handkerchief, shivered, rose to her feet.

'Well,' she said, in a voice much like normal. 'Bridey is one for bombshells, isn't he?'

I followed her into the house and to her room; she sat at her looking-glass. 'Considering that I've just recovered from a fit of hysteria,' she said, 'I don't call that at all bad.' Her eyes seemed unnaturally large and bright, her cheeks pale with two spots of high colour, where, as a girl, she used to put a dab of rouge. 'Most hysterical women look as if they had a bad cold. You'd better change your shirt before going down; it's all tears and lipstick.'

'Are we going down?'

'Of course, we mustn't leave poor Bridey on his engagement night.'

'When I went back to her she said: 'I'm sorry for that appalling scene, Charles. I can't explain.'

Brideshead was in the library, smoking his pipe, placidly reading a detective story.

'Was it nice out? If I'd known you were going I'd have come, too.'

'Rather cold.'

'I hope it's not going to be inconvenient for Rex moving out of here. You see, Barton Street is much too small for us and the three children. Besides, Beryl likes the country. In his letter papa proposed making over the whole estate right away.'

I remembered how Rex had greeted me on my first arrival at Brideshead as Julia's guest. 'A very happy arrangement,' he had said. 'Suits me down to the ground. The old boy keeps the place up; Bridey does all the feudal stuff with the tenants; I have the run of the house rent free. All it costs me is the food and the wages of the indoor servants. Couldn't ask fairer than that, could you?'

'I should think he'll be sorry to go,' I said.

'Oh, he'll find another bargain somewhere,' said Julia; 'trust him.'

'Beryl's got some furniture of her own she's very attached to. I don't know if it would go very well here. You know, oak dressers and coffin stools and things. I thought she could put it in mummy's old room.'

'Yes, that would be the place.'

So brother and sister sat and talked about the arrangement of the house until bedtime. 'An hour ago,' I thought, 'in the black refuge in the box hedge, she wept her heart out for the death of her God; now she is discussing whether Beryl's children shall take the old smoking-room or the school-room for their own.' I was all at sea.

'Julia,' I said later, when Brideshead had gone upstairs, 'have you ever seen a picture of Holman Hunt's called "The Awakened Conscience"?'

'No.'

I had seen a copy of *Pre-Raphaelitism* in the library some days before; I found it again and read her Ruskin's description. She laughed quite happily.

'You're perfectly right. That's exactly what I did feel.'

'But, darling, I won't believe that great spout of tears came just from a few words of Bridey's. You must have been thinking about it before.'

'Hardly at all; now and then; more, lately, with the Last Trump so near.'

'Of course it's a thing psychologists could explain; a preconditioning from childhood; feelings of guilt from the nonsense you were taught in the nursery. You do know at heart that it's all bosh, don't you?'

'How I wish it was!'

'Sebastian once said almost the same thing to me.'

'He's gone back to the Church, you know. Of course, he never left it as definitely as I did. I've gone too far; there's no turning back now; I know that, if that's what you mean by thinking it all bosh. All I can hope to do is to put my life in some sort of order in a human way, before all human order comes to an end. That's why I want to marry you. I should like to have a child. That's one thing I can do. ... Let's go out again. The moon should be up by now.'

The moon was full and high. We walked round the house; under the limes Julia paused and idly snapped off one of the long shoots, last year's growth, that fringed their boles, and stripped it as she walked, making a switch, as children do, but with petulant movements that were not a child's, snatching nervously at the leaves and crumbling them between her fingers; she began peeling the bark, scratching it with her nails.

Once more we stood by the fountain.

'It's like the setting of a comedy,' I said. 'Scene: a Baroque fountain in a nobleman's grounds. Act one, sunset; act two, dusk; act three, moonlight. The characters keep assembling at the fountain for no very clear reason.'

'Comedy?'

'Drama. Tragedy. Farce. What you will. This is the reconciliation scene.'

'Was there a quarrel?'

'Estrangement and misunderstanding in act two.'

'Oh, don't talk in that damned bounderish way. Why must you see everything second-hand? Why must this be a play? Why must my conscience be a pre-Raphaelite picture?'

'It's a way I have.'

'I hate it.'

Her anger was as unexpected as every change on this evening of swift veering moods. Suddenly she cut me across the face with her switch, a vicious, stinging little blow as hard as she could strike.

'Now do you see how I hate it?'

She hit me again.

'All right,' I said, 'go on.'

Then, though her hand was raised, she stopped and threw the half-peeled wand into the water, where it floated white and black in the moonlight.

'Did that hurt?'

'Yes.'

'Did it? ... Did I?'

In the instant her rage was gone; her tears, newly flowing, were on my cheek. I held her at arm's length and she put down her head, stroking my hand on her shoulder with her face, cat-like, but, unlike a cat, leaving a tear there.

'Cat on the roof-top,' I said.

'Beast!'

She bit at my hand, but when I did not move it and her

teeth touched me, she changed the bite to a kiss, the kiss to a lick of her tongue.

'Cat in the moonlight.'

This was the mood I knew. We turned towards the house. When we came to the lighted hall she said: 'Your poor face,' touching the weals with her fingers. 'Will there be a mark tomorrow?'

'I expect so.'

'Charles, am I going crazy? What's happened tonight? I'm so tired.'

She yawned; a fit of yawning took her. She sat at her dressing table, head bowed, hair over her face, yawning help-lessly; when she looked up I saw over her shoulder in the glass a face that was dazed with weariness like a retreating soldier's, and beside it my own, streaked with two crimson lines.

'So tired,' she repeated, taking off her gold tunic and letting it fall to the floor, 'tired and crazy and good for nothing.'

I saw her to bed; the blue lids fell over her eyes; her pale lips moved on the pillow, but whether to wish me good night or to murmur a prayer – a jingle of the nursery that came to her now in the twilight world between sorrow and sleep: some ancient pious rhyme that had come down to Nanny Hawkins from centuries of bedtime whispering, through all the changes of language, from the days of pack-horses on the Pilgrim's Way – I did not know.

Next night Rex and his political associates were with us.

'They won't fight.'

'They can't fight. They haven't the money; they haven't the oil.'

'They haven't the wolfram; they haven't the men.'

'They haven't the guts.'

'They're afraid.'

'Scared of the French; scared of the Czechs; scared of the Slovaks; scared of us.'

'It's a bluff.'

'Of course it's a bluff. Where's their tungsten? Where's their manganese?'

'Where's their chrome?'

'I'll tell you a thing ...'

'Listen to this; it'll be good; Rex will tell you a thing.'

'... Friend of mine motoring in the Black Forest, only the other day, just came back and told me about it while we played a round of golf. Well, this friend driving along, turned down a lane into the high road. What should he find but a military convoy? Couldn't stop, drove right into it, smack into a tank, broadside on. Gave himself up for dead. ... Hold on, this is the funny part.'

'This is the funny part.'

'Drove clean through it, didn't scratch his paint. What do you think? It was made of canvas – a bamboo frame and painted canvas.'

'They haven't the steel.'

'They haven't the tools. They haven't the labour. They're half starving. They haven't the fats. The children have rickets.'

'The women are barren.'

'The men are impotent.'

'They haven't the doctors.'

'The doctors were Jewish.'

'Now they've got consumption.'

'Now they've got syphilis.'

'Goering told a friend of mine ...'

'Goebbels told a friend of mine ...'

'Ribbentrop told me that the army just kept Hitler in power so long as he was able to get things for nothing. The moment anyone stands up to him, he's finished. The army will shoot him.'

'The Liberals will hang him.'

'The Communists will tear him limb from limb.'

'He'll scupper himself.'

'He'd do it now if it wasn't for Chamberlain.'

'If it wasn't for Halifax.'

'If it wasn't for Sir Samuel Hoare.'

'And the 1922 Committee.'

'Peace Pledge.'

'Foreign Office.'

'New York Banks.'

'All that's wanted is a good strong line.'

'A line from Rex.'

'And a line from me.'

'We'll give Europe a good strong line. Europe is waiting for a speech from Rex.'

'And a speech from me.'

'And a speech from me. Rally the freedom-loving peoples of the world. Germany will rise; Austria will rise. The Czechs and the Slovaks are bound to rise.'

'To a speech from Rex and a speech from me.'

'What about a rubber? How about a whisky? Which of you chaps will have a big cigar? Hullo, you two going out?'

'Yes, Rex,' said Julia. 'Charles and I are going into the moonlight.'

We shut the windows behind us and the voices ceased; the moonlight lay like hoar-frost on the terrace and the music of the fountain crept in our ears; the stone balustrade of the terrace might have been the Trojan walls, and in the silent park might have stood the Grecian tents where Cressid lay that night.

'A few days, a few months.'

'No time to be lost.'

'A lifetime between the rising of the moon and its setting. Then the dark.'

CHAPTER IV

'AND of course Celia will have custody of the children.'

'Of course.'

'Then what about the Old Rectory? I don't imagine you'll want to settle down with Julia bang at our gates. The children look on it as their home, you know. Robin's got no place of his own till his uncle dies. After all, you never used the studio, did you? Robin was saying only the other day what a good play-room it would make – big enough for Badminton.'

'Robin can have the Old Rectory.'

'Now with regard to money, Celia and Robin naturally don't want to accept anything for themselves, but there's the question of the children's education.'

'That will be all right. I'll see the lawyers about it.'

'Well, I think that's everything,' said Mulcaster. 'You know, I've seen a few divorces in my time, and I've never known one work out so happily for all concerned. Almost always, however matey people are at the start, bad blood crops up when they get down to detail. Mind you, I don't mind saying there have been times in the last two years when I thought you were treating Celia a bit rough. It's hard to tell with one's own sister, but I've always thought her a jolly attractive girl, the sort of girl any chap would be glad to have – artistic, too, just down your street. But I must admit you're a good picker. I've always had a soft spot for Julia. Anyway, as things have turned out everyone seems satisfied. Robin's been mad about Celia for a year or more. D'you know him?'

'Vaguely. A half-baked, pimply youth as I remember him.'

'Oh, I wouldn't quite say that. He's rather young, of course, but the great thing is that Johnjohn and Caroline adore him. You've got two grand kids there, Charles. Remember me to Julia; wish her all the best for old times' sake.'

'So you're being divorced,' said my father. 'Isn't that rather unnecessary, after you've been happy together all these years?'

'We weren't particularly happy, you know.'

'Weren't you? Were you not? I distinctly remember last Christmas seeing you together and thinking how happy you looked, and wondering why. You'll find it very disturbing, you know, starting off again. How old are you – thirty-four? That's no age to be starting. You ought to be settling down. Have you made any plans?'

'Yes. I'm marrying again as soon as the divorce is through.'

'Well, I do call that a lot of nonsense. I can understand a man wishing he hadn't married and trying to get out of it – though I never felt anything of the kind myself – but to get rid of one wife and take up with another immediately, is beyond all reason. Celia was always perfectly civil to me. I had quite a liking for her, in a way. If you couldn't be happy with her, why on earth should you expect to be happy with anyone else? Take my advice, my dear boy, and give up the whole idea.'

'Why bring Julia and me into this?' asked Rex. 'If Celia wants to marry again, well and good; let her. That's your business and hers. But I should have thought Julia and I were quite happy as we are. You can't say I've been difficult. Lots of chaps would have cut up nasty. I hope I'm a man of the world. I've had my own fish to fry, too. But a divorce is a different thing altogether; I've never known a divorce do anyone any good.'

'That's your affair and Julia's.'

'Oh, Julia's set on it. What I hoped was, you might be able to talk her round. I've tried to keep out of the way as much as I could; if I've been around too much, just tell me; I shan't mind. But there's too much going on altogether at the moment, what with Bridey wanting me to clear out of the house; it's disturbing, and I've got a lot on my mind.'

Rex's public life was approaching a climacteric. Things had not gone as smoothly with him as he had planned. I knew nothing of finance, but I heard it said that his dealings were badly looked on by orthodox Conservatives; even his good qualities of geniality and impetuosity counted against him, for his parties at Brideshead got talked about. There was always too much about him in the papers; he was one with the Press lords and their sad-eyed, smiling hangers-on; in his speeches he said the sort of thing which 'made a story' in Fleet Street, and that did him no good with his party chiefs; only war could put Rex's fortunes right and carry him into power. A divorce would do him no great harm; it was rather that with a big bank running he could not look up from the table.

'If Julia insists on a divorce, I suppose she must have it,' he said. 'But she couldn't have chosen a worse time. Tell her to hang on a bit, Charles, there's a good fellow.'

'Bridey's widow said: "So you're divorcing one divorced

man and marrying another. It sounds rather complicated, but
my dear" – she called me "my dear" about twenty times – "I've
usually found every Catholic family has one lapsed member,
and it's often the nicest." '

Julia had just returned from a luncheon party given by Lady
Rosscommon in honour of Brideshead's engagement.

'What's she like?'

'Majestic and voluptuous; common, of course; husky voice,
big mouth, small eyes, dyed hair – I'll tell you one thing, she's
lied to Bridey about her age. She's a good forty-five. I don't see
her providing an heir. Bridey can't take his eyes off her. He was
gloating on her in the most revolting way all through luncheon.'

'Friendly?'

'Goodness, yes, in a condescending way. You see, I imagine
she's been used to bossing things rather in naval circles, with
flag-lieutenants trotting round and young officers on-the-make
sucking up to her. Well, she clearly couldn't do a great deal of
bossing at Aunt Fanny's, so it put her rather at ease to have me
there as the black sheep. She concentrated on me in fact, asked
my advice about shops and things, said, rather pointedly, she
hoped to see me often *in London*. I think Bridey's scruples only
extend to her sleeping under the same roof with me. Apparently
I can do her no serious harm in a hat-shop or hairdresser's or
lunching at the Ritz. The scruples are all on Bridey's part,
anyway; the widow is madly tough.'

'Does she boss him?'

'Not yet, much. He's in an amorous stupor, poor beast, and
doesn't quite know where he is. She's just a good-hearted
woman who wants a good home for her children and isn't going
to let anything get in her way. She's playing up the religious
stuff at the moment for all it's worth. I daresay she'll go easier
when she's settled.'

The divorces were much talked of, among our friends; even
in that summer of general alarm there were still corners where
private affairs commanded first attention. My wife was able to
make it understood that the business was at the same time a

matter of congratulation for her and reproach for me; that she had behaved wonderfully, had stood it longer than anyone but she would have done. Robin was seven years younger and a little immature for his age, they whispered in their private corners, but he was absolutely devoted to poor Celia, and really she deserved it after all she had been through. As for Julia and me, that was an old story. 'To put it crudely,' said my cousin Jasper, as though he had ever in his life put anything otherwise: 'I don't see why you bother to marry.'

Summer passed; delirious crowds cheered Neville Chamberlain's return from Munich; Rex made a rabid speech in the House of Commons which sealed his fate one way or the other; sealed it, as is sometimes done with naval orders, to be opened later at sea. Julia's family lawyers, whose black, tin boxes, painted 'Marquis of Marchmain', seemed to fill a room, began the slow process of her divorce; my own, brisker firm, two doors down, were weeks ahead with my affairs. It was necessary for Rex and Julia to separate formally, and since, for the time being, Brideshead was still her home, she remained there and Rex removed his trunks and valet to their house in London. Evidence was taken against Julia and me in my flat. A date was fixed for Brideshead's wedding, early in the Christmas holidays, so that his future step-children might take part.

One afternoon in November Julia and I stood at a window in the drawing-room watching the wind at work stripping the lime trees, sweeping down the yellow leaves, sweeping them up and round and along the terrace and lawns, trailing them through puddles and over the wet grass, pasting them on walls and window-panes, leaving them at length in sodden piles against the stonework.

'We shan't see them in spring,' said Julia; 'perhaps never again.'

'Once before,' I said, 'I went away, thinking I should never return.'

'Perhaps years later, to what's left of it, with what's left of us ...'

A door opened and shut in the darkling room behind us.

Wilcox approached through the firelight into the dusk about the long windows.

'A telephone message, my Lady, from Lady Cordelia.'

'Lady Cordelia! Where was she?'

'In London, my Lady.'

'Wilcox, how lovely! Is she coming home?'

'She was just starting for the station. She will be here after dinner.'

'I haven't seen her for twelve years,' I said – not since the evening when we dined together and she spoke of being a nun; the evening when I painted the drawing-room at Marchmain House. 'She was an enchanting child.'

'She's had an odd life. First, the convent; then, when that was no good, the war in Spain. I've not seen her since then. The other girls who went with the ambulance came back when the war was over; she stayed on, getting people back to their homes, helping in the prison-camps. An odd girl. She's grown up quite plain, you know.'

'Does she know about us?'

'Yes, she wrote me a sweet letter.'

It hurt to think of Cordelia growing up 'quite plain'; to think of all that burning love spending itself on serum-injections and de-lousing powder. When she arrived, tired from her journey, rather shabby, moving in the manner of one who has no interest in pleasing, I thought her an ugly woman. It was odd, I thought, how the same ingredients, differently dispensed, could produce Brideshead, Sebastian, Julia, and her. She was unmistakably their sister, without any of Julia's or Sebastian's grace, without Brideshead's gravity. She seemed brisk and matter-of-fact, steeped in the atmosphere of camp and dressing-station, so accustomed to gross suffering as to lose the finer shades of pleasure. She looked more than her twenty-six years; hard living had roughened her; constant intercourse in a foreign tongue had worn away the nuances of speech; she straddled a little as she sat by the fire, and when she said, 'It's wonderful to be home,' it sounded to my ears like the grunt of an animal returning to its basket.

Those were the impressions of the first half hour, sharpened by the contrast with Julia's white skin and silk and jewelled hair and with my memories of her as a child.

'My job's over in Spain,' she said; 'the authorities were very polite, thanked me for all I'd done, gave me a medal, and sent me packing. It looks as though there'll be plenty of the same sort of work over here soon.'

Then she said: 'Is it too late to see nanny?'

'No, she sits up to all hours with her wireless.'

We went up, all three together, to the old nursery. Julia and I always spent part of our day there. Nanny Hawkins and my father were two people who seemed impervious to change, neither an hour older than when I first knew them. A wireless set had now been added to Nanny Hawkins' small assembly of pleasures – the rosary, the Peerage with its neat brown-paper wrapping protecting the red and gold covers, the photographs, and holiday souvenirs – on her table. When we broke it to her that Julia and I were to be married, she said: 'Well, dear, I hope it's all for the best,' for it was not part of her religion to question the propriety of Julia's actions.

Brideshead had never been a favourite with her; she greeted the news of his engagement with: 'He's certainly taken long enough to make up his mind,' and, when the search through Debrett afforded no information about Mrs Muspratt's connexions: 'she's caught him, I daresay.'

We found her, as always in the evening, at the fireside with her teapot, and the wool rug she was making.

'I knew you'd be up,' she said. 'Mr Wilcox sent to tell me you were coming.'

'I brought you some lace.'

'Well, dear, that is nice. Just like her poor Ladyship used to wear at mass. Though why they made it black I never did understand, seeing lace is white naturally. That is very welcome, I'm sure.'

'May I turn off the wireless, nanny?'

'Why, of course; I didn't notice it was on, in the pleasure of seeing you. What have you done to your hair?'

'I know it's terrible. I must get all that put right now I'm back. Darling nanny.'

As we sat there talking, and I saw Cordelia's fond eyes on all of us, I began to realize that she, too, had a beauty of her own.

'I saw Sebastian last month.'

'What a time he's been gone! Was he quite well?'

'Not very. That's why I went. It's quite near you know from Spain to Tunis. He's with the monks there.'

'I hope they look after him properly. I expect they find him a regular handful. He always sends to me at Christmas, but it's not the same as having him home. Why you must all always be going abroad I never did understand. Just like his Lordship. When there was that talk about going to war with Munich, I said to myself, "There's Cordelia and Sebastian and his Lordship all abroad; that'll be very awkward for them."'

'I wanted him to come home with me, but he wouldn't. He's got a beard now, you know, and he's very religious.'

'That I won't believe, not even if I see it. He was always a little heathen. Brideshead was one for church, not Sebastian. And a beard, only fancy; such a nice fair skin as he had; always looked clean though he'd not been near water all day, while Brideshead there was no doing anything with, scrub as you might.'

'It's frightening,' Julia once said, 'to think how completely you have forgotten Sebastian.'

'He was the forerunner.'

'That's what you said in the storm. I've thought since, perhaps I am only a forerunner, too.'

'Perhaps,' I thought, while her words still hung in the air between us like a wisp of tobacco smoke – a thought to fade and vanish like smoke without a trace – 'perhaps all our loves are merely hints and symbols; vagabond-language scrawled on gate-posts and paving-stones along the weary road that others have tramped before us; perhaps you and I are types and this sadness which sometimes falls between us springs from disappointment in our search, each straining through and beyond the other, snatching a glimpse now and then of the shadow which turns the corner always a pace or two ahead of us.'

I had not forgotten Sebastian. He was with me daily in Julia; or rather it was Julia I had known in him, in those distant Arcadian days.

'That's cold comfort for a girl,' she said when I tried to explain. 'How do I know I shan't suddenly turn out to be somebody else? It's an easy way to chuck.'

I had not forgotten Sebastian; every stone of the house had a memory of him, and hearing him spoken of by Cordelia as someone she had seen a month ago, my lost friend filled my thoughts. When we left the nursery, I said, 'I want to hear all about Sebastian.'

'Tomorrow. It's a long story.'

And next day, walking through the wind-swept park, she told me:

'I heard he was dying,' she said. 'A journalist in Burgos told me, who'd just arrived from North Africa. A down-and-out called Flyte, who people said was an English lord, whom the fathers had found starving and taken in at a monastery near Carthage. That was how the story reached me. I knew it couldn't be quite true – however little we did for Sebastian, he at least got his money sent him – but I started off at once.

'It was all quite easy. I went to the consulate first and they knew all about him; he was in the infirmary of the head house of some missionary fathers. The consul's story was that Sebastian had turned up in Tunis one day in a motor bus from Algiers, and had applied to be taken on as a missionary lay brother. The Fathers took one look at him and turned him down. Then he started drinking. He lived in a little hotel on the edge of the Arab quarter. I went to see the place later; it was a bar with a few rooms over it, kept by a Greek, smelling of hot oil and garlic and stale wine and old clothes, a place where the small Greek traders came and played draughts and listened to the wireless. He stayed there a month drinking Greek absinthe, occasionally wandering out, they didn't know where, coming back and drinking again. They were afraid he would come to harm and followed him sometimes, but he only went to the church or took a car to the monastery outside the town. They loved him there. He's still loved, you see, wherever he goes, whatever condition he's in. It's a thing about him he'll never lose. You should have heard the proprietor and his family talk of him, tears running down their cheeks; they'd clearly robbed him right and left, but they'd looked after him and tried to make him eat his food. That was the thing that shocked them about him; that he wouldn't eat; there he was with all that money, so thin. Some of the clients of the place came in while we were talking in very peculiar French; they all had the same story; such a *good* man, they said, it made them unhappy to see him so low. They thought very ill of his family for leaving him like that; it couldn't happen with their people, they said, and I daresay they're right.

'Anyway, that was later; after the consulate I went straight to the monastery and saw the Superior. He was a grim old Dutchman who had spent fifty years in Central Africa. He told me his part of the story; how Sebastian had turned up, just as the consul said, with his beard and a suitcase, and asked to be admitted as a lay brother. "He was very earnest," the Superior said' – Cordelia imitated his guttural tones; she had an aptitude for mimicry, I remembered, in the school-room – "Please do not think there is any doubt of that – he is quite sane and quite in earnest." He wanted to go to the bush, as far away as he could get, among the simplest people, to the cannibals. The Superior said: "We have no cannibals in our missions." He said, well, pygmies would do, or just a primitive village somewhere on a river, or lepers, lepers would do best of anything. The Superior said: "We have plenty of lepers, but they live in our settlements with doctors and nuns. It is all very orderly." He thought again, and said perhaps lepers were not what he wanted, was there not some small church by a river – he always wanted a river you see – which he could look after when the priest was away. The Superior said: "Yes, there are such churches. Now tell me about yourself." "Oh, I'm nothing," he said. "We see some queer fish," Cordelia lapsed again into mimicry; "he was a queer fish but he was very earnest." The Superior told him about the novitiate and the training and said: "You are not a young man. You do not seem strong to me." He said: "No, I don't want to be trained. I don't want to do things that need training." The Superior said: "My friend, you need a missionary for yourself," and he said: "Yes, of course." Then he sent him away.

'Next day he came back again. He had been drinking. He said he had decided to become a novice and be trained. "Well," said the Superior, "there are certain things that are impossible for a man in the bush. One of them is drinking. It is not the worst thing, but it is nevertheless quite fatal. I sent him away." Then he kept coming two or three times a week, always drunk, until the Superior gave orders that the porter was to keep him out. I said, "Oh dear, I'm afraid he was a terrible nuisance to you," but of course that's a thing they don't understand in a place like that. The Superior simply said, "I did not think there was anything I could do to help him except pray." He was a very holy old man and recognized it in others.'

'Holiness?'

'Oh yes, Charles, that's what you've got to understand about Sebastian.

'Well, finally one day they found Sebastian lying outside the main gate unconscious, he had walked out – usually he took a car – and fallen down and lain there all night. At first they thought he was merely drunk again; then they realized he was very ill, so they put him in the infirmary, where he'd been ever since.

'I stayed a fortnight with him till he was over the worst of his illness. He looked terrible, any age, rather bald with a straggling beard, but he had his old sweet manner. They'd given him a room to himself; it was barely more than a monk's cell with a bed and a crucifix and white walls. At first he couldn't talk much and was not at all surprised to see me; then he was surprised and wouldn't talk much, until just before I was going, when he told me all that had been happening to him. It was mostly about Kurt, his German friend. Well, you met him, so you know all about that. He sounds gruesome, but as long as Sebastian had him to look after, he was happy. He told me he'd practically given up drinking at one time while he and Kurt lived together. Kurt was ill and had a wound that wouldn't heal. Sebastian saw him through that. Then they went to Greece when Kurt got well. You know how Germans sometimes seem to discover a sense of decency when they get to a classical country. It seems to have worked with Kurt. Sebastian says he became quite human in Athens. Then he got sent to prison; I couldn't quite make out why; apparently it wasn't particularly his fault – some brawl with an official. Once he was locked up the German authorities got at him. It was the time when they were rounding up all their nationals from all parts of the world to make them into Nazis. Kurt didn't want to leave Greece, but the Greeks didn't want him, and he was marched straight from prison with a lot of other toughs into a German boat and shipped home.

'Sebastian went after him, and for a year could find no trace. Then in the end he ran him to earth dressed as a storm-trooper in a provincial town. At first he wouldn't have anything to do with Sebastian; spouted all the official jargon about the rebirth of his country, and his belonging to his country, and finding self-realization in the life of the race. But it was only skin deep with him. Six years of Sebastian had taught him more than a year of Hitler; eventually he chucked it, admitted he hated Germany, and wanted to get out. I don't know how much it was simply the call of the easy life, sponging on Sebastian, bathing in the Mediterranean, sitting about in cafés, having his shoes polished. Sebastian says it wasn't entirely that; Kurt had just begun to grow up in Athens. It may be he's right. Anyway, he decided to try and get out. But it didn't work. He always got into trouble whatever he did, Sebastian said. They caught him and put him in a concentration camp. Sebastian couldn't get near him or hear a word of him; he couldn't even find what camp he was in; he hung about for nearly a year in Germany, drinking again, until one day in his cups he took up with a man who was just out of the camp where Kurt had been, and learned that he had hanged himself in his hut the first week.

'So that was the end of Europe for Sebastian. He went back

to Morocco, where he had been happy, and gradually drifted down the coast, from place to place, until one day when he had sobered up – his drinking goes in pretty regular bouts now – he conceived the idea of escaping to the savages. And there he was.

'I didn't suggest his coming home. I knew he wouldn't, and he was too weak still to argue it out. He seemed quite happy by the time I left. He'll never be able to go into the bush, of course, or join the order, but the Father Superior is going to take charge of him. They had the idea of making him a sort of under-porter; there are usually a few odd hangers-on in a religious house, you know; people who can't quite fit in either to the world or the monastic rule. I suppose I'm something of the sort myself. But as I don't happen to drink, I'm more employable.'

We had reached the turn in our walk, the stone bridge at the foot of the last and smallest lake, under which the swollen waters fell in a cataract to the stream below; beyond, the path doubled back towards the house. We paused at the parapet looking down into the dark water.

'I once had a governess who jumped off this bridge and drowned herself.'

'Yes, I know.'

'How could you know?'

'It was the first thing I ever heard about you – before I ever met you.'

'How very odd. ...'

'Have you told Julia this about Sebastian?'

'The substance of it; not quite as I told you. She never loved him, you know, as we do.'

'*Do*'. The word reproached me; there was no past tense in Cordelia's verb 'to love'.

'Poor Sebastian!' I said. 'It's too pitiful. How will it end?'

'I think I can tell you exactly, Charles. I've seen others like him, and I believe they are very near and dear to God. He'll live on, half in, half out of, the community, a familiar figure pottering round with his broom and his bunch of keys. He'll be a great favourite with the old fathers, something of a joke to the novices. Everyone will know about his drinking; he'll disappear for two or three days every month or so, and they'll all nod and smile and say in their various accents, "Old Sebastian's on the spree again," and then he'll come back dishevelled and shame-faced and be more devout for a day or two in the chapel. He'll probably have little hiding places about the garden where he keeps a bottle and takes a swig now and then on the sly. They'll bring him forward to act as guide, whenever they have an English-speaking visitor, and he will be completely charming so that before they go, they'll ask about him and perhaps be given a hint that he has high connexions at home. If he lives long enough, generations of missionaries in all kinds of remote places will think of him as a queer old character who was somehow part of the Home of their student days, and remember him in their masses. He'll develop little eccentricities of devotion, intense personal cults of his own; he'll be found in the chapel at odd times and missed when he's expected. Then one morning, after one of his drinking bouts, he'll be picked up at the gate dying, and show by a mere flicker of the eyelid that he is conscious when they give him the last sacraments. It's not such a bad way of getting through one's life.'

I thought of the youth with the teddy-bear under the flowering chestnuts. 'It's not what one would have foretold,' I said. 'I suppose he doesn't suffer?'

'Oh, yes, I think he does. One can have no idea what the suffering may be, to be maimed as he is – no dignity, no power of will. No one is ever holy without suffering. It's taken that form with him. ... I've seen so much suffering in the last few years; there's so much coming for everybody soon. It's the spring of love ...' and then in condescension to my paganism, she added: 'He's in a very beautiful place, you know, by the sea – white cloisters, a bell tower, rows of green vegetables, and a monk watering them when the sun is low.'

I laughed. 'You knew I wouldn't understand?'

'You and Julia ...' she said. And then, as we moved on towards the house, 'When you met me last night did you think, "Poor Cordelia, such an engaging child, grown up a plain and pious spinster, full of good works"? Did you think "thwarted"?'

It was no time for prevarication. 'Yes,' I said, 'I did; I don't now, so much.'

'It's funny,' she said, 'that's exactly the word I thought of for you and Julia. When we were up in the nursery with nanny. "Thwarted passion," I thought.'

She spoke with that gentle, infinitesimal inflexion of mockery which descended to her from her mother, but later that evening the words came back to me poignantly.

Julia wore the embroidered Chinese robe which she often used when we were dining alone at Brideshead; it was a robe whose weight and stiff folds stressed her repose; her neck rose exquisitely from the plain gold circle at her throat; her hands lay still among the dragons in her lap. It was thus that I had rejoiced to see her nights without number, and that night, watching her as she sat between the firelight and the shaded lamp, unable to look away for love of her beauty, I suddenly thought, 'When else have I seen her like this? Why am I reminded of another moment of vision?' And it came back to me that this was how she had sat in the liner, before the storm; this was how she had looked, and I realized that she had regained what I thought she had lost for ever, the magical sadness which had drawn me to her, the thwarted look that had seemed to say, 'Surely I was made for some other purpose than this?'

That night I woke in the darkness and lay awake turning over in my mind the conversation with Cordelia. How I had said, 'You knew I would not understand.' How often, it seemed to me, I was brought up short, like a horse in full stride suddenly refusing an obstacle, backing against the spurs, too shy even to put his nose at it and look at the thing.

And another image came to me, of an arctic hut and a trapper alone with his furs and oil lamp and log fire; everything dry and ship-shape and warm inside, and outside the last blizzard of winter raging and the snow piling up against the door. Quite silently a great weight forming against the timber; the bolt straining in its socket; minute by minute in the darkness outside the white heap sealing the door, until quite soon when the wind dropped and the sun came out on the ice slopes and the thaw set in a block would move, slide, and tumble, high above, gather weight, till the whole hillside seemed to be falling, and the little lighted place would open and splinter and disappear, rolling with the avalanche into the ravine.

CHAPTER V

My divorce case, or rather my wife's, was due to be heard at about the same time as Brideshead was to be married. Julia's would not come up till the following term; meanwhile the game of General Post – moving my property from the Old Rectory to my flat, my wife's from my flat to the Old Rectory, Julia's from Rex's house and from Brideshead to my flat, Rex's from Brideshead to his house, and Mrs Muspratt's from Falmouth to Brideshead – was in full swing and we were all, in varying degrees, homeless, when a halt was called and Lord Marchmain, with a taste for the dramatically inopportune which was plainly the prototype of his elder son's, declared his intention, in view of the international situation, of returning to England and passing his declining years in his old home.

The only member of the family to whom this change promised any benefit was Cordelia, who had been sadly abandoned in the turmoil. Brideshead, indeed, had made a formal request to her to consider his house her home for as long as it suited her, but when she learned that her sister-in-law proposed to install her children there for the holidays immediately after the wedding, in the charge of a sister of hers and the sister's friend, Cordelia had decided to move, too, and was talking of setting up alone in London. She now found herself, Cinderella-like, promoted *châtelaine*, while her brother and his wife who had till that moment expected to find themselves, within a matter of days, in absolute command, were without a roof; the deeds of conveyance, engrossed and ready for signing, were rolled up, tied, and put away in one of the black tin boxes in Lincoln's Inn. It was bitter for Mrs Muspratt; she was not an ambitious woman; something very much less grand than Brideshead would have contented her heartily, but she did aspire to find some shelter for her children over Christmas. The house at Falmouth was stripped and up for sale; moreover, Mrs Muspratt had taken leave of the place with some justifiably rather large talk of her new establishment; they could not return there. She was obliged in a hurry to move her furniture from Lady Marchmain's room to a disused coach-house and to take a furnished villa at Torquay. She was not, as I have said, a woman of high ambition, but, having had her expectations so much raised, it was disconcerting to be brought so low so suddenly. In the village the working party who had been preparing the decorations for the bridal entry, began unpicking the Bs on the bunting and substituting Ms, obliterating the Earl's points and stencilling balls and strawberry leaves on the painted coronets, in preparation for Lord Marchmain's return.

News of his intentions came first to the solicitors, then to Cordelia, then to Julia and me, in a rapid succession of contradictory cables. Lord Marchmain would arrive in time for the wedding; he would arrive after the wedding, having seen Lord and Lady Brideshead on their way through Paris; he would see them in Rome. He was not well enough to travel at all; he was just starting; he had unhappy memories of winter at Brideshead and would not come until spring was well advanced and the heating apparatus overhauled; he was coming alone; he was bringing his Italian household; he wished his return to be unannounced and to lead a life of complete seclusion; he would give a ball. At last a date in January was chosen which proved to be the correct one.

Plender preceded him by some days; there was a difficulty here. Plender was not an original member of the Brideshead household; he had been Lord Marchmain's servant in the yeomanry, and had only once met Wilcox on the painful occasion of the removal of his master's luggage when it was decided not to return from the war; then Plender had been valet, as, officially, he still was, but he had in the past years introduced a kind of suffragan, a Swiss body-servant, to attend to the wardrobe and also, when occasion arose, lend a hand with less dignified tasks about the house, and had in effect become major-domo of that fluctuating and mobile household; sometimes he even referred to himself on the telephone as 'the secretary'. There was an acre of thin ice between him and Wilcox.

Fortunately the two men took a liking to one another, and the thing was solved in a series of three-cornered discussions with Cordelia. Plender and Wilcox became joint grooms of the chambers, like 'Blues' and Life Guards with equal precedence, Plender having as his particular province his Lordship's own apartments and Wilcox a sphere of influence in the public rooms; the senior footman was given a black coat and promoted butler, the nondescript Swiss, on arrival, was to have plain clothes and full valet's status; there was a general increase in wages to meet the new dignities, and all were content.

Julia and I, who had left Brideshead a month before, thinking we should not return, moved back for the reception. When the day came, Cordelia went to the station and we remained to greet him at home. It was a bleak and gusty day. Cottages and lodges were decorated; plans for a bonfire that night and for the village silver band to play on the terrace, were put down, but the house flag, that had not flown for twenty-five years, was hoisted over the pediment, and flapped sharply against the leaden sky. Whatever harsh voices might be bawling into the microphones of central Europe, and whatever lathes spinning in the armament factories, the return of Lord March-main was a matter of first importance in his own neighbourhood.

He was due at three o'clock. Julia and I waited in the drawing-room until Wilcox, who had arranged with the sta-tionmaster to be kept informed, announced 'the train is sig-nalled', and a minute later, 'the train is in; his Lordship is on the way.' Then we went to the front portico and waited there with the upper servants. Soon the Rolls appeared at the turn in the drive, followed at some distance by the two vans. It drew up; first Cordelia got out, then Cara; there was a pause, a rug was handed to the chauffeur, a stick to the footman; then a leg was cautiously thrust forward. Plender was by now at the car door;

another servant – the Swiss valet – had emerged from a van; together they lifted Lord Marchmain out and set him on his feet; he felt for his stick, grasped it, and stood for a minute collecting his strength for the few low steps which led to the front door.

Julia gave a little sigh of surprise and touched my hand. We had seen him nine months ago at Monte Carlo, when he had been an upright and stately figure, little changed from when I first met him in Venice. Now he was an old man. Plender had told us his master had been unwell lately: he had not prepared us for this.

Lord Marchmain stood bowed and shrunken, weighed down by his great-coat, a white muffler fluttering untidily at his throat, a cloth cap pulled low on his forehead, his face white and lined, his nose coloured by the cold; the tears which gathered in his eyes came not from emotion but from the east wind; he breathed heavily. Cara tucked in the end of his muffler and whispered something to him. He raised a gloved hand – a schoolboy's glove of grey wool – and made a small, weary gesture of greeting to the group at the door; then, very slowly, with his eyes on the ground before him, he made his way into the house.

They took off his coat and cap and muffler and the kind of leather jerkin which he wore under them; thus stripped he seemed more than ever wasted but more elegant; he had cast the shabbiness of extreme fatigue. Cara straightened his tie; he wiped his eyes with a bandanna handkerchief and shuffled with his stick to the hall fire.

There was a little heraldic chair by the chimney-piece, one of a set which stood against the walls, a little, inhospitable, flat-seated thing, a mere excuse for the elaborate armorial painting on its back, on which, perhaps, no one, not even a weary footman, had ever sat since it was made; there Lord Marchmain sat and wiped his eyes.

'It's the cold,' he said. 'I'd forgotten how cold it is in England. Quite bowled me over.'

'Can I get you anything, my lord?'

'Nothing, thank you. Cara, where are those confounded pills?'

'Alex, the doctor said not more than three times a day.'

'Damn the doctor. I feel quite bowled over.'

Cara produced a blue bottle from her bag and Lord Marchmain took a pill. Whatever was in it, seemed to revive him. He remained seated, his long legs stuck out before him, his cane between them, his chin on its ivory handle, but he began to take notice of us all, to greet us and to give orders.

'I'm afraid I'm not at all the thing today; the journey's taken it out of me. Ought to have waited a night at Dover. Wilcox, what rooms have you prepared for me?'

'Your old ones, my Lord.'

'Won't do; not till I'm fit again. Too many stairs; must be on the ground floor. Plender, get a bed made up for me downstairs.'

Plender and Wilcox exchanged an anxious glance.

'Very good, my Lord. Which room shall we put it in?'

Lord Marchmain thought for a moment. 'The Chinese drawing-room; and, Wilcox, the "Queen's bed".'

'The Chinese drawing-room, my lord, the "Queen's bed"?'

'Yes, yes. I may be spending some time there in the next few weeks.'

The Chinese drawing-room was one I had never seen used; in fact one could not normally go further into it than a small roped area round the door, where sight-seers were corralled on the days the house was open to the public; it was a splendid, uninhabitable museum of Chippendale carving and porcelain and lacquer and painted hangings; the Queen's bed, too, was an exhibition piece, a vast velvet tent like the *baldacchino* at St Peter's. Had Lord Marchmain planned this lying-in-state for himself, I wondered, before he left the sunshine of Italy? Had he thought of it during the scudding rain of his long, fretful journey? Had it come to him at that moment, an awakened memory of childhood, a dream in the nursery – 'When I'm grown up I'll sleep in the Queen's bed in the Chinese drawing-room' – the apotheosis of adult grandeur?

Few things, certainly, could have caused more stir in the house. What had been foreseen as a day of formality became one of fierce exertion; housemaids began making a fire, removing covers, unfolding linen; men in aprons, never normally seen, shifted furniture; the estate carpenters were collected to dismantle the bed. It came down the main staircase in pieces, at intervals during the afternoon; huge sections of Rococo, velvet-covered cornice; the twisted, gilt and velvet columns which formed its posts; beams of unpolished wood, made not to be seen, which performed invisible, structural functions below the draperies; plumes of dyed feathers, which sprang from gold-mounted ostrich eggs and crowned the canopy; finally, the mattresses with four toiling men to each. Lord Marchmain seemed to derive comfort from the consequences of his whim; he sat by the fire watching the bustle, while we stood in a half circle – Cara, Cordelia, Julia, and I – and talked to him.

Colour came back to his cheeks and light to his eyes. 'Brideshead and his wife dined with me in Rome,' he said. 'Since we are all members of the family' – and his eye moved ironically from Cara to me – 'I can speak without reserve. I found her deplorable. Her former consort, I understand, was a seafaring man and, presumably, the less exacting, but how my son, at the ripe age of thirty-eight, with, unless things have changed very much, a very free choice among the women of England, can have settled on – I suppose I must call her so – *Beryl*. ...' He left the sentence eloquently unfinished.

Lord Marchmain showed no inclination to move, so presently we drew up chairs – the little, heraldic chairs, for everything else in the hall was ponderous – and sat round him.

'I daresay I shall not be really fit again until summer comes,' he said. 'I look to you four to amuse me.'

There seemed little we could do at the moment to lighten the rather sombre mood; he, indeed, was the most cheerful of us. 'Tell me', he said, 'the circumstances of Brideshead's courtship.'

We told him what we knew.

'Match-boxes,' he said. 'Match-boxes. I think she's past child-bearing.'

Tea was brought us at the hall fireplace.

'In Italy,' he said, 'no one believes there will be a war. They think it will all be "arranged". I suppose, Julia, you no longer have access to political information? Cara, here, is fortunately a British subject by marriage. It is not a thing she customarily mentions, but it may prove valuable. She is legally Mrs Hicks, are you not, my dear? We know little of Hicks, but we shall be grateful to him, none the less, if it comes to war. And you,' he said, turning the attack to me, 'you will no doubt become an official artist?'

'No. As a matter of fact I am negotiating now for a commission in the Special Reserve.'

'Oh, but you should be an artist. I had one with my squadron during the last war, for weeks – until we went up to the line.'

This waspishness was new. I had always been aware of a frame of malevolence under his urbanity; now it protruded like his own sharp bones through the sunken skin.

It was dark before the bed was finished; we went to see it, Lord Marchmain stepping quite briskly now through the intervening rooms.

'I congratulate you. It really looks remarkably well. Wilcox, I seem to remember a silver basin and ewer – they stood in a room we called "the Cardinal's dressing-room", I think – suppose we had them here on the console. Then if you will send Plender and Gaston to me, the luggage can wait till tomorrow – simply the dressing case and what I need for the night. Plender will know. If you will leave me with Plender and Gaston, I will go to bed. We will meet later; you will dine here and keep me amused.'

We turned to go; as I was at the door he called me back.

'It looks very well, does it not?'

'Very well.'

'You might paint it, eh – and call it the *Death Bed*?'

'Yes,' said Cara, 'he has come home to die.'

'But when he first arrived he was talking so confidently of recovery.'

'That was because he was so ill. When he is himself, he knows he is dying and accepts it. His sickness is up and down; one day, sometimes for several days on end, he is strong and lively and then he is ready for death, then he is down and afraid. I do not know how it will be when he is more and more down. That must come in good time. The doctors in Rome gave him less than a year. There is someone coming from London, I think tomorrow, who will tell us more.'

'What is it?'

'His heart; some long word at the heart. He is dying of a long word.'

That evening Lord Marchmain was in good spirits; the room had a Hogarthian aspect, with the dinner-table set for the four of us by the grotesque, *chinoiserie* chimney-piece, and the old man propped among his pillows, sipping champagne, tasting, praising, and failing to eat, the succession of dishes which had been prepared for his homecoming. Wilcox had brought out for the occasion the gold plate, which I had not before seen in use; that, the gilt mirrors, and the lacquer and the drapery of the great bed and Julia's mandarin coat gave the scene an air of pantomime, of Aladdin's cave.

Just at the end, when the time came for us to go, his spirits flagged.

'I shall not sleep,' he said. 'Who is going to sit with me? Cara, *carissima*, you are fatigued. Cordelia, will you watch for an hour in this Gethsemane?'

Next morning I asked her how the night had passed.

'He went to sleep almost at once. I came in to see him at two to make up the fire; the lights were on, but he was asleep again. He must have woken up and turned them on; he had to get out of bed to do that. I think perhaps he is afraid of the dark.'

It was natural, with her hospital experience, that Cordelia should take charge of her father. When the doctors came that day they gave their instructions to her, instinctively.

'Until he gets worse,' she said, 'I and the valet can look after him. We don't want nurses in the house before they are needed.'

At this stage the doctors had nothing to recommend except

to keep him comfortable and administer certain drugs when his attacks came on.

'How long will it be?'

'Lady Cordelia, there are men walking about in hearty old age whom their doctors gave a week to live. I have learned one thing in medicine; never prophesy.'

These two men had made a long journey to tell her this; the local doctor was there to accept the same advice in technical phrases.

That night Lord Marchmain reverted to the topic of his new daughter-in-law; it had never been long out of his mind, finding expression in various sly hints throughout the day; now he lay back in his pillows and talked of her at length.

'I have never been much moved by family piety until now,' he said, 'but I am frankly appalled at the prospect of – of Beryl taking what was once my mother's place in this house. Why should that uncouth pair sit here childless while the place crumbles about their ears? I will not disguise from you that I have taken a dislike to Beryl.

'Perhaps it was unfortunate that we met in Rome. Anywhere else might have been more sympathetic. And yet, if one comes to consider it, where could I have met her without repugnance? We dined at Ranieri's; it is a quiet little restaurant I have frequented for years – no doubt you know it. Beryl seemed to fill the place. I, of course, was host, though to hear Beryl press my son with food, you might have thought otherwise. Brideshead was always a greedy boy; a wife who has his best interests at heart should seek to restrain him. However, that is a matter of small importance.

'She had no doubt heard of me as a man of irregular life. I can only describe her manner to me as roguish. A naughty old man, that's what she thought I was. I suppose she had met naughty old admirals and knew how they should be humoured ... I could not attempt to reproduce her conversation. I will give you one example.

'They had been to an audience at the Vatican that morning; a blessing for their marriage – I did not follow attentively –

something of the kind had happened before, I gathered, some previous husband, some previous Pope. She described, rather vivaciously, how on this earlier occasion she had gone with a whole body of newly married couples, mostly Italians of all ranks, some of the simpler girls in their wedding dresses, and how each had appraised the other, the bridegrooms looking the brides over, comparing their own with one another's, and so forth. Then she said, "This time, of course, we were in private, but do you know, Lord Marchmain, I felt as though it was I who was leading in the bride."

'It was said with great indelicacy. I have not yet quite fathomed her meaning. Was she making a play on my son's name, or was she, do you think, referring to his undoubted virginity? I fancy the latter. Anyway, it was with pleasantries of that kind that we passed the evening.

'I don't think she would be quite in her proper element here, do you? Who shall I leave it to? The entail ended with me, you know. Sebastian, alas, is out of the question. Who wants it? *Quis*? Would you like it, Cara? No, of course you would not. Cordelia? I think I shall leave it to Julia and Charles.'

'Of course not, papa, it's Bridey's.'

'And ... Beryl's? I will have Gregson down one day soon and go over the matter. It is time I brought my will up to date; it is full of anomalies and anachronisms ... I have rather a fancy for the idea of installing Julia here; so beautiful this evening, my dear; so beautiful always; much, much more suitable.'

Shortly after this he sent to London for his solicitor, but, on the day he came, Lord Marchmain was suffering from an attack and would not see him. 'Plenty of time,' he said, between painful gasps for breath, 'another day, when I am stronger,' but the choice of his heir was constantly in his mind, and he referred often to the time when Julia and I should be married and in possession.

'Do you think he really means to leave it to us?' I asked Julia.

'Yes, I think he does.'

'But it's monstrous for Bridey.'

'Is it? I don't think he cares much for the place. I do, you know. He and Beryl would be much more content in some little house somewhere.'

'You mean to accept it?'

'Certainly. It's papa's to leave as he likes. I think you and I could be very happy here.'

It opened a prospect; the prospect one gained at the turn of the avenue, as I had first seen it with Sebastian, of the secluded valley, the lakes falling away one below the other, the old house in the foreground, the rest of the world abandoned and forgotten; a world of its own of peace and love and beauty; a soldier's dream in a foreign bivouac; such a prospect perhaps as a high pinnacle of the temple afforded after the hungry days in the desert and the jackal-haunted nights. Need I reproach myself if sometimes I was taken by the vision?

The weeks of illness wore on and the life of the house kept pace with the faltering strength of the sick man. There were days when Lord Marchmain was dressed, when he stood at the window or moved on his valet's arm from fire to fire through the rooms of the ground floor, when visitors came and went – neighbours and people from the estate, men of business from London – parcels of new books were opened and discussed, a piano was moved into the Chinese drawing-room; once at the end of February, on a single, unexpected day of brilliant sunshine, he called for a car and got as far as the hall, had on his fur coat, and reached the front door. Then suddenly he lost interest in the drive, said 'Not now. Later. One day in the summer,' took his man's arm again and was led back to his chair. Once he had the humour of changing his room and gave detailed orders for a move to the Painted Parlour; the *chinoiserie*, he said, disturbed his rest – he kept the lights full on at night – but again lost heart, countermanded everything, and kept his room.

On other days the house was hushed as he sat high in bed, propped by his pillows, with labouring breath; even then he wanted to have us round him; night or day he could not bear to be alone; when he could not speak his eyes followed us, and if anyone left the room he would look distressed, and Cara, sitting often for hours at a time by his side against the pillows with an arm in his, would say, 'It's all right, Alex, she's coming back.'

Brideshead and his wife returned from their honeymoon and stayed a few nights; it was one of the bad times, and Lord Marchmain refused to have them near him. It was Beryl's first visit, and she would have been unnatural if she had shown no curiosity about what had nearly been, and now again promised soon to be, her home. Beryl was natural enough, and surveyed the place fairly thoroughly in the days she was there. In the strange disorder caused by Lord Marchmain's illness, it must have seemed capable of much improvement; she referred once or twice to the way in which establishments of similar size had been managed at various Government Houses she had visited. Brideshead took her visiting among the tenants by day, and in the evenings, she talked to me of painting, or to Cordelia of hospitals, or to Julia of clothes, with cheerful assurance. The shadow of betrayal, the knowledge of how precarious were their just expectations, was all one-sided. I was not easy with them; but that was no new thing to Brideshead; in the little circle of shyness in which he was used to move, my guilt passed unseen.

Eventually it became clear that Lord Marchmain did not intend to see more of them. Brideshead was admitted alone for a minute's leave-taking; then they left.

'There's nothing we can do here,' said Brideshead, 'and it's very distressing for Beryl. We'll come back if things get worse.'

The bad spells became longer and more frequent; a nurse was engaged. 'I never saw such a room,' she said, 'nothing like it anywhere; no conveniences of any sort.' She tried to have her patient moved upstairs, where there was running water, a dressing-room for herself, a 'sensible' narrow bed she could 'get round' – what she was used to – but Lord Marchmain would not budge. Soon, as days and nights became indistinguishable to him, a second nurse was installed; the specialists came again from London; they recommended a new and rather daring treatment, but his body seemed weary of all drugs and did not respond. Presently there were no good spells, merely brief fluctuations in the speed of his decline.

Brideshead was called. It was the Easter holidays and Beryl was busy with her children. He came alone, and having stood silently for some minutes beside his father, who sat silently looking at him, he left the room and, joining the rest of us, who were in the library, said, 'Papa must see a priest.'

It was not the first time the topic had come up. In the early days, when Lord Marchmain first arrived, the parish priest – since the chapel was shut there was a new church and presbytery in Melstead – had come to call as a matter of politeness. Cordelia had put him off with apologies and excuses, but when he was gone she said: 'Not yet. Papa doesn't want him yet.'

Julia, Cara, and I were there at the time; we each had something to say, began to speak, and thought better of it. It was never mentioned between the four of us, but Julia, alone with me, said, 'Charles, I see great Church trouble ahead.'

'Can't they even let him die in peace?'

'They mean something so different by "peace".'

'It would be an outrage. No one could have made it clearer, all his life, what he thought of religion. They'll come now, when his mind's wandering and he hasn't the strength to resist, and claim him as a death-bed penitent. I've had a certain respect for their Church up till now. If they do a thing like that I shall know that everything stupid people say about them is quite true – that it's all superstition and trickery.' Julia said nothing. 'Don't you agree?' Still Julia said nothing. 'Don't you agree?'

'I don't know, Charles. I simply don't know.'

And, though none of us spoke of it, I felt the question ever present, growing through all the weeks of Lord Marchmain's illness; I saw it when Cordelia drove off early in the mornings to mass; I saw it as Cara took to going with her; this little cloud, the size of a man's hand, that was going to swell into a storm among us.

Now Brideshead, in his heavy, ruthless way, planted the problem down before us.

'Oh, Bridey, do you think he would?' asked Cordelia.

'I shall see that he does,' said Brideshead. 'I shall take Father Mackay in to him tomorrow.'

Still the clouds gathered and did not break; none of us spoke. Cara and Cordelia went back to the sickroom; Brideshead looked for a book, found one, and left us.

'Julia,' I said, 'how can we stop this tomfoolery?'

She did not answer for some time; then: 'Why should we?'

'You know as well as I do. It's just – just an unseemly incident.'

'Who am I to object to unseemly incidents?' she asked sadly. 'Anyway, what harm can it do? Let's ask the doctor.'

We asked the doctor, who said: 'It's hard to say. It might alarm him of course; on the other hand, I have known cases where it has had a wonderfully soothing effect on a patient; I've even known it act as a positive stimulant. It certainly is usually a great comfort to the relations. Really I think it's a thing for Lord Brideshead to decide. Mind you, there is no need for immediate anxiety. Lord Marchmain is very weak today; tomorrow he may be quite strong again. Is it not usual to wait a little?'

'Well, he wasn't much help,' I said to Julia, when we left him.

'Help? I really can't quite see why you've taken it so much to heart that my father shall not have the last sacraments.'

'It's such a lot of witchcraft and hypocrisy.'

'Is it? Anyway, it's been going on for nearly two thousand years. I don't know why you should suddenly get in a rage now.' Her voice rose; she was swift to anger of late months. 'For Christ's sake, write to *The Times*; get up and make a speech in Hyde Park; start a "No Popery" riot, but don't bore me about it. What's it got to do with you or me whether my father sees his parish priest?'

I knew these fierce moods of Julia's, such as had overtaken her at the fountain in moonlight, and dimly surmised their origin; I knew they could not be assuaged by words. Nor could I have spoken, for the answer to her question was still unformed; the sense that the fate of more souls than one was at issue; that the snow was beginning to shift on the high slopes.

Brideshead and I breakfasted together next morning with the night-nurse, who had just come off duty.

'He's much brighter today,' she said. 'He slept very nicely for nearly three hours. When Gaston came to shave him he was quite chatty.'

'Good,' said Brideshead. 'Cordelia went to mass. She's driving Father Mackay back here to breakfast.'

I had met Father Mackay several times; he was a stocky, middle-aged, genial Glasgow-Irishman who, when we met, was apt to ask me such questions as, 'Would you say now, Mr Ryder, that the painter Titian was more truly artistic than the painter Raphael?' and, more disconcertingly still, to remember my answers: 'To revert, Mr Ryder, to what you said when last I had the pleasure to meet you, would it be right now to say that the painter Titian ...' usually ending with some such reflection as: 'Ah, it's a grand resource for a man to have the talent you have, Mr Ryder, and the time to indulge it.' Cordelia could imitate him.

This morning he made a hearty breakfast, glanced at the headlines of the paper, and then said with professional briskness: 'And now, Lord Brideshead, would the poor soul be ready to see me, do you think?'

Brideshead led him out; Cordelia followed, and I was left alone among the breakfast things. In less than a minute I heard the voices of all three outside the door.

'... can only apologize.'

'... poor soul. Mark you, it was seeing a strange face; depend upon it, it was that – an unexpected stranger. I well understand it.'

'... Father, I am sorry ... bringing you all this way ...'

'Don't think about it at all, Lady Cordelia. Why, I've had bottles thrown at me in the Gorbals. ... Give him time. I've known worse cases make beautiful deaths. Pray for him ... I'll come again ... and now if you'll excuse me I'll just pay a little visit to Mrs Hawkins. Yes, indeed, I know the way well.'

Then Cordelia and Brideshead came into the room.

'I gather the visit was not a success.'

'It was not. Cordelia, will you drive Father Mackay home when he comes down from nanny? I'm going to telephone to Beryl and see when she needs me home.'

'Bridey, it was horrible. What are we to do?'

'We've done everything we can at the moment.' He left the room.

Cordelia's face was grave; she took a piece of bacon from the dish, dipped it in mustard and ate it. 'Damn Bridey,' she said, 'I knew it wouldn't work.'

'What happened?'

'Would you like to know? We walked in there in a line; Cara was reading the paper aloud to papa. Bridey said, "I've brought Father Mackay to see you"; papa said, "Father Mackay, I am afraid you have been brought here under a misapprehension. I am not *in extremis*, and I have not been a practising member of your Church for twenty-five years. Brideshead, show Father Mackay the way out." Then we all turned about and walked away, and I heard Cara start reading the paper again, and that, Charles, was that.'

I carried the news to Julia, who lay with her bed-table amid a litter of newspapers and envelopes. 'Mumbo-jumbo is off,' I said. 'The witch-doctor has gone.'

'Poor papa.'

'It's great sucks to Bridey.'

I felt triumphant. I had been right, everyone else had been wrong, truth had prevailed; the threat that I had felt hanging over Julia and me ever since that evening at the fountain, had been averted, perhaps dispelled for ever; and there was also – I can now confess it – another unexpressed, inexpressible, indecent little victory that I was furtively celebrating. I guessed that that morning's business had put Brideshead some considerable way further from his rightful inheritance.

In that I was correct; a man was sent for from the solicitors in London; in a day or two he came and it was known throughout the house that Lord Marchmain had made a new will. But I was wrong in thinking that the religious controversy was quashed; it flamed up again after dinner on Brideshead's last evening.

'... What papa said was, "I am not *in extremis*, I have not been a practising member of the Church for twenty-five years."'

'Not "*the* Church", "*your* Church".'

'I don't see the difference.'

'There's every difference.'

'Bridey, it's quite plain what he meant.'

'I presume he meant what he said. He meant that he had not been accustomed regularly to receive the sacraments, and since he was not at the moment dying, he did not mean to change his ways – *yet*.'

'That's simply a quibble.'

'Why do people always think that one is quibbling when one tries to be precise? His plain meaning was that he did not want to see a priest that day, but that he would when he was "*in extremis*".'

'I wish someone would explain to me,' I said, 'quite what the significance of these sacraments is. Do you mean that if he dies alone he goes to hell, and that if a priest puts oil on him –'

'Oh, it's not the oil,' said Cordelia, 'that's to heal him.'

'Odder still – well, whatever it is the priest does – that he then goes to heaven. Is that what you believe?'

Cara then interposed: 'I think my nurse told me, someone did anyway, that if the priest got there before the body was cold it was all right. That's so, isn't it?'

The others turned on her.

'No, Cara, it's not.'

'Of course not.'

'You've got it all wrong, Cara.'

'Well, I remember when Alphonse de Grenet died, Madame de Grenet had a priest hidden outside the door – he couldn't bear the sight of a priest – and brought him in *before the body was cold*; she told me herself, and they had a full Requiem for him, and I went to it.'

'Having a Requiem doesn't mean you go to heaven necessarily.'

'Madame de Grenet thought it did.'

'Well, she was wrong.'

'Do any of you Catholics know what good you think this priest can do?' I asked. 'Do you simply want to arrange it so that your father can have Christian burial? Do you want to keep him out of hell? I only want to be told.'

Brideshead told me at some length, and when he had finished Cara slightly marred the unity of the Catholic front by saying in simple wonder, 'I never heard that before.'

'Let's get this clear,' I said; 'he has to make an act of will; he has to be contrite and wish to be reconciled; is that right? But only God knows whether he has really made an act of will; the priest can't tell; and if there isn't a priest there, and he makes the act of will alone, that's as good as if there were a priest. And it's quite possible that the will may still be working when a man is too weak to make any outward sign of it; is that right? He may be lying, as though for dead, and willing all the time, and being reconciled, and God understands that; is that right?'

'More or less,' said Brideshead.

'Well, for heaven's sake,' I said, 'what is the priest for?'

There was a pause in which Julia sighed and Brideshead drew breath as though to start further subdividing the propositions. In the silence Cara said, 'All I know is that *I* shall take very good care to have a priest.'

'Bless you,' said Cordelia, 'I believe that's the best answer.'

And we let the argument drop, each for different reasons, thinking it had been inconclusive.

Later Julia said: 'I wish you wouldn't start these religious arguments.'

'I didn't start it.'

'You don't convince anyone else and you don't really convince yourself.'

'I only want to know what these people believe. They say it's all based on logic.'

'If you'd let Bridey finish, he would have made it all quite logical.'

'There were four of you,' I said. 'Cara didn't know the first thing it was about, and may or may not have believed it; you knew a bit and didn't believe a word; Cordelia knew about as much and believed it madly; only poor Bridey knew and believed, and I thought he made a pretty poor show when it came to explaining. And people go round saying, "At least Catholics know what they believe." We had a fair cross-section tonight –'

'Oh, Charles, don't rant. I shall begin to think you're getting doubts yourself.'

The weeks passed and still Lord Marchmain lived on. In June my divorce was made absolute and my former wife married for the second time. Julia would be free in September. The nearer our marriage got, the more wistfully, I noticed, Julia spoke of it; war was growing nearer, too – we neither of us doubted that – but Julia's tender, remote, it sometimes seemed, desperate longing did not come from any uncertainty outside herself; it suddenly darkened, too, into brief accesses of hate when she seemed to throw herself against the restraints of her love for me like a caged animal against the bars.

I was summoned to the War Office, interviewed, and put on a list in case of emergency; Cordelia also, on another list; lists were becoming part of our lives once more, as they had been at school. Everything was being got ready for the coming 'Emergency'. No one in that dark office spoke the word 'war'; it was taboo; we should be called for if there was 'an emergency' – not in case of strife, an act of human will; nothing so clear and simple as wrath or retribution; an emergency; something coming out of the waters, a monster with sightless face and thrashing tail thrown up from the depths.

Lord Marchmain took little interest in events outside his own room; we took him the papers daily and made the attempt to read to him, but he turned his head on the pillows and with his eyes followed the intricate patterns about him. 'Shall I go on?' 'Please do if it's not boring you.' But he was not listening; occasionally at a familiar name he would whisper: 'Irwin ... I knew him – a mediocre fellow'; occasionally some remote comment: 'Czechs make good coachmen; nothing else'; but his mind was far from world affairs; it was there, on the spot, turned in on himself; he had no strength for any other war than his own solitary struggle to keep alive.

I said to the doctor, who was with us daily: 'He's got a wonderful will to live, hasn't he?'

'Would you put it like that? I should say a great fear of death.'

'Is there a difference?'

'Oh dear, yes. He doesn't derive any strength from his fear, you know. It's wearing him out.'

Next to death, perhaps because they are like death, he feared darkness and loneliness. He liked to have us in his room and the lights burnt all night among the gilt figures; he did not wish us to speak much, but he talked himself, so quietly that we often could not hear him; he talked, I think, because his was the only voice he could trust, when it assured him that he was still alive; what he said was not for us, nor for any ears but his own.

'Better today. Better today. I can see now, in the corner of the fireplace, where the mandarin is holding his gold bell and the crooked tree is in flower below his feet, where yesterday I was confused and took the little tower for another man. Soon I shall see the bridge and the three storks and know where the path leads over the hill.

'Better tomorrow. We live long in our family and marry late. Seventy-three is no great age. Aunt Julia, my father's aunt, lived to be eighty-eight, born and died here, never married, saw the fire on beacon hill for the battle of Trafalgar, always called it "the New House"; that was the name they had for it in the nursery and in the fields when unlettered men had long memories. You can see where the old house stood near the village church; they call the field "Castle Hill", Horlick's field where the ground's uneven and half of it is waste, nettle, and brier in hollows too deep for ploughing. They dug to the foundations to carry the stone for the new house; the house that was a century old when Aunt Julia was born. Those were our roots in the waste hollows of Castle Hill, in the brier and nettle; among the tombs in the old church and the chantry where no clerk sings.

'Aunt Julia knew the tombs, cross-legged knight and doub-leted earl, marquis like a Roman senator, limestone, alabaster, and Italian marble; tapped the escutcheons with her ebony cane, made the casque ring over old Sir Roger. We were knights then, barons since Agincourt, the larger honours came with the Georges. They came the last and they'll go the first; the barony goes on. When all of you are dead Julia's son will be called by the name his fathers bore before the fat days; the days of wool shearing and the wide corn lands, the days of growth and building, when the marshes were drained and the waste land brought under the plough, when one built the house, his son added the dome, his son spread the wings and dammed the river. Aunt Julia watched them build the fountain; it was old before it came here, weathered two hundred years by the suns of Naples, brought by man-o'-war in the days of Nelson. Soon the fountain will be dry till the rain fills it, setting the fallen leaves afloat in the basin; and over the lakes the reeds will spread and close. Better today.

'Better today. I have lived carefully, sheltered myself from the cold winds, eaten moderately of what was in season, drunk fine claret, slept in my own sheets; I shall live long. I was fifty when they dismounted us and sent us into the line; old men stay at the base, the orders said, but Walter Venables, my commanding officer, my nearest neighbour, said: "You're as fit as the youngest of them, Alex." So I was; so I am now, if I could only breathe.

'No air; no wind stirring under the velvet canopy. When the summer comes,' said Lord Marchmain, oblivious of the deep corn and swelling fruit and the surfeited bees who slowly sought their hives in the heavy afternoon sunlight outside his windows, 'when the summer comes, I shall leave my bed and sit in the open air and breathe more easily.

'Who would have thought that all these little gold men, gentlemen in their own country, could live so long without breathing? Like toads in the coal, down a deep mine, untrou-bled. God take it, why have they dug a hole for me? Must a man stifle to death in his own cellars? Plender, Gaston, open the windows.'

'The windows are all wide open, my lord.'

A cylinder of oxygen was placed beside his bed, with a long tube, a face-piece, and a little stop-cock he could work himself. Often he said: 'It's empty; look nurse, there's nothing comes out.'

'No, Lord Marchmain, it's quite full; the bubble here in the glass bulb shows that; it's at full pressure; listen, don't you hear it hiss? Try and breathe slowly, Lord Marchmain; quite gently, then you get the benefit.'

'Free as air; that's what they say – "free as air". Now they bring me my air in an iron barrel.'

Once he said: 'Cordelia, what became of the chapel?'

'They locked it up, papa, when mummy died.'

'It was hers, I gave it to her. We've always been builders in our family. I built it for her; in the shade of the pavilion; rebuilt with the old stones behind the old walls; it was the last of the new house to come, the first to go. There used to be a chaplain until the war. Do you remember him?'

'I was too young.'

'Then I went away – left her in the chapel praying. It was hers. It was the place for her. I never came back to disturb her prayers. They said we were fighting for freedom; I had my own victory. Was it a crime?'

'I think it was, papa.'

'Crying to heaven for vengeance? Is that why they've locked me in this cave, do you think, with a black tube of air and the little yellow men along the walls, who live without breathing? Do you think that, child? But the wind will come soon, tomorrow perhaps, and we'll breathe again. The ill wind that will blow me good. Better tomorrow.'

Thus, till mid-July, Lord Marchmain lay dying, wearing himself down in the struggle to live. Then, since there was no reason to expect an immediate change, Cordelia went to London to see her women's organization about the coming 'emergency'. That day Lord Marchmain became suddenly worse. He lay silent and quite still, breathing laboriously; only his open eyes, which sometimes moved about the room, gave any sign of consciousness.

'Is this the end?' Julia asked.

'It is impossible to say,' the doctor answered; 'when he does die it will probably be like this. He may recover from the present attack. The only thing is not to disturb him. The least shock will be fatal.'

'I'm going for Father Mackay,' she said.

I was not surprised. I had seen it in her mind all the summer. When she had gone I said to the doctor, 'We must stop this nonsense.'

He said: 'My business is with the body. It's not my business to argue whether people are better alive or dead, or what happens to them after death. I only try to keep them alive.'

'And you said just now any shock would kill him. What could be worse for a man who fears death, as he does, than to have a priest brought to him – a priest he turned out when he had the strength?'

'I think it may kill him.'

'Then will you forbid it?'

'I've no authority to forbid anything. I can only give my opinion.'

'Cara, what do you think?'

'I don't want him made unhappy. That is all there is to hope for now; that he'll die without knowing it. But I should like the priest there, all the same.'

'Will you try and persuade Julia to keep him away – until the end? After that he can do no harm.'

'I will ask her to leave Alex happy, yes.'

In half an hour Julia was back with Father Mackay. We all met in the library.

'I've telegraphed for Bridey and Cordelia,' I said. 'I hope you agree that nothing must be done till they arrive.'

'I wish they were here,' said Julia.

'You can't take the responsibility alone,' I said; 'everyone else is against you. Doctor Grant, tell her what you said to me just now.'

'I said that the shock of seeing a priest might well kill him; without that he may survive this attack. As his medical man I must protest against anything being done to disturb him.'

'Cara?'

'Julia, dear, I know you are thinking for the best, but, you know, Alex was not a religious man. He scoffed always. We mustn't take advantage of him, now he's weak, to comfort our own consciences. If Father Mackay comes to him when he is unconscious, then he can be buried in the proper way, can he not, Father?'

'I'll go and see how he is,' said the doctor, leaving us.

'Father Mackay,' I said. 'You know how Lord Marchmain greeted you last time you came; do you think it possible he can have changed now?'

'Thank God, by his grace it is possible.'

'Perhaps,' said Cara, 'you could slip in while he is sleeping, say the words of absolution over him; he would never know.'

'I have seen so many men and women die,' said the priest; 'I never knew them sorry to have me there at the end.'

'But they were Catholics; Lord Marchmain has never been one except in name – at any rate, not for years. He was a scoffer, Cara said so.'

'Christ came to call, not the righteous, but sinners to repentance.'

The doctor returned. 'There's no change,' he said.

'Now doctor,' said the priest, 'how would I be a shock to anyone?' He turned his bland, innocent, matter-of-fact face first on the doctor, then upon the rest of us. 'Do you know what I want to do? It is something so small, no show about it. I don't wear special clothes, you know. I go just as I am. He knows the look of me now. There's nothing alarming. I just want to ask him if he is sorry for his sins. I want him to make some little sign of assent; I want him, anyway, not to refuse me; then I want to give him God's pardon. Then, though that's not essential, I want to anoint him. It is nothing, a touch of the fingers, just some oil from this little box, look it is nothing to hurt him.'

'Oh, Julia,' said Cara, 'what are we to say? Let me speak to him.'

She went to the Chinese drawing-room; we waited in silence; there was a wall of fire between Julia and me. Presently Cara returned.

'I don't think he heard,' she said. 'I thought I knew how to put it to him. I said: "Alex, you remember the priest from Melstead. You were very naughty when he came to see you. You hurt his feelings very much. Now he's here again. I want you to see him just for my sake, to make friends." But he didn't answer. If he's unconscious, it couldn't make him unhappy to see the priest, could it, doctor?'

Julia, who had been standing still and silent, suddenly moved.

'Thank you for your advice, doctor,' she said. 'I take full responsibility for whatever happens. Father Mackay, will you please come and see my father now,' and without looking at me, led him to the door.

We all followed. Lord Marchmain was lying as I had seen him that morning, but his eyes were now shut; his hands lay, palm upwards, above the bed-clothes; the nurse had her fingers on the pulse of one of them. 'Come in,' she said brightly, 'you won't disturb him now.'

'D'you mean . . . ?'

'No, no, but he's past noticing anything.'

She held the oxygen apparatus to his face and the hiss of escaping gas was the only sound at the bedside.

The priest bent over Lord Marchmain and blessed him. Julia and Cara knelt at the foot of the bed. The doctor, the nurse, and I stood behind them.

'Now,' said the priest, 'I know you are sorry for all the sins of your life, aren't you? Make a sign, if you can. You're sorry, aren't you?' But there was no sign. 'Try and remember your sins; tell God you are sorry. I am going to give you absolution. While I am giving it, tell God you are sorry you have offended him.' He began to speak in Latin. I recognized the words '*ego te absolvo in nomine Patris* . . .' and saw the priest make the sign of the cross. Then I knelt, too, and prayed: 'O God, if there is a God, forgive him his sins, if there is such a thing as sin,' and the man on the bed opened his eyes and gave a sigh, the sort of sigh I had imagined people made at the moment of death, but his eyes moved so that we knew there was still life in him.

I suddenly felt the longing for a sign, if only of courtesy, if only for the sake of the woman I loved, who knelt in front of me, praying, I knew, for a sign. It seemed so small a thing that was asked, the bare acknowledgement of a present, a nod in the crowd. I prayed more simply; 'God forgive him his sins' and 'Please God, make him accept your forgiveness.'

So small a thing to ask.

The priest took the little silver box from his pocket and spoke again in Latin, touching the dying man with an oily wad; he finished what he had to do, put away the box and gave the final blessing. Suddenly Lord Marchmain moved his hand to his forehead; I thought he had felt the touch of the chrism and was wiping it away. 'O God,' I prayed, 'don't let him do that.' But there was no need for fear; the hand moved slowly down his breast, then to his shoulder, and Lord Marchmain made the sign of the cross. Then I knew that the sign I had asked for was not a little thing, not a passing nod of recognition, and a phrase came back to me from my childhood of the veil of the temple being rent from top to bottom.

It was over; we stood up; the nurse went back to the oxygen cylinder; the doctor bent over his patient. Julia whispered to me: 'Will you see Father Mackay out? I'm staying here for a little.'

Outside the door Father Mackay became the simple, genial man I had known before. 'Well, now, and that was a beautiful thing to see. I've known it happen that way again and again. The devil resists to the last moment and then the Grace of God is too much for him. You're not a Catholic I think, Mr Ryder, but at least you'll be glad for the ladies to have the comfort of it.'

As we were waiting for the chauffeur, it occurred to me that Father Mackay should be paid for his services. I asked him awkwardly. 'Why, don't think about it, Mr Ryder. It was a pleasure,' he said, 'but anything you care to give is useful in a parish like mine.' I found I had three pounds in my note-case

and gave them to him. 'Why, indeed, that's more than generous. God bless you, Mr Ryder. I'll call again, but I don't think
the poor soul has long for this world.'

Julia remained in the Chinese drawing-room until, at five
o'clock that evening, her father died, proving both sides right in
the dispute, priest and doctor.

Thus I come to the broken sentences which were the last
words spoken between Julia and me, the last memories.

When her father died Julia remained some minutes with his
body; the nurse came to the next room to announce the news
and I had a glimpse of her through the open door, kneeling at
the foot of the bed, and of Cara sitting by her. Presently the two
women came out together, and Julia said to me: 'Not now; I'm
just taking Cara up to her room; later.'

While she was still upstairs Brideshead and Cordelia arrived
from London; when at last we met alone it was by stealth, like
young lovers.

Julia said: 'Here in the shadow, in the corner of the stair – a
minute to say good-bye.'

'So long to say so little.'

'You knew?'

'Since this morning; since before this morning; all this year.'

'I didn't know till today. Oh, my dear, if you could only
understand. Then I could bear to part, or bear it better. I
should say my heart was breaking, if I believed in broken
hearts. I can't marry you, Charles; I can't be with you ever
again.'

'I know.'

'How can you know?'

'What will you do?'

'Just go on – alone. How can I tell what I shall do? You
know the whole of me. You know I'm not one for a life of
mourning. I've always been bad. Probably I shall be bad again,
punished again. But the worse I am, the more I need God. I
can't shut myself out from his mercy. That is what it would
mean; starting a life with you, without him. One can only hope

to see one step ahead. But I saw today there was one thing unforgivable – like things in the school-room, so bad they were unpunishable, that only mummy could deal with – the bad thing I was on the point of doing, that I'm not quite bad enough to do; to set up a rival good to God's. Why should I be allowed to understand that, and not you, Charles? It may be because of mummy, nanny, Cordelia, Sebastian – perhaps Bridey and Mrs Muspratt – keeping my name in their prayers; or it may be a private bargain between me and God, that if I give up this one thing I want so much, however bad I am, he won't quite despair of me in the end.

'Now we shall both be alone, and I shall have no way of making you understand.'

'I don't want to make it easier for you,' I said; 'I hope your heart may break; but I do understand.'

The avalanche was down, the hillside swept bare behind it; the last echoes died on the white slopes; the new mound glittered and lay still in the silent valley.

EPILOGUE
Brideshead Revisited

'THE worst place we've struck yet,' said the commanding officer; 'no facilities, no amenities, and Brigade sitting right on top of us. There's one pub in Flyte St Mary with capacity for about twenty – that, of course, will be out of bounds for officers; there's a Naafi in the camp area. I hope to run transport once a week to Melstead Carbury. Marchmain is ten miles away and damn-all when you get there. It will therefore be the first concern of company officers to organize recreation for their men. M.O., I want you to take a look at the lakes to see if they're fit for bathing.'

'Very good, sir.'

'Brigade expects us to clean up the house for them. I should have thought some of those half-shaven scrim-shankers I see lounging round Headquarters might have saved us the trouble; however ... Ryder, you will find a fatigue party of fifty and report to the Quartering Commandant at the house at 1045 hours; he'll show you what we're taking over.'

'Very good, sir.'

'Our predecessors do not seem to have been very enterprising. The valley has great potentialities for an assault course and a mortar range. Weapon-training officer, make a recce this morning and get something laid on before Brigade arrives.'

'Very good, sir.'

'I'm going out myself with the adjutant to recce training areas. Anyone happen to know this district?'

I said nothing.

'That's all then, get cracking.'

'Wonderful old place in its way,' said the Quartering Commandant; 'pity to knock it about too much.'

He was an old, retired, re-appointed lieutenant-colonel from some miles away. We met in the space before the main doors, where I had my half-company fallen-in, waiting for orders. 'Come in. I'll soon show you over. It's a great warren of a place, but we've only requisitioned the ground floor and half a dozen bedrooms. Everything else upstairs is still private property, mostly cram-full of furniture; you never saw such stuff, priceless some of it.

'There's a caretaker and a couple of old servants live at the top – they won't be any trouble to you – and a blitzed R.C. padre whom Lady Julia gave a home to – jittery old bird, but no trouble. He's opened the chapel; that's in bounds for the troops; surprising lot use it, too.

'The place belongs to Lady Julia Flyte, as she calls herself now. She was married to Mottram, the Minister of whatever-it-is. She's abroad in some woman's service, and I try to keep an eye on things for her. Queer thing the old marquis leaving everything to her – rough on the boys.

'Now this is where the last lot put the clerks; plenty of room, anyway. I've had the walls and fireplaces boarded up you see – valuable old work underneath. Hullo, someone seems to have been making a beast of himself here; destructive beggars, soldiers are! Lucky we spotted it, or it would have been charged to you chaps.

'This is another good-sized room, used to be full of tapestry. I'd advise you to use this for conferences.'

'I'm only here to clean up, sir. Someone from Brigade will allot the rooms.'

'Oh, well, you've got an easy job. Very decent fellows the last lot. They shouldn't have done that to the fireplace though. How did they manage it? Looks solid enough. I wonder if it can be mended?

'I expect the brigadier will take this for his office; the last did. It's got a lot of painting that can't be moved, done on the walls. As you see, I've covered it up as best I can, but soldiers get through anything – as the brigadier's done in the corner. There was another painted room, outside under pillars – modern work but, if you ask me, the prettiest in the place; it was the signal office and they made absolute hay of it; rather a shame.

'This eyesore is what they used as the mess; that's why I didn't cover it up; not that it would matter much if it did get damaged; always reminds me of one of the costlier knocking-shops, you know – "*Maison Japonaise*" ... and this was the ante-room ...'

It did not take us long to make our tour of the echoing rooms. Then we went outside on the terrace.

'Those are the other ranks' latrines and wash-house; can't think why they built them just there; it was done before I took the job over. All this used to be cut off from the front. We laid the road through the trees joining it up with the main drive; unsightly but very practical; awful lot of transport comes in and out; cuts the place up, too. Look where one careless devil went smack through the box hedge and carried away all that balustrade; did it with a three-ton lorry, too; you'd think he had a Churchill tank at least.

'That fountain is rather a tender spot with our landlady; the young officers used to lark about in it on guest nights and it was looking a bit the worse for wear, so I wired it in and turned the water off. Looks a bit untidy now; all the drivers throw their cigarette-ends and the remains of the sandwiches there, and you can't get to it to clean it up, since I put the wire round it. Florid great thing, isn't it? ...

'Well, if you've seen everything I'll push off. Good day to you.'

His driver threw a cigarette into the dry basin of the fountain; saluted and opened the door of the car. I saluted and the Quartering Commandant drove away through the new, metalled gap in the lime trees.

'Hooper,' I said, when I had seen my men started, 'do you think I can safely leave you in charge of the work-party for half an hour?'

'I was just wondering where we could scrounge some tea.'

'For Christ's sake,' I said, 'they've only just begun work.'

'They're awfully browned off.'

'Keep them at it.'

'Rightyoh.'

I did not spend long in the desolate ground-floor rooms, but went upstairs and wandered down the familiar corridors, trying doors that were locked, opening doors into rooms piled to the ceiling with furniture. At length I met an old housemaid carrying a cup of tea. 'Why,' she said, 'isn't it Mr Ryder?'

'It is. I was wondering when I should meet someone I know.'

'Mrs Hawkins is up in her old room. I was just taking her some tea.'

'I'll take it for you,' I said, and passed through the baize doors, up the uncarpeted stairs, to the nursery.

Nanny Hawkins did not recognize me until I spoke, and my arrival threw her into some confusion; it was not until I had been sitting some time by her fireside that she recovered her old calm. She, who had changed so little in all the years I knew her, had lately become greatly aged. The changes of the last years had come too late in her life to be accepted and understood; her sight was failing, she told me, and she could see only the coarsest needlework. Her speech, sharpened by years of gentle conversation, had reverted now to the soft, peasant tones of its origin.

'. . . only myself here and the two girls and poor Father Membling who was blown up, not a roof to his head nor a stick of furniture till Julia took him in with the kind heart she's got, and his nerves something shocking. . . . Lady Brideshead, too, Marchmain it is now, who I ought by rights to call her Ladyship now, but it doesn't come natural, it was the same with her. First, when Julia and Cordelia left to the war, she came here with the two boys and then the military turned them out, so they went to London, nor they hadn't been in their house not a month, and Bridey away with the yeomanry the same as his poor Lordship, when they were blown up too, everything gone, all the furniture she brought here and kept in the coach-house. Then she had another house outside London, and the military took that, too, and there she is now, when I last heard, in a hotel at the seaside, which isn't the same as your own home, is it? It doesn't seem right.

'. . . Did you listen to Mr Mottram last night? Very nasty he was about Hitler. I said to the girl Effie who does for me: "If Hitler was listening, and if he understands English, which I doubt, he must feel very small." Who would have thought of Mr Mottram doing so well? And so many of his friends, too, that used to stay here? I said to Mr Wilcox, who comes to see me regular on the bus from Melstead twice a month, which is very good of him and I appreciate it, I said: "We were entertaining angels unawares," because Mr Wilcox never liked Mr Mottram's friends, which I never saw, but used to hear about from all of you, nor Julia didn't like them, but they've done very well, haven't they?'

At last I asked her: 'Have you heard from Julia?'

'From Cordelia, only last week, and they're together still as they have been all the time, and Julia sent me love at the bottom of the page. They're both very well, though they couldn't say where, but Father Membling said, reading between the lines, it was Palestine, which is where Bridey's yeomanry is, so that's very nice for them all. Cordelia said they were looking forward to coming home after the war, which I am sure we all are, though whether I live to see it, is another story.'

I stayed with her for half an hour, and left promising to return often. When I reached the hall I found no sign of work and Hooper looking guilty.

'They had to go off to draw the bed-straw. I didn't know till Sergeant Block told me. I don't know whether they're coming back.'

'Don't know? What orders did you give?'

'Well, I told Sergeant Block to bring them back if he thought it was worthwhile; I mean if there was time before dinner.'

It was nearly twelve. 'You've been hotted again, Hooper. That straw was to be drawn any time before six tonight.'

'Oh Lor; sorry, Ryder. Sergeant Block –'

'It's my own fault for going away. . . . Fall in the same party immediately after dinner, bring them back here and keep them here till the job's done.'

'Rightyoh. I say, did you say you knew this place before?'

'Yes, very well. It belongs to friends of mine,' and as I said the words they sounded as odd in my ears as Sebastian's had done, when, instead of saying, 'It is my home,' he said, 'It is where my family live.'

'It doesn't seem to make any sense – one family in a place this size. What's the use of it?'

'Well, I suppose Brigade are finding it useful.'

'But that's not what it was built for, is it?'

'No,' I said, 'not what it was built for. Perhaps that's one of the pleasures of building, like having a son, wondering how he'll grow up. I don't know; I never built anything, and I forfeited the right to watch my son grow up. I'm homeless, childless, middle-aged, loveless, Hooper.' He looked to see if I was being funny, decided that I was, and laughed. 'Now go back to camp, keep out of the C.O.'s way, if he's back from his recce, and don't let on to anyone that we've made a nonsense of the morning.'

'Okey, Ryder.'

There was one part of the house I had not yet visited, and I went there now. The chapel showed no ill-effects of its long neglect; the *art-nouveau* paint was as fresh and bright as ever; the *art-nouveau* lamp burned once more before the altar. I said a prayer, an ancient, newly-learned form of words, and left, turning towards the camp; and as I walked back, and the cook-house bugle sounded ahead of me, I thought:

'The builders did not know the uses to which their work would descend; they made a new house with the stones of the old castle; year by year, generation after generation, they enriched and extended it; year by year the great harvest of timber in the park grew to ripeness; until, in sudden frost, came the age of Hooper; the place was desolate and the work all brought to nothing; *Quomodo sedet sola civitas*. Vanity of vanities, all is vanity.

'And yet,' I thought, stepping out more briskly towards the camp, where the bugles after a pause had taken up the second call and were sounding 'Pick-em-up, pick-em-up, hot potatoes', 'and yet that is not the last word; it is not even an apt word; it is a dead word from ten years back.

'Something quite remote from anything the builders

intended, has come out of their work, and out of the fierce little human tragedy in which I played; something none of us thought about at the time; a small red flame – a beaten-copper lamp of deplorable design relit before the beaten-copper doors of a tabernacle; the flame which the old knights saw from their tombs, which they saw put out; that flame burns again for other soldiers, far from home, farther, in heart, than Acre or Jerusalem. It could not have been lit but for the builders and the tragedians, and there I found it this morning, burning anew among the old stones.'

I quickened my pace and reached the hut which served us for our ante-room.

'You're looking unusually cheerful today,' said the second-in-command.

ABOUT THE INTRODUCER

SIR FRANK KERMODE, formerly Lord North-cliffe Professor at London University, is now Professor at Cambridge and Columbia Universities. His books include *The Sense of an Ending*, *Romantic Image*, and *Continuities*.

TITLES IN EVERYMAN'S LIBRARY

CHINUA ACHEBE
Things Fall Apart

THE ARABIAN NIGHTS
(tr. Husain Haddawy)

MARCUS AURELIUS
Meditations

JANE AUSTEN
Emma
Mansfield Park
Northanger Abbey
Persuasion
Pride and Prejudice
Sense and Sensibility

HONORÉ DE BALZAC
Cousin Bette
Eugénie Grandet
Old Goriot

SIMONE DE BEAUVOIR
The Second Sex

WILLIAM BLAKE
Poems and Prophecies

JORGE LUIS BORGES
Ficciones

JAMES BOSWELL
The Life of Samuel Johnson

CHARLOTTE BRONTË
Jane Eyre
Villette

EMILY BRONTË
Wuthering Heights

MIKHAIL BULGAKOV
The Master and Margarita

SAMUEL BUTLER
The Way of all Flesh

ITALO CALVINO
If on a winter's night a traveler

ALBERT CAMUS
The Stranger

WILLA CATHER
Death Comes for the Archbishop

MIGUEL DE CERVANTES
Don Quixote

GEOFFREY CHAUCER
Canterbury Tales

ANTON CHEKHOV
The Steppe and Other Stories
My Life and Other Stories

KATE CHOPIN
The Awakening

CARL VON CLAUSEWITZ
On War

SAMUEL TAYLOR COLERIDGE
Poems

WILLIAM WILKIE COLLINS
The Moonstone
The Woman in White

JOSEPH CONRAD
Heart of Darkness
Lord Jim
Nostromo
The Secret Agent
Typhoon and Other Stories
Under Western Eyes

DANIEL DEFOE
Moll Flanders
Robinson Crusoe

CHARLES DICKENS
Bleak House
David Copperfield
Great Expectations
Hard Times
Little Dorrit
Nicholas Nickleby
Oliver Twist
A Tale of Two Cities

DENIS DIDEROT
Memoirs of a Nun

JOHN DONNE
The Complete English Poems

FYODOR DOSTOEVSKY
The Brothers Karamazov
Crime and Punishment

W. E. B. DU BOIS
The Souls of Black Folk